JP. Anne

D1461204

ABOUT THE AUTHOR

Peter Gray has been writing in various guises since he was twelve years old and he has never been able to stop. From plays to magazine articles Peter has produced a plethora of work.

His first Sam Series book 'A Certain Summer' had excellent reviews, one from TV presenter and ex England soccer coach Bob Wilson who grew up in the same area and could easily identify with the characters in the book and loved its humour.

With many short stories, articles and celebrated Mummers Plays, plus many touring productions under his belt. Peter is always busy writing something or other. He has also acted in and directed some of those productions and one such production played at Warwick Castle for six full seasons. He has also written several scripts for advertisements, mostly with a humorous theme as well as celebrated live shows for the stage.
Other books by the same author can be found on his website listed below.

He now lives in the Highlands of Scotland.

For more information please visit
www.petergrayauthor.co.uk.

ALSO BY PETER GRAY

A Certain Summer
Sam's Kingdom
With Feeling

FROM THE AVALON SERIES

The Drums of Drumnadrochit
Auld Clootie
The Brollachan
The Black Clan
Caledonian Flame - out November 2019

The Drums
of
Drumnadrochit

by
Peter Gray

Tricky Imp Publishing

The Drums of Drumnadrochit

First edition first published December 2016
Revised April 2018
This revised edition July 2019

Tricky Imp Publishers
Highlands, Scotland.
Email: books@trickyimppublishing.co.uk

A CIP catalogue record for this title is available from
The British Library.

ISBN: 978-0-9572668-3-4

Cover design and artwork by the author.

More Information at:
www.petergrayauthor.co.uk
www.trickyimppublishing.co.uk

Printed and bound in the UK by 4 Edge.

Preface

James Avalon had been living in my mind for a few years, sometimes not under that particular name but there nonetheless. His shape was not fully formed until later, and even then a literal metamorphosis took place before he finally became the prominent character in this series.

I never saw him as a hero or even a role model, in some ways I think initially he had many faults and aspects to his psyche that were less than salubrious but as his path was set to paper I began to see him differently.

I hope that he isn't too much of a compromise but this is how he evolved over the planning stages and I have grown to like him - eventually.

There are always problems in setting a contemporary novel in real places, the obvious ones are that it has to be accurate to the real world at the moment that it happens. That is reasonably easy but there were a few surprises along the way. The most compromised part of such a writing is not to be too close to actual people and so to steer well clear of this, I decided to make some of the police procedures and departments slightly different to how they are in the real world. Nothing too obtuse but enough of a disparity to make sure no one in the real world thought the story in any way involved them.

However, there are a few 'real' people in the story who gave me permission to be included and I hope they enjoy the part they play in this drama.

Peter Gray. June 2016.

Chapter One

Avalon pressed himself into the straw bales as several shots struck the soft barricade with a terrifying thud. Nervously he looked down to check his weapon for ammunition and satisfyingly noticed it was almost full. This did nothing to calm his nerves however as several more shots struck the flimsy cover. Once more he checked the weapon and trying to find a more comfortable position to ready himself for the onslaught that would surely come, he noticed that his mouth was dry and it was making swallowing difficult. Squashing himself even further into the dirt and the straw bales, he gasped at the air, which seemed to refuse to enter his body. From the corner of his eye, he noticed movement on the ridge behind him, it was the only remaining member of his team, Paul Staunton. A stocky, broad Staffordshire man with the 'devil may care' attitude and a brutish approach to police work. Avalon looked once again down towards his gun and wondered what the hell he was doing here, he had completed no training for this kind of caper, not like Staunton who had been fully trained in the use of handguns and siege tactics. Detective Sergeant James Avalon was just a normal detective, more at home with paperwork and leads to follow than full out combat. He hated all types of guns and usually let the others do the gung-ho stuff, he was just a normal copper really. If Avalon was truthful with himself he wasn't even a proper policeman at all, he just didn't have the right temperament to mindlessly, follow orders, which was his main problem. But here he was, on what would normally be a lovely day, glancing over at the remaining member of his team, Detective Sergeant Paul Staunton who was loosing off shots like a wild man and then ducking down behind the ridge.

'For Christ's sake Avalon, I need cover!' growled out Staunton as he wildly fired his gun towards the enemy. Avalon could sense the panic in Staunton's voice, he had bawled out Avalon's name instead of the disparaging nickname he had received at the office. Avalon could do little, every time he tried to move several shots thumped into the barricade or whined past just over the top. Once again he looked down to his weapon and once again he pushed himself deeper into the barricade. Sensing Avalon's panic and realising that he was pinned down, Staunton made a break from cover and ran along the ridge firing his weapon over the top of Avalon's flimsy barricade, screaming as he ran. Avalon reacted by shooting blindly over the barricade in an effort to support Staunton and somehow the big detective got behind a large tree and regained his breath. The area was wooded but most of the trees offered little shelter yet somehow, Staunton had found the excellent cover of a large sycamore. He too was firing blindly from the tree now and then as several shots struck the tree from the direction of their assailants. Avalon knew he had to act. It wasn't like him to just give up when the odds were against him. It was his job to work with the cards stacked on the other side and here he was hiding like a child, behind soft cover that would very soon cease to provide any protection. It was time. If he could just make a difference maybe he and Staunton could move forward and take out the three enemies over on the other side of the small clearing. He was now wishing he had gone for the firearms training he had been offered but he hated the whole idea so much that he had refused and was only here now because the team was short of staff. Avalon didn't like Staunton very much but he could tell he was becoming exasperated by inactivity and would soon make a push on his own. Avalon knew it was now or never. He took deep breaths and tried to swallow once more but it felt like he had a mouth full of hot sand. Avalon knew he had more in him, maybe it was time to reach deep into his soul and prove it. Somewhere in the distance he heard a Robin singing, a stark contrast to what he had to do next. With a nervous wave, he signalled to Staunton that he was ready as several more shots hit the straw bales. Staunton mouthed a silent countdown from five and then,

'Go!' he screamed. Avalon just leaped up and ran past several small trees firing as he went. He couldn't actually see the enemy but he could hear their shots whizzing past and he loosed off several rounds in the direction they seemed to come from. Just in front, he saw a gully, a slight indent in the ground and he made for that. If he could shoot from there, he and Staunton would be able to enfilade from either side and maybe take out all three shooters.

Avalon was now beginning to feel less nervous and was thinking like the detective he knew he was but as he was just about to dive for the indent, he saw movement just ahead. One shooter had moved, and he was directly ahead of him. Avalon instinctively brought up his gun and shot, just at the moment the assailant did the same, and as he dived for the indent, he didn't know if he had hit the shooter or not. The ground was damp where the woodland drained its excess water down into the stream some forty yards away. Avalon hoped that he could somehow pull the moisture into his body through osmosis but he couldn't and he could feel his breath hot in his nose and mouth. He felt stronger now though as the adrenaline gave him the buzz he needed. It was then he considered that if he had not shot the enemy attacker, then the assailant could be hunting him at that moment. Avalon gripped the gun tightly and looked around. He heard shots whizzing here and there over to the right which meant Staunton was still in the game and was giving as good as he got. If he could only take out the shooter close by, the odds would be equal and that meant that they would have a fighting chance. He lifted himself clear of the cool, damp leaf litter and peered over the top of the rise and there he saw the enemy shooter trying to outflank him. Avalon jumped up to a low crouch, moved quickly to a mound of earth and shot twice at the enemy who was still crawling along on his belly. The first shot struck the enemy in the buttocks and the second in the back. He had done it! the numbers were equal, even if he did feel bad about the first shot in the assailant's backside.

Turning to find cover, he heard the shot before it struck and he leaped in a vain hope it would miss him. As he landed on the ground back in the damp gully, he knew he had been hit. It didn't hurt as much as he had expected, but he could feel somewhere in his lower stomach, a slight pain. As he laid in the indent, he put his hand down to where the shot had struck and felt a sticky wetness.

'Shit!' he spat as he considered the stupidity of what he had done. He thought it over and over in his mind, the hesitation just because he had shot the victim in the backside, enough time for one of the other shooters to take aim and pull the trigger. Staunton was now alone but the harsh reality struck home he had failed. He had got it wrong and now it was all over and he once more felt the sticky patch where he had been shot to confirm he was truly hit. He looked at his hand and sure enough, the yellow, gooey mess showed that he was indeed shot in the stomach and all he could do was lay there and wait for the end. He could hear over to the right the fight was still going on but at least Avalon had taken out one of the enemy and that was slightly gratifying, leaving Staunton with an easier job. Avalon remained looking at the sky breathing deeply and wondering how Staunton would now deal with the other two but to his surprise, he thought he could hear someone creeping towards him. He tried to move his head to one side to look down, past his body, to the direction of the sound, a sort of soft rustle, like the leaf litter was being moved by something, or someone creeping towards him. He moved his position an amount and then he saw the person he had shot, carefully and slowly crawling towards him. That wasn't right, the enemy was dead, one shot is a kill, but he put two into that person. True, one wasn't a traditional point of entry for a kill shot and it must have hurt but the second one was into the area of the spine. But still, the person

11

crawled towards him, slowly, but with a determination that wasn't easily stopped. Avalon looked around for his gun, it was just out of reach but he stretched out just... a... little more... and then a hand reached down from above him and picked up the gun. It was a tall figure wearing a red sash standing directly above and pointing the gun at him.

'You're dead,' he quietly said and then looked over to the crawling figure before repeating the phrase, picking up the enemy gun and tramping off in the direction of the fight that was surprisingly still going on. Avalon once again lay back and glanced up at the blue sky until yet again he heard the determined exertions of the enemy corpse that just refused to die.

'Looks like you got me, I'm Nina,' came a whispered voice. Avalon sat up and looked to his left to see the other person looking at him through misted eye goggles. 'Oh sorry,' continued the crawling figure as the goggles were removed and a hand was offered. It was a woman. It had been hard to tell under the camouflage suit and the eye protection but the forty-something face, with smears of sweat and eye make-up, was smiling as the hand was still being proffered. Avalon shook it as he said.

'Avalon,' then he revised it to, 'James.' He used his first name so little he had to dredge the corners of his mind to remember what it was. Only his ex-wife called him James, and he saw her rarely these days. After he had said it he still wondered if that was correct, and maybe he should have said Jim, to be less formal? He didn't particularly like Jim, so it would have to be James.

'It's my first time, how about you?' she asked.

Avalon took a second or two to understand what she meant.

'Sorry?' he asked to be sure.

'Paint-balling, it's my first time. How about you?' she asked in a quiet voice as further shots could be heard over the other side of the woodland.

'Oh yeah, sorry, yes... first time for me too. The others have been before but the first for me,' explained Avalon with a slight embarrassment now he realised he had shot this woman in the posterior. 'Sorry about the first shot,' he apologised rolling his eyes. She appeared not to realise at first and then seemed to grasp what he meant. 'The guns are not particularly accurate, I mean I didn't mean to er...' He pointed to his own bottom to try to make sense without going into an embarrassing explanation

'Oh, it's fine, it stings a bit, but I'll survive.' There was irony in the comment but Avalon just smiled. 'Are you all from the same company?' she asked as she made herself comfortable.

'Sort of,' smiled Avalon. 'We're all coppers.'

'Really?' replied Nina with a start. 'Oh wow,' she grinned before adding, 'you should have kicked our arses then shouldn't you? Maybe we could get you for cheating.' She was still smiling.

'Cheating?' laughed Avalon. 'We're not Special Branch or the SFO, we just work in a cramped office in Wolverhampton.'

'Oh, well, it still has some cachet, taking on the Police Force,' she grinned. It was about then Avalon realised he maybe should have made up some lie. It just wasn't in his nature, the truth came easier than lies. Lies were for the criminal, the truth mattered and he believed in it strongly.

'Well, I suppose I did kick, or rather shoot, your arse,' he smiled trying to make light of the situation and in an effort to make her forget about the fact they were police. In the distance, a whistle blew which signified that the game was over and someone had won.

'Oh, I wonder who takes the trophy?' smiled Nina.

'Well,' began Avalon, 'I don't know who you have on *your* team but they will be hard pushed to beat Staunton, he's like Rambo.'

'He must be the big chap, I think he took most of our team out,' and just as if on cue Staunton stamped past.

'We won Spook,' he spat as he walked past the two figures. 'You took your time though,' he added without looking back.

'Spook?' Nina inquired, 'is that your nickname?' Avalon was visibly uncomfortable with the question and Nina noticed. 'Er, sorry, I shouldn't pry.' Avalon gave a weak smile and stood.

'I suppose we should go.... seeing as it's all over.' She nodded and the two of them turned to walk back to the barn that stood in the field by the woodland. To their left, three figures came from the trees, one of them looked like he had been given the once over by an eager painter and decorator, probably suffering from Obsessive Compulsive Disorder as there didn't seem to be much of his body that didn't sport at least one layer of yellow paint. The only place that didn't show yellow was around the eyes where the face protector had been, which was now being carried by the marshal and it too was covered in yellow goo. Obviously, Staunton, not

14

being satisfied with winning, had emptied the whole gun on the unfortunate chap and almost drowned him in paint.

'Your teammate is a little thorough,' commented the marshal as he walked past with raised eyebrows. Crosley was walking past too. Crosley was one of Avalon's team, he was the one who had arranged the trip and he flashed an embarrassed grin towards Avalon as he walked to the barn. Avalon didn't mind Crosley, he was hard-working and tried to get the team to bond together at work and away from it but he was fairly new and no one really took him seriously.

'I suppose he was confirming the kill,' Crosley offered with a slight smirk and he continued following the yellow drip line on the ground.

'I suppose we will be banned from here too,' whispered Avalon to Nina.

'You get banned a lot then?' smiled Nina.

'Yeah, particularly when Staunton attends.' He turned and followed the painted man. 'It could be a really bad case of jaundice I suppose,' continued Avalon as an afterthought.

'Possibly,' replied Nina with a gentle laugh.

Back in the barn they all handed back their camouflage coveralls and goggles and sat at a long table with a hot drink. Nina was a plain woman but out of the camouflage coveralls Avalon was surprised he had mistaken her for a man. She was slightly built but had a shape that was not at all manly. He looked her over for what he considered was far too long and he tried to conceal it by asking her a question.

'So where are you from... I mean where are you

all from?'

'Oh,' she smiled, 'we work for a cardboard container company, we're mainly from the accounts department.'

'And where in the country is that?' he asked a little more confidently.

'Solihull,' she nodded.

'Oh,' replied Avalon with nowhere else to go conversationally. He looked down at the terrible coffee he had already decided to leave and with no other ideas added, 'You have travelled about the same distance as us then.' She nodded with some disinterest. Since his divorce three years ago, Avalon had not really dusted off his ego and gone looking for female companionship and now it was showing like a tattoo on the forehead. He was out of practice, out of kilter and out of time. His party were leaving and without doubt, if he wasn't on the minibus soon, he would be left behind.

'Well, nice to meet you Nina.' He held out his hand, which she took.

'Nice to meet you too James,' she smiled again. Avalon thought the name sounded stupid, he would leave it at 'Avalon' next time, if there *was* a next time. His work meant he had little time of his own, which was why his wife was 'ex' after all.

He sat in the minibus ignoring the chat from his 'team' for he knew he was considered very much an outsider. At least once he heard the word 'Spook', the derogatory name most of them called him just prior to a burst of laughter. It was his own fault, he knew that. He had never been all that friendly with his colleagues and his approach had been wrong from the very start of his career. Through the bus window, he watched people

16

going on with their 'easy' lives, going to the pub, the shop, to work and he wondered how many of them were happy. He certainly wasn't and he felt that all too familiar explosive undercurrent flowing. That was bad, he always went too far when he let the inner anger out. He took deep breaths and kept quiet and just sat staring out of the window. There it was again that name 'Spook' and another round of laughter. Before Avalon could put a noose on his mouth, it had spoken.

'Staunton, how many hits did you make today?' Staunton was taken aback a little but turned to Avalon and said.

'I dunno, I would have to think about it.'

'What about you Green?' Avalon looked at the pale-faced man who was a particular pain to him and glared.

'Er,' stammered Green, 'none, but they're not exactly accurate are they?' he said in his defence.

'Well, I got one kill,' grinned Crosley, 'accurate or not.' Avalon then looked over to Ellis who knew what was coming and just shrugged and said.

'Zero.' Avalon then looked over to Presley who just held up a single finger.

'No one over-performed then,' insisted Avalon, 'me and Crosley took out one each and Staunton took the rest so let's get the facts right before anyone points any fingers.' There was silence, just the monotone droning of the minibus engine and the road noise. The other faces looked back at Avalon with surprise and shock, all except Staunton who was still counting his hits.

'I think about forty-five,' he eventually replied. Crosley then broke the silence of the others and explained.

'Er, we weren't taking the pee, I was just telling the others about the comment you made about the Jaundice.' Avalon shrunk back into himself. He had made a grave error, was it any wonder that they disliked him? He quickly tried to think of a way out of it but he couldn't and so he tried to make light of the situation.

'And Staunton, your score was five, not forty-five. You only get one point for the kill, the other forty shots were just window dressing.' The comment brought a couple of smiles as Staunton broke into his customary verbal abuse but Avalon had already gone back to his window. What an idiot he was. Why couldn't he put the expertise from his career into his life? What was wrong with him? He was a good detective, he knew that, even if other people didn't realise it but luck didn't shine on him. The only time he actually cracked a difficult case, 'fate' or something similar, made sure the whole thing was altered out of proportion. He had made the wrong career decisions that was clear but at nearly forty years old it was a bit late to realise it and even later to do anything about it. What could he do if he left the force anyway? He had no other skills, and he had no other interests. His private life was a sad, lame affair without hobbies or adventure. He went back to his terrace house at night, cooked a simple meal, usually from tins and sat watching the television with a glass of single malt whisky, sighing and shaking his head at the utter rubbish he was watching.

As the minibus pulled into the car park near the office, he knew he had to change something. He knew if he didn't get out of the job or at least move to another area, the situation would deteriorate. As they walked from the minibus to their cars, only Crosley acknowledged him with a nod and so he slumped into the car and watched them drive off. He sat there, the only car left in the small car park and rested his chin on the steering wheel. He thought back, he tried to think of happier times. He thought all the way back to his marriage, his college days and his childhood and one thing was clear. The source of all his problems lay with the job. His wife had gone, he had no friends, no life and no hope and it was all because of the job. He had to get out. He had to decide when to do it and to his surprise, as he leaned back into the seat, taking deep breaths he was beginning to feel better already. Just the thought of making a decision at last made him feel more positive. The only thing missing was a little reassurance. His ex-wife was usually the one for that but lately even she had been a little impatient with him. She was probably the only friend he had, she had left him of course, but they had never really fallen out. They had argued but who doesn't? In fact, they had thrown things at each other, well she had thrown things at him mostly and he had tried to catch them trying not to break them but wasn't that how all married couples acted? Wasn't it?

Avalon drove home and tried to forget about his troubles. He went back to his terrace house, cooked a simple meal mainly from tins and sat watching the television with a glass of single malt, sighing and shaking his head at the utter rubbish he was watching... again.

Monday morning came around all too soon and Avalon entered the cramped office from which he and eight other people worked, he sat at his desk and checked his emails. Green sat opposite and once again hummed the theme tune to the movie 'Ghostbusters' which always irritated Avalon but today more so.

'You know Green, that joke is sort of wearing really thin after two years.'

'I know,' grinned Green not bothering to look away from the screen of the computer, 'but it still amuses me.' Avalon sighed and shook his head in disbelief that someone with the intelligence to be a detective could be so stupid as to run a tedious joke for two years and still get something from it. The Ghostbusters theme had become a part of Avalon's life, it was just a series of musical notes but in the order that made up 'that' tune, it made him angry. He decided that today he knew he would do something he would regret if he stayed in the office and so he went to get a coffee from the terrible vending machine in the lobby of the building. He hardly ever drank the chemical concoction, but it was an excuse when he needed to retreat from the office and he cradled the plastic cup in his hands benefiting from a warmth he didn't receive from the job. He walked down the corridor and found himself in the vehicle compound behind the building where it was relatively quiet. He sat on a low wall and took deep breaths of the cool air and thought about his position and what had brought him to this point. It had been a long journey, but the problems had started just over two years ago. He had been with the West Midlands Police for about a year at the time, his previous experience had been unremarkable. A murder case or two but nothing high profile or even particularly taxing but he had been reasonably happy with the work and as he thought about it, he was feeling unsure about exactly what had caused his fortunes to change. Certainly his early career had been happy enough, he had joined the police in his home county of Norfolk when he was twenty-six, not long after studying law and economics and trying several jobs that just didn't suit him. He had made ends meet during his studying by working as a motorcycle courier and then as an emergency courier for blood and vital organs. He loved riding, and he considered it a great way to make money though his own bike was nothing special. He couldn't remember who but someone suggested that he applied to the police as a Motorcycle Officer but the thought of 'pounding the beat' during training didn't appeal. With no other ideas or interest in any other work, he eventually joined up and donned the uniform of a police constable, just to make his way to the motorcycle section. He spent just over two years with the Norfolk force through which time he found that it wasn't as bad as he had thought as long as he kept a close ear to the ground. He was an accidental police officer, he just wanted to get his hands on one of those big police bikes. He soon realised it wasn't that easy as there were long waiting lists but after another eight months, he moved to Lincolnshire to take up a post there riding a big Honda.

He took a sip of the fast cooling coffee but winced at its pungent 'twang'. He then smiled as he remembered his time with the Lincolnshire Police and his life during that period. He felt warm memories flooding over him, good times in his work and his private life. He had enjoyed it so much he had continued with the bike section for almost four years until he was ready for something new, and as he thought, he wondered if it was time for another change.

Avalon looked over to the far end of the vehicle

compound and noticed a police bike by the wall and for a moment, he considered going over to take a closer look, but then resisted as he saw a mechanic walk over to it. Instead, he thought about the moment that a notice came through at his police station, a small poster detailing the benefits of joining the CID. Just before his thirty-third birthday, he had heard about the lack of detectives on the force and just for a moment, considered this as a career change. Due to the rumours that being a detective wasn't all it was cracked up to be, Avalon had resisted the change, but he eventually felt his career in the bike section had become stale and so he applied to take the exams and passed them quite easily. He was eventually accepted into the CID and moved back to Norfolk to take up a post as Detective Constable, working around Norwich centre.

As Avalon thought of those days he remembered both good and bad times but it made him smile. He stood and walked around the vehicle compound and saw two of the engineers working on a van, they looked up to him questioningly so he nodded to them and returned inside realising it was this place, this station where his life had been turned upside down. He emptied the remains of the coffee over a pot plant by the door and walked slowly back to the office with his hands thrust deep into his pockets. Once again he thought about his recent history and the day he had arrived at Wolverhampton, after his application had been approved. He had thought that the move to the West Midlands Police would turn his career around, and in some ways, it did. The cases he worked on at Wolverhampton were generally run-of-the-mill as the longer served officers worked on the major cases but he persevered and eventually found himself moved to a new team under DS Staunton. His section was running a case where three jewellery shops had been attacked and the crimes all had the same modus operandi. One was in Dudley, one in Cradley Heath and the other in Blackheath. On one occasion three masked men had been foiled during their attack and a few clues had been gathered but there were no real suspects for the crimes.

'That was it,' thought Avalon to himself as he returned to his desk and sat, 'that was the moment my life changed, that damn St Mary's case.' He looked down at his screen but the only images he saw were from inside his thoughts. About six months into the case, the gang had struck again, this time they had changed their tactics and firearms were brandished. This put a whole new aspect onto the crime and pressure was put on Staunton's team to find them before they used the guns in anger, but nothing concrete turned up and the team went back to basics. Avalon was tasked with trying to track down if any of the plunder had cropped up with known fences and handlers but by chance he scanned through the local press to find pawnbrokers. One small article caught his eye. It was nothing to do with the crimes and he only read it because it wasn't all that far from his home. It was an article about a ghost that had been seen on several occasions within the grounds of Saint Mary's Church, which the newspaper had reported, had appeared after the site had been given permission for redevelopment. The church had been vacant for some time and on several occasions developers had tried to purchase the land for housing. Every time the locals had objected on various grounds, one, being 'that the dead should be allowed to rest in peace', as the graveyard contained departed relatives of many local people. The developers had said they would pay to have all the remains removed but the local populace were up in arms about it. Then without warning, the council sanctioned demolition of the church and gave permission to build, although the graveyard would remain untouched, though the headstones would be removed. The article Avalon read said the locals had now taken the matter to the high court and were awaiting a decision. The ghost, it seemed, was haunting the grounds since the decision to go ahead with the development. This part of the article got Avalon thinking. It was incorrect. He had heard about a ghost being seen previous to this event and though it was to be expected that the locals would use the sighting to their purpose, Avalon had decided to visit the offices of the newspaper to look through back editions to find out when the ghost was first seen. He didn't know why, he had a feeling at the back of his mind that something was tickling his detective gland. He had smiled when he saw that the sightings had begun sometime earlier, just after the start of the jeweller robberies. At first Avalon saw no connection between a sighting of a ghost and a trio of armed robbers and he dare not share the information with the rest of the team because he would be ridiculed, but he could see a sort of chronological connection with ghost sightings and the attacks. He tucked it away and waited to see what happened.

In April of that year, a new sighting of the ghost was reported, a seventeen-year-old girl returning from a late party had been scared out of her wits by a white figure floating through the grounds and though the locals attributed it to a review of their case, Avalon expected a new jewellery shop attack. He mentioned to Staunton that he thought an attack was imminent but Staunton took it with a pinch of salt and forgot about it but two days after, another attack was reported and this time a gun was discharged. No one was hurt but Staunton's team was under tremendous pressure and firearms officers were put on alert. Avalon didn't believe in ghosts but he conducted a door-to-door visit in the area of Saint Mary's church and found several eyewitnesses including the seventeen-year-old girl and they all seemed sure that they had seen a floating figure. He decided that a night-time visit to the church was in order. The grounds were pitch black but an asphalt path cut through the grounds from one line of terraces to another and a second path ran down from the church to Church Lane. The church, though boarded up and sealed, had been breached several times in the past and was now in poor condition. Avalon circled its perimeter but found, and saw, nothing. He sauntered around the grounds but saw no one, it was obvious people had stopped moving through the churchyard after dark.

He began to get cold and tired, he was also bored, and he realised that the odds of the ghost appearing when he was there were quite remote. Left in the dark with his thoughts, he considered that if there was a link with the robberies and the ghost, the said ghost might be 'packing heat' as they say in old gangster movies. Avalon decided that his sojourn in the church grounds was utterly stupid and had no logic to connect it with the case at hand. He decided to remove his backside from the large gravestone he was resting on and get some much-needed sleep. As he stood and walked away, the ground seemed to give under his weight. He at first put it down to a soft grave but on closer inspection, he realised it was at the rear of the headstone, not the front, where the grave would normally be. Using his small flashlight, he examined the place and found that below the leaf litter, the grass had been disturbed. Below that, there were some short wooden boards. He carefully lifted one of the boards and saw heavy-duty plastic sheet below. He turned off his torch instinctively and glanced around the churchyard to check for other people and then examined the plastic without removing it. What he saw made him shudder slightly. Guns, several guns sealed in plastic bags. He replaced the boards and the grass and took another turn around the churchyard before leaving for home. He was excited and worried at the same time. From there on, his detective mode kicked in and all he had to do was report what he had found to Staunton who was in charge of the case, set up surveillance on the churchyard and wait for the crooks to turn up, which is what he and Staunton did. The gang, prior to another attack, went to retrieve the guns for the job and one of them was dressed in a shabby white glowing suit and a top hat of all things. He was carrying a skateboard which was how they simulated the hovering ghost along the asphalt paths, a ruse to make sure that no one was watching the accomplices retrieve or hide the weapons. The surveillance team followed them back to their places of residence and arrests were made.

They had cracked the case, Avalon had his name in the papers and it should have been good for his career, indeed he was promoted to Detective Sergeant but his career seemed to stall, mainly due to the 'fame' that had brought his promotion. The problem was that the papers told of the 'Jewel Heist Gang' being foiled by detectives from the local CID and the 'Saint Mary's Church

Spectre' as it became called by the press, was cracked by a *'Ghost-busting Detective with a King Arthur connection.'* They may as well have put, 'Phantom zapped by Merlin.' Thereafter, Avalon became the 'Ghost-buster' in his office and when they tired of that, they took to calling him 'Spook'. It may have been dropped eventually but when a local drug ring was thwarted by Avalon and Crosley it was found that some pushers had been practising Devil Worship under the influence of narcotics in the basement of a disused public house. The press had a field day. *'Satanists foiled by Detective Ghost-buster'* and *'The Ghostbusters Nail Devilish Drug Gang.'* were just two of the credibility destroying headlines. Avalon found out that being likened to the Ghostbusters did relatively nothing to further a career as a detective and the part that galled him the most, was that it was a sheer accident he found the arms cache in the Saint Mary's case. True, the crime was solved but who was going to let him ever lead a case now? No one it seemed, including the Detective Chief Inspector who did everything possible to keep him out of the front line.

Since then, Avalon had become bored and disillusioned with the work and was sliding down a slippery slope of depression. That was almost two years ago and Avalon wanted out, he was reduced to being the third detective on minor cases, which put him in the same category as the tea lady but working more hours. Some of it was his own fault, he realised that, but he had values and morals that would not let him compromise when it came to the job. It made some people dislike him, particularly Staunton and his new sidekick Green.

27

Avalon sat, as he sometimes did, gazing out of the office window trying to find the motivation to type up a mundane report about a disturbance outside a pub on Wood Street where a man had been attacked with a wooden club. It was more of the same and it bored him.

'Avalon,' came a voice cutting through his thoughts. 'the DCI wants to see you in his office.' It was Crosley and Avalon had a good idea of what it was about. The rare times the Detective Chief Inspector wanted to see him was when he was in trouble. As he entered the office, he noticed Staunton sat at the edge of the desk looking through notes.

'You wanted to see me sir?' asked Avalon

'Sit down Avalon,' came the brusque reply. There was a quiet in the room that Avalon found distasteful and when the DCI looked up, he continued in the same manner. 'DI Staunton tells me you will not overlook DC Green's forgetfulness.' Avalon expected trouble when he had decided not to play ball on a minor internal cover-up.

'I can't overlook it sir, Green failed to log important evidence, and that is a serious error. If I was not to mention it in my report, I would be not doing my job correctly.'

'For Christ's sake Avalon it's only a minor error, and the evidence wasn't even slightly important to the case.' Avalon nodded in agreement.

'That's true sir but if it could be missed on a simple case like a robbery, it could happen on something major.' The DCI sighed and looked to Staunton.

'There is nothing we can do, if Avalon wishes to make this into a bigger mess than it already is, then there is nothing further to be said.'

'Christ Avalon, just for once play for the team,' spat Staunton. Avalon grinned slightly at Staunton.

'The *team* doesn't pay my wages, the public does, and that is where my responsibility lies.' Staunton glared at Avalon as the DCI announced.

'Get back to whatever you were doing Avalon, I'll have a word with the officer involved.'

As Avalon left the office, he felt the glares of the two men burning into the back of his head. The silence seemed to escort him to the door and push him out. He felt angry that they would expect him to put his principles on the line for the sake of an incompetent officer who would one day become a liability. He was about to take his seat at his desk when he heard Staunton's booming voice call across the room.

'Avalon! This will come back to haunt you, you know that.' Avalon turned to see Staunton hurrying towards him. He felt trouble approach. Staunton came right up to him, his face almost pressing on Avalon's as he continued. 'Why don't you just leave Spook? You've never fit in here and you'll never be trusted by the team.' Avalon kept the gaze on the big man as he replied.

'Team? There is no team. You and Green make sure of that.' He blinked and continued. 'And step back, your breath is as toxic as your leadership.' Staunton's face was purple and Avalon thought for a moment that Staunton wouldn't be able to resist violence, but he did... just. He stepped back a pace and took a deep breath.

'If you want war, I'll give you war,' he eventually said. Avalon gave a slight smile though inside he could feel his heart beating violently.

'You don't have the IQ to get the better of me

Staunton. You better go off and make some clever friends.' Avalon could feel himself deliberately trying to goad Staunton. Did he feel that subconsciously this was his way out? It didn't work however because Staunton turned and walked out without saying a word. Green cut in after Staunton left.

'You are treading very dangerous ground Avalon you better-' but Avalon cut him short.

'Green, if I want to contact you, I will send for a medium.' The venom in the outburst shut Green up without another word. For the next hour, the office was silent and Avalon sat pondering his future. He was thirty-nine years old, life was passing him by, he lived alone, he ate alone and he almost worked alone. He had no social life and no future. He did, however, have a pristine, 1956 Triumph Thunderbird in a lock-up garage but he rarely rode it. Instead, he used the Ford Mondeo which was beginning to look rather shabby, like Avalon. He even liked the area he lived in and its people, he found the Black Country humour was very much to his taste. He didn't want to move away, but the job was becoming worthless. He had just about calmed down when his internal phone rang.

'Avalon,' he automatically said as he lifted the receiver.

'DC Avalon? This is Rod Moore in the DLO's office, can you come down when you have a minute?' Why would the Divisional Liaison Officer be contacting him? He told Moore he would attend straight away and then made his way to the office.

'Ah, Detective Avalon,' smiled the man behind a small desk in an equally small office, 'the Chief pointed me in your direction last week as a candidate for a police conference.'

'Did he now?' replied Avalon with some doubt in his voice. Given the recent interview with the DCI he considered that was odd timing. 'Last week you say?' Moore nodded as he quickly went over details on his computer screen. Avalon was usually the one to draw the short straw, as most officers hated conferences but *he* didn't mind them, it was a way to get away from the office for a day.

'What's it about this time?' asked Avalon with disinterest. Moore looked back up to his screen.

'It's about policing methods with respect to refugees that are entering the country from France,' replied Moore.

'Sounds exceedingly tedious,' groaned Avalon.

'Probably, but this one is in Edinburgh so there will be three days away and some expenses,' replied the officer trying to make it sound a little better.

'Edinburgh? typical,' spat Avalon, 'a conference about the policing of refugees and held about as far away as you can get from Dover.'

'Well, you know how it is, one of the Chief Constable's probably has a bit of skirt up there,' smiled the DLO.

'Yes, and his name is probably Angus,' frowned Avalon and then wondered if the Chief would still want him to go after he had refused to play ball concerning Detective Green. 'Have you spoken to the Chief today about it?' he asked. Moore shook his head.

'You have to be there next Wednesday,' he explained.

'Wednesday? That's a bit short notice isn't it?' asked Avalon raising his voice a little.

'Do you want me to tell him you don't want to go?' Avalon stared at Moore for a moment and then suddenly formed an idea. 'No, I'll certainly go. I'm not promising to stay awake though,' smiled Avalon to hide the doubt he had.

'Good,' said Moore returning the smile, 'I think they forgot about it, I told them it was coming up last month.' He shrugged and then continued. 'All the info is on the front desk along with your ID.' With a slight hesitation, Avalon said.

'Okay, I'll let the Chief know when I see him,' and he left. He walked slowly down the corridor and realised that this could be a bit of good luck, it would give him some breathing space and time to think. He certainly didn't want to be in the office any more than he needed to be and with the pressure from his superiors, it was best that he had some time away from the station. Anyway, Avalon had plans. 'If she can swing it,' he thought with a slight grin and he made his way to the front desk to pick up all the details for the conference.

'Is there a package or something for me Gary?' Avalon got along fine with the uniform officers at the station and the desk sergeant turned to see who was behind him, he was dealing with an elderly woman who seemed to be in some distress.

'Oh, Jim, yes, the DLO shoved a folder under the desk there for you.' The desk sergeant was pointing down to his right and he returned to the old lady.

'So, at what time was that?' the desk sergeant asked the woman as he once again readied his note pad.

'Well officer, I would think about...' her wobbly voice trailed off as she tried to recollect something. Avalon peered into his folder and looked through the brochures and other details for his trip. 'About half-past three,' continued the old lady. Avalon peered over to her as he replaced the items back in the folder for further reading at home.

'Half-past three,' repeated the sergeant as he wrote it down. He then looked up to her and said, 'I will get someone to come down and see you, in the meantime have a sit down and I'll get you a cuppa.' He smiled warmly at her.

'Problems?' asked Avalon with a passing interest.

'Oh, this is Mrs...' the desk Sergeant looked down at his notes, the Biro still hovering over the pad. 'Skilling, she's here to report a lost child.'

'Oh,' replied Avalon slightly more interested, as the woman must have been in her late seventies and was well past bearing children. Then he reproached himself for the inward giggle. The desk sergeant was now on the phone and asking for one of the PCs to see him on the desk. He popped the phone down and then turned back to the woman who was still standing by the desk, trying to make sense of all he had just said on the phone.

'So Mrs Skilling, just to confirm, you say it was somewhere on Clarkwell Street?'

'Well, I'm sure I don't know exactly, the chemist is on Clarkwell Street so I expect he was there but I really can't say, he could have gone anywhere.' She seemed very distraught.

'Well, I have sent for someone to see you, the quicker we get this sorted the better...' The sergeant tailed off as Avalon stepped up to the counter.

'How old was the child Mrs Skilling?' The woman seemed to be getting more upset and was showing some panic. The sergeant offered the information from his notepad.

'Just a baby really, about two and a half, fair hair and name of Clifton.' The sergeant turned the page. 'Last seen at three-thirty heading off towards the shopping precinct.' Avalon gulped. What the hell was a child of that age doing walking about on its own? And could a child of that age walk at all? He didn't know, he didn't have any children.

'That seems odd,' he said.

'Well, it's not a usual name I admit,' replied the sergeant with a slight frown.

'I mean the fact that the baby was going off to the shops,' added Avalon with a slight amount of venom in his voice.

'It's his father's fault,' demanded the woman wringing her hands. Avalon turned to her. He was about to ask more questions but she continued staring straight at Avalon. 'His mother wanted to call him David but his father was a fan of Bernie Clifton.'

'You mean the comedian who used to ride about on an emu?' asked the sergeant.

'I think you will find officer,' replied the woman, with a slight hesitation in her voice, 'it was an ostrich, it was Rod Hull who had an emu.'

'I meant,' interrupted Avalon with a bit too much impatience in his voice. He calmed his tone down a little and began once more. 'I meant, it seems odd that a child so young was out on his own.'

'Oh, he wasn't Mr Avolot.' Avalon was thinking the woman was crazy and had made this all up. 'He was with his grandfather, my husband and he was in a pushchair, not walking.' Avalon half expected the dry tones of the desk sergeant to ask, 'Your husband was in a pushchair?' but thankfully, he didn't.

'So your husband was with him?' The woman nodded, her eyes like dull grey saucers. 'So we are looking for two missing persons?'

'No, my husband is at home.' She then pointed to the sergeant's note pad. 'As I said, he suffers from...' She trailed off at this point and seemed to be thinking of something. 'Oh, I can't remember what it's called, but it's the loss of memory.' Avalon sighed, it was like the start of a bad joke.

'Alzheimer's?' offered Avalon.

'No,' insisted the woman shaking her head and looking at the floor. Avalon tried again.

'Dementia?' The woman shook her head again and then looked up with her crooked index finger almost pointing skyward.

'Oh, I can't remember what it's called,' she suddenly replied impatiently. 'Does it matter what it's called? Anyway, I told him he shouldn't do it but he said he was fine and my son-in-law said he was only going to the chemist a few hundred yards away so what could go wrong?' She looked at the floor again. 'I can't remember what for, cough medicine I think, or was it corn plasters? I can't remember but it should have only taken him fifteen minutes.' She looked up to Avalon again. 'After an hour or so we began to worry and my son-in-law and my daughter went to look for him in their car.'

'But you just said we weren't looking for two people, you said your husband was at home,' insisted Avalon picking up the sergeant's notes.

'He is, when he came back without Clifton I decided to walk down here to you,' she insisted.

'So was the pushchair with him or was it

missing?' asked Avalon not sure what was happening anymore.

'Oh it was missing, he was pushing a lawnmower instead.' For several seconds and for much longer than he should have, Avalon stared blankly at the old woman. She just stared back. Eventually she added. 'Oh, and when I asked him why he had the lawnmower he just asked, 'So didn't I go out with it then?''

'A lawnmower?' asked Avalon with his surprise unchecked. The sergeant cut in at this point and read from his notes once more.

'The mower it seemed had a flex, so it was electric.' Avalon frowned at the sergeant.

'Is that important?' he asked sarcastically.

'Well, yes it is actually,' replied the sergeant equally sarcastic. 'It means it wasn't the one belonging to Mr Skilling as he had one of those push types.'

'Oh yes,' interrupted the old woman, 'it was a brand new one, not at all like the old thing we have.' Avalon cast her a weak smile and asked.

'So let me get this right Mrs Skilling, your husband went out with his young grandson in a pushchair to go to the chemist, and he came back an hour later with a lawnmower?'

'Yes,' she nodded and then looked back down at the floor, 'it's terrible isn't it?'

'Ah Robinson,' exclaimed the sergeant as a woman PC arrived at the desk, 'will you please take Mrs Skill-' the desk phone rang. 'Oh excuse me,' and he answered the call. Avalon took over.

'Mrs Skilling here is reporting a child missing, will you take her to get a cup of tea and then run her home?' The female PC nodded and looked to the old

36

woman with a smile.

'Come on love, let's get you a nice hot cuppa,' but before they could leave, the sergeant replaced the phone on the hook and said.

'That was an interesting call.' Avalon could see satisfaction on the sergeant's face.

'So?' he asked.

'Well, the DIY shop in the precinct, has reported a very odd theft.' He closed his notebook as a gesture. Avalon thought he knew what was coming. 'It seems at about three o'clock, a Qualcast electric lawn mower was stolen from their display in front of the shop. They were temporarily off their guard because of the discovery of a young child in a pushchair hidden behind a pile of plant pots.' Avalon allowed a slight smile to lurk about on his face. He shrugged and picked up his folder and thrust it under his arm. The desk sergeant turned to the female PC.

'PC Robinson, will you please take Mrs Skilling home and see if you can get a number for her daughter if they haven't arrived back, give them a call and let them know what's happened.'

'Yes Sarge, what about the child?' she asked as she gently took the old lady by the arm.

'I'll get another car to go down there, the kid should be back in half an hour.'

'Okay Sarge,' the PC replied, and she turned to walk the old lady through the office door but the lady stopped and turned.

'Thank you, officer and Mr Overlot,' she began, and then after a moment, she asked. 'Do you think they will let us keep the lawnmower?'

'I doubt it Mrs Skilling,' replied the sergeant as

the doors swung closed. The sergeant picked up the phone and dialled, then turned to Avalon. 'It's a horrible thing that dementia, my uncle's got it.' Avalon nodded and sighed.

'Yes, it's the black death of the twenty-first century. It attacks without prejudice, without reason and crosses social and economic barriers.' Avalon ceased as the sergeant arranged for the child to be collected and then he hung up and rested his elbows on the desk and his head on his hands.

'Hmm,' was all that the sergeant said. Avalon was still staring at the office doors as he concluded.

'None of us know who will suffer with it and who will escape but ultimately it's fatal and affects the whole family.' For a moment they both stood silent and staring into nothingness until the sergeant broke the quiet with.

'Black Death, wasn't that the Pubolic Plague?' Avalon decided that if the sergeant was going to single-handedly dismantle the English language, it was time to leave.

~~~~~~

'So what do you think?' asked Avalon. His ex-wife Carol was sitting in the easy chair, cradling her cup of tea with both hands, wondering why Avalon was asking her to go with him. They were in her flat, a place Avalon had visited frequently, but a place he never really felt comfortable. He didn't know why.

'I'm suspicious,' she frowned.

'I just thought it was a great opportunity for us to see your parents and we could go out like we used to.'

Avalon was referring to the times they would visit her family and then go out into Edinburgh at night. Avalon's wife wasn't actually Scottish but her mother was. She had married an English train driver from Norfolk and he had transferred to Edinburgh some years ago after Carol had left home. When they had retired, they decided to move to Eyemouth, just over an hour along the coast from Edinburgh.

They both remembered those times in Edinburgh with a fondness and she was tempted. Carol had not remarried and to Avalon's knowledge did not see anyone on a regular basis and Avalon harboured thoughts of them getting back together. He thought that a trip back up north may do the trick. He got on well with her parents and in his mind, it was a chance to have a few days away from it all.

'So what's the catch?' she asked.

'I have to go to a conference on Wednesday and Thursday but the rest of the time is ours. I've put a couple of days leave in too so we can stay over the weekend.' The last part he said a little more quietly than the rest.

'That's new for you, having time off to be with me, maybe you should have tried that some time ago.'

'Please...' barked Avalon. He then added in a quieter tone. 'Please let's not make this into an argument, I know my flaws, I just want you to come with me.' He saw her distrusting look and added with his hands held aloft. 'I promise there is no hidden agenda.' He slowly let his hands fall and added. 'In any case, I haven't seen your parents since their anniversary two years ago.' Carol looked at him under the slightly frowning lids of her eyes and eventually said.

'Well, I suppose I could put a few days leave in too.' She took a small diary from a nearby drawer. 'What's the date?' At this point, Avalon looked slightly embarrassed and went quiet. He coughed and then said quickly and quietly.

'Next Wednesday.'

'What?' laughed Carol, 'you must be joking, I can't arrange it for Wednesday.'

'I know it's short notice but I have only just been told,' he explained apologetically.

'James, I can't, I just can't,' she said. Avalon looked disappointed, it was clear he expected her to go. He eventually sighed and said.

'I thought it was a long shot, but I really thought it would be nice.' She noticed him rest his hands on his knees, a sign she knew well, it meant he was about to get up. Before he did, she said.

'You can't expect me to drop everything just because you have to go north.' As expected, he was on his feet and looking down at her with a slight nod.

'It was worth asking,' he said with a shrug. She sighed as he walked to the door.

'Look,' she began. 'I can't promise but I may be able to call in a favour.' Avalon visibly brightened. 'But,' she insisted pointing directly at him, 'if there is a whiff of an ulterior motive I will come straight back.'

'There isn't, I promise.' It wasn't exactly the truth, but neither was it a lie. He had reasons but no ulterior motive.

'Okay,' she said. 'I'll try to sort out a few days off and I'd better let my folks know,' and picked up her phone. 'I'll do it now, they'll think we're crazy coming up without any warning, they'll need time to sort out the spare room.' She dialled and was soon speaking to her mother to make the arrangements and Avalon sat again as he remembered that the sofa bed in her mother's lounge was very uncomfortable, he thought about taking something better to lie on. His eyes scanned the room looking at *her* 'things' and how they were laid out. He looked at the way her touches made it obviously a woman's home, so much at odds with how Avalon had his rooms. He saw her individuality in the way she made home comforts and the items she kept by her, the way the cushions were arranged, the curtains and the pictures. There was nothing of their life together at all and now Avalon realised why he never felt comfortable, there was nothing of *him* in the flat. Nothing to say she had ever been married to him and everything in the room seemed to be 'just so' as if it wasn't possible to move anything. He picked up a tiny vase and looked at the base as if he knew what he was looking at and replaced it in a slightly different position. He wondered if she would notice.

'Okay, that's lovely,' she suddenly said. 'Bye, love you too,' and she placed the phone by her side and looked over to Avalon. 'Yes, she says it will be fine. She also said it would be lovely to see you again.'

'Why not, we always got on?' smiled Avalon. Carol nodded, she wasn't going to tell him that her mother had always taken *his* side when they were splitting up. She noticed the vase and moved it back to where it had previously been. Avalon smiled.

'Does the vase have a special place then?' he grinned.

'Yes, it goes exactly there, if you move it you can see I haven't dusted for two days.'

'Oh,' replied Avalon slightly crestfallen.

'And if you are going to try to cause problems before we are even on the way I suggest you call it off now.' Avalon apologised and decided to leave, cursing himself all the way back home.

The following Tuesday they were on their way and trying to make it a pleasant trip with Avalon driving and Carol reading a map.

'Why can't you have a satnav like a normal person?' she asked.

'No adventure in it, anyway I don't want to end up in a loch or something.'

'They are perfectly accurate, it's all hogwash about people getting lost using them.'

'Well, I would rather use my brain than just have someone or *something* telling me where to go and what to do,' insisted Avalon.

'I was under the impression you didn't like making decisions, I used to make all your decisions so I don't see why you-'

'No you didn't,' interrupted Avalon, giving her a quick glance.

'Of course I did,' she snapped. Avalon fell quiet, he was planning to ask her advice on issues during the trip and pursuing this conversation would jeopardise his case.

'Yes, sorry. You did indeed help me make my mind up on several occasions.' Neither was happy with the explanation but neither thought it was a good idea to continue. There was silence for several minutes and Avalon thought of turning the radio on but didn't want to give any cause for argument or disagreement. It was a six-hour drive, which was long enough to remarry and get divorced again and so he hummed a tune in his head. By the time there were in the Lake District, both of them had become tired of the silence and Carol began telling Avalon about the comings and goings of where she worked. He feigned interest for a while but the personal lives of the staff of a large opticians, didn't 'enthuse' him for very long and after he had suffered about forty miles of it, he switched his brain off and just drove.

'Well, there's no need to look so bored,' she eventually said. Avalon bit his lip.

'Here we go again,' he thought to himself. In an effort to change the subject and to get himself out of an argument he said.

'I'm packing up the job.' There was a short silence until Carol replied with.

'Where are you thinking of going?' There was an amount of doubt in the question that Avalon could perceive.

'I mean, packing it up, as in doing something else,' he added. There was more silence this time broken with a stifled, but false laugh.

'To do what, exactly?'

'Dunno, I just know I have to get out of that job.' She seemed to be thinking, Avalon could almost feel it but he could also see by her body language she was agitated. 'So, what are you thinking?' he asked. She took a deep breath, looked over to him and then back to the road before a deep sigh and then.

'What am I thinking?' She spoke in such a way Avalon knew the next few minutes were going to be traumatic. 'I'm thinking of all the times I asked you to quit the job and you refusing, of the times when you could have done something else rather than see our

43

relationship crumble, I'm thinking what could have been avoided if you had taken this decision before. I'm thinking if you pack it up now, everything we went through, all the heartache, all the fights, all the bloody lies we told our friends were a waste of time and were for nothing.' She folded her arms with a snap and then unfolded them just as quick to wag a finger at Avalon. 'If you chuck that job now, I will never, ever forgive you.' She refolded her arms and stared out of the side window. Avalon took a deep swallow and thought of a reply.

'I was wrong I admit it, but the job has become worse, the workload is higher, the hours are longer and the paperwork is-'

'Sod the paperwork!' she screamed, 'you go through all this, the last ten years of hell of trying to better yourself, getting married, divorced and only now when there is only *you* to think about, you decide the time is right to throw it all up in the air.' It had been a long time since Avalon had seen her this angry. He looked at a passing sign because he knew exactly what was coming next. 'Turn around, I want to go back.'

'I can't, we're on a motorway and the next junction is twenty miles ahead.' He tried to keep his voice calm.

'Then as soon as we reach it, head south,' she said and he could feel her gaze burning into him. He had twenty miles to try to defuse the situation. He left it for some time before he spoke and when he did, he turned to glance at her. There were a few tears on her face and for a moment it put him off track.

'I admit that...' He paused for a moment and thought deeply. 'I admit that everything that happened to us was my fault and I regret it all, all that is except our

44

marriage.' He looked ahead and tried to find the right way to say what he needed to tell her. 'I feel so bad about it and I can't change things, I can only say it was my fault and I should have done something about it.' She remained quiet, which was worrying for Avalon. 'I'm sorry for it all but I want to put it right.' This caused a reaction, quite an animated reaction.

'Don't tell me you're sorry, never tell me you're sorry. It's too late to put it right and you need to know that.' Avalon took a glance at her. She was furious, and he considered it was time to keep quiet. 'I don't care if you pack up your job. Do what you like but leave me out of your life.' He felt her turn back to stare through the side window. What was it that made him such an idiot in his personal life? He was a good detective but he couldn't blend the two parts of his life together to make them both bearable. In the next few miles, he made a decision. It was time for big changes, not small ones. He indicated to turn off the motorway and pulled up the ramp and onto the roundabout and into a services car park. They were not even halfway, and the journey had turned into a nightmare. Avalon stopped the car and got out, he then walked around to the boot and took out his case and then opened the passenger door and crouched down to speak to Carol.

'As I said, I can't undo what is done. I'm sorry but that is all I can do. You go back, I can't,' and he stood and began walking to the café. He ordered coffee and sat by a window, thinking through the next few hours. He would call a taxi to take him to the nearest train station and catch a train to Edinburgh, from there he had no further plans for the moment. As he sipped the coffee, he watched a Jackdaw searching the car park for something to eat. He felt a little like that bird, just going through the motions of keeping alive and yet not knowing what it was to live. He felt the chair move to his side, it was Carol.

'A bit melodramatic, but a clever move.' Her face was passive but Avalon kept quiet. 'So what now?' she asked looking at him. Avalon shrugged. 'I'm off to see your parents and then go to a conference,' he replied showing no emotion. She looked down at the floor. 'Coming?' he added. She nodded.

Chapter Two

A very large, blue road sign that stood as high as a sizeable house, close to Gretna Services announced the crossing of the border into Scotland but there was still a considerable way left to travel. The journey had been quiet since the argument earlier, but both Avalon and Carol were becoming bored with the silence. It was she that broke it.

'Can you remember the first time I brought you up to see my parents?'

'Yes,' replied Avalon, a slight smile growing on his face, 'it was just before I became a detective, I was still working for the bike section, I think I had applied to CID by then though.' He hesitated as the memory flooded back. 'It was Christmas and we were going up there for a week.'

'Yes, that's it,' nodded Carol with a smile, 'I remember you couldn't wait to meet them, you were telling everyone you had the job, even though you had only just applied,' she smiled. Avalon laughed and looked over to her.

'Yeah, and I made the mistake of telling your dad I was going to be a detective when we got there too.'

Avalon laughed again and turned his gaze back to the endless road.

'Oh yeah, what was it he said to you?' Carol put her index finger to her lip as she tried to recall the conversation. She frowned a little trying to remember it.

'Ah, well, he gave me a glass of sherry and sat me down by the Christmas tree,' Avalon glanced back to her to see if she remembered but there was still doubt on her face, 'can't you recall it?' She shook her head as she pursed her lips. Avalon laughed as he related the story. 'Well, he sat beside me with a very serious face and I thought he was going to give me all the stuff about taking care of his daughter and all that.'

'A bit late then,' interrupted Carol, 'we had been married for eight months.'

'I know,' grinned Avalon, 'but I couldn't have imagined at the time what he was going to say.' Avalon laughed and shook his head as he recalled the detail. 'He looked into my eyes and with the sternest expression you could imagine he said, 'I have something very unfortunate to tell you, seeing as you will soon be a detective and all that.' Carol burst out laughing at this point.

'I sort of remember it now but go on.' Avalon continued.

'He said, *Just three days ago, I came home to find a terrible crime had been committed.*' You know he looked so serious about it too,' laughed Avalon as he copied the Norfolk accent. 'I just sat there, goggle-eyed wondering what he would say, and then he said with a frown, *'I came home to find all the doors and windows wide open and everything inside had gone, not a thing was left.'* Avalon tried his best to keep the serious voice of his father-in-law but Carol was almost in tears trying to hold back the laughter, 'I looked at him and with a shocked expression I just said 'Everything - gone?' As Carol recalled the whole story, she was almost sobbing with laughter. Avalon continued. 'I wanted to tell him how sorry I was, in truth I was shocked that he could take it so well, and then came the conclusion.' Avalon took a deep breath before he continued to mimic the voice of his ex-father-in-law as he said, '*Yes, at Christmas too, everything was gone, with all the windows wide open, who could do such a thing... to an advent calendar?*' Carol was positively apoplectic now and Avalon felt tears of laughter forming in his eyes.

It was a few miles further on before all the laughter had gone and the mood inside the car had changed totally.

'We used to laugh a lot at one time,' smiled Carol.

'Yeah, but things change,' replied Avalon. 'We get older, we make mistakes and we have to deal with it.' He flashed her a quick smile, 'We just *have* to deal with it,' he added. They were both quiet for ten minutes or so until Avalon broke it with a question.

'Why did they go to Eyemouth?'

'Why not?' asked Carol, 'they like the coast and it's not that far from Edinburgh, it seems the perfect place for them.' Carol looked over to him and asked. 'I thought you liked it there?'

'I do,' nodded Avalon, 'I love the coast, but it doesn't seem that it's quite your dad, he likes towns and cities.'

'He likes activity, yes, but he also loves the coast too.' There was another small patch of silence until

Avalon said wistfully.

'You know, he predicted all this.'

'Who predicted all what?' asked Carol trying to get more comfortable.

'Your dad and us splitting up.' answered Avalon, flashing her a quick glance.

'When? How?' she stuttered.

'Oh some time ago, I think it was when we came up for that summer break, just after I got this job.'

'So what did he say?' she shuffled even more uncomfortable now. The idea, that her father saw the bust-up before it happened, unnerved her.

'Well, he didn't just burst out with it. It was when we all went into Edinburgh and you and your mum went off shopping.'

'Yes I recall, you two went to the pub,' smiled Carol trying to put a brave face on information she was sure she didn't need to know.

'Yes, we did but after a quick drink, we took a turn around the gardens and sat on a bench.' Avalon stopped the story to overtake a short line of trucks on the motorway. After a quick glance in the rear-view mirror, he continued. 'He said that as you get older, you think about missed opportunities and how maybe you would do things differently.'

'I'm not sure you should tell me this,' interrupted Carol.

'It's nothing critical, it was just his way of starting the conversation,' smiled Avalon, trying to put her mind at rest. It didn't seem to work as her body language seemed to be tense and she fidgeted and folded her arms. 'He spoke of how people can lose track of what their aims and dreams are and how we become too embroiled in the trivia of day to day living.' Avalon gave her a quick glance after checking the road ahead.

'So what's all this got to do with him predicting our divorce?' she asked slightly agitated. Avalon sighed and explained further.

'Well, he said that there were two professions he had noticed that had a social curse with them. He said one was Publican, and the other was Police Detective,' he hesitated, to see if there was a reaction, but he couldn't sense one so he continued, 'he said the former was a job with too many opportunities and the latter too few.'

'Well I hope you know what he meant because I don't,' she frowned. Avalon thought for a moment, then said.

'Your dad is a perceptive and canny man, I didn't understand at the time and thought he was talking rubbish but his words struck me just about the time of our divorce.' Avalon indicated to overtake more traffic and then drifted back to the inside lane. 'I now see what he meant, he was talking about the fact that a lot of publicans get divorced because the nature of that job means you meet lots of the opposite sex, and it's your job to pander to their needs.' He let the image sink in but she interrupted.

'So, what has that got-'

'Let me finish,' insisted Avalon, he waited for a moment and then continued, 'on the other hand, a police detective is usually with his own sex in less than salubrious surroundings. Hence, one has many opportunities, the other doesn't.'

'Sounds like a load of rubbish to me,' sighed Carol.

'Not so, I know what he means now. There are no distractions for a detective, he goes to work for long hours and comes home trying to forget about the day, trying to keep his working life from his family. Trying to forget.' He gave her another glance as she said,

'I know it's difficult, and I know it's not all your fault.' Avalon didn't want to get into another conversation on the subject, so he interrupted her again.

'Let's not go down that route, I'm just explaining what your dad predicted, *he* saw the potential for disaster, we didn't.' She sighed and folded her arms again and then, just as quickly, dropped them by her side on the seat. After a minute or two, she opened the glove box and pulled out a bag of sweets. She opened it and popped one in her mouth.

'Do you want a sweet?' she asked. Avalon shook his head and kept driving. They spent the rest of the journey in silence.

~~~~~~

Carol's parents lived on the edge of Eyemouth and as Avalon pulled up at the front gate of the little bungalow, he said.

'Looks like he eventually painted the fence.' The wooden fence was a vivid light blue colour, it looked odd and very out of place. They got out of the car and pulled out some light luggage but as they walked up the short path, the front door opened and Carol's parents came out to meet them.

'Ooh look at y' wee lambs, I bet you're exhausted,' smiled Margaret, in her light Scottish accent as she hugged her daughter. Her father then hugged and kissed her as Margaret hugged Avalon. 'You look a wee bit thin James,' she said looking him over.

'Take no notice lad, you look fine to me, how are you?' asked Colin, as he shook Avalon warmly by the hand.

'I see you got the fence done finally.' he smiled at Colin.

'Yeah, the colour was not my choice.' He nodded towards his wife.

'Ah, he was going to paint it a dull broon colour, aufy drab I thought,' she explained. Colin just looked at Avalon and said.

'Scottish,' he shrugged and rolled his eyes, 'everything has to have bright colours,' he added as they walked into the house.

After the welcome and the initial conversation about the journey, Avalon announced he was going for a walk to have a look around Eyemouth, not for any other reason than to allow the family to catch up and have some time alone. He strolled down the hill into the centre, past the little museum and down to the quayside. The town still clung on to a fishing industry and Avalon liked to sit at the bridge and watch the boats manoeuvring in and out of what seemed a tiny space. If he didn't get too close to the processing yard and the smell of rotting fish, the sights and sounds could be particularly relaxing. He then took a walk down the quay and onto the seafront, he leaned on the seawall to contemplate his future. What would he do if he left the police force? There was now some doubt where previously there had been a direction. Did he really need to leave the force? After all, he had just let the job get on top of him, as Carol had said many times, he was too inflexible. Maybe if he had been a little easier going with his fellow officers from the start, things wouldn't have gone so bad for him, it was his own fault, he knew that, but it was his nature to do the job to the best of his ability. The more he glanced out and watched the sea breaking onto the sand, the more he realised that all he needed to do was move to another police force. There were so few detectives it would be relatively easy, latest estimates were that there was a shortfall of several thousand experienced detectives. That was a great problem to many forces, as with the long hours, poor pay and far too much paperwork, very few police officers were making the move to the CID. He jumped from his thoughts to walk down the beach and picking up a couple of pebbles and tossing them into the water, he realised he was just skirting over the problem. Those were the major reasons he was sick of the job. Things in the force were getting worse, not better, and he knew he was kidding himself that the job would be any easier with another force. With so few detectives, everyone was overworked, so how would he ever be able to recover a private life for himself unless he left? As he walked back up the hill, he had decided the time had come for a change and he would give notice as soon as he returned.

The following morning, they drove to Dunbar to have a relaxing day, so the four of them called at a twee little café on the main street and ordered coffee. Avalon was planning to catch the train into Edinburgh from Dunbar to save parking problems and as he had never been to Dunbar, he thought he would familiarise himself with the place. The weather was pleasant and Avalon liked the town but it wasn't long before Colin motioned with his hand that, a 'dram' may be on offer. Avalon surreptitiously nodded and Colin announced,

'We could go for a pint while these two do some shopping don't you think?' to no one in particular.

'Sounds good to me,' agreed Avalon as if the idea hadn't been in his head previously.

'Och, you two get off, we'll see you later,' cooed Margaret in her soft burr. The two men strode off to a pub that was obviously well known to Colin as he went straight to it. It was clear why too, Colin liked 'real ale' and though Avalon wasn't keen and preferred a single malt, he decided to go with a half pint of beer as he was driving. They stood at the bar by the door, after Colin had taken three or four gulps and half emptied the glass, he turned to Avalon and asked.

'So how's James, what are you up to these days?'

'Oh, you know,' he sighed, 'the same old crap, work, bed, work, bed.' He too took a sip of beer and then added. 'I go to the toilet on occasions too.'

'Nothing changes then?'

'No, not really,' sighed Avalon again not wanting to get into a depressing conversation that proved even more conclusively how boring his life was. 'What about you?' he asked to change the subject.

'Well, if it's excitement you want, stay clear of Eyemouth,' he grinned. Avalon nodded and looked around the pub, it was busy enough and comfortable, Avalon felt relaxed, maybe *too* relaxed, as he decided to let Colin into his thoughts. Standing there, listening and taking in the comings and goings of a quiet, Scottish coastal town, he heard himself say.

'I'm packing up the police.' For a moment there

was no response and then gradually, Colin turned to him.

'Does Carol know?'

'Yes, we had an argument about it on the way up.'

'To be expected,' said Colin taking another gulp of beer. 'By, that's hit the spot,' he added and ordered another. 'You?' he then asked pointing at Avalon's almost full glass.

'No, better not,' he replied. Colin paid for the new drink and motioned to a seat by the bar and the two of them sat.

'What're going do?' asked Colin.

'No idea,' replied Avalon shrugging, 'I just know I have to sort my life out and the police force is no place to do that.' Colin made a slight noise at this, like a sniff with a hum included. Avalon was unsure what it meant but expected the older man to impart some words of wisdom. He wasn't disappointed.

'Well,' Colin sighed at length, 'maybe it's for the best.' He took another drink. 'Y' know, when I was about your age, I wondered about my life. Yeah, I had a great family, a friend and wife and a wonderful daughter but there always seemed to be something missing.' Colin looked around the small bar. 'When you sit in a place like this, it's easy to think that there isn't much to life anyway. You take in the passing of other people, having a chat and a beer and you can easily think this is as good as it gets,' he took yet another drink, as if to confirm it, 'but when you're younger and you sit in the cab of a diesel locomotive, watching the world pass by the window and yet not seeing any of it, you start to wonder.' Avalon sensed a break and used it to say.

'Odd that, because I thought you of all people,

were content.'

'Me?' Colin laughed slightly. 'Show me a content man and I'll show you an empty husk of a person.' He turned to Avalon and continued, 'Life isn't about watching the world pass by your cab window lad, it's about opening the bloody door and jumping off the train and if you feel the time has come for change, then just do it.' He picked up his glass and gestured a toast. 'To the future, be a participant, not a spectator.' Avalon picked up his glass and repeated,

'The future!' Both glasses returned to the table and Colin, once more, looked at Avalon.

'I know you have expectations of getting things back together with Carol but don't let that stand in the way of what you have to do.'

'I did have, but I think...' Avalon hesitated, then continued, 'I think I've ruined any chance of that to be honest.'

'Right then,' offered Colin with a hint of determination in his voice. 'Do you fancy a drink at home?' Avalon thought it was a good idea.

'Certainly, we could stop off somewhere to grab a bottle of something.'

'No need,' grinned Colin, 'I have a lonely bottle of Bowmore in the cupboard.' They both drank up and went back to the town to find the two women.

~~~~~~

Avalon wasn't a great fan of trains but he had decided that driving to Dunbar and catching the train into Edinburgh was preferable to trying to find parking in the city. Oddly, the train had been on time and he considered that it could be a coincidence or, maybe Scottish trains were run slightly better than in the south, either way, he found the 'James McIntyre Conference Centre' in plenty of time for a coffee before it began. It was going to be tedious he knew, but it had been a means to an end and here he was, with a break away from the office in Wolverhampton, drinking a reasonable cup of coffee in quiet surroundings. There were just the comings and goings of the other people at the conference, most of them employed by the police service in one way or another. Avalon considered that he could tell what job they had by the way they walked. There was a Detective Sergeant and there was an inspector. He wondered if he had the CID gait and thought about trying to change the way he walked. To his right, there was a chap in a dark blue suit, carrying a coffee and a newspaper, he had the conference ID lanyard around his neck and a folder stuffed under the same arm that carried the coffee. That meant to Avalon that the newspaper was the more important document and the folder was to do with the conference. He looked tired and under pressure.

'Definitely CID,' thought Avalon to himself, 'probably a sergeant, or maybe an inspector due to the quick movement of his eyes.' Avalon noticed he was searching the room for a place to sit and yet had passed by an empty table, he was now working his way towards Avalon. The man raised his eyebrows and Avalon returned a tight-lipped smile as the man came to the table.

'Do you mind?' he asked, as he sat.

'No, not at all, be my guest.' The man carefully placed the cup, folder and newspaper on the table. He then reached his hand across and said.

'Andrew Davies.' Avalon shook the hand, replying with,

'Avalon,' there was a slight hesitation before he offered, 'James Avalon.' The man looked to be searching his mind for something and then, as the look of realisation came across his face, he attempted a slight gesture with his hand holding out two fingers to point at Avalon.

'It's an unusual name and I expect there is more than one family with it, but...' Avalon sighed inwardly as he anticipated what was coming. 'are you, by any chance, the DS Avalon from the West Midlands?' The man was readying a slight smile and Avalon began to regret coming, was he never to shake off the spectre of the Ghostbusters?

'Yes,' he replied as he took a drink of his coffee.

'I thought it would be, that was an amazing insight to tie in the church with the jewel gang.' The man seemed genuinely animated as Avalon tried to brush over the event and for a moment the tiredness seem to fall from the man's face.

'Just one case that hit the news,' he sighed.

'Oh, yes,' replied Davies as he saw the ambivalence in Avalon's face, 'but nevertheless, it was a brilliant piece of detective work.' Avalon didn't know how the national papers had covered it but to his own mind, he knew the case had been cracked by pure chance, detective work had nothing to do with it. He shrugged and took another drink. 'You have quite a reputation for that kind of case,' added Davies realising that Avalon was somewhat disinterested. Avalon just smiled and nodded. 'That kind of case,' sounded very much like this Davies was accusing him of being incapable of proper detective work.

'I do sometimes work on ordinary cases you know,' he replied but this time without the smile.

'Oh, of course,' stuttered Davies, 'I didn't mean to...' He stopped and then leaned on the table, 'I'm sorry.' He began again. 'I must have sounded like an idiot going on about something in the past. It's just that we were talking about you and that case last week.' Davies tried a slight smile.

'We?' asked Avalon.

'In my office,' replied the man, 'one of the cases we are running at the moment has some...' he broke off for a second, 'anomalies that reminded one of the team of your old case and he mentioned it.'

'Oh.' nodded Avalon still unimpressed.

'We're so swamped at the moment, everyone has become a little disoriented by it. One of the team brought up your name. Ironic really that I should bump into you.' He stopped and sipped at his own coffee.

'Yeah, I think we're all overworked at the moment,' replied Avalon, watching the man check his watch as he replaced the cup on the table.

'I suppose we had better get off,' he said pointing to the exit. Indeed, it was about time for the conference to begin and they walked into the hall together.

It was a boring affair with very few people interested in the problems over in Calais and Dover. Every force had its own issues, without bringing any more to the table, several speakers came to the stage, but no one really listened to any of them. When it was over, Avalon looked at his watch and considered a drink before the journey back, but then he realised he still had to drive back from Dunbar. Maybe he could get Carol to drop him off tomorrow.

'Got time for another coffee?' asked Davies. Avalon considered it for a moment why not? What else was he going to do for forty minutes? The two of them set off towards the cafe and immediately Davies began to speak.

'Look, I've been thinking.' Avalon was quite unsure of what was coming, but he listened. 'I was wondering if you would consider helping out on this case for a few weeks,' he then added quickly as an aside, 'if your people can spare you, of course.' Avalon smiled.

'Well, it's not my decision as you know and I'm absolutely sure they wouldn't let me, we are pulled out too.'

'Of course, we all are these days, it's a big problem,' there was a pause, 'but what if I could swing it?' He raised his eyebrows a little as they stopped at the cafe entrance, 'would you think about it?' Avalon realised he was serious. This wasn't someone having a laugh, this wasn't someone calling him Spook because they saw him as an outsider. This was someone interested in him for his abilities. Or was it?

'Well,' began Avalon with a hint of inevitability, 'for starters, I don't know who you are, where you are from and what the case is. Secondly, it's more likely that you will find that Bergerac is a real copper, and he's here at the conference than you'll get my Inspector to agree to let me help, so I would probably say, forget it.' Davies just smiled.

'Sorry, I seem to be leaving you in the dark a great deal today, I'm Detective Inspector Davies of 'B' Section, Inverness.' He held out his hand again.

'Oh,' replied Avalon shaking his hand once more, 'Inverness?' he added, knowing it was north of their current position but not knowing exactly where. 'But you're not...' Davies interrupted.

'Scottish? No, I'm from Yorkshire originally but moved up ten years ago.' He held his arm out towards the cafe and they moved inside as he spoke and Avalon followed. 'I do like it up there but we are sadly understaffed and just lately we have had, what you may describe as, a crime wave. We can't understand it but there you go.' They walked to the counter and Davies ordered, then he continued. 'One or two important cases are being left on the back burner it's so bad.' Avalon took his coffee as he considered that in his office, *that* was always the case. The lesser crimes waited until there was time to get to them. Davies continued. 'This one particular case has baffled the team and though we are working on it as time allows, your take on it would be interesting, to say the least.' He stopped and nodded to a table, 'Shall we?' Avalon moved off and they sat. 'We could do with someone with your particular experience to give it a once over.'

'What do you mean?' asked Avalon stirring in his sugar.

'Well, some people,' he glanced up to Avalon with a look that said 'you can count me out of that demographic', 'seem to think that there is some kind of legend attached to the case and even a few of the team are beginning to think it has a hint of oddness to it.'

'Do they think like that up there then?' asked Avalon frowning.

'No not usually, they like their legends of course and after all, Inverness is the land of the Loch Ness

Monster, but they are usually level-headed, pragmatic and realistic.' Davies dropped his guard for a moment and Avalon could see, the man was not just tired, he looked totally drained. It was a hard life anywhere in Britain and if they were really busy at his section, then the fact he was at this conference, probably meant he was attending in his own time. Avalon looked at his watch, he would have to leave soon, and so he concluded the little conversation.

'Well, as I said, we're all pretty busy so I doubt that anyone in their right mind would agree to move an officer at the moment, no matter how temporarily.' Avalon omitted to mention he was planning on leaving the force.

'Well, there are ways. We have issued many secondments before and though there's always loads of paperwork, they can be very beneficial to all parties.'

'Yeah, but secondments are usually for specialists,' insisted Avalon.

'Not always,' replied Davies, 'but then again, you *are* a specialist.' He gave a smile before taking another drink. 'If you're not interested, I understand,' he concluded.

'It's not that, I just don't know how you could swing it in such a short time,' replied Avalon.

'There are ways to short track it but you would have to be sure you wanted to do it.' Avalon thought about it for a moment and then drank his coffee. What had he got to lose? He was going to hand his notice in anyway, this at least gave him some hope, and time to think.

'Why not? if you can sort it, I'll certainly give it a try.'

'The only drawback is that when you return to your force, they may reassign you, same pay grade of course but it stands to reason, if they bring someone in, you may not get your old post back,' frowned Davies. Avalon didn't say anything about that, he didn't tell Davies he didn't want the damn post back, so he stood holding his hand out.

'Well, I am interested for sure but I have a train to catch, are you here tomorrow?' Davies shook the hand and said,

'Probably, as long as I don't get called back, this damn conference couldn't have come at a worse time.' They said their goodbyes and Avalon began the journey back to Dunbar and then to Eyemouth where he had a late dinner with the family and an early night.

The following day was much of the same as Avalon had decided not to ask Carol to drive him to Dunbar. He caught the train into Edinburgh then made his way to the conference centre and the café for a preparatory drink, to help him through the tedium of the day. The conference menu for the day was even more stale, with talks by this Chief of Police and that, several Police Federation speakers and various other members of the police force. Avalon didn't see any sign of Andrew Davies that morning and so he made his way to the conference hall alone. Most of the speeches were about long hours, too much paperwork, lack of clothing allowances and sundry other issues, which to Avalon's jaundiced eye, seemed like preaching to the converted. Everyone knew the problems, what they needed was someone to do something about it.

One female Chief Inspector took the podium to

tell the assembled crowd how they needed more experienced police officers to take up the cause and join the ranks of the CID, Avalon laughed at the seemingly random way in which her talk had followed directly after a Detective Inspector bemoaning the exact reasons no one wanted to be a detective. He found he was looking at his watch with a regularity which may be noticed in a room that contained a great number of detectives, but he also noticed he wasn't the only one. He calculated that, as long as he did a bit of research on the subjects, he could easily leave around noon and make his way back to Eyemouth. There was little of any interest anyway and so, during one of the too-few breaks, he made his way towards the door and into the foyer. There, he saw Andrew Davies talking on his phone and when Davies saw Avalon, he dropped his serious face and smiled, held the phone to his chest and whispered.

'Have you got a minute?' and returned to the phone. Avalon stood and waited, while Davies continued the call, which had the word 'Sir' contained often enough for it to be one of his commanding officers on the other end.

'Sorry about that,' he said as he finished the call, 'have you got time for a drink?' He motioned in the café's direction. Avalon nodded, he wasn't keen on staying more than he had to but he wanted to hear what the man had to say. They were served at the till and Avalon offered to pay but Davies wouldn't hear of it and they moved to a bar area as most of the tables were already taken.

'I had a word with the Chief this morning about what we talked of yesterday.' It seemed Davies was certainly taking the issue more seriously than Avalon was.

'Oh, was that who you were just talking to?' he asked without any real interest.

'Yes, but not about that,' smiled Davies. 'The Chief is all for it and says he'll do what he can.'

'Which is almost nothing,' thought Avalon, but all he said was, 'Okay.' He said it in an almost questioning way but he could think of nothing to add and simply shrugged his shoulders.

'We have started the ball rolling with the paperwork just in case. It's a long shot, I know, but there's nothing to lose.' Avalon was on the verge of telling Davies that he was quitting the force but a little piece of old advice from his ex-wife cut in through his memory and told him not to volunteer information. He had to admit that in the past, he had freely given information to colleagues and it had always cost him. No more. Information was power, he knew that really, and he was beginning to correct his mistakes and create a new Avalon, this Avalon would be more careful about what he said.

'We are so short of officers...' there was a pause, 'it would be a real bonus to have someone with your background working with us.'

'As you said, every force is under the cosh and that's why I think my branch will never agree,' shrugged Avalon, trying to justify his lack of enthusiasm.

'I don't think that is the problem, we can issue the paperwork to get you up for ten weeks or so, the trick is short tracking the system and we may have to pull strings for that.'

'It hardly seems worth the hassle,' smiled Avalon.

'Don't sell yourself short James.' Davies meant

it, but Avalon couldn't imagine what Davies thought he could do for them. 'So are you off back to the West Midlands after this?' asked Davies.

'No, I'm having a few days in Eyemouth with the ex-wife and her family.' Avalon almost visibly cringed as he said it. So 'what happened to the new Avalon?' he thought to himself, as he cursed inwardly. He shook his head as he considered what that whole statement gave away. 'Well, I er...' he stuttered, trying to find the words to make the situation seem better, 'we still get on fine and I still keep in touch with her parents... it's, well...' and he shrugged, as Davies took a sip from his coffee, watching Avalon over the rim of his cup with piercing, but friendly, blue eyes. Davies nodded and then, just for a moment, he seemed to drift off, before saying quietly.

'Yes, the job can take a harsh toll on family life.' He looked down to his cup for some few seconds. It didn't take the mind of a detective to see that Davies was under some kind of personal pressure too. He seemed to jump slightly as he said. 'Well, it's nice you both still get on,' replacing the cup on the saucer.

'It is,' but Avalon gave nothing else away. Davies looked down to his cup again, the tiredness seemed to wash over him, like a cloud and then he looked up and said.

'Look, I could do with your phone number.' Avalon took out his phone and looked for the number, as he had no idea what it was. Davies copied the digits onto his phone, and said, 'Great, I'm not sure if your people will play ball but we'll give it a shot. Nothing ventured....' Avalon placed the phone back in his pocket as Davies continued. 'If I can get someone back at the office to push this, you never know,' he let it sink in, then continued, 'so what day do you go back?'

'We're travelling back on Saturday, I'm at work on Monday morning, so I've got a lot to do when I get back.'

'Talking of which,' said Davies, and he drained the dregs of his cup with alacrity, 'I have to go.' He looked at his watch and held out his hand. 'I'll try to call you before you go back south but great to meet you anyway and you never know, we may still work together.' Avalon shook his hand with genuine friendship, he had grown to like the man for his affable nature.

'Yeah, I look forward to that,' smiled Avalon, and they parted company, with Avalon realising he hadn't had time to question Davies about the case. He left the building and called off at a small whisky shop he had noticed earlier, to see if he could find a bottle of single malt he had promised himself. Few shops seemed to sell exactly what he was looking for but to his surprise, this one did. He paid just over £190 to walk out of the shop with a particular twenty-five-year-old whisky. He smiled as he walked, it wasn't in his nature to smile just after parting with so much money, and it was a great deal of cash for a single bottle, but it *was* in his nature to smile about the thought of sampling his favourite tipple.

On the train back, he pulled the bottle out of its bag, looked at the light, amber fluid and read every word on the label and then it was carefully replaced into the bag and gently rest at his side.

Friday morning was reasonably warm and, once again, Avalon set off to the railway station at Dunbar, the difference was, today there was no conference and he was having a day in Edinburgh with Carol. They were going to try to have a pleasant day visiting the places they had once frequented years before. After departing the train at Waverly Station, they crossed the bridge and passed the Wellington Statue then headed into the old town. There were quite a few changes in the city since he had last been, the most obvious addition were the trams. A contentious project, only recently completed, but they turned their back on the new part of the town, to search out the old, in search of places they shared in their memories. The area they were heading for was the Grassmarket, once a place where many a felon met their end, hanging from a gallows, now just another part of the city, popular with tourists due to its history. Avalon saw buildings and pubs that he remembered but there was a great deal of change. The Grassmarket certainly had its tourism, but the old town still had its bustling drinking houses and music scene, yet there was something lacking. A sense that everything now ran to schedule, there was no spontaneity, no 'edge' and everything seemed very expensive. A clean, clinical feel was what they both felt but the pleasure of remembering and chatting about the times they had, and the characters they recalled, made for a most pleasurable day and Avalon suggested lunch in one of the pubs in the Grassmarket. The interior was dark but pleasing, with plenty of character and they sat, rested, and talked. After their meal was finished, Carol tentatively asked Avalon about his plans.

'So, when are you going to tell them you are leaving?' Avalon's eyes darted up from his glass on the table that was still almost full.

'When I get back, I suppose,' he replied taking a

sip of the beer. It wasn't his favourite tipple, but he tried to stay off the whisky at lunchtime. She looked more intently at him and as he looked back into her eyes, he began to realise something, something he had known for some time but had refused to admit. He hadn't *wanted* to admit it. They were never going to get back together and if he carried on pursuing it, he knew he would lose her as a friend, as well as a wife. He couldn't bear that, she had been, and still was, the best friend he had, probably, the only friend, and he had to start treating her as such. Inside, his stomach bucked and baulked at the thought of having to give her up, but there was no other way.

'Actually, I've got something to tell you,' he began but quickly added, with a gesture that expressed doubt, 'I mean it may come to nothing but it has been offered.' He knew that was probably an exaggeration, but he didn't want to come over somewhat morose and wished to keep the mood upbeat.

'Go on then,' she smiled, 'or do I have to ask questions like usual?'

'No,' he grinned, 'I just want to make it clear, there is nothing confirmed.' He waited a second before continuing. 'One of the people I met at the conference asked if I would work on a case with their section if he could get me transferred temporarily.' Carol let the smile subside. Avalon wondered if he had misjudged it.

'Well, that's good isn't it?' she eventually said.

'Yes, I think it is,' shrugged Avalon, 'it's in Scotland though.' He waited for her reaction. She opened her eyes wide, and a broad smile erupted, as she said.

'Brilliant! That could be so good for you, a new start. That's what you need.'

'Well, don't look so eager to see the back of me,' smiled Avalon. She laughed.

'No, I mean that couldn't be better for *you*, but...' a stain of doubt came over her features, 'why would someone ask you? Are you sure they are genuine?'

'Yeah, pretty sure,' shrugged Avalon, 'he said he knew of me from the papers, you know, after the Saint Mary's Church thing?' Avalon had always wanted to choke in the past when he spoke of it but this time he brushed it off, 'and, he said they had a case where my experience would be of use.' He felt excited and took another drink.

'It sounds like it's just what you need, have you told him you would take it?'

'Sort of,' replied Avalon, replacing his glass on the table, 'there is nothing concrete but his boss is up for the idea. The problem is they need someone now and the paperwork with these things takes forever.' There was a slight silence before he continued. 'With our office being pulled out at the moment, well we always are, I can't see them agreeing to it.' Carol softened her smile, making small creases around her eyes which gave away a look of genuine happiness for him.

'I don't know, they might,' she said.

'Well if they don't, I *will* hand my notice in, that's for sure.'

'So when will you find out?' she inquired.

'I don't know, he said he would try and call before we went back but I expect he has loads of other things on his plate.' Avalon once again remembered how Davies looked terribly tired when his guard was down.

'Well fingers crossed for you,' she said. Avalon finished his drink with an edge of finality that pleased

71

him. He felt better than he had for some time. He actually considered things were going to change, whether for the better or not, he didn't know but on the bright side, he didn't care.

They left the pub and made their way back to the station and caught the train back to Dunbar. Before going back to the car, Avalon suggested going down to the harbour. There was something about old harbours that gave him a sense of warmth, somewhere that he could gather his thoughts. Maybe it was the fact that these were the places that so many mariners and fishermen had gone about their work, not sure if they would ever return to see their loved ones again. It was probably the harshness of the life that had been lived at the ports over the years that brought him down to earth, either way, he had noticed on previous occasions that sitting at the dockside, brought clarity of thought. They walked down towards the ruin of the castle and sat on a bench that overlooked the harbour and an old ship's screw that was now on display as a historical exhibit. There was a slight aroma of fishing, that salty, fishy smell that can only be found in that kind of place, a place where fishing was still practised and nets and baskets littered the harbour. Avalon took a deep breath.

'That ought to be a bad smell, but I love it,' he smiled.

'The fishy smell you mean?' asked Carol.

'Yeah, sort of, but to me it smells of the sea.'

'Well, there is a good reason for that,' she began, he knew what was coming but he let it go, 'you see that big bluish-grey thing over there? Well that, for your information, *is* the sea.' Avalon looked out beyond the harbour, took another deep breath, exhaled, and said,

'They see the form of air, but mortals breathing it drink the whole summer down into the breast. The lavish pinks, the field new-mown, the ravishing sea smells, the wood fire smoke that whispers rest.'

'My god,' exclaimed Carol, 'poetry?'

'I love poetry, you know that,' he replied looking directly at her.

'Yes, but do you know how long it is since you quoted any?' He shrugged and looked back out towards the sea before continuing,

'The tremor on the rippled pool of memory that, from each smell in widening circles goes, the pleasure and the pang, can angels measure it?' and with this, he looked to her, *'An angel has no nose.'* He touched her lightly on the tip of her nose, before smiling and saying, 'far too long I'm thinking.' He stood and leaned on the heavy shaft of the ship's screw, 'but something has changed,' he added.

'So what is it?' she asked. He turned to her, folded his arms, and said.

'To be honest, I can't remember, but it's CS Lewis.'

'No, what's changed? Not the name of the bloody poem,' she sighed.

'Oh, I don't know.' He turned back to look out to the sea again. She stood and joined him, as she knew she wouldn't be able to hear what he said with his back turned. 'I think it's being here, in such a place as this, it clears the mind, it makes me sane again.'

'It's a pity you can't bottle it, maybe you wouldn't be in this position if you could.' She folded her arms and looked out trying to imagine what he saw in a little harbour town.

'Probably,' he replied, 'but if I could bathe in this all the time, I wouldn't know how special it was, would I?' She shrugged and looked around. She couldn't see anything, just a pile of old fishing paraphernalia and noticed far too many 'odd' odours to make it pleasant. As she was just thinking that she would like to walk back to the car, Avalon began again.

'*Far richer they! I know the senses, witchery, guards us like air, from heavens too big to see,*' he was looking out beyond the harbour and out to sea, '*imminent death to man that barbed sublimity, and dazzling edge of beauty unsheathed would be.*'

'Have you done?' she asked, turning to him with her arms still folded.

'On being human,' he replied.

'What?'

'The name of the poem, On Being Human, by CS Lewis,' he added.

'You know all that stuff flies over my head. It flies over so often I think poems use my head to find their way home.'

'You don't need poetry when you have a strange mind,' smiled Avalon, as he walked away.

'Hang on, who's got a strange mind?' she said as she followed and called after him, 'it's you that thought that 'Grand Budapest Hotel' was a good film.'

~~~~~~

Avalon and his ex-wife had said goodbye to her parents and were travelling south to return to the West Midlands, but still, there had been no call from Davies. Avalon hadn't really expected it and he wasn't all that

74

bothered, he just wasn't looking forward to telling them back at the station that he was quitting the force and didn't really know when he ought to do it. He knew there would be a scene when he did but there was one aspect of it he would enjoy, he could actually tell them what he really thought. The sense of release was palpable, and he was feeling stronger and more decisive by the hour, the idea of quitting as soon as he arrived on Monday morning, was becoming the most obvious option. Yes, he ought to wait to see if Davies rang but in the back of his mind, he knew that call would never come and the feeling of freedom he had been thinking about leaving the force overrode all others. As they left the motorway, after seven hours on the road, Avalon turned down a side road and said,

'I'll just top up with fuel so I don't have to do it Monday morning.' Carol nodded and sat in the car while he filled up. To her left, at the rear of the petrol station, some horrible little adolescent was giving a mother with a child a great deal of trouble for bumping into him. It hadn't been her fault, the teenager had been engrossed with his phone and hadn't seen the woman, but as always, the innocent party gets attacked because they are not as strong. Carol sat in her sadness, shaking her head, as she watched the woman backing off to protect the child but then she saw a man was going over to help. 'Ah, that's good,' she thought, just before she realised it was Avalon. Before she could get out of the car, Avalon had backed his forearm over the chest of the teenager, slipped his leg behind the youth, and forced him over onto his back, he dropped like a sack of wet manure. Then Avalon's foot came crashing down on the hand of the youth, the one that had been holding the phone, making the prostrate attacker scream out with agony.

'Help, help call the police!' screamed the youth in panic. Avalon pulled out his warrant card and stuffed it roughly into the face of the horror-stricken youth.

'Oh look, we're here, that was quick wasn't it?' hissed Avalon, bringing more pressure onto the youth's hand.

'James, James.' Avalon turned to see Carol looking at him with a worried face. He looked down at the prostrate figure that was now in tears. He let the pressure off the hand, which revealed a broken phone, and what could have been a broken hand. He put his warrant card away and bent down to the youth.

'Please remember to tell everyone how quickly we responded to your call,' he spat, 'we sometimes get bad press,' he concluded. As he stood, he noticed a few people standing around including the manager of the petrol station. The woman who had been the target of the youth smiled at him and nodded, the petrol station manager looked over to the now swearing, youth and said to Avalon.

'I knew someone would slip, it's obvious when the soapy water from the car wash runs down over the oil, Bam!' and he emphasised the last word, by slamming his fist into the palm of his other hand. 'Typical as well that just here there are no CCTV cameras, so we will never know how he managed to fall.' Avalon nodded grimly and returned to the car. Carol sat beside him and waited until they had left the forecourt and then set about him.

'What do you think you are doing?' She turned to him. Avalon sat quietly. 'If that gets out, you will be sacked and that will affect your pension, not to mention a day in court and maybe a prison sentence.' She was still glaring at him. He turned to her and smiled.

'I know, but I don't care.'

'Well, I'm glad you think it's amusing but I don't. I have never seen you like that.' She looked back to the road ahead. Avalon was still smiling but instinct made him check the mirror. There was no one there, and he didn't expect to see anyone following him, but this was something he had wanted to do for years. It felt good, like a release of pressure and it was a feeling he hadn't experienced for many, many years. The rest of the journey was quiet and Avalon noticed that Carol had been sitting with her arms folded which, to him, meant she was furious, or upset, or both. She was right of course, if he was reported he was as good as sunk but by the comments of the garage manager, he considered that he stood a good chance of getting away with that strange bout of chivalry, saving a damsel in distress was part of his job anyway, sort of.

Oddly, Carol didn't mention the incident, but she did seem rather cool when he dropped her off at her place, then he thanked her for helping make the time in Scotland pleasant and he drove off to his house.

It was strange to be back there, after the few days at the coast in Scotland, the old house seemed a little dismal and foreboding and as he poured a glass of his newly acquired whisky, he sat at the dining table, turned on his laptop and scoured the seemingly hundreds of emails but nothing of real interest showed itself. Just odd messages from the office, and spam. He picked up a folder he had made notes in, and, on a new sheet, jotted down the main points of the conference so he could type it up later. After about fifteen minutes contemplating the tedium that he was going to have to go back to on Monday, he was slipping back into his old self, so he made a light snack and put the TV on. Some inane programme was playing in the background as Avalon began to return to the idea of keeping his job. Was he running scared? Was he 'shooting up' the feeling of freedom rather than believing he had any options? It was possible, and the doubt began to cloud his judgement once more. He turned off the TV, finished his glass of whisky, and then went to bed in the hope that he would dream of a new adventure that may come his way. He didn't however, he dreamed instead of being in the local Morison's supermarket, stark naked, pushing a shopping trolley full of ready meals but unable to get to the checkout without bumping into anyone. Why was it that he had such stupid dreams? Did everyone dream of being naked in public places or was it just him, stifling some weird fetish that he didn't realise he had?

Sunday arrived, Avalon assessed his future again and readied himself for Monday morning, whatever it would bring. He got all the work out of the way he needed to do, and by lunchtime, he considered that he could relax for the rest of the day and give himself time to think. He thought of going to the chip-shop for his lunch but then realised the 'chippy' would be closed, so his next best option was going to be out of a tin as he hadn't had time to go shopping. Normally, Avalon hated spaghetti in all its forms, so why the hell did he actually have a tin of the stuff in his cupboard? He certainly hadn't bought it and as he was the only person living there, he had to assume that the tin had appeared by means unexplained. Maybe the tin had been caught up in some experiment in the future and been transported there, or maybe a balloon of 'dark matter' had floated by and caused some temporal instability that had allowed the tin to appear in his house. On closer examination, it was clear that both options were probably not the case, as the 'use by' date was still valid.

'What the hell?' asked Avalon, but there was no one there to answer. He placed the tin on the kitchen worktop and looked for something else, which ended up as beans on toast after thawing out half a frozen loaf from the freezer. Anything rather than spaghetti. He carried the food and the tin containing the spaghetti, placing it carefully on the table, glancing at it now and then, just in case it mysteriously disappeared, to reappear back in the cupboard. He turned on the TV again and ate the meal, watching more inane rubbish that he was amazed by.

'Who the hell watches this junk?' he asked himself, not considering that *he* was actually watching it. A programme where a so-called 'Celebrity Chef' was showing a 'Celebrity Gardener' how to cook what he had grown and, presumably, the 'Celebrity Gardener' would show the 'Celebrity Chef' how to grow peas in the next show. Avalon considered that there were very few 'Celebrity Coppers' on the television, other than the fictional ones of course. Was there a gap in the market he wondered? He passed a thought through his mind, a mind that was becoming more adventurous every day, and that thought was of a TV programme where a 'Celebrity Copper' and a 'Celebrity Chef' team up to catch a 'Celebrity Villain'.

'You're nicked sunshine,' hissed Avalon between

bites of beans on toast, 'and when we get you back to the cells, we're gonna show you how to make the perfect flan.' He giggled to himself and finished his food. He then stood and decided that the programmes were not worth his attention and the TV would be got rid of. He was making decisions he never thought he had the power to make. Things were changing and the speed of the change was gathering momentum. He considered taking the television down to the firearms team and asking them to shoot it, but after consideration, they would just tell him it wasn't a proper, designated target or something similar. Throw it off a cliff? Not likely, as there were very few cliffs in Wolverhampton. Well, it would just have to sit there in the corner and collect dust. He may find some other piece of furniture to take its place later. Avalon washed the plate he had used, made a cup of tea and sat in the easy chair. He then realised he was looking at the blank screen of the TV, so he got up, found his leather jacket and walked to his lockup garage, pulled the Triumph out and went for a gentle ride around the outskirts of the town. He loved that bike, the smell, the noise, the feel of the thing were all very nostalgic and relaxing. It wasn't a bad day, he lifted the visor of his crash helmet and enjoyed the afternoon. It was then the phone rang from his inside pocket. It was such a surprise to him, who the hell was ringing him on a Sunday anyway? He pulled over into a lay-by close to the Bilbrook Canal and answered it after taking his helmet off.

'Avalon.' He said in a monotone voice.

'Hello, James, it's Andrew.' Avalon had no idea who Andrew was, he had only just worked out who James was.

'Sorry?' he replied, in a questioning tone.

'It's Andrew, Andrew Davies, we met in Edinburgh.' Then it clicked, this was Detective Inspector Davies of the Inverness police force, the person he never thought he would hear from again.

'Oh,' there was some hesitation, many thoughts were whizzing through his mind, 'er hello, how are you?'

'Great, yeah I'm fine. Er listen,' Avalon detected a doubt in the man's voice, as if Davies was about to tell him that it couldn't be done. 'I'm sorry to call on your day off but I just had a call from the Chief, he says he managed to swing it and he wants you to come up to see how you fit in.' Avalon suddenly felt rather sick. His stomach jumped up into his throat with this information. Avalon held hopes that things would change but lack of any real conviction had left him sitting on the fence about what he would do if that chance came.

'Oh, oh, I see,' stuttered Avalon.

'I know it's a bit sudden and I realise you will probably want to think it over but...'

'No, it's not that, it's...' Avalon had stalled, but he didn't really know why. Wasn't this what he had wanted? He was taken aback, and it took some moments to rationalise the situation. Luckily his instincts were at hand to take over. 'Yeah, I'd love to.' He gulped at the words he had just spoken.

'Great, I'll make some arrangements,' replied Davies.

'Erm, when will this be, I mean when will I be starting?' he asked, still reeling from the newness of the situation.

'As soon as you can get here, when you're ready,'

came the reply.

'But I have to tell everyone at the station and make arrangements for...' He was going to say, make arrangements for someone to take over his work but that wasn't important, as there was nothing critical he was working on at the moment. Davies spoke again.

'Well, they will know the situation by the time you get there I would think, so it's just down to tidying loose ends and then,' Davies hesitated now, 'well, packing,' he laughed. Avalon thanked Davies for all the trouble and told him he would ring back Monday afternoon to arrange the changeover. In the meantime, the transfer was only a short period, just ten weeks, but it was a further leap away from his old job. He got off the bike, opened his leather jacket and walked across the field, then sat by the canal on a sloping concrete bank taking it all in. How quickly this had happened, were things changing for Avalon? Was this a renaissance for him? He then found the need to tell Carol. He rang her number and she answered.

'Hello, it's James, are you alone?'

'Are you checking up on me?'

'No silly, I just have something to tell you and didn't want you to say 'I'll call you back',' he laughed to make light of it.

'Yes, I'm alone, what do you have to tell me?'

'Firstly, I want to apologise for the incident in the petrol station, you were right, I shouldn't have done it.'

'Well,' began Carol, 'it seemed out of character, but I understand there are sides of you I don't see, the policeman for instance.'

'Well, if I was honest, all you ever saw was the policeman, that was the problem,' admitted Avalon.

'So you mean the person at the petrol station was the *real* you?' she asked, with a slight emphasis on 'real'.

'Yes, no, er well, something in between I suppose, but that's a conversation for another time. What I wanted to tell you was that I got it.'

'Got what?' she asked.

'The secondment, the temporary job in Inverness.' There was a smile on his lips as he said it.

'Oh, brilliant, I'm so pleased for you,' she said and Avalon could tell she meant it.

'It's only for ten weeks I think but it will give me time to sort my life out I'm sure.'

'Hopefully, but remember, this is a new start, be yourself rather than super-cop.' There was a real sincerity in her voice but Avalon still laughed at the super-cop. 'When do you go?' she asked.

'As soon as I can sort everything out. I'd go now if it was possible.' As he said it, he heard a bleeping in his ear but didn't know where it was coming from. There was no one else on the canal side, so it must be his phone.

'Well if there's anything I can help with just let me know,' she said.

'I will, we should try to meet up before I go.'

'Yes, we could do.'

'Okay,' added Avalon with the bleeping still audible. What the hell was that noise? 'I'll phone later and arrange something,' he had an afterthought, 'you have been a great friend to me through my problems Carol, I just want to say,' he hesitated, 'I still love you. I will always love you and I'm not trying to creep I just want to tell you how I feel.' There was silence. He wondered if he had overstepped the mark. More silence.

'Hello, are you okay?' he asked with a troubled voice. Yet more silence. Avalon looked at the phone. 'Battery Dead' said the legend, before it too, went out through lack of power.

'Damn phone!' he spat as he tossed it down by his side. Typical, he finally said what he ought to have said every day they had been married and the damn phone was dead. Maybe she did hear it, then again... There was a gentle plop. 'Was it a fish?' thought Avalon, as he leaned over to look into the canal? Then it became obvious that a fish hadn't caused the sound but the stupid phone. It had steadily but determinedly, slid down the bank and into the canal. Well, it was certainly dead now and would remain dead under three feet of water. Avalon sighed as he walked back to the bike, maybe this change was going to be harder to maintain than he thought.

~~~~~~

On Monday morning, the office was the same stuffy pit of despair that he remembered, no one spoke to him, but that was usual and, fortunately, Staunton was on the phone and so ignored him. It was clear they did not know about his move and he began to wonder if Davies had pulled a really sick joke on him. His desk was covered in other people's junk as usual, but this morning Detective Sergeant Avalon was different, this Avalon simply placed his arm behind the pile and pushed it all off the desk and onto the floor. The clatter made everyone look for a moment and then, in came PC Duckworth and said.

'DS Avalon, the Chief Inspector wants to see you in the office.' There were a few smirks and grins but Avalon nodded and made his way to the office, leaving all the rubbish on the floor. The Chief Inspector was a little grim behind the desk as he said.

'Well Avalon, I don't know who your friends are in Scotland, but I had a phone call yesterday, Sunday of all days, to inform me you had been seconded to Inverness nick for a project they had you earmarked for.' This felt odd as if he had gone behind their backs. 'It seems it was logged months ago but we have no record of it, do you know about this?' Avalon was speechless, the people in Scotland must have falsified paperwork to make it happen.

'Erm,' he hesitated, he didn't want to lie, but the truth was implausible. 'Well sir, I have been asked, but I thought it would be stopped at this end, so I didn't mention it.' The Chief made a 'harrumph' sound.

'We didn't have much say in the matter, it was all cut and dry, from above by the look of it.' Avalon shrugged.

'I don't understand that, sir.'

'Avalon,' replied the Chief, 'I think you know more than you are saying but we'll deal with this later, for now, you better clear your desk and make arrangements.'

'I *have* cleared my desk, sir,' replied Avalon almost smiling.

'You have, have you? Well, this isn't over, I will have words with a few people and find out what you are up to.' Avalon went off to clear his lockers and his drawers with the others in the room giving each other questioning looks. Green then burst into the room and announced.

'Well, well, Spook is going to Jockland, it seems they have lost the Loch Ness Monster.' Avalon smiled at him and then pressed his face up to Green's. Green now looked nervous at this unfamiliar, mean-looking, Avalon. Avalon wasn't handsome, but neither was he ugly, he had a face that was anonymous, a blank canvas. However, he could mould it to look right for the mood he was in, and at the moment, it was like a Halloween mask and Green panicked slightly.

'That's right Green, they have lost it, they were going to ask you, but the Chief told them there was no use because you couldn't find your dick in a dark room.' There was a ripple of laughter and Avalon walked out of the room, tossing his office keys on Staunton's desk. Staunton looked up at him.

'How have you wangled this Avalon?'

'Read under section ninety-seven of the Police Act under employment legislation. There, under contracts of employment to other police-related UK organisations to meet the need for,' here, Avalon paused. 'And, I quote, *specific expertise*.' He put great emphasis on the last two words of a paragraph he had researched the night previous. Then he left. It was done, he was on his way.

Chapter Three

Avalon didn't know if he had done everything he needed to do. As he sat behind the wheel of his car, hurtling up the M6 motorway towards the 'wild north', he wondered if a detective ought to be more organised. He would be away from home for quite a while, at least for ten weeks or so and that needed a great deal of thought, not just the passing consideration he had made about the affair. Yes, he had asked Carol to keep an eye on his house and the lock-up garage where his treasured Triumph motorcycle was kept, but had he covered every other angle? The little things that usually get forgotten about bothered him but he couldn't think of anything he had missed. The more he thought about it, the more he realised that the reason he was in such a confused state, was due to him hardly ever going away for any extended period before. That realisation made him sigh. He then pressured himself more by considering that he would have to look around for a flat or a house to rent in the north. That was a daunting prospect to him.

'Don't worry. Time will tell and if you have forgotten something, it's too late now!' he thought to himself, or had he just said that? Yes he had, he was noticing he was talking more and more these days when he should just be thinking.

'I'll have to stop that,' he said and then laughed about the humour of the statement. He still couldn't shake the thought that he had forgotten to do something, and he was still trying to remember what it was by the time he reached Scotch Corner.

He stopped for a break soon after on the Cumbrian Moors and a bite to eat, a sandwich purchased from a service station earlier and looked out from the lay-by onto the moors beyond. As far as the eye could see was moorland, nothing like the landscape of Wolverhampton, and Avalon breathed the air through the open window. It was enough to tease him out of the car seat and to prompt him to prop his backside on the bonnet of his scruffy, blue Mondeo, and ponder the majesty of the scene. Another car pulled up behind in the lay-by and a woman with a small child got out to tend the fussing brat in the seat beside her. When she had admonished the boy, she made her way back to her seat, noticing Avalon watching her.

'Kids,' she smiled rolling her eyes, 'you know what it's like.' She smiled as she sat in the driver's seat and carefully drove away. No actually, Avalon didn't know what it was like, it seemed to him the job he did stopped that becoming a reality. Inside he considered the 'motherly' looking woman and her feral child and wondered if he really wanted that sort of life anyway. He wanted Carol and her 'devil-may-care' outlook, that's why he had married her, true she would have been happy to have been a mother but there had never been time. Between work and the arguments, they had never sat down to seriously consider a family, probably for the best too, for any children would now have a broken home to look forward to. But then again, didn't most children? In Avalon's line of work, he saw victims and perpetrators who were single mothers, stepfathers and runaways. Families with several children without a single, shared surname between them and, more than that, a toxic environment which would ensure that they too would probably live their lives in crime. Some rose above it but with a poor start to life, most neglected children seemed to end up at one or the other end of a violent crime in Avalon's experience. He glanced once again over the moors and tried to convince himself he was an outsider, nothing that 'normal' life had to offer was for, or available to him. His future relationships would have to take that into account.

He reached into the rear of the car and brought out a bottle of water, which he raised to his lips. He drank greedily and then broke off to look both ways up and down the road, watching all those 'normal' people going about their 'normal' lives, not knowing what was around the corner for them. Maybe some of them would end up in criminal cases that *he* would work on, who could tell? Were they victims or perpetrators? He wondered if that might be the problem with his outlook. Did he see any other type of person? Victims, criminals and innocent bystanders. Yes, bystanders. But who the hell wanted to be a bystander?

He took another drink and placed the bottle back into the car. He then looked down and saw a small pebble on the ground. He picked it up, its smooth surface felt nice to the touch but at its rear there was a part where some of it had been broken off and a rough inner core could be felt. It was to Avalon a good representation of his past life, no, more accurately a representative of *him*. A smooth outer, with a rough core. Who was he kidding? He had made a hash of his life in many ways. He looked one last time out onto the moors of Cumbria then down to the pebble.

'Bye!' he said calmly and then threw the pebble as far as he could onto the moors.

Avalon made a second stop, just after Glasgow. He was in new territory now, he had been to Edinburgh plenty of times but from here the route lead north on roads he had never travelled before. As he sat in the services car park drinking a reasonable coffee from an unreasonable plastic cup, he began to wish he had a satnav in the car instead of an AA map book. True, the untidy morass of post-it notes all over the dashboard and windscreen were fewer than when he set out, but there were still lots of them. He opened the map book and after seeing how much further he still had to go and almost spilling his drink from the shock, he settled into the idea that he was still only about halfway. He checked the route up the A9 and then threw the map book in the back seat and studied his post-it directions. It seemed straightforward, if not tiresome but he decided the music would be a must and found a couple of CD's to play when he became more tired. The coffee was finished and off he set, threading his way along the Clyde valley and around the quickly rising hills. The views of this part of Scotland made the journey a little easier to cope with but it soon became a monotonous trip once more and Avalon reached for the radio button along with the volume.

The A9 seemed to go on forever and with speed restrictions, it wasn't long before a train of vehicles backed up behind slower trucks. Several times, Avalon watched as irate drivers took risks to pass the slower traffic and he tucked the information away for his return visit. Through seas of forested hillsides, he continued and now and then, he looked down to check on his post-it notes for reassurance. He was beginning to wish he had not taken this job and wondered if he should split the journey for the return route. As he looked down at the nearest post-it note to try and figure out how far was left, he had a feeling something was wrong and as he looked up he saw a car on *his* side of the road coming towards him. In a split second, he assessed the situation but he had nowhere to go, as there was an Armco barrier to his left with a narrow verge. He mounted the small verge and just about missed the other car, a side mirror exploding on impact. The poor old Mondeo had lost its mirror years ago on the back streets of Wolverhampton, so the plastic parts that were flying to oblivion were from the idiot who was speeding off with no intention of stopping. Avalon considered racing after him but the extra work made him think twice and instead, he pulled into a left turn to catch his breath. He got out and sniffed the Highland air and leaned on the boot of the car looking up the A9. He would give anything to be in Inverness now, a meal and a hot shower were all he wanted. He glanced around from the hillside opposite to the little white painted village down the road he had just parked on, nestling in a glorious valley. He looked again at the white painted village. It had something familiar about it, the odd shaped towers gave it away and Avalon realised this was a distillery. He looked at the signpost across the road but had to walk down the verge a little to read it. Avalon just couldn't believe his eyes. The sign said, 'Dalwhinnie' and as he read it, a smile came to his face. He walked back to the car looking down at the white buildings of the distillery and opened the boot of the vehicle. He reached into his case and pulled out the bottle of Dalwhinnie he had purchased in Edinburgh and held it up towards the hills on the opposite side of the valley.

'Cheers,' he smiled. 'If this isn't an omen I don't know what is.' and he replaced the bottle into the case.
He knew he hadn't time to visit the distillery, but he drove down to it as a sort of pilgrimage, a Cathedral of Whisky at the edge of the little village of eighty or so people, dubiously twinned with Las Vegas. He then continued on his way up the A9 with a renewed enthusiasm, watching out for crazy drivers coming towards him.

Avalon was tired, bored and ready to give in just as he saw the sign that said he was about to enter Inverness, he now had the unenviable task of finding the Bed and Breakfast he had booked previously. The address was Urquhart Road and Avalon wasn't even sure how to pronounce it but he called at a service station and asked how he might get there. The young chap was kind enough to sketch out a small map, which Avalon transferred to yet another post-it note but by now there was plenty of space on the dashboard. He set off and was pleasantly surprised by what he could see of Inverness, it was bustling but had a very open aspect and seemed reasonably well planned. He found Urquhart Road, a strange mix of stone cottages and 1930's housing on a wide boulevard, and he also found the B&B quickly. He lugged his bags into the porch. A fussy Scotswoman came out to book him in and show him around the place.

'Ah, Mister Avalon, you are with us for five nights I believe,' rang out her tinkling voice. It was certainly Scottish but not as broad as Avalon had expected.

'Yes, indeed. I may need a few nights longer if that suits. I don't quite know how long I will require.'

'Of course, but be sure to let us know as soon as y' can because it can be busy at this time o' the year.'

'I certainly will, I suspect I will be able to let you know tomorrow evening.'

'That'll be fine. Well, this is your room,' she said as she let him into the place he would live for the next few days. It was light and well-furnished and seemed scrupulously clean. Avalon liked it and said so. He placed his case on the chair and a bag on the floor.

'I have more luggage but I'll bring it in sometime in the morning,' he explained.

'That's fine. Here are your keys and there is the menu for breakfast, if you have any special requests just let us know.'

'I'm sure it will be just fine,' he smiled. He could have eaten it there and then but he considered a meal out close by. He asked about restaurants and she jotted down directions to one she said was good.

'I'll leave you to it then Mr Avalon,' she hesitated and little, then continued, 'it's a very unusual name if you don't mind me saying.'

'I don't and it is,' he smiled, 'I'll tell you about it sometime.' She smiled back.

'Okay, I'll look forward to that. I'll let you get

settled in, as you have come some way I believe.'

'Yes, Wolverhampton,' he nodded.

'My,' her eyes widened, 'that is a long way. Well, I hope you enjoy your holiday.' Avalon didn't bite. Landladies of your typical B&B have a way of extracting as much information out of a person as they can with so few questions. Avalon considered that many understaffed police forces could make up their detective shortfall by employing a hand full of B&B landladies.

After she had left, he unpacked and placed his bottle of single malt on the closed-over fireplace. He was planning a glass for later. He showered then sat on the bed and considered his position. In the morning he was going to find the police station and enter into a new contract with himself. He was going to start as he meant to go on. He would show only his real self and promised his inner 'Id' that he would change his attitude to life, totally. He had to start immediately and he worked everything out that night. It was such an intense self-interview that he never made it to the restaurant and after he dressed, he went to the car to find the remaining sandwich from earlier in the day. He sat in the window seat with a cup of tea and a cheese and lettuce sandwich that had entered into its later life and he smiled out towards Scotland. This was his new beginning and he now knew he was ready. A small glass of single malt made him feel that he had conquered all his fears and he would attack the morning with a vigour he had never shown before.

~~~~~~

Scottish sparrows it seems do not have any

particular accent but they are just as noisy, if not more so, as English ones. Several of them were holding parliament just above his open window, which ensured Avalon was well awake before his phone alarm went off. After a wash and shave, he made his way downstairs and ordered a full English breakfast. As he ate, he could feel his new self, wanting to have a little fun. There were a few others at breakfast, so it had to be tame and polite. When Jeanie, the landlady, served him he had a question for her.

'Aye, ask away,' she smiled.

'I was just wondering about this wonderful repast you have delivered,' he pointed to the plate, 'seeing as we are in Scotland, why is it called Full English? Shouldn't it be Full Scottish?' She smiled with a bright twinkle in her blue eyes.

'No, Mr Avalon. It's called full English because that's what it is. If you look further down the menu, there's 'Full Scottish'.' She bent to point at the menu though her diminutive stature meant is wasn't much of a bend. 'And they are quite different,' she added as she turned and disappeared through the swinging door to the kitchen. Avalon decided two things. Always read menus fully and watch these Scottish people, they may have a few surprises.

He was supposed to be at the police station for nine thirty, so he was in plenty of time. He looked through the free brochures in the B&B and luckily, one of them had a small but reasonably detailed street map of the centre of Inverness. He studied it and tried to memorise as much as he could but he decided to ask Jeanie the best way to get there. Her face gave nothing away when he mentioned the police station and she helpfully drew the best route in Biro on his little map. He thanked her and retired to his room to get ready for his day.

From the outside, the police station looked modern and purpose-built, so much removed from the office he was used to in Wolverhampton and with a slight nervousness, Avalon walked through the door. There were two uniformed officers at the desk, one being a sergeant, Avalon headed straight for him as the officer looked up.

'Detective Sergeant Avalon to see Detective Chief Inspector Anderson,' announced Avalon as matter-of-fact as he could be.

'Oh aye,' nodded the sergeant, 'we were expecting you. There's your ID here somewhere.' The sergeant had a very 'broad' Scottish accent, more the sort of sound that Avalon had expected. The officer handed Avalon a lanyard with his ID and asked him to sign into the daybook and then added.

'The 'Chief' is in but I'm no' sure if he's alone or not.' He then picked up the phone.

'Sergeant Avalon to see the DCI.' There was a pause and then he continued. 'Okay, thanks.' The officer replaced the phone and asked Avalon to wait. 'They're sending somebody down for y'.' He motioned to the seats. 'You can tek' a seat if y' like, it could be a time.' The officer raised his eyebrows as if to say 'it's always like this' and so, Avalon sat. 'D' y' want a cuppa?' asked the sergeant. Avalon gave a weak smile but refused. Twenty minutes later he was being led up a flight of stairs, higher into the building by a uniformed officer that looked like he should still be at school. The 'uniform' knocked and entered and lead Avalon in.

'Ah, Sergeant Avalon, welcome. Detective Chief Inspector Anderson.' The man behind the desk stood and offered a broad smile and his hand. Avalon took it as he heard the door close behind him.

'Nice to be here at last sir,' smiled back Avalon.

'I bet, it's a long haul from Brum.' The voice was definitely English even if the man wasn't. Pushed to one side, Avalon could clearly read, 'DCI Alan Anderson' on a small nameplate.

'Yes, I was surprised how long it actually took me.'

'Well, you're here now and we have plenty for you to do.' Anderson looked down to the mass of paperwork on his desk. 'If we all get on well together, of course.' He smiled up at Avalon. 'I'll not bore you with any details, suffice to say, we are really pulled out at the moment, so if you have no objections, we'll make this informal and just get you settled in.' He looked back up to Avalon. 'I've heard good things about you, so I'm sure you will fit in. I think Andrew has some plans for you.' Avalon wasn't sure if the interview was over or not but assuming 'Andrew' was Andrew Davies, Avalon just nodded. The 'Chief' suddenly became animated once more and added. 'I'm afraid with things as they are, you may find the situation here is not quite what you expected and I'll be the first to admit it. I wish your introduction to Inverness could have been a little less rushed but I'm sure you'll cope.' He had picked up the phone as he spoke and almost without a pause he said,

'Can you ask Andrew to come over?' and the phone went down. 'Well,' he continued as he stood. Avalon saw the chief's hand extend once more, so he

97

also stood and shook it. The interview was really over now, a much, stilted version of what he had expected. Were they really so busy that even interviews were an unnecessary evil? 'Andrew will show you around I'm sure and I hope you enjoy your time with us.' Avalon thought it was an odd expression under the circumstances but he replied with.

'Thank you sir, I'm sure I will.' There was a light tap at the door then it opened carefully to reveal the face of Andrew Davies, looking much more tired than when Avalon had last seen him in Edinburgh. He smiled warmly and shook his hand.

'Glad to have you on board.' Davies ushered him out and down one of the corridors into the heart of the building. It was busy in the extreme, many people milling about with almost every office bulging with officers, computers and paperwork. 'I'll take you down to meet C section, you'll be working with them, or at least part of that section.' He sighed before he continued. 'We are so busy it's hard to know where one section ends and the other begins.' They turned a corner and came to a small office that contained four people and all the equipment and furniture crammed in. Everyone in there seemed to be buried in paperwork and all looked tired and overworked.

'People, this is DS James Avalon,' announced Davies. All looked up, one said 'hello', one gave a slight smile but the other two just continued with their work. 'It's too cramped in here for you to join them,' said Davies frowning a little, 'but I'll find somewhere for you tomorrow.'

'I think cubicle three in the ladies is still free,' said a deep Scottish voice. It came from a ginger-haired chap of about thirty years old, thin and pale but with ferocious blue eyes.

'Wrong,' said another voice from behind a computer screen, 'it's been booked for the Christmas party.' Davies began to point to the man.

'That voice of reason came from DC Ross.' explained Davies. Ross was a well-built Scotsman of around thirty-five but Avalon could make no other assessment as the head returned to its position behind the screen. Davies continued to point to the others as he introduced them. 'That ginger object in the corner is DS Wilson,' Wilson nodded to Avalon, 'this, is DC MacDonald,' added Davies pointing to a chubby-faced man that looked in his mid-twenties. His face seemed too wide as his body was of normal build, which made him look 'top heavy'. 'And this is DC Frazer.' Avalon had already noticed that Frazer was female, a slightly built woman with a drawn face that was difficult to age. She turned and gave a brief, forced smile.

'When Frazer started she was a man but they've worked the balls off her,' added Wilson.

'Thank you Wilson for bringing down the tone of the office,' said Davies.

'Office? I'd love an office,' replied Ross.

'As you can see,' said Davies to Avalon, 'we are struggling for room, our usual office has become a mini incident room so we are spread out a little.' Avalon sensed that Ross was going to add something but Davies continued before he could speak. 'DS Murrey and DC McGill are out this morning but you will possibly meet them tomorrow.'

'Aye we have to take it in turns as there're only four seats,' added Ross.

'What would we do without your humour Ross?' asked Davies.

'I'd call it a statement o' fact, not humour,' chipped in MacDonald.

'When have you ever used fact in your work Mac?' quipped Davies. MacDonald didn't answer, he just rolled his eyes and continued with his work. Davies ushered Avalon away and continued with the tour.

'They're under a great deal of pressure, you've seen how they have to work but with you here we may be able to split the section in two.' Davies didn't explain his thinking, he just continued showing Avalon around. When they reached the restroom, Avalon noticed that this too was being used for storage. Davies poured two cups of coffee and sat. Avalon joined him.

'Obviously we can't make you up to DI, I would like to, it's not possible on secondment but I would like you to run your own show if I can get the 'old man' to sanction it.' Avalon nodded. The thought of running his 'own show' with all the possibilities that came with it was the icing on the cake. 'You'll be working under a very competent detective,' continued Davies, 'Detective Inspector Robert Lasiter. He's considered hard-nosed but I've known him since I've been up here and he's one of the best. I wanted you in B section but Robert needs the help at the moment.'

'I'm sure I'll fit in soon enough,' smiled Avalon. Davies patted Avalon's shoulder in a friendly way.

'I think you will James and if things cool down, I'll move you into my section later,' he returned the smile. 'Well, unless you have any issues or questions I'll get on and we'll see you about eight o'clock in the morning.' Avalon nodded and they said their goodbyes,

Avalon was shown downstairs but as he walked into the foyer, he stopped at the front desk to question the sergeant.

'Have we got an A to Z for Inverness at the station?'

'So you're in then?' questioned the desk sergeant reaching behind the desk for a map.

'It seems so,' answered Avalon raising his brow.

'We certainly need more hands here,' replied the sergeant, passing Avalon the map. 'It's not brilliant but it has all the landmarks and road names on there.' He offered his hand as he added, 'Gregory, Sergeant Bob Gregory.' Avalon shook his hand.

'Well, you know my name,' he smiled.

'Aye, Avalon, it's an unusual name is it not?' asked the sergeant. Avalon nodded as he looked at the map. 'Do you go by James or Jim?' Avalon thought for a moment. He had always hated 'Jim' but this was a new start, maybe it required a new name.

'Either,' grinned Avalon, 'I've been called so many things in the past, James or Jim will seem quaint.' The sergeant nodded.

'Back in the mornin' then?'

'Yes,' replied Avalon as he made for the door. 'I suppose I'll have to work for a living now.'

Avalon walked around the town to try to become at least slightly conversant with its layout and as he did, he thought about his day. All in all, the station seemed to work well even though it was busy and cramped. He had met most of the people he would be working with and he saw no real issues there, but he knew there would be surprises and he had to be ready for them. He had to work out an approach, there had to be an easy way of changing his 'style'. What was his problem after all? To be truthful to himself, James Avalon, was the problem, if he had more of the detective in his private life he knew he could do better. Maybe that was the answer. Leave James Avalon in England and let Detective Sergeant Jim Avalon loose in Scotland. It was worth a try.

The next morning at breakfast, Avalon was alone, save for Jeanie fussing about in the dining room and her husband Reg cooking in the kitchen. This time he had read the menu fully and noticed that Full Scottish included haggis and something called 'tattie scones' but Avalon stuck with the straightforward English style.

'So you're a police officer Mr Avalon?' asked the inquisitive Jeanie.

'What makes you say that?'

'Oh, well, the fact of ye' wanting the police station, the Inverness map by your side and the black tie,' she smiled.

'The black tie?' he asked playfully.

'Aye, it's either a funeral or the police with such a tie.' She smiled as she removed his plate. Avalon thought about this, he had plenty of ties and hardly ever wore the black one, maybe he would change it before he left. Jeanie returned with a second pot of coffee. 'Not only that Mr Avalon, you sort of look like a detective.' Avalon smiled at this. His previous consideration that B&B landladies had a sort of supernatural observation had been confirmed once more but for the life of him, he had never considered that he *looked* like a detective.

'I could just be a sales rep, or even an insurance advisor for the police,' he mused.

'Aye, that could be, but for one reason,' she was obviously teasing as she made her way back to the kitchen. She turned just short of the door. 'When you sent your original email for the booking, it said 'Detective Sergeant James Avalon, West Midlands Police'.' She gave him a cheeky wink and slid into the kitchen.

~~~~~~

'Morning Jim, I'll get O-K down tae sort y' out,' said the desk sergeant picking up the internal phone.

'Pardon?' asked Avalon resting his briefcase on the desk.

'O-K, sorry, Constable Kirk sorts all the mince out round here.' Avalon just stared at the officer blankly and just as he was about to ask what the hell he was talking about, the Sergeant spoke on the phone. 'O-K, get yer arse doon here, y'er man's arrived.' He replaced the phone and looked at Avalon. 'She'll be here in a mo, she'll sort y' out.' Avalon was still no wiser until a female uniformed officer entered the room. 'Oh, she's here. This is Constable Kirk, she will sort out all your keys and authorisation.' Avalon saw a small-built female officer with lank, blonde hair pulled tightly back into a short ponytail. 'This is DS Avalon.' She gave a cursory smile and then snapped.

'This way Sergeant,' and she turned on her heels and set a quick pace. In one of the interview rooms, at the rear of the building, she had placed a small box on a table and began to open it and pull some items out. 'This es your pass ID and your keys. They are labelled with numbers and the code for the numbers is on this card.'

She hardly stopped for breath and Avalon guessed she was a hard-worked officer and didn't like wasting time. 'This es your phone and et already has most of the main numbers on there. This es your pager and I'll warn you DI Lasiter es a stickler for his officers keeping these by them.' She continued in this matter-of-fact way until the box was empty and all the items were either on the table or in Avalon's pockets. She then looked up to him. 'If there are no questions, please sign this form tae say you are in possession of the items.' He signed it without a word. She picked up the form, glanced at the signature and then gave out a mechanical smile saying, 'Welcome tae Inverness nick.' then she once again spun on her heels and walked off, adding. 'I'll let DI Lasiter know you're ready.' Avalon picked up the remaining items from the table and looked at his reflection in the two-way mirror. The blue tie was certainly a better choice, and he was reasonably pleased with the way this 'born again detective' looked. Business-like, but not too harsh. Avalon had never really been happy with his reflection, he knew a few women had thought him handsome in a rugged way but he considered he was severe to look at, his nose was three sizes too large and his skin was rough and leathered. Now he had to deal with the thought that he *looked* like a detective and that brought a slight frown to his face. He patted down his short hair and then glanced around the little room and noticed even here the place was used for storage with chairs and filing cabinets against the walls. The oddest thing was that there was a computer on the interview table and a trailing cable running out which meant that the door could not be closed. He followed the cable through the doorway and noticed it went into the next room, which also had the door slightly ajar. He then noticed footsteps coming down the corridor. A man of approximately Avalon's height was coming towards him, he had a natural look of authority and his face was making a slight smile. This must be DI Lasiter Avalon thought.

'Nice tae meet y' at last.' His accent was a thick Scottish type, the sort of accent people copy when they tell a story which includes a generic Scotsman.

'Detective Inspector Lasiter?' asked Avalon as he shook the strong hand.

'Aye, that's right. I can see why y' became a detective,' he smiled, and he held his hand towards the room Avalon had just left and so they re-entered, Lasiter sitting on one of the chairs. 'I know it's less than perfect but needs must.' In a flash, Avalon understood. This was *his* new office, an interview room. He shrugged, what could he say. 'As soon as somethin' crops up we'll get y' moved upstairs.'

'It'll be fine,' nodded Avalon.

'No, it's not fine an' a' wish there was more a could offer y' but as things stand we hav'tae make do.' Avalon smiled slightly and nodded. He thought he would strike straight away while he had the upper hand.

'So what are your plans for me?' Lasiter's face showed a little stress at this and his shoulders slumped visibly.

'Look Avalon, I'll be straight with y'. Davies es a brilliant officer and a good mate but he can be a bit,' he paused for a second, 'a bit, enthusiastic en his approach.' Avalon was struggling a little with the accent but he got the gist of what Lasiter had said.

'He seems a nice chap, I agree,' nodded Avalon knowing what was coming but hoping he was wrong.

'Aye, he es that. What I'm sayin' es that a don't know what he's told y' but the truth es y' here because we are short o' bodies. A think he told y' that we had somethin' special for y' but we need y' where we need you.' Avalon considered this for a moment and it was something that had passed through his mind on occasions but now he was here, he would make the best of it. He conjured up a slight smile.

'Well he did say there was a particular case he wanted me on but I'm here to help out however that manifests itself. You give me the job and I'll complete it.' Avalon was quite shocked by the new attitude, it was something he never knew he had inside him. Lasiter gave a genuine smile and grasped Avalon by the shoulder.

'I can see why Davies wanted you on the team now. A detective by nature, it's a truly rare thing.' He stood and gave a quick look around the room. 'I'll get Constable Kirk to get y' all the trimmings in here and leave y' tae settle en.' He then looked back at Avalon. 'Good tae have y' on-board.' He turned and then stopped as if he had remembered something. 'Oh, and just watch PC Kirk, she's a grafter, but she has a wicked sense o' humour,' and he left.

Soon after, Constable Kirk arrived and asked what he needed and in a very short time she was acquiring the necessary items without showing anything of a glimmer of humour as Lasiter had suggested. Avalon moved the filing cabinet to cover part of the two-way mirror opposite so he didn't see his reflection every time he turned. He repositioned the computer and the telephone, jotting down all the internal numbers on a notepad. When he had finished, the room looked more like home but the idea of not being able to close the door didn't appeal. He didn't quite know why as he had always previously worked in an open office. Still, PC Kirk had told him that she was trying to get a Wi-Fi connection if they had suitable security for it. For now, he found a rubber doorstop which he placed under the cable to prevent it being damaged and at least the slightly open door meant he could see activity in the corridor. Behind him the CCTV camera showed it was not live, but he turned it toward the wall anyway, he just didn't like the idea of anyone watching him all day. Then he afforded himself a moment to sit and look around. It wasn't a large room but looking at the rest of the building, he probably had more space than anyone. Through the crack of the open door, he watched several uniformed PC's walk past making quick glances through the slightly open door and then another who seemed to be trying to catch the others up and he noticed this one also give a cursory glance into Avalon's room. He thought it odd, as the corridor didn't really go anywhere in particular. He was already on his guard when he saw PC Kirk coming down the corridor carrying what seemed to be a computer screen. She entered the room pushing the door with her foot and placed the screen on the other side of the interview table. She then left and came back soon with the tower unit to match.

'So you've got to change the whole thing?' he asked.

'What? Er no, sorry sir, this es for someone else,' she then left again and returned quickly with all the extra ancillaries for the machine and began to lay them on the desk. Avalon tried to ignore her and pretended to be doing something on his computer but when she closed the door, as far as she could and began to assemble the machine, he couldn't help himself.

'Are you saying I'll be sharing with someone?'

'Aye I would think so,' she smiled, 'you can't expect to have this cavernous space to yerself.' Her gaze kept on him for more time than was comfortable so he broke the glance with a question.

'Does everyone around here call you Okay, or did I hear that wrong?' She turned on the machine to boot it up and stood closer to Avalon with her thigh resting on the edge of the table.

'Aye, et's what they call me alight.' Avalon sensed a trap as she slid slightly towards him.

'So this may be a silly question but why?' he asked having already worked out that he needed to be on his guard. She slid her hand across the desk catching Avalon's Biro and touching his hand gently and then brought the cap end of the Biro to her bottom lip.

'Et's what I always say,' she purred looking deep into his eyes, 'I just can't say no, I just say, okay!' Avalon swallowed and gave her a slight smile, stood then walked the two paces to the filing cabinet and straightened his tie in the two-way mirror above it. Then casually took out his comb and ran it twice through his hair before replacing it in his jacket pocket. He then sighed, shifted his focus from his reflection to somewhere beyond the glass into the room beyond and knocked hard on the mirror with his knuckles.

'You lot get back to work,' he called out. It was a gamble but one that paid off as he heard several feet scuttling off up the corridor from the room behind the two-way mirror. He turned to see PC Kirk trying to leave. 'Wait!' he called. He pointed to the computer on the opposite side of the desk. A slightly embarrassed Kirk turned and looked at the machine.

'Er, I don't know sir,' she said flatly and shaking her head, 'DI Lasiter told me to set et up in here.' Avalon just nodded and walked back to his seat but he was surprised to see the constable still standing by the now open door. 'Et's my initials sir,' she paused to make sure he knew what she meant, 'Olivia Kirk.' Avalon nodded.

'I see, O-K,' he sighed again and looked down to his keyboard and without looking back at her said, 'Carry on PC Kirk.' PC Olivia Kirk left the office.

~~~~~~

Avalon had made his way around the Police cyberspace and found all the sections he needed on his computer by the time a knock came at the opening door. It was DC Ross and he had bundles of files under both arms.

'It looks like I have to babysit you,' he announced.

'So I'm guessing this is your seat,' said Avalon nodding to the computer opposite.

'Yeah,' replied Ross dropping the files on the desk and slumping down into the seat.

'So what are we working on?' asked Avalon peering around his screen.

'First, I have to show you the system.' Ross pulled a file from the pile and held it up. 'This number in the corner is the case file number, and it corresponds to a file in the database on your computer. If you want to cross reference anything, or add to it, make sure you have that correct file number opened first.'

'Seems simple enough,' agreed Avalon.

'Oh aye, simple enough but it's just more paperwork for the poor bluebottle.' Avalon wanted to explain that information is their greatest tool but it would seem naïve. It was the same in every police force, paperwork was the bane of the job, but they couldn't function without it.

'So where do we start?' he asked instead.

'Well, seeing as you're so eager we'll start with this.' Ross had a slight Scottish burr to his voice but it was easy to understand for Avalon. The DC tossed the file he had been holding onto Avalon's side of the desk.

'I'm not wasting my time reading twenty pages of notes,' frowned Avalon, 'tell me about it.' Ross stared at him for a moment and then shrugged. He pulled back the file and opened it.

'Attempted jewellery robbery,' he began, 'the 'perps' stole a red Vauxhall Astra and tried to ram-raid a jewellers in the town. The car turned up four days later in Fort William burned to a crisp.' Ross tossed a photograph of the crime scene. There was a great deal of smashed glass and plastic but it seemed the two bollards in the front of the shop had taken most of the damage. Avalon had a quick glance at the map of Scotland PC Kirk had pinned to the wall for him.

'Is that it?' asked Avalon with a frown, 'I was under the impression we were CID.' Ross just shrugged and pointed to the pile of files.

'There are twenty other cases like this here.'

'But this is legwork for the uniform section surely,' exclaimed Avalon.

'Tell that to the Detective Chief Inspector.'

'Is this what you have been working on?'

110

'No, I was working on a major case until I was told to babysit you,' frowned Ross. Avalon sighed, picked up his pen and tapped it several times on the desk. He leaned back in his chair and asked.

'So why has the DI asked me to work on this?' Ross gave a slight grin.

'Maybe he thinks that you need easing in gently or maybe...' he paused for a second or two, 'for some other reason.' Avalon was becoming irritated by Ross and his anger was welling up inside.

'Okay,' he shrugged and stared at Ross, 'clues?' he asked simply.

'Nothing. Nothing at the scene, and nothing in the car.'

'Any conclusions been put forward?' Avalon asked placing the photograph on the desk.

'The original conclusion was that some teenagers stole the car for a joyride, decided to do the jewellers but didn't have the brains to work out the bollards would stop them,' sighed Ross.

'Any connection with Fort William?' asked Avalon.

'The car was stolen from that area,' replied Ross with a bored look.

'So why has this even been brought to us?' asked Avalon, 'it's not much more than car theft.' Ross sighed again and in his clear but dry Scottish accent said.

'Well, you may ask. DI Lasiter thinks it is yet another crime instigated by one gang.'

'And you don't think so?' asked Avalon.

'I don't know,' shrugged Ross, 'DI Lasiter wanted to know why a car would be rammed into the bollards trying to break into a jewellers but still be in a good enough condition to drive all the way to Fort William.'

'Well, he has a point,' agreed Avalon, 'so what links this with a gang?' Ross didn't speak he just slowly pushed the pile of files towards Avalon. 'So all these files relate to crimes that DI Lasiter thinks are connected to this attempted ram-raid?'

'Yeah,' nodded Ross, 'but if it is the same gang, they need a new M.O. because more than half of their attacks fail.' Avalon leaned back in his chair.

'Doesn't that seem odd in itself?' he asked.

'Maybe the criminal just isn't what he used to be,' replied Ross as he also leaned back. 'To be honest, no one gives a damn. Like you said, it's work for the uniforms.' Avalon wondered if he was getting all the information and he looked down at the serial number on the file and entered it into the computer. The reading was matter-of-fact with no speculation and no other details than basics. No forensic material had been found at any of the sites that could link anyone to the crimes. All the so-called 'linked crimes' were ram-raids, petty break-ins and other minor offences that looked small beer for the CID. After twenty minutes of reading and studying, Avalon once more leaned back in his chair.

'This doesn't make sense. I know I'm new but even if there is a gang at work here it doesn't warrant a major investigation.' Ross just glared back at him making no other comment than a slight sniff. Avalon was puzzled, so he stood and left the office to find his immediate senior. He found DI Lasiter in his office with the ginger-haired Wilson.

'DI Lasiter, can I have a word?' asked Avalon.

'Yeah o' course, what's on yer mind?'

'These cases that you have sent me, they are so obviously staged that I'm wondering if this is some kind of joke.'

'Och, has the bumble-headed idiot not told you the rest of it?' Lasiter sighed and rested his hands on the desk. 'Okay, Gordon, fill James in with the details, I'm off to kick Ross' arse,' and with this, he stood and left. The ginger-haired detective pointed to a chair.

'You best tak a seat, this may take some time.'

'Go on,' said Avalon his interest now piqued.

'The files y' have are linked to other crimes, or at least DI Lasiter thinks they are but he can't go official on that for many reasons.'

'Well Ross told me that they are linked but petty break-ins and failed ram-raids seem a little tame for this department,' frowned Avalon.

'Ross has got a wasp up his arse at the moment and et sounds like he has only brought some of the files. Did you see the files on the three burglaries in town?'

'I didn't see them, no,' frowned Avalon.

'Ah, Ross is going to get intae some serious trouble.' Wilson glanced to the door for a second before continuing. 'Well, the files you have are considered to be closely linked tae three break-ins en the centre of the town.' Avalon nodded but he still wasn't convinced about the importance of the crime. 'The general consensus es that they are also linked to a spate of protection racket reports en the city and local area.'

'Protection rackets?' smiled Avalon.

'Aye, serious threats on the three reported incidents too.' Wilson broke off to look back at the door. Avalon shrugged. 'One of the burglaries involved an assault and we think several assaults have taken place within this protection racket scam but the victims hav'nae come forward.'

'So you think some businesses are not reporting incidents and these attacks are part of the same gang?' he asked. Wilson nodded.

'Maybe, we're not all convinced but there's a wee bit of oddness to et. Mind, don't tell the DI I told you this, he goes scranny when anyone mentions et.'

'Go on,' insisted Avalon leaning forward so he could speak more quietly.

'DI Davies wanted you tae work on another case but Lasiter talked him out of et.' Wilson lowered his voice to a whisper. 'Some people are sayin' that the recent spate of crimes are linked to the incidents down at...' he tailed off at this point as the door opened. It was Lasiter with a reddish glow to his face, which probably meant he had given Ross a ticking off.

'I'm sorry about that idiot Ross. I'll assign someone else t' help y',' he insisted as he took his seat.

'Er, if you don't mind sir,' interrupted Avalon. 'I would rather keep Ross.' Lasiter stared at Avalon for a few seconds and then shrugged.

'I'm guessing that look on your face means y' are insistent about et,' he sighed, 'Fine, probably best for y' to put yer foot down from the start.' Then he nodded. 'I admire that.'

'Thank you,' nodded Avalon.

'I'll get someone to bring you the rest of the files,' added Lasiter as Avalon rose to leave.

As Avalon returned to his office, Ross was coming in the opposite direction carrying some of the files.

'Where are you off to?' asked Avalon.

'Well,' replied Ross with a very false grin, 'since you went off to tell daddy about me he's been over and smacked my legs.' The stupid smile dropped as he concluded with, 'so you'll be please to know I'm out of your hair.'

'No, you're not,' insisted Avalon.

'What?' questioned Ross with a frown.

'I told him you were staying. What's the matter don't you like my new office?' Avalon walked past Ross and into the interview room where he stood looking at the map on the wall. Ross stood at the open door. 'So why did you not bring in the other files that are part of this case?'

'You're a detective, you figure it out,' sneered Ross. Avalon pointed to the chair opposite and he sat on his. For a moment Ross leaned on the doorframe but then decided to sit, tossing the files onto the desk. Avalon had two options, he could berate Ross and tell him what a complete arse he was, or he could try to win him over. He decided on the latter keeping the former as plan 'B'.

'So what's your story Ross?' he asked glaring at the man.

'Eh?'

'What's your story?' Avalon placed his hands at the back of his head and leaned back in his seat as if to say 'we go no further until I know'.

'My story? Bloody hell, are you an agony aunt?'

'You said you are here to babysit me. That isn't true.' Avalon kept his gaze fixed on Ross. 'I'm here to babysit you.' Once again Avalon found himself gambling with someone, twice in one day? This was becoming a habit.

'What do you mean by that?' There was a look of suspicion on Ross' face.

'It means whatever you want it to mean. You know where I'm from. The West Midlands Police has had its problems too.' Ross didn't blink. He just stared at Avalon. 'West Midlands CID have big fish to fry and I mean big!' Avalon allowed himself some artistic license. 'This so-called 'crime wave' you have here is nothing compared to what some offices in Wolverhampton and Birmingham have to deal with, so consider who is babysitting who here.' He left a pause for effect. 'And that is without including Internal investigations which can be a real drain on both sides of the fence.'

'So you are saying you are here for internal investigations?' laughed Ross which began to anger Avalon and he could feel the irritation deep inside.

'Worried?' questioned Avalon. Ross shot to his feet. Avalon had gone too far. 'Sit down Ross,' he said calmly. Ross eventually sat but kept his eyes on Avalon.

'If you are some kind of spook I'm out of here now.' Avalon inwardly baulked at the word. There was a silence for several seconds. Ross looked away then looked back at Avalon. 'My issues are nothing to do with anyone but myself, you can beat your chest all you like about your part of the world but it's no holiday camp here either.'

'I'm not internal, I was brought here to help out so just tell me what your problem is so we can move on,' insisted Avalon trying to find a way out of the hole he had dug for himself.

'This is the problem,' he said slapping his hand on the files, 'I spend five years in uniform and came into

116

this branch of the force with the promise of a better job. It was a lie, the job stinks and we shouldn't be dealing with crap like this.'

'So you want to be working on big cases?' Avalon asked sitting forward a little.

'It's nothing to do with that. You don't know the score here, it's all gone tits up since the uniform issues.' Avalon was silent. There was nothing he could say because he didn't know what Ross meant. Ross saw something in Avalon's face. He grinned. 'You don't know do you?' he laughed, 'you don't know what's happened. That's hilarious, but to be expected.' Avalon waited for a few seconds but Ross' body language said it all. He was angry.

'Yeah, so it's a crap job, but although you have to pass exams to get here, there are no exams to go back to uniform. It's easy, you just transfer,' insisted Avalon. Ross folded his arms and calmed a little.

'I'll tell you something Avalon. I came to CID because I believed I could make a difference. I believed I was above corruption and all the other things that the public love to accuse us of but over the years I have come to see the job as just a tool of the government, nothing to do with solving crimes.'

'I would agree with that,' nodded Avalon, 'I think every copper would say there is truth in that, you're not a special case.'

'But I *want* to do my job. I thought I *was* doing my job until some uniform coppers got sent down and then two more have been suspended. Now we are told that the whole of the area is being looked at, so the police commissioner comes over and gives us a lecture about having to help out with crap like this.' Once again he banged the pile of files.

'Then do it. Do your job and stop whining about having to do things that you think are below you.' Ross shook his head with a look of disdain but Avalon continued. 'Yeah, I know you think you are special, that's why the uniforms don't like us that much. They think we are sat on our hairy arses watching television repeats of Morse so we can look the part. But you can't blame the uniforms because they are at the limit too and understaffed and yes, they think *we* are the enemy.' Avalon took a breath. 'I have seen DC's in previous forces that watch so many detective drama's they see John Nettles as a role model. When they have to help pull a rotting corpse out of a drainage ditch they get on their high horse about getting stains on their Matalan suits.'

'So what's your story?' asked Ross with his arms still folded.

'The same as you, to do my job as best I can because I still believe that someone has to do it, no matter how crappy it gets.'

'So, why the secondment, do you have some skeleton in the cupboard?' Ross leaned forward. Avalon slowly shook his head but was trying to work out a way to explain without telling him a downright lie.

'This job cost me my marriage, mainly because my private life was non-existent. I made mistakes and I regret that but I still think this job is too important to walk away from. No skeletons, just long shadows.' The two glared at each other. Ross stood and left the room. Avalon sighed and rested his head in his arms, here he was again, new job, new life, same mistakes. He stared at the strip light and emptied his head of everything.

'Nice speech,' he told himself and then took off his jacket and hung it on the back of his chair. He hadn't even told Ross the truth at any level, he *did* have skeletons, but he had locked them away deep in the corners of his mind. One of them still came out to haunt him on occasions and woke him at night in a cold sweat, it was a constant reminder that the world can be a very bad place. He sighed and realised he would have to go and see Lasiter and tell him he had failed with Ross. Then the door was flung open and Ross walked in carrying more files.

'These are the three burglaries in town, this is an attack on a shopkeeper in the suburbs. I think there are so many similarities that there is a possibility of a tie,' he sat and without giving Avalon any eye contact he busied himself on his computer.

'Right,' said Avalon grinning inside, 'let's plot all these on the map and cross reference anything you have to match them up. I'll have a nose through the case files.' For the best part of an hour, Avalon and the newly inspired Ross, went through the files one by one to try to find anything that had been missed. There was nothing. Ross threw the final file on the desk and sighed deeply.

'Nothing, absolutely nothing.' Avalon bit his top lip, there was certainly nothing to find that hadn't already been noted.

'What about the shop owners that refused to be intimidated?' he put forward.

'Well, there's nothing there. As their statements say, they phoned the police straight away, and they were left alone by the gang.' Avalon sat quietly. He suddenly leaned forward and typed something into the computer. He made a 'Ah-um' sound and then once again went quiet.

'Yes, you're right. Isn't that odd, more than a coincidence I mean?'

'Well, I suppose it is, but it just means that whoever did this was frightened off a bit by the possibility of police involvement,' added Ross with some doubt in his voice.

'But that's odd too.' Avalon looked up to Ross. 'Think about it, the business people who told the 'perps' they were going to report them to the police were left alone...' Avalon tailed off and waited for Ross to catch up.

'You think the gang were informed by someone inside the police?' he eventually concluded. Avalon raised his eyebrows a little. Ross looked worried.

'Hell's bells, if there is a mole in the police, there will be hell to pay. The chief is having kittens over the last few arrests and we'll never find homes for any more.'

'Well, let's not jump to an obvious conclusion, I'll go and have a word with the three people who reported the threats and find out what they did.' Ross nodded, it was too early to point any fingers and the way this was going, there were more directions than fingers.

'What do you want me to do?' asked Ross. Avalon looked back at the map as he pulled on his jacket.

'Give forensics a call and see if they had any hunches about the three burned-out cars from previous cases. I know they'll say they work with facts only but give it a go.' He straightened his tie in the mirror. 'Oh, and see if you can get 'O-K' to find us a coffee machine. I think better with the smell of good coffee.' Ross didn't know whether to laugh about the fact he knew PC Kirk's nickname or about the suggestion of a coffee machine. He resisted however as he saw Avalon was serious.

'That won't be easy,' he said.

'It's just a coffee machine, not the 'Stone of Destiny',' and he left.

Avalon decided there was a visit he had to make before he went to find the three businesses that reported being attacked. He drove to find a shop where he could buy a satnav for his car. It was obvious, in the long term it would save him a great deal of time and it was probably worth the money, and it would look better than the three-year-old, dog-eared AA map-book in the back seat.

Ross had his head buried between files and his computer screen when DC MacDonald walked into the interview room that was now Avalon's office.

'Hey Ross, I like the new office, plenty o' room and the added benefit o' no windae.'

'What? Oh aye, plenty of room, better than the Cupboard I suppose.' The Cupboard was the name they gave to the small office they usually worked out of. Ross went back to his work.

'So how's the new boy?' asked MacDonald.

'Oh, y' know, English and full of shite,' replied Ross.

'Aye, goes with the territory.' Ross seemed distracted a little. MacDonald sensed Ross didn't want to talk and so he turned to leave.

'Okay, I can tak a hint,' he grinned. Ross turned round to him and asked.

'Hey Mack, can you remember the drugs bust we

made last year and that forensics chap who examined the burned out car said he could always find evidence?'

'Aye, what about it?' asked MacDonald.

'As I remember, he was trying to get the fire services to use less water to put the fires out.'

'Aye, he said it washes away any evidence.'

'I thought that's what he said,' replied Ross, and he went back to the computer. MacDonald shrugged and said.

'So aye ye found somethin' then, on the burned out cars?' asked MacDonald.

'Probably not but I have to make a few calls,' replied Ross, and he picked up the phone. He was still on it long after MacDonald had left and Avalon returned.

'Okay, if you can send me that over as soon as?' asked Ross to someone on the phone. 'Aye, that's right, thanks,' and he replaced the handset. Avalon was standing by the filing cabinet with his hands in his pockets.

'Anything?' he asked.

'Aye, well, maybe. I talked to forensics about the car wrecks, the reason they could find nothing was that the cars had been cleaned.'

'What you mean before they were burned?' asked Avalon.

'Before and after. Forensics put in their report that ammonia was found in the wrecks which is used in cleaning fluids.'

'And explosives,' added Avalon.

'Yeah but in this case they think the upholstery was cleaned with ammonia-based products. Too little upholstery left and too little evidence to be sure though.' Avalon nodded.

'And after?' he asked with a puzzled expression.

'All those car wrecks were flushed out with water.'

'Well, you can blame the fire service for that.'

'Not at all,' insisted Ross who seemed to be sniffing something, 'they rarely use water on car fires now and in any case, one of them was found burned out without the fire service being called.'

'And it was flushed out?' asked Avalon. Ross nodded. 'Then how the hell do you flush out a burning car with water without putting the fire out?'

'Forensics made a guess on that, the burned plastic found in the debris may have been plastic containers that held water rather than the petrol that started the fires.' Ross began sniffing again.

'If we can prove this, we can be sure that this wasn't some adolescent boy racer stealing cars for an occasional ram-raid,' announced Avalon.

'Too right, but why would you have containers of water in a car you were about to burn?' Ross stopped and curled up his nose, 'And what is that bloody awful smell?' Avalon seemed distant at first but then he acted.

'Oh, this?' he pulled out a paper bag and revealed a small black, card box. He opened the top flap of the box and the smell became stronger as he pulled out a black bottle with white writing on it.

'Dark Ice?' said Ross as he read the label on the bottle, 'what is it?'

'Parfum pour homme,' grinned Avalon.

'What?' asked Ross with a stifled laugh.

'Aftershave, cologne, de-stinker, whatever you want to call it,' replied Avalon.

'Sarge, we really have to get you some therapy,

you can't go around wearing this junk. It smells like cleaning fluid.' Avalon was taken aback slightly. Ross had called him 'Sarge'. Was this the sign of a truce?

'It's not for me Ross, I thought it was more you.' Ross turned his nose up further as the bottle was examined. Avalon took the bottle back and placed it on the desk. 'This, my friend is evidence. I'm not sure of what yet but we have to keep it in mind.'

'Not difficult with a pong like that.' Ross looked up to Avalon. 'Well, why evidence?'

'I had a talk with all the businesses who were threatened, and they all confirmed that they warned the crooks that they would be contacting the police,' began Avalon. 'I really don't think that it would be enough to put them off though, it wouldn't make any sense.' He paused and Ross nodded, then he continued to explain. 'The owner of one of the family-run businesses actually threw one of the crooks out and I have asked him to come in to help make a photofit.'

'The notes say they were wearing heavy disguises,' added Ross.

'True but the one they threw out lost part of his disguise and one of the sons got a good look at him. It really seems to me that these protections racketeers didn't seem to have their heart in the work and were too easily put off, 'Avalon sat, 'But the jewel in the crown is this bottle. One of the owners was a woman called Anne McLeod, and she told me she phoned the police whilst they were actually in her shop. They left, but she remembered that there was a lingering smell for sometime after.' Ross said nothing, he just pointed to the black bottle. 'Exactly,' smiled Avalon.

'But by itself, it means nothing,' frowned Ross.

'True,' admitted Avalon, 'but, she told me she thought it must be a new scent because she hadn't smelled it before and low and behold, I went down the street, into the chemist and asked if there was a new aftershave on the market. I was told this was it but it wasn't very popular.'

'I'm not surprised,' laughed Ross.

'I bought this and took it back to Miss McLeod and she confirmed it was the exact odour,' confirmed Avalon.

'So now we are looking for a crook with no sense of smell,' grinned Ross.

'Well, probably but the sheer coincidence of this makes it worth keeping in mind.' Ross nodded and picked up the phone.

'Who are you calling?' asked Avalon. Ross looked up and said.

'Bomb disposal, we need someone to get rid of this bottle.'

Chapter Four

Craig Nisbett always walked his dog through the fields at the rear of his house in the evenings. He didn't dislike his wife watching so much television, he just wished on some occasions, she would watch something that *he* liked too. For that reason, his life, after the evening meal, which was always at six o'clock on the dot, was regulated to the extreme. They would eat and then she would sit in front of the TV for the rest of the evening, he would wash the pots. He would then log on to his laptop and make his usual trip around the internet forums that he was a member of, six of them all dedicated to the ubiquitous Ford Escort. Craig also owned one of the said vehicles, a 1974, four-door version painted in electric blue with the 'quirky' square headlights. That was the next port of call after he had checked his emails, mainly from other escort owners, he would look around the treasured car in its tiny garage. He would usually sit in the car for a few minutes taking in the nostalgic aroma, a smell of the past from when his father owned a very similar car and would take them on trips to the coast and into the mountains. His little car was his world. He could forget about his job, his wife, her stupid TV programmes and the bills and demands that seemed to arrive daily. His only other concern in life was his dog. His dog was called 'Hannu', a little Shetland Sheepdog, named after the Finnish rally driver Hannu Mikkola who had helped make the Ford Escort famous many years previous. Craig and Hannu always walked across the fields around the same time and at this time of year, it was still reasonably light. The sun had long since set but in the dull, blue light of the evening, most things could be seen clearly. Hannu was good company for Craig and he thought the world of her, he certainly thought more about the dog than his wife. Craig sat on a broken part of the fence where a crossbeam made a perfect seat. He sat there almost every evening at this time and looked down across the Great Glen, with the inky water of Loch Ness hidden in the valley below. That same view had been available to him most of his life but it never failed to impress him. The dog went on sniffing the same things it did every night and Craig kept to his normal schedule and hoped tonight he wouldn't hear it. For months that awful noise had been heard many times and every time something had gone wrong in the world. Locally the sound was dreaded by almost all that heard it and to Craig, it meant a violation of his private world. The night was eerily quiet and in the back of his mind, he knew that this was a perfect night for that sound to shudder down the valley, so much so, that for the first time he could remember, he decided to return a little early. He crossed the field and over the fence onto a public footpath which passed a copse of trees and back to the road. It wasn't much of a road but it was a quicker route back to his house. As he walked out onto the asphalt, he turned to look for the dog but couldn't see her. She was usually close by, so this worried Craig.

'Hannu! Hannu!' he called but saw nothing. What little light there had been was now just about gone but her characteristic . movement could not be seen anywhere. 'Hannu, come on old girl,' he called a little louder. Nothing. Carefully he traced his steps back onto the footpath but still, he could see no sign of her, then to his right he heard a noise that sounded like the dog walking through the undergrowth.

'Hannu, are y' there?' he called but if the dog was over by the copse of trees, she wasn't moving anymore. With trepidation, Craig climbed over the fence and made his way towards the copse of trees and peered into its black centre.

'Hannu, come on girl, let's go,' he called once more. There was still no sign of the dog. He didn't want to go into that dark space within the trees, it was calling him, but he hated the idea. His feelings told him there was something bad in there, but what if the dog was in trouble? He called several times, a little quieter but still nothing. Then he heard it. That terrible sound that reverberated down the valley, a distant sound but with a thud that seemed to enter the bloodstream. A double thud like the heartbeat of some monstrous Kraken and he looked over to the dark mass of the hills to the southwest where the direction the sound seemed to come from. It was time to go and he knew he would have to steel himself to enter that copse, so with a determination he never knew he had, he launched himself into the briars and looked around in the gloom. The ground felt softer where it neared the edge of the drainage ditch and there, some yards away he saw something that was lighter in colour. He wanted to believe it was Hannu, but the shape wasn't moving and his heart began to sink. He closed in on the shape and then to his right he saw movement, just a slight movement but movement nonetheless. He squinted, it looked like his dog, yes it was, and the dog was sitting quietly looking from the light coloured shape back to him. He couldn't make out detail on Hannu but the white blaze on her face made it clear it was her. So what was the shape on the ground? Craig began to feel sick. He moved forward and noticed the object looked like a blanket, so he touched the corner and lifted it. He couldn't quite tell what it was and so he decided to go back and fetch a torch. He moved to the dog, caught hold of her collar, and led her away. Back home, he locked Hannu in the kitchen and went to the garage to fetch a torch. He tried the torch, and it worked. For several minutes he tried to pluck up the courage to return to the copse but eventually he replaced the torch on the shelf and went for a bath as he always did. He was exactly twelve minutes later than normal and his wife had noticed.

Avalon hadn't been in the interview room which doubled as his temporary office, for more than about ten minutes before Davies knocked and entered.

'How are you settling in James?' Avalon smiled as he hung his jacket on the back of the chair.

'Very well thank you. I think I just about know where everything is now.'

'I see you even have a coffee machine, even I don't have that luxury,' shrugged Davies. Avalon sat and laughed.

'I work better when I smell the stuff even if I'm

not drinking it.' Davies nodded and looked around the room.

'We're still working on an office for you but it's taking time to move things around.'

'Don't worry, we're coping. A window would be nice but it's fine for now,' admitted Avalon. Davies looked a little more serious as he said.

'I'm starting to feel that I got you here under false pretences, the case I wanted you to work on has been shelved for the time being as there is so much to do. We're going to have a meeting about it this morning, it's in the restroom so we can get everyone in.'

'Oh right,' replied Avalon trying to look animated. The truth was, Avalon was used to morning meetings about current cases, he thought it was standard practice.

'So we'll see you in there about nine thirty then? Oh, and bring Ross.' Davies looked at the empty chair where Ross should have been. 'Where is he by the way?'

'Ross?' asked Avalon, 'oh, I sent him on an errand, he should be back soon.' Davies didn't ask what the errand was and Avalon didn't look like he was about to say, so he turned to leave. In the doorway, he stopped and said,

'I'll get the cleaners to come in while the meeting is on, there is a really odd smell in here don't you think?' Avalon took a quick glance at the filing cabinet that housed the Dark Ice Aftershave and quickly replied with,

'Oh, don't worry, It's probably me I had a curry last night.'

Five minutes after Davies left, DC Ross arrived, he said nothing and just sat in his chair. Avalon played it cool, he didn't look at Ross and didn't ask anything. After a minute or so he just said.

'There's a conference at zero, nine-thirty hours.' For a moment Ross didn't react, then he said.

'Okay.' There was a little more silence then Avalon stood and put on his jacket.

'Davies asked where you were.'

'What did you tell him?' asked Ross looking up at Avalon.

'I said you were on an errand for me.' Avalon poured himself a coffee and turned to Ross raising his eyebrows whilst pointing to the cup. Ross nodded. Then as Avalon poured out another coffee Ross said.

'Thanks.'

'It would be easier to lie if you keep me in the loop.'

'I was stuck in traffic,' replied Ross with a little venom in his voice.

'In Inverness? I don't think so,' laughed Avalon as he handed Ross his cup. 'You don't know what traffic is up here.' Avalon took a sip of his coffee and sat, but he moved the seat so he could see Ross behind his computer screen.

'I think we need to talk to forensics about this plastic found in the burned cars,' he said. Ross looked over to him.

'Personally, even with this, I don't think the case is worth putting any serious time into.' Avalon just shrugged.

'I admit that it doesn't have the hallmark of the crime of the century but it has piqued my interest. Why would someone go to the trouble of stealing cars, carry out some half-hearted ram-raids and then drive the cars to isolated spots so they could torch them leaving no evidence?'

'I have no idea,' began Ross, 'but there is a queue of more important cases and in my opinion we should be working on those.' Once again Avalon shrugged taking more sips of coffee.

'Maybe, but as of yet, these are all the cases we have been given.'

'*You* have been given, I was working on other things and I expect to be back on them when they let you loose.' Avalon laughed. He drained his cup and stood up to place it on the top of the filing cabinet.

'Well,' he began, 'how do I get in touch with forensics?' Ross looked up with a frown.

'So you want to go through with this?' he asked. Avalon just stared blankly at him. 'Okay, it's up to you.' Ross scribbled down a name and an address for the forensics team. 'They work off-site at that address, there are four in the lab but Sarah Underwood is the head forensics science officer, she co-ordinates most of the cases.' Avalon read the address and had no idea where it was but it would be a great trial for his new satnav system. 'You'll also have to let them know you are going, it's not high security but as they don't know who you are...' Ross broke off and sat back.

'Okay, I'll ring later and arrange it.'

'Oh, and I may as well tell you,' began Ross with a smile, 'don't get any ideas with Miss Underwood.'

'What do you mean?' asked Avalon with a doubtful expression.

'I'm just saying.'

'It sounds like you have a thing for Miss Underwood,' smiled Avalon, reading the scrap of paper

Ross had given him.

'I certainly haven't but you'll find out,' and Ross picked up his cup to drink with a grin. Avalon looked at his watch.

'It's nearly time, we better get off to the restroom.' Ross nodded and stood. 'Oh, and DI Davies got a whiff of the Quatermass Experiment in the filing cabinet.'

'What did he say?' asked Ross.

'I managed to put him off by saying I had eaten a curry last night.'

'Bloody 'ell, remind me never to go for a curry with you.'

'Okay everyone,' said Davies looking around the room, 'this morning's complement is a little larger than usual, as myself and DI Lasiter want you all in on this.' He looked around to Lasiter. 'Robert?' he said. Lasiter stood and Davies sat.

'Right, as an update I want y's to know how the investigations are goin' so that we are all up tae speed on what's going on,' he paused and looked down to a sheet of paper in his hand. 'Unfortunately, B section are drawing blanks on the two abductions and the computer data robberies, and the two robberies at gunpoint are much the same. We do have a new witness who has come forward but we are waiting for a report on that.' He stopped for breath. 'The uniform branch have all but closed the paintings and jewel robbery cases, for lack of evidence, and they say that they are too busy with more section twenty attacks in the town and two major RTCs on the A9.' Lasiter picked up another sheet with an audible sigh. 'The two arson attacks from two weeks ago

133

have drawn very little from the Fire Brigade investigations and their arson officer is asking for backup, I have declined and told them it will have to wait.' Lasiter looked down at an officer who Avalon had seen and assumed to be DS Murrey. 'Tom, have you got anything on the fraud case yet?'

'Sorry Governor, we are all out at the moment, Callum is going over the details later but without more people we can't get very far.' Lasiter nodded and sighed again.

'Aye a' know laddie.' He looked up. 'Where's Frazer?'

'Here boss.' Came the voice of the diminutive DC Frazer. Her hazel eyes flashed around with a hint of doubt.

'Ah Megan, what have you and MacDonald got at the moment?' Lasiter knew there was too much work for C Section but he had to ask, it was his job. Frazer pulled a notebook out and read from it.

'Other than the cases we are active on, we have two rapes, seven S-twenty assaults, five S-eighteen assaults, a holdup with a firearm that has just come en an' another case that we can't talk about as et's internal.'

'Hey, Frazer, you forgot about the missing cat on Fairfield Road,' grinned Wilson. There was a ripple of laughter.

'I didn't mention it because the Chief Constable wanted you specifically on that one.' There was more laughter. Avalon was impressed that even with the pressure to get results, the team still had time for humour. It was new to him, people usually burned out under this much pressure.

'Okay, calm down people. We'll have to reshuffle again,' announced Lasiter.

'There is also the request for a liaison with the coastguard and the uniform branch want assistance with a surveillance,' added Davies.

'Surveillance? What's that for?'

'It sounds like it could be related to the fraud case we've been dealing with, so it might be in our interests,' replied Davies.

'Dear god it gets better,' groaned Lasiter, 'okay we'll try to deal with the most pressing issues and consolidate other cases for a later date.' Lasiter then looked around and Avalon felt his eyes rest momentarily on him.

'I think Andrew, we need to consider y'r idea. DI Davies has suggested splitting the sections and concentrating on the cases we can get ticks for.' There were a few sighs around the room. 'Yeah, a' know how y' feel about et but we have to do et.' Lasiter looked at his sheets and then said. 'Right, DS Murrey and DC McGill will team up with DC Frazer, I want you t'-' there was an interruption by a uniformed Sergeant.

'Sorry sir but we have a report of a body somewhere near Abriachan.'

'Where?' asked Lasiter.

'Et's on the banks of the loch,' replied the Sergeant.

'Has anyone gone?' asked the DI.

'Aye, responders have gone out to secure the scene but there isn't anybody else left.'

'Shite,' exclaimed Lasiter brushing his hand over his forehead, 'okay, thanks McNeill, we'll get someone out there.' The sergeant nodded and left. Lasiter mumbled something to himself and then looked straight at Avalon.

'DS Avalon, drop what y're working on, you and Ross take a trip out to Abriacherwatsit. Don't do any more than y' have tae an' please come back and tell me et's a suicide.' Avalon nodded and stood, Ross was already up and making his way to the door. After picking up a 'scenes of crime kit', they made their way to Avalon's car.

'Is this yours?' asked Ross.

'Yeah, why?' asked Avalon with a slight frown.

'I win twenty quid then, I bet it was yours.' Avalon wasn't sure what he meant, but he got in and asked Ross how to spell the name of the place that the Sergeant had given them for the satnav.

'Just drive down the A82 and look for blue flashing lights,' said Ross flippantly. This they did and as they progressed along the road, Avalon was struck by the beauty of the area, the green of the lush vegetation, the almost blue, hue of the heather and the sparkling reflections cast on the water that seemed to be everywhere. Yes, the sky seemed to be a constant pall of grey but there was a natural beauty that was intoxicating. As they moved along the road, Avalon noticed the watercourse to the left was broadening out and it struck Avalon what it may be.

'Is that what I think it is?' he asked pointing to the water.

'What do you think it is?' asked Ross.

'Loch Ness?'

'Then it's what you think it is,' replied Ross unconcerned.

'I've never seen it before,' admitted Avalon.

'It's just water, there's plenty of it too, this is just

a tiny bit of it,' explained Ross, glancing quickly over to it.

'It certainly looks big,' agreed Avalon taking the odd peep between the trees.

'Big?' questioned Ross, 'that doesn't really do it justice. If you stand in a particular spot at one end, you can't see land at the other.'

'Impressive, the curve of the earth I suppose,' suggested Avalon.

'Aye, that or the rain,' quipped Ross, and he continued with, 'Someone once calculated that if all the water was removed, the Loch could hold all the bodies of all the people of the whole world.'

'I somehow don't think that it would be quite the tourist trap that the monster provides thought,' smiled Avalon. Ross nodded.

'It would be one hell of a murder investigation too,' he said.

'What's your take on the monster then?' asked Avalon, 'being local and all that.' Avalon felt Ross glance at him for a moment.

'I would like to think it was real, but come on, look at the facts.' He looked back to the water. 'It's a great setting for it and it brings in a lot of money to the local economy and in Scotland that is important. If people ask I say yeah, it's real.' Avalon nodded, he knew what he was getting at. 'The problem is that a Norwegian company are scanning and plotting the whole loch and that will be bad for the area.'

'Why?' asked Avalon.

'Well, if they turn round and say there is no monster, we can kiss goodbye to fifty million pounds of tourism a year,' frowned Ross.

'They have tried it before but tourists still come,' added Avalon.

'Maybe, we'll know soon enough, they started last week.' Avalon was about to ask further questions but he noticed a small side road up a steep hill blocked off with cones and police tape.

'Looks like this is it,' he said as a slight drizzle began to fall.

Avalon was apprehensive as he turned on the windscreen wipers and pulled off the main road, through the police roadblock. It was some time since he had worked on a case with a body. The road looked daunting too. It was a very narrow, steep lane with small passing places and the Mondeo was struggling a bit. They continued on through the trees and the soft drizzle until after many twists and turns, they seemed to be nearing the summit. As they came out of the trees, the road levelled out and swept to the right onto the fields and moorland. Avalon saw two uniformed officers standing by a police van and there was a Scenes of Crimes Officer suiting up already.

'It looks like SOCO aren't as busy as us then,' quipped Avalon as he pulled into a small parking area that became a forest track. In the field, he noticed two other people who he assumed to be the other scenes of crime officers as one was carrying camera kit. He got out of the car and noticed one of the police officers walking towards him. The PC gave a quick smile and raised his eyebrows a little as he approached. Avalon gave a slight nod and said instinctively.

'Avalon, Wolv...' he had to stop himself abruptly, his automated response had to be altered slightly, 'sorry, Detective Sergeant Avalon, Inverness CID. This is DC

Ross,' he announced. It sounded odd to him, yet slightly exotic.

'Ye must be new,' said the officer in a Scottish lilt.

'Very,' nodded Avalon.

'PC Dodds.' The officer said and then added. 'Welcome to Inverness though I'm no' sure this es the best sort of Scottish welcome.'

'What do we have?' asked Avalon.

'A body of a male about twenty-five tae thirty-five years old, wrapped in a blanket,' answered the PC.

'Foul play?' asked Ross.

'Aye, it certainly looks like et.' The officer looked round to the black van parked in the road. 'SOCO have still got to seal the site but at first glance et looks like a heid injury.'

'Who found the body?' asked Avalon. The PC pulled out his notebook and read.

'A Mr Craig Nisbett seems to have found the body last night but for reasons unknown, he didn't report et until this mornin'.' Avalon frowned a little.

'That seems a bit odd,' he mused.

'Aye but et seems the drums were playing again last night. It probably scared him off.'

'Sorry?' asked Avalon.

'It's a bit of a local mystery Sarge,' interrupted Ross, 'there have been sounds of drums in the hills every time there is a crime.'

'So why wasn't I told about this?' asked Avalon. Ross looked at Avalon and then quickly glanced at the uniformed officer. Avalon understood the meaning and so they moved slightly away from the PC. Ross shrugged as he explained.

'I don't know, I suppose the DI thought you would hear about it soon enough. He took everyone off the case a few days ago.' Avalon thought for a moment but decided to pursue the issue later.

'We better go and see Mr Nisbett then,' he demanded, and he returned to the PC to ask the way.

The tiny bungalow was set a hundred yards or so from the road and was plain in styling, a feature that continued indoors, where, in the main room, a giant flat screen television dominated the small space. Opposite Avalon and Ross sat Mr and Mrs Nisbett, he small and lithe, she large and homely.

'So, Mr Nisbett,' asked Avalon to the worried-looking man, 'why didn't you report the body as soon as you found it?'

'Well... well,' he seemed very unsure and looked constantly at his wife for reassurance, 'well I did'nea know what it was, it was dark and I was out with Hannu, my dog.' Avalon looked for a dog but didn't see one. 'I found her watching over what looked like erm, a pile of rubbish.' He stopped to take a breath and a quick look at his wife. 'I lifted the blanket a bit and saw a foot and a leg, but at first I thought it may be a drunk or a tramp.'

'Et's because he's yella!' cut in his wife with a strong accent, 'He told me this mornin' what he found, he also told me he came back for a torch but thought better o' et.' His wife turned to him in disgust, then back to Avalon. 'I knew somethin' was wrong this morning, so I made him tell me. We went o'er and saw the bundle. I've seen enough CSI programmes tae know not tae touch anythin'.'

'Quite,' smiled Avalon.

'Is this true Mr Nisbett?' asked Ross who was

140

writing down the interview.

'Y-yes,' stuttered the man.

'Do you always walk your dog in that field Mr Nisbett?' asked Avalon. The man nodded.

'Ev-ery night at the same taime detective,' added his wife.

'But detective,' began Nisbett, 'a heard the drums y' see, a was afraid.' Avalon looked sternly at the man and then asked.

'Is that the first time you heard them?' The man shook his head with a quick nervous movement.

'No, it seems most nights they sound off.'

'Et's all shite if ye ask me,' interrupted the wife, 'I mean, drums from a phantom drummer? Get real.'

'So you don't believe it then Mrs Nisbett?' asked Avalon.

'No, and no one wi' an ounce of brain would either,' she said stabbing her chubby fingers towards her head. Avalon showed little reaction to the story himself, he just asked to see the dog which had been put in another room, just to corroborate the story, and then they went to talk to the scenes of crime people. As they walked over to the spot, Avalon asked a few questions of Ross.

'So what is the real reason I was kept out of the loop about the drums?'

'As far as I know you weren't kept out of the loop. It's orders of DI Lasiter. He thought that the growing legend was putting people off the job at hand, so he told us all to drop the idea that the drums linked anything.'

'But that's not good practice, what if there is something that links, or even helps solve something?'

'Well, with respect, that's something you'll have to take up with DI Lasiter,' replied Ross.

'So this must be what Wilson was going to tell me,' added Avalon, more to himself. He shrugged the 'drum' issue off for the moment but he knew he would need to ask more questions.

The area near where the body was found had been taped off and only one police officer remained but the three SOCO team members were still processing the scene. Avalon looked over but couldn't attract their attention so he called.

'Detective Avalon,' he announced. One of the men in white coveralls looked over and came towards him. 'Detective Sergeant Avalon,' he repeated.

'Hello detective, I'm John McFarlaine, Inverness SSD. I know Detective Ross, but I haven't met you, new are you?'

'Yes, very,' he repeated, 'do you have anything for me and can we take a look?'

'Yes by all means, the surrounding area has been processed, we are now examining the body.' They climbed over the fence and began to walk to the copse of trees. 'He's a white male probably in his early thirties, approximately five feet nine and one hundred and sixty pounds in weight, long brown hair with some facial hair.'

'And the cause of death?' asked Avalon.

'Hard to say until the body is examined but I would say a head wound by the amount of matted blood in the hair.' As they crouched to make their way into the trees, McFarlaine continued. 'He's wrapped in a wool blanket and I *suspect* he didn't receive the injury here.' He made a great emphasis on the word 'suspect'. Both

Ross and Avalon understood what he was trying to say.

'So it looks like foul play?' asked Ross.

'That's what it looks like but the autopsy will shed more light on that.' McFarlaine saw one of his team nod his head. 'We're about to turn the body if you would like to give a hand,' he asked. Avalon thought the word 'like' under these circumstances was misplaced but it would confirm whether this was the place the man died, or not. The blanket which was brightly multi-coloured, had already been moved from part of the body by the team and the initial evidence gathering was done. They still had to look under the body however, so when they were all in position, the body was rolled slightly to one side and the photographer took several shots.

'Yes, as I thought, there is very little blood here, so make what you will of that,' said McFarlaine. Avalon looked at the clothing of the man and said to Ross.

'He looks like a...' he paused for a moment trying to think of the correct word but he could find none, 'well... a hippy.'

'Maybe homeless or living rough I would suggest,' added McFarlaine. Ross was looking at a small badge that was fixed to the man's waistcoat.

'I know where he's come from, this badge is a big clue,' added Ross looking at the unusual dress. The clothes looked well-worn yet much of them had bright colours and his socks were candy-striped. His hair looked unkempt and his short wispy beard had beads knotted into a small plait. 'I reckon he's from the camp up by Ardendrain. He's wearing a badge, that probably came from the festival up there,' he added.

'What festival?' asked Avalon, as he stood.

'Every year they have a UFO spotting camp up

on the hill, he looks like he may be part of that, it certainly fits,' explained Ross.

'Yes,' nodded McFarlaine, 'it could be.' Ross looked at Avalon and nodded sideways just very slightly and Avalon understood.

'We'll leave you to finish off, we'll be by the van.' Avalon said to McFarlaine and he and Ross moved out of the copse.

'What is it?' asked Avalon.

'B section have been working on several abductions from that camp, Lasiter said this morning that they have dropped the case for now.'

'Explain,' insisted Avalon.

'Three weeks ago, just after the camp began, a male went missing, no one saw him leave, he just went missing in the night. Others reported seeing spinning lights across the valley,' Ross laughed, 'they said it was a UFO.'

'Go on,' insisted Avalon without a smile. Ross stopped laughing and continued.

'The man appeared back at the camp three nights later, convinced he had been abducted by aliens. No further investigation was pursued as most people thought he was mad or drunk. Then, a week later another person went missing, this time a female under the same conditions, flashing lights and weird noises in the forest.' He saw no reaction in Avalon's face. 'So, again, the female turns up several days later at the camp and swears she was experimented on by aliens.'

'Is that it?' Avalon asked glaring at Ross.

'Well, the police doctor checked her over and did find small incisions and needle marks and they found some odd compounds in her blood but even she admitted to taking drugs at the camp so it was ignored,' Ross sighed. 'Then a day after that, another man went missing, just as strange lights were seen in the forest but this time someone heard a man scream out. A small amount of blood was found near the area but nothing else. He has been listed as a missing person.'

'And you think this might be him?' asked Avalon. Ross nodded.

'Could be.'

'Well, if they found blood at the site, then it will be simple enough to tie it to this body, this may have to be handed back to 'B' section.' Ross agreed just as his pager went off. Avalon saw Ross reading the pager but remembered he had left his in the car, he also remembered what PC Kirk had told him about keeping it with him.

'Something big has gone off, they want us back, but we can't leave yet can we?' asked Ross.

'Not really, we'll have to wait for the coroner's van to arrive to remove the body, there's only one uniform left here. Best phone in though and explain, I'll have a word with the PC.' Ross nodded and pulled out his phone while Avalon went to talk to Dodds.

'Well the others have had to respond to something in the town,' said PC Dodds in answer to why there was only one PC on duty, 'they say they'll send someone out as soon as, but I doubt it,' he added. Avalon returned to Ross and the two of them had a quick look around the area as Ross began to explain.

'It's a major robbery, a security van has been stolen. They want us back.' There was a look of excitement on his face.

'Hells bells,' exclaimed Avalon, 'what next?' He turned and noticed what looked like the coroner's van coming up the road, so he walked over to the PC. 'We're going to have to leave you to sort this out, make sure you let Nisbett know, he will be required to make a full statement back at the station.'

'Aye okay sergeant, they'll be done here soon enough and it must be a big job in Inverness with all the chatter on the radio,' explained Dodds.

'Did you hear anything?' asked Ross.

'Not much,' replied Dodds as he curled his nose, 'they are just saying it's a major incident.' Avalon let out a big sigh.

'We really need to get statements from all the houses around here, I don't like leaving without covering everything,' he said.

'There aren't that many houses up here, a couple over there and a caravan or two in the moorland,' pointed Dodds.

'Well, it will have to wait,' answered Avalon, and he turned to walk to the car as the light drizzle ceased completely.

Avalon and Ross made their way carefully back down the hill along the narrow road seeing the vast expanse of the loch ahead and below them. At the bottom, Ross moved the cones blocking the way onto the main road and they made their way back to base.

'It's going to be a long day,' Avalon quipped.

On the way back to the station, Avalon once again asked Ross about the so-called 'drums' that had been heard.

'People up at the camp and even down in the

146

village say they heard the drums on the night of the abductions,' explained Ross.

'Drums? strange lights? How the hell, can this link to a dead man in a copse of trees and why doesn't Lasiter want this in the open?' sighed Avalon. 'So what were the theories before Lasiter closed it down?'

'Most people are linking it to a legend from the Jacobite risings but the official word is that it is coincidental.'

'Coincidental? How can that be? The noise is heard every time there is an incident? It sounds more than coincidental,' frowned Avalon.

'Well that was what we thought but after plotting a calendar of events and cross-referencing the incidents with the sounds, there *are* discrepancies,' insisted Ross.

'I would still like to look at this. Do we have a recording of the sounds?'

'What? you mean, has the perpetrator done a YouTube video?'

'Don't get smart Ross, I'm serious. Check the internet I'm betting someone has posted a recording on there from a mobile phone. It would make a change from videos of dancing cats and children falling over,' insisted Avalon.

'Right, I'll check on it. Anything else?'

'Yeah, where is this list of events you spoke about?'

'In the files, I think,' replied Ross.

'We need that too and I still have to go and see the forensics people about the plastic found in the cars.'

'The DI told us to drop that,' insisted Ross.

'No, he told me to drop it, your name wasn't mentioned,' Avalon grinned, Ross sighed, 'where are the sounds heard mostly?' continued Avalon. Ross looked over to him and nodded towards the back of the car.

'Back where we just came from.' Avalon looked wide-eyed at Ross. 'Well not exactly there but in the village a mile or two further on, Drumnadrochit.'

'You 're joking right?' asked Avalon with a grin.

'No, why? We plotted where the sounds had been reported and the centre of the area is Drumnadrochit. You must have heard of Drumnadrochit?' said Ross with a questioning look.

'It rings a bell, but the sound of *drums* in *Drum*-nadrochit?' He put emphasis on the word drum in both cases. Ross looked out of the windscreen in silence for several seconds and then turned to Avalon and said.

'You probably won't believe this but until now no one has made that connection.' He turned back to look ahead and then added. 'But then again, there are many places around here that have 'drum' in their name, it's Gaelic for 'ridge'.' Ross hesitated as if trying to remember something. 'I think Drumnadrochit translates to 'Ridge of the Bridge'.'

'Very poetic but is the drum legend from there?' asked Avalon.

'No, miles away. It comes from Culloden, just after the battle. Look it up on the internet,' said Ross.

'Well, I've heard of Culloden obviously but nothing about a drum,' added Avalon.

'It's a sad moment in Scotland's history, we were fighting an insignificant nation called England somehow we managed to get our arses kicked.'

'My recollection of the history is that your own people kicked your arse, it may have been financed by the English but most of the Government forces were

Scottish.'

'It's more complex than that but to be honest, my history isn't up to much,' frowned Ross.

'Do you know enough to say where the drum comes into it?' demanded Avalon.

'I don't know all the details of the legend but as far as I remember the old drummer of Gillies MacBean followed him into the fight and beat his drum as MacBean struck down dragoon after dragoon until a heap of his enemy laid around him. Eventually, MacBean was overpowered and killed as was the drummer who had never struck a blow in the fight. The drummer's mother was said to be a witch, she took his shattered body, and his drum, back to her hut on the moor. There she cursed the English and empowered the drum with the curse too and buried his smashed body on the south bank of Loch Ness on MacBean land.' Avalon listened to the story with interest, Ross continued. 'It has been said, that if the drum is beaten, an Englishman somewhere dies. Another legend is that if Scotland is at risk from her enemies, the ghost of MacBean's drummer will find the drum and march the Scottish nation into battle.'

'It's an Arthurian type of legend then?' said Avalon, 'the legend of King Arthur is similar, if England is in trouble, he will come back to lead them.'

'Tosh though after all,' shrugged Ross. Avalon nodded. Ross looked around at him. 'The thing is, many people still believe if the drum is heard, evil will befall someone, and in this case, it certainly seems to have some truth.' Ross folded his arms.

'So you believe it?' smiled Avalon.

'Course not, but some do, I think that's why

Lasiter stopped it as a separate investigation.' Avalon asked why it had been a CID investigation anyway. Ross took a deep breath and answered.

'Well, when it started it seemed that every time it was heard, some crime happened in the Highlands, as the amount of crime intensified, so did the nights the drum was heard.'

'So,' began Avalon, 'it was assumed that whoever was making the drum sound was probably the same person or persons who were committing the crimes?' Ross nodded tightening his lips slightly, then added.

'It didn't hold water though, we plotted dates and times of the crimes with a rough date and time of the drums and though they were sometimes fairly accurate, they were also sometimes wildly off.'

'So it was dropped?' asked Avalon glancing at Ross who nodded again.

'Davies thought there was more to it though and I think that's when Wilson brought up your name in conversation.' Ross looked over to him. 'He said you were the Ghost-busting detective.' On any other occasion, Avalon would have gone off like a Roman Candle, but with his new character and outlook, he just smiled a little and shook his head. Things *had* changed. 'I think Lasiter must have eventually convinced Davies that it wasn't worth following due to the workload and the Detective Chief Inspector agreed.'

'But they needed extra hands to pump the sinking ship so they continued to rush through my secondment,' added Avalon.

'Possibly,' said Ross. Avalon stared at the road as he said.

'The very deep did rot, Oh Christ! that ever this

150

should be.' Ross frowned deeply and turned to Avalon.

'What's that? Some religious stuff?' he asked. Avalon gave him a quick glance then shook his head.

'Not unless your religion is Samuel Taylor Coleridge,' he said, 'it's a poem, The Ancient Mariner.'

'Oh,' said Ross and continued to look at the car in front. Avalon grinned slightly then repeated the phrase, this time with a little more passion.

'*The very deep did rot, Oh Christ! that ever this should be. Yea, slimy things did crawl with legs, Upon the slimy sea.*' Ross shrugged a little then said.

'Well, it's not exactly 'Skillet' but I suppose it would work with a decent tune behind it.'

'What's skillet?' asked Avalon pulling in at the station, but it would have to wait.

By the time Avalon and Ross had arrived, there was a conference just about drawing to a close with everyone who was available and so they crept in through the door and stood at the back.

'So, for now, we will have to wait for DI Lasiter and DC Frazer to phone the details in,' Davies, who was looking particularly stressed, was running the conference, 'so are there any questions?'

'Do we just wait or shall we carry on regardless?' asked Wilson.

'Just carry on but be ready to move if we need you and don't leave the station.' The meeting broke up at this and Davies walked over to Avalon and Ross.

'So what's the score over at Abriachan?' he asked.

'One dead male, possible foul play,' frowned Avalon.

'Great,' sighed Davies deeply.

'It looks like he could be the missing man from the UFO camp,' added Ross.

'Were there any press there? asked Davies. Avalon shook his head. 'Good, we'll keep that one from them for now.'

'I'm guessing we hand this back to B section Boss,' shrugged Ross but Davies bit his bottom lip and thought for a moment.

'No, I know they looked into the prior missing persons but I'll have a word with DI Lasiter and keep you on this. You know the score down there, so keep with it.' He turned to leave and seemed to remember something. 'I know you're busy but if you get chance, the chappy who had the paintings stolen a few weeks ago has made an official complaint about the officers that attended his crime scene,' Davies looked sheepish and slightly apologetic, 'if you get a minute will you look into it?' Ross shrugged and then said,

'From what I can gather from the uniform team that attended, he was a pain in the arse.'

'I know, I heard but if you can?' He turned to leave.

'DI Davies?' Davies stopped and turned back to Avalon, he seemed impatient to leave, 'Sorry to bother you about this but can we keep the burned car wrecks file for now?'

'If you think it's worth it, I'll go with your judgement James but don't get bogged down with it.' Avalon nodded and gave a fake smile and Davies left.

'You won't leave that one will you?' frowned Ross as they returned to their office.

'No, not yet, I still want to talk to the forensics,

not that we can go anywhere now,' replied Avalon as they entered.

'We have to get rid of that poison in the black bottle, this whole room stinks,' frowned Ross.

'Yes, it is pretty ripe, well we better make a start on the paperwork for the body at Abriachan.' Avalon was surprised that he could remember the name and then he asked.

'Is it me or does Davies look ill?' Without looking at Avalon Ross said.

'DI Davies has a lot of pressure at the moment from here and at home from what I have heard.' Avalon decided not to ask further questions on the subject.

Two hours later, information was trickling back to the station that the 'major incident' in Inverness was an audacious security truck robbery and most of B section had been called in to help. What this meant for Avalon and Ross was that, though they may not have to work on the robbery, they would certainly have to take on some of the other cases of B section, as well as their own.

'We probably need to make some moves on this car-wrecks case before we get hit with the extra workload,' sighed Avalon leaning back in his chair and loosening his tie.

'I think we should shelve it,' replied Ross still hidden behind his computer screen. Avalon stretched his legs then stood.

'I know you do but I still think there's something we are not seeing here.' Avalon looked in the two-way mirror and ran his fingers through his hair then re-tightened his tie. 'I'll have a quick trip over to forensics before the excrement hits the turbine.' He pulled on his jacket and looked down to Ross. 'Have you done the report?'

'Just about,' nodded Ross still typing and looking at the screen, 'I thought we were supposed to stay here?'

'I'll see Davies first, I can't see us being needed at the moment.' Ross gave a slight nod.

'What do you want me to do?' Avalon thought for a moment then reached for the door.

'It might be worth looking at the file on the artwork thefts if we are going to look at the complaint about the uniform section.' Ross nodded and said.

'Yeah, okay, another pointless waste of time.'

'I agree,' said Avalon, 'I'll be as quick as I can,' and he left to find Davies.

~~~~~~

Avalon pulled his car into the parking bay at the forensics lab and was satisfied by the performance of his new satnav. Davies had told him to be as quick as he could as there could be some follow up work on the robbery case. Avalon knew from experience that the officer in charge would want to gather as much information as they could before a regular team was put on the case, so he doubted there would be any movement on that until the morning. He was shown into the building by an eager-faced young man, who introduced himself as Hendry and he was shown into the main lab area. The lab was pretty much like any other forensics lab and Avalon had seen plenty of those during his career. This lab did have one major difference to all the others, Miss Sarah Underwood. She was, to Avalon's eye, a joy to behold, not a stunning or classical beauty but a very attractive woman in many ways. Her make-up emphasised that attractiveness and made the overall image difficult to look away from, Avalon took it all in. The hair was dark but probably coloured as there was a purple, raven tinge to it and was cut at a medium length in a very good style. She looked up from her desk and smiled, not an over-ambitious smile but it did the trick.

'Hello Detective...' there was a pause as she glanced to her notepad, 'Avalon,' she added and held out her hand. 'Forgive me for not standing but I have to finish this report.' Her accent was Scottish but slight, probably local, as Avalon was beginning to recognise the relaxed tones of Inverness.

'No need to apologise Miss Underwood, you must be very busy,' smiled Avalon.

'Pull up a seat,' she pointed to a chair, 'what can I do for the latest addition to the area?' She watched him as he moved the chair and seated himself. Her cool brown eyes looked straight at him.

'I'm trying to establish a few connections between the burned-out cars you examined recently, the ones suspected of being involved in the ram-raids.' She nodded but said nothing. Avalon continued. 'The report says that some plastic residue was found that was consistent with the type of five-gallon liquid containers sold by garden centres and such like.'

'That's correct,' she nodded again but added no more.

'Is there any way of finding out what was in those containers?' he asked.

'Not really, you have to understand, that with so much heat, what little plastic we found, was melted. We

155

did several tests to find out what the plastic was and spectrometer tests proved, without doubt, it was from the containers as you have suggested. Whatever liquid was in them was boiled out or burned away but there were traces of chemicals in most of the vehicles.'

'I see,' replied Avalon a little crestfallen.

'What I can tell you is that some of the same containers were used to start the fire as we found evidence of accelerant in their remains but at least one did not contain accelerant or any other flammable material, it did, however, contain traces of chemicals which were probably in the containers originally,' she added.

'And can you be sure that some containers did not contain any accelerant?' asked Avalon a little more optimistic.

'Of course. The difference between the residue of burned plastic through contact with accelerant is very different to that which is simply melted,' she replied with a slight frown. Avalon considered this for a moment he knew he had to ask the right questions, as forensics deal in facts, nothing more.

'Are there any conditions, in your opinion, where a plastic container such as this would not burn in such a hot fire.' She gave a slight smile.

'You are asking me why the plastic didn't burn?'

'Sort of,' nodded Avalon. She looked at her computer screen for a moment and then swung the swivel chair round to face him.

'I can't even begin to understand why we found what we found, and there are no real facts to substantiate any theories but as the case stands, there are signs that at least one container had water or something water-based within it. But that is in the report.'

'Could they have been placed to wash away evidence during the fire?' suggested Avalon. She raised her eyebrows and then shrugged.

'Possibly, but in truth it would most likely have the opposite effect, it would wash the evidence out of the car before it was consumed by the fire.' Avalon nodded and then she added. 'As we also examine the residue from under and around the car, any items would still be found.' Avalon felt slightly cheated, he was hoping for something more useful. As it stood, it looked like this was a dead end and there was no way to even link any single burned car to the others, even if they were positive the same people were responsible.

'Well, thank you for your time Miss Underwood,' smiled Avalon as he stood.

'My pleasure,' she said smiling back, 'I'm sorry I can't do anymore for you but if you need any further help...' she didn't elaborate and Avalon could think of no reason to stay any longer, though he wished he could.

~~~~~~

'Okay,' admitted Avalon throwing a folder on the table, 'I admit defeat on this one.' Ross gave the folder a cursory glance. It was the combined notes for the burned car cases and, it seemed, at last, Avalon had bowed to the inevitable. Ross just looked back to his computer.

'Good,' he said, 'What did you think of Sarah Underwood?' Avalon removed his jacket and slumped in his chair.

'She seems good at her job and works in a logical manner, all in all, she is what you expect from the

157

forensics service.' Avalon knew what Ross was getting at but he was playing it carefully.

'I didn't mean that and you know it,' replied Ross glancing around the screen of the computer. Avalon just gave Ross a questioning look. Ross shook his head and said. 'You know you are so full of shite.'

'I'm sure, Detective Constable Ross, I don't know what you mean.' Avalon placed his hands behind his head and tried to relax. It had been a long day already and there was still too much of it left.

'So,' began Ross as he too leaned back, 'you are telling me that after meeting Sarah Underwood, a female that just about every copper in Inverness has tried to get off with, you have nothing more to say than,' Ross stopped to change to an English accent, 'She works in a logical manner?' Ross made a slight sneer and finished with 'Bullshit!' returning to his Inverness accent.

'I admit that she is an attractive woman but I like to keep a professional attitude whenever I can.' Avalon was still taking in the fact that she had obviously refused everyone that had asked to date her. 'Anyway, she's a little,' Avalon paused, 'too young for an old stager like me I would have thought.' Ross laughed.

'So how old do you think she is?' he asked with a questioning grin.

'I'd say...' Avalon paused again, this time to consider, 'maybe late twenties.'

'She's thirty, never married, and no one has ever seen her with a man,' insisted Ross.

'That doesn't mean anything, she probably keeps her private life private,' offered Avalon.

'There's more to it than that if you ask me,' replied Ross, his eyes showing his thoughts, 'I would say there aren't many at this nick that haven't tried to ask her out and to this date she has never said yes.' Avalon shrugged. He smiled a little then asked,

'So you asked her?'

'Maybe,' replied Ross looking away from Avalon's gaze.

'So what happened?'

'She just told me that she didn't date police officers,' frowned Ross.

'Well, there you are,' said Avalon, 'it shows she's a sensible girl. She doesn't want to jeopardise her professional life by bringing more instability into it.'

'Say what you like, I think she's not into men and I'm not the only one that thinks it,' insisted Ross moving back behind his computer screen. 'A bloody shame though if you ask me,' he added. Avalon had indeed been taken by her looks, she was a very attractive woman, but it was likely, even if she was into men, police officers were off limits. He couldn't blame her, he thought what a miserable life his ex-wife Carol had endured being married to one. He shrugged off his thoughts and said.

'Did you check the internet for recordings of the drums?' Ross peered from behind his screen with a questioning look.

'Oh, aye,' he eventually replied as he grasped the meaning of the question, 'There are a couple but only one where you can hear it well.' Ross made some taps on his keyboard and then said. 'Here come and look.' Avalon stood and walked round to Ross' side of the table and looked at the screen. There was a very shaky image of some green hills taken from a phone at dusk and a woman's voice talking. In the background, a couple of deep booms were heard and the woman's voice said.

'There, there it was again.' There was a moment as the phone was pointed in a different direction and the booms were heard once more, like an enormous heartbeat. There the video stopped. The title of the video was 'Booms at Loch Ness'.

'Do we know where that was taken?' asked Avalon. Ross nodded slightly.

'Sort of, in the comments, someone has written, 'the sounds were coming from the hills above Urquhart Castle'.'

'Where's that?' asked Avalon remembering that the road he was staying at was Urquhart Street.

'Close to Drumnadrochit,' replied Ross turning to Avalon.

'Hmm,' mused Avalon, 'we need to visit Drumnadrochit.'

'You love poking sticks at dead horses don't you?' said Ross looking back to his screen. Avalon didn't reply, he returned to his seat and once again leaned back. He then looked up to the map on the wall and reached over and ran his finger down it.

'The scale of this map isn't ideal for pinpointing areas,' said Avalon, more to himself than Ross. Ross looked at him and suggested.

'There is a map with a larger scale in the restroom.' Avalon nodded and left. He was gone just over a minute but returned with the map from the restroom, complete with its board, and began taping it to the wall. Ross shook his head as he watched. Avalon stood back from the map and then turned to Ross.

'Have we got any pins?' Ross stared at him blankly, 'for the map I mean,' he pointed but Ross continued the blank stare. Avalon picked up the phone

160

and looked for a particular internal number. He dialled it and then said.

'PC Kirk?' there was a slight pause, 'O-K, do we have any board pins, the coloured sort?' There was another pause, this time a little longer, 'Would you? Oh thanks,' and he replaced the handset on the phone. He then stood and looked closely at the map. There was a knock at the door and both Ross and Avalon looked to see who it was. It was PC Kirk and she was shaking a large box of coloured pins.

'Thanks,' smiled Avalon, and he immediately tipped out some of the pins on the table and began to place them in the map. Both Ross and Kirk watched but Avalon seemed to be puzzling.

'Problems?' grinned Ross.

'I can't find the places, I don't know where to look.'

'What are y' after?' asked Kirk stepping closer.

'Drumnadrochit and...' Avalon couldn't remember the name of the place, 'the UFO camp.' Kirk picked up several pins and studied the map and placed two of them at separate points. 'And now Urquhart Castle and the place the body was found,' he looked over at Ross for the name of the locus.

'Abriachan,' said Ross and Kirk forced in two more pins. Avalon looked closely and then pushed in another pin, saying,

'That is where the terrified Mr Nisbett heard the drums the night he found the body,' then he stood back and looked at the map just as the phone rang. Avalon didn't react so Ross answered.

'DC Ross,' was his abrupt reply, 'Er, yes he is, who shall I say is calling,' he added. Avalon looked

161

round. Ross looked at Avalon and held the phone out towards him.

'It's Sarah Underwood...' he paused for a moment, 'for you.' Avalon raised his eyebrows and then took the phone from Ross.

'Hello, DS Avalon.' There was a long pause before he said. 'Do you know where this was by any chance?' There was another long pause. 'Well thanks for that,' a short pause and then, 'on the contrary, it may make a difference. Yes, again thank you, bye.' Avalon passed the phone back to Ross and moved to the map.

'Miss Underwood recalled something after I left. It seems there was a burned-out car found over a year ago on one of the back roads and it had some hallmarks of this case,' he said still facing the map.

'Probably,' shrugged Ross, 'some kid steals a car, drives it until it runs out of fuel and then torches it. So what?' Avalon turned to Ross.

'Well, this one had burned plastic containers inside and some clothing was found.' Avalon waited for Ross to catch up but he didn't. 'Forensics were asked to look at it because it looked suspicious,' added Avalon.

'Sorry, it doesn't ring any bells. I'll check,' said Ross, and he busied himself on the computer.

'I remember that,' added Kirk. Avalon turned to her, forgetting she was still in the room. 'I was sent out to a car blaze with PC Richards. It was on the A833, down a wee side road. It was well burned by the time we got there but Richards was concerned that a pile of smouldering clothes in the back was a body.' Kirk looked from Avalon to Ross and back. 'The fire brigade arrived just after us and they made et safe so with a stick we tried to lift the clothing without touching any

162

potential evidence, we just saw melted plastic.'

'I've found it on the database,' said Ross looking at the computer screen, 'the containers were badly melted but after forensics checked it over, they said they were probably empty when the fire was started.'

'That's what Sarah Underwood said and there were no signs of accelerant in the remains of the plastic,' agreed Avalon. Ross just nodded then added.

'The car had been stolen two days previously from Inverness.' Avalon looked pensive, then he asked.

'Why was no connection made with this?'

'Well,' began Ross, 'why would there be? It was a car blaze someone torched a stolen car that had some empty plastic containers inside it. It was a local police matter and it would still be if it happened again.' Avalon stared at Ross for a few moments and then quickly turned to Kirk and asked,

'Can you remember where it was?' Kirk nodded and answered.

'Yeah, et's a while ago but there isn't much on that road and only a few side roads.'

'Stick a pin where you think the car was found,' instructed Avalon pointing to the map. PC Kirk chose a pin and traced her finger along the A833 until she found the spot and then she carefully pushed it in, to mark the place. Avalon looked at the map and held his chin with his hand. Then he nodded and turned to Ross resting his hands on the edge of the table.

'You're wrong. I'm not poking sticks at dead horses. This horse is far from dead DC Ross. This is very much alive and kicking.'

Chapter Five

Scotland has its own peculiar weather systems, the weather can change from one extreme to the other without any warning and you can experience all four seasons in one day. For Avalon, this brought on an amount of confusion regarding what to wear and when, it also restricted accurate predictions on suitable attire for the day.

In his first few days there, Scotland had provided almost every kind of weather condition and he decided that a small kitbag with emergency equipment and clothing in the boot of his car was a good idea. He was also thinking about that car. Were they really taking bets at the station to see whose car the old blue Ford was? Well, he had just shelled out several hundred pounds for a satnav system, the idea of spending the amount of cash needed for a new vehicle just wasn't going to evolve anytime soon. There was also the need to find a flat or house for the rest of the time he was in the country as Jeanie's B&B would not suffice for the full ten weeks he had been seconded for, he needed a kitchen and the freedom the little room on Urquhart Street didn't offer. He had been busy in the evenings looking for apartments, brushing up on the differing nature of Scottish law as it applied to his job and he was also researching Scottish history, just in case it gave him an edge. Better to know it than not. Yes, he needed to find a place to rent, the privacy and flexibility was important and although he was certainly happy with the service at the B&B, his late nights and early starts would soon become awkward. He even enjoyed Jeanie's morning questions they reminded him of why he did the job. Jeanie's world was so unlike the grim world Avalon lived in during his office hours. The constant pressure to get results, the burned-out cars and the dead body in the copse and yet, she was very much 'in the know' about what was going on outside the bubble she lived in.

'So, are y' going to try the Scottish breakfast Mr Avalon?' she smiled.

'Not this morning Jeanie but I will certainly give it a go before I leave.' Avalon smiled back. When she brought his plate from the kitchen containing his breakfast, she casually said,

'Bon appetite.' Avalon answered with,

'Merci, je suis affame.' Margaret raised her eyebrows and replied,

'Ah, vous avez talents chaches.' Avalon shrugged and picked up his knife and fork.

'I'm sorry madame but my enthusiasm outweighs my talent. That is just about my whole French repertoire,' he laughed, bowing slightly.

'I speak just about enough to converse with French guests but it serves,' she laughed and walked back towards the kitchen door. As she reached it, she turned with a slight frown. 'I was thinking about you yesterday,' she admitted.

'Really?' said Avalon, about to start his meal.

'Yes, we heard all the commotion and then the police cars whizzing about.' The frown was still playing across her brow.

'Oh yes, there was a robbery of some sort in the town,' nodded Avalon, looking down at his waiting fried tomatoes.

'Yes, I heard on the radio, something about a security van I believe. I said to Reg, I bet Mr Avalon is having to deal with that.' The frown subsided.

'Erm,' began Avalon, 'no, actually I didn't have to deal with that, though we had to return to the station just in case we were needed.' He smiled hoping that would do. It seemed to work as she paused a little and then retreated to the kitchen. By the time Avalon had finished, and she came out with his second pot of coffee, she had more questions.

'It seems a bit on the adventurous side for round here.'

'Sorry?' asked Avalon questioningly.

'The security van robbery, maybe it's someone out of the area, probably Glasgow.' She placed the coffee on the table and removed his plate.

'You may be right. I'm sure the chaps at the station will have it wound up in a few days,' he smiled.

'I don't want to question the ability of your fellow officers Mr Avalon,' she began stroking the used milk jug like it was a magic lantern, 'but somehow, I suspect it will be you that solves it.' Avalon broke into a wide smile.

'I'm not even on the case and I can assure you that the team dealing with it are the best.'

'Probably,' she nodded but didn't explain herself

166

further, and then returned to the kitchen.

At the station, Avalon received both bad and good news.

'So which do you want first?' asked Ross. Avalon sighed and shook his head.

'Well, it better be the bad news first,' he replied folding his arms.

'But not today,' replied Ross with no further explanation.

'What?' asked Avalon.

'That's the bad news,' smiled Ross sitting at his desk.

'Oh, I see, so what's the good news?' frowned Avalon.

'We are getting a new office,' was the reply. Avalon was still in the dark but he did notice that Ross had included himself with the word 'we.' That made Avalon feel he was going down the correct route, he was beginning to feel he had just about shaken the spectre of his past.

'So, when?' asked Avalon, also sitting down. Ross looked around his screen and replied.

'Probably next week, they're setting it up over the next few days.'

'Great,' nodded Avalon, 'let's hope it has a window.' Ross nodded and smiled just as his phone rang.

'Hello, DC Ross.' There was silence but Avalon watched Ross' eyes, he gave nothing away and Avalon couldn't guess what the call was. 'Yeah, okay, thanks for that.' He put the phone on the desk. 'That was the coroner's office.'

'Oh?' said Avalon questioningly, 'any news?'

'Yeah,' began Ross, 'the body *is* that of the missing man from the UFO camp. An unemployed gardener from Dumfries.'

'A long way from home,' replied Avalon looking up at the wall map. Ross nodded and continued.

'Aye, the coroner says it's too early to confirm the details, but he thinks the man died sometime during Monday night and was moved to the spot the following day. There is no doubt that he died elsewhere.' Avalon nodded slowly.

'Cause of death?' he asked, raising his eyebrows.

'Blunt force trauma.'

'So it's a murder then?' sighed Avalon, though he had known that all along. Ross nodded then added,

'They'll have the official results after the weekend.' Avalon stared into space then said,

'Well, we better take a trip up to the campsite then.' Ross just nodded he wasn't looking forward to that. 'Oh, and did you find the file out, the one we have to check up on for DI Davies?'

'Yes, I did but I know about the case, the man is a total arse, we have had dealings with him before.' frowned Ross.

'Is it on the way?' asked Avalon.

'Sort of,' shrugged Ross.

'Right, you can fill me in on the way to the campsite and this time *you* drive.'

Avalon was quite taken by Ross' BMW and, as they cruised down the main road, he found himself looking around it as Ross explained the details of the man they were about to see.

'Damian Tennant, real name Clive Smith. Easy to

see why he changed his name. Born in York 1966, he made his money on the television and radio as a presenter and magician.'

'I'm thinking *just* television here Ross, because I'm also thinking a radio magician isn't going to be riveting listening,' interrupted Avalon without emotion.

'No, I mean he worked on both, television latterly as a magician,' explained Ross.

'Yeah, I've seen him, he was quite popular a few years ago. Didn't he make Jonathon Ross disappear on live TV?' asked Avalon with disinterest.

'Yeah, he brought the annoying shite back again though didn't he?'

'So what's his story here then?' asked Avalon.

'He bought a big house near here some years ago where he collects a few things like artwork and pretty girls. Some weeks ago, he had two paintings stolen, but we hadn't got enough bodies for the case, so the Chief said the uniform branch would have to deal with it,' explained Ross quickly glancing over.

'Normal practice I would have thought, it's not really serious enough for CID when it's busy,' shrugged Avalon.

'True, but Mr Tennant thought *he* was serious enough for CID treatment and he gave the uniform lot hell. They eventually told him that the case was still open but there was little chance of finding the culprits.' Avalon sniffed and nodded.

'So Tennant went ballistic and made a complaint to the Chief of Police that he received a less than adequate service?' he surmised.

'More or less correct,' agreed Ross.

'So here we are?' sighed Avalon. Ross nodded.

169

'Do you think he got a good service DCRoss?' Ross looked over to Avalon with doubt.

'Well, if you mean are the uniforms capable, I'd say yes they are. I know we have our tiffs with them but they can cover a bloody robbery for Christ's sake.' Avalon kept quiet. Ross wondered what he was thinking but Avalon seemed to read his mind.

'Do you know what I'm wondering?' he asked. Ross shrugged as if he didn't care. 'I'm wondering what this does,' and he pressed a small button on the dashboard of the car. Slowly a panel opened and revealed the CD player. 'I like that, I wonder if I can get one for my CD?'

'Your car has a CD?' asked Ross with a grin.

'Of course, no expense spared on the building of the Ford Mondeo.' Ross just shook his head and then pressed the button to hide the CD once more. Avalon looked out of the side window and then leaned forward to look up at the hills. Ross felt he was agitated about something but before he could ask, Avalon asked a question.

'Isn't Beauly around here somewhere?'

'Not that far, why?' asked Ross.

'Oh, I considered paying a visit there.'

'Beauly, why Beauly? It's pleasant enough I suppose but I doubt it has anything you'd be interested in.'

'The priory actually,' explained Avalon abruptly.

'Well, there is that, but it's a ruin.'

'Yeah, I know. It used to be a Valliscaulian monastery apparently.'

'You've lost me now. I really have no idea what you are talking about,' frowned Ross. Avalon looked

170

quickly over to Ross and at last decided to explain his interest.

'It's a poetry connection, in 1818 Keats and Charles Brown visited the priory and, urged on by Keats, Brown wrote a poem about the place. I always wondered what it was about the ruin that inspired them.'

'I can't imagine. I've never seen it but it's nothing grand as I recall from photos,' replied Ross remembering something from his school days, 'surely the poem explains it.'

'Not really,' answered Avalon, 'its unequivocal title is, *'On Some Skulls in Beauly Abbey, near Inverness'*.'

'Well, I can safely say that if there were any skulls, there we would probably be involved by now,' then Ross turned to Avalon and concluded with, 'ask Frazer, she is from Beauly.'

'Oh, well maybe I will.'

'Is it any good? The poem I mean,' asked Ross. Avalon shrugged and turned to look out of his side window.

'Not particularly but that's just my opinion.'

'Wasn't he in that Peanuts cartoon serial?' asked Ross.

'Who?' questioned Avalon with a frown.

'Charlie Brown?' asked Ross glancing towards him. Avalon didn't bother to answer, he just returned his gaze to the passenger window.

The gate at the end of the drive of Damian Tennant's house was chained and locked so they left the car and climbed over the gate. The drive was short but so covered with trees that the large house was only visible as they turned a corner.

'Nice,' nodded Avalon as he looked over the impressive manor-style building, 'odd why he keeps the gate chained though.'

'Probably to stop any more of his paintings going walkabout. Some of the uniform lot say he's a paranoid,' explained Ross as he stopped where a large garage faced towards the house. He looked to Avalon and said, 'It's funny really,' Avalon stopped too and looked at Ross.

'What is?' he asked.

'Someone made the magicians paintings disappear,' Ross smiled and added, 'watch this.' Ross pulled a pound coin from his pocket and held it between the forefinger and thumb of the right hand while passing his left hand over it, as if to grab it. Then he showed the open left hand empty. Avalon patted the other hand and said.

'Schoolboy stuff, give me the coin.' Ross frowned at Avalon's dismissal of the trick and handed him the coin and Avalon performed the same trick in what seemed to be the identical manner to Ross.

'Yeah, very impressive,' shrugged Ross, 'so you can do it too.' Avalon then showed *both* hands empty. Ross gaped as Avalon continued to walk.

'How?' he paused and then followed Avalon, 'how did you do that?'

'Night shifts long ago, with nothing to do, make for some strange hobbies,' grinned Avalon. Ross was so amazed by the trick that he forgot that Avalon still had his coin. 'Come on, let's see if he's in,' added Avalon. They knocked at the door and then rang the bell. The door opened almost immediately

'Who the hell are you?' asked the tall, gaunt man

in a very aggressive manner. Avalon frowned deeply and produced his identification card.

'DS Avalon, Inverness CID,' he said with a stern but friendly tone, 'this is Detective Const-' Avalon tried to continue but the man interrupted

'So, 'DS Avalon, Inverness CID, are you working on the premise of 'better late than never' or is this for something else?' Avalon was already on level three of his 'loss of patience'.

'If you mean am I here to investigate your original theft, no, the uniform branch are fully equipped to handle that,' replied Avalon.

'Obviously not, as they don't seem to have caught anyone,' said Tennant.

'We are here because a complaint was filed against the officers involved in the case,' interjected Ross.

'Well, is it surprising when-' this time Ross interrupted the aggressive man.

'I'm sorry sir we can only discuss the matter with Mr Tennant.' The man was caught off guard for a moment but then his fury was unleashed.

'Who bloody god damn do you think I am?' he screamed. Avalon thought Ross' approach was clever, ruinous to the cause, but clever.

'Well sir, we haven't been able to establish that yet,' added Ross in a matter-fact-way. The man's face was gradually turning purple.

'There is no wonder that you can't solve a simple burglary when you don't even know who I am,' he growled.

'Are we supposed to sir?' added Ross but Avalon could see Ross had tied the man in knots and the next thing was a likelihood that he would snap. Avalon took over.

'If you are Damien Tennant, then could we come in and talk about the nature of your complaint?' he asked.

'No, no, NO!' cried Tennant. 'Go, get off my property and I'll pursue this with the Chief Constable,' he screamed. Avalon decided that there was nothing further to be gained and simply said,

'If you wish that, we will go,' he and Ross turned to leave. Tennant called some other threats but neither Ross nor Avalon had the time to waste on the rude man. As they walked away, the garage at the side of the drive was now facing them and one of the large doors was open, revealing a motorcycle. Ross saw it first.

'Look at that, an old Harley isn't it?' Avalon looked over to see the green bike sideways on, in the front part of the large garage.

'Nope,' he said as he continued walking.

'What is it then?' asked Ross stopping to take a further look. Avalon stopped too and walked up to Ross.

'That, my unenlightened Scottish friend, is a Sunbeam S-Seven, about 1951 I think, finished in mist green,' smiled Avalon glancing wistfully at the bike. He nudged Ross and nodded to keep walking.

'1952 actually,' came a voice, it was Tennant, and he was approaching, 'you certainly know your motorcycles Detective.' The man seemed calm and was walking towards them as if the incident earlier had never happened.

'I know a little,' nodded Avalon, 'I'm no expert, but it is an interest.'

'Do you own one?' asked Tennant, now wearing

a thin smile.

'Yes, not a Sunbeam,' nodded Avalon, 'a Triumph Thunderbird,' he hesitated a moment, then added, 'in black.'

'Ah, the 'Blackbird' as we used to call them,' grinned Tennant nodding, 'a very fine bike indeed. Do you still ride it?' he asked.

'Now and then,' nodded Avalon, 'do you?' he glanced over to the green motorbike.

'Sadly not as often as I would like but when the sun shines and I feel like some inspiration, I still take to the road.' He looked over to the bike and held out his hand towards the garage. 'Take a closer look if you wish,' he offered.

'Thanks,' nodded Avalon, 'but we are very busy, maybe some other time.' Avalon wanted to look the bike over but he knew Tennant's type, he would be all 'chummy' and then report to the Chief that all they wanted to do was look at the bike. No fear, Avalon wasn't falling for that. He knew who this man was inside and didn't want to talk with him any more than he had to. 'Do you wish to talk about the complaint now because we really have to-' Tennant held up his hand as if to stop Avalon.

'Yes, Detective Avalon, I understand,' he said smiling, 'I was a little upset and I'm sorry I raised my voice. It's just, with all the crime around here, I was worried that I may be the target again.'

'Well, I'm sure that whoever broke into your home will be caught soon enough,' nodded Avalon.

'Please, come to my house and I will explain my concerns,' Tennant said, holding his hand out again, this time towards the grand house. Avalon would have liked to have just left, but he had a job to do and so he agreed. Ross was even less enthusiastic and Avalon was sure he heard him sigh. Once inside the house they were shown to a large room Tennant described as the 'sitting room'. It was well furnished with many lavish trinkets and paintings on the walls. Tennant offered them whisky but Avalon insisted tea would be fine. Tennant was gone for just a few seconds and so Avalon assumed there must be someone else in the house.

'So, Mr Tennant,' began Avalon as the man returned, Ross automatically took out his notebook and Tennant's eyes flicked quickly to it, 'you made a complaint about the officers in charge of the investigation of your burglary.'

'Yes,' nodded Tennant as he sat, 'I didn't think they knew what they were doing, they looked for fingerprints and left the house in a complete mess and stomped about in the garden but in the end I was left with a 'Crime Number' on a card and a whole lot of mess to clean up.'

'Well,' nodded Avalon, 'it can be a time of upheaval and though all of us try to be sympathetic to the victims, we do have procedures that look a little disruptive to the untrained eye.'

'But Detective Avalon, they still seem to be no further down the road to catching the criminals responsible,' replied Tennant. Avalon gave a quick glance to Ross who knew what it meant.

'You can be sure Mr Tennant,' he began, 'that they haven't forgotten you and they have to work with what they have. No clues or fingerprints were found. It was a professional job but the thieves *will* make a mistake.' Avalon saw the man become slightly agitated

176

once more, so tried to placate him a little. He had noticed photographs around the room of Tennant with several celebrities.

'Is that Daniel Craig in the photo with you?' Avalon was pointing to a framed picture on the wall.

'Yes, it is. We were at a charity event some years ago,' nodded Tennant.

'So you got to meet James Bond?' added Ross.

'Yes, it was just after he was first cast for the role.' It was clear Tennant was easily distracted by conversation that allowed his ego to run free.

'You don't do much television now do you?' commented Ross but Avalon decided to soften the approach somewhat by adding.

'Did you decide to retire?' Tennant thought for a moment but then, a small, but well-presented woman came into the room with a tea tray. She was somewhat younger than Tennant and Avalon watched for anything that may lead to the assumption that she was his wife. The tea was poured and handed around then the woman left, with Tennant giving the slightest nod to her. Tennant waited for her to leave and then turned to Avalon.

'To answer your question, I certainly retired from television, the problem is, some of the 'big shot' magicians in America began to ruin the whole industry by making jet aircraft disappear or the Statue of Liberty.'

'But isn't that just looking for a bigger trick,' questioned Avalon.

'That's just the point detective. It's a trick,' replied Tennant. He sighed a little then continued. 'If we make a particular playing card appear from out of a pack, it's magic, if we make London Bridge disappear, it's a trick. People know London Bridge hasn't moved,

177

so it has to be an optical illusion.' Tennant looked around the room. 'I can do a little thing that may explain it.' He stood and fetched a gold cup, a sort of a chalice from the mantel over the fireplace and placed it on a coffee table. He then looked at Ross and said. 'Choose one of those Satsumas from that bowl.' Ross did and placed it on the table, just as Tennant passed the cup to Avalon to examine. It was a heavy ceramic item with a gilt finish, a sort of Arabic style to its decoration. Tennant took the cup back and covered the Satsuma with the upturned bowl. 'So gentlemen, where is the fruit?' asked Tennant. Avalon gave a slight grin.

'Well, normally I would have said under the cup but seeing as it's you asking...' Avalon tailed off and shrugged. Tennant reached out and lifted the cup, the fruit was still there.

'You see detective, you expect a trick, so you expect the fruit to have vanished, it clearly didn't.' Tennant let the cup cover the fruit once more.

'I'm not sure what you're getting at,' Avalon shook his head a little.

'The point is yet to be made,' Tennant continued, 'when someone says he is going to make Tower Bridge disappear and then he seems to accomplish that, the audience know they have been conned. Why? Because they know that the bridge hasn't moved and it will re-appear soon after.' Tennant raised his eyebrows and let his hand grasp the upturned cup once more. 'But, when someone says he is going to make something disappear, and it stays missing,' Tennant paused to lift the cup revealing the fruit had gone, 'it's pure magic.' He tossed the cup to Avalon, who examined it and then passed it to Ross. 'The public wants magic but television executives want tricks. I'm a magician not a trickster.'

'So you gave it up?' asked Avalon. There was quite a pause.

'I wouldn't say I have given it up. I am still looking for the perfect illusion, any magician who says otherwise is a liar. If I could make something large disappear for good and no one could work it out, I could then retire.'

'Maybe you should have done that with Jonathan Ross,' quipped Ross. Tennant laughed.

'So you don't like your namesake?' Tennant asked. Ross just shrugged he didn't want to voice his opinions to Tennant.

'So, back to business Mr Tennant,' said Avalon after finishing his tea, 'from what we can see of the police procedure in the burglary, everything was done in accordance with this kind of investigation.' He placed his cup and saucer down on the table. 'The complaint will still be investigated but it could slow any further inquiries down in the case of your burglary.' Tennant nodded.

'Yes, I can see that. I may, therefore, consider retracting my complaint.' Avalon gave a slight smile.

'So we must get on now but if you wish to discuss anything further, you can contact either myself or Detective Constable Ross on this number.' Avalon stood and handed him a card, then turned to leave.

'There is one thing Detective,' said Tennant. Avalon turned for a moment as the man stood to let them out. 'What do you make of the drums we keep hearing along the glen?' Avalon took a quick glance at Ross, then answered,

'It isn't something the police are dealing with if

that's what you are asking Mr Tennant.'

'Why is that? most people seem to think that it is an omen of doom and closely connected to all the crimes that seem prevalent at the moment?' Avalon smiled a little and then said,

'It isn't a crime to make a noise, even a loud one and even if someone reports it as a nuisance, it would be a council issue to begin with, not a police matter.' Avalon waited for a reaction but there wasn't one. Tennant just said,

'I see, well thank you for coming to see me.' Then the two detectives left. As Ross and Avalon walked down the drive, Ross said,

'He is seriously odd.' He glanced over to Avalon. 'I don't know how he did that trick though.' Avalon looked back over to Ross.

'He's odd sure enough,' agreed Avalon, 'but does fame damage the psyche so much?'

~~~~~~

Sarah Underwood looked up from the lens of the microscope and stood.

'Yes, you're right,' she said to her colleague 'it doesn't match anything else we have seen.' The colleague sat where Sarah had been and looked up.

'So do y' want me tae find a textile match?' he asked.

'Yes,' replied Sarah, 'if we can narrow down what exactly this fibre has come from, then at least we have something to work with. I can't imagine why there isn't more.' Sarah went back to her own desk and began to write up what they had found from the evidence collected. All the items were from the body found at Abriachan, including the clothes worn by the man and the blanket he was wrapped in. There were also test samples from around the site and the same thing was becoming clear, there was virtually no DNA evidence other than that belonging to the man. Hundreds of dog hairs were found indicating that the man probably owned a dog or was with a dog for some extended time before his death, as many of the hairs were found within his clothing. Just two human hairs not consistent with the dead man were found on his person but finding a match from the campsite would be the job of the police. All she could do was record them. The only anomaly was a single fibre collected from the blanket that didn't match the dead man's clothing or the blanket itself. Not much but it may prove an outside influence if nothing else. All she could do now was return all the items and samples back to their bags and boxes and have them returned to the police evidence archive.

The visit from the new detective, Detective Sergeant Avalon had also started her thinking about the burned car-wrecks case. There was something about the one found a year earlier that was nagging at the back of her mind and she decided to bring up the notes on her computer to see if there was anything that had been missed. She read through them. There wasn't much as it had just been written off as a car theft and the evidence had since been destroyed, but she still couldn't shake the feeling there was something she was missing. She decided to check the notes on the more recent ones, but again, there was no evidence of any kind to really link them to either the previous car fire or any other car theft. The only constant was the burned and melted plastic found inside the wrecks. She couldn't even link the type of plastics as the previous evidence had gone and there was no way to check it. She sat and pondered the situation and wondered why Avalon had seen something in the case. Obviously, he wouldn't express any theories he had but he must have some reason for it. For now, she put the thoughts aside and continued to write up the report on the case at hand just as her colleague returned.

'I think I have a match,' he said. Sarah looked at his findings and said.

'Well, it's not much, but it's a start.'

~~~~~~

'I didn't know you were a biker,' said Ross, as he was about to drive into Drumnadrochit.

'I wouldn't call myself a biker, I just have a bike,' said Avalon as he scanned the little village at the shore of Loch Ness.

'So you don't ride it much then?' asked Ross.

'Not much, I take it out now and then in the summer.'

'I like the summer,' began Ross, 'it's my favourite day of the year.' Avalon smiled at this.

'Well, I suppose if I lived in Scotland, I would probably have to rethink my motorcycling future.' Ross turned off the road onto the A833 and began the fifteen-minute journey to the UFO campsite. Once clear of Drumnadrochit, with its shops and tourist signs dedicated to the Loch Ness Monster, they climbed steadily up the valley and through plantation woodland skirting the edge of the hillside. Avalon was struck once again with the beauty of the landscape and as if on cue, the sun peeped out from the Ross-shire 'perma-cloud' and shone down onto the Highlands, showing its majesty in full glory. Avalon wished he had time to explore it but he forced himself back into 'detective mode' and asked,

'Isn't this the road where PC Kirk was sent to the car fire last year?'

'Aye it is but I don't know exactly where it was,' replied Ross.

'Odd though that it's the same road as the UFO camp,' mused Avalon.

'Abriachan is just over the hill too,' added Ross pointing to the hilltop.

'Hmm,' sighed Avalon as he considered if there was any sort of link, 'is there a direct route from this road, to where the body was found?' he eventually asked.

'Sort of, it's not direct but you can cut across,' explained Ross just as they came across a hand-painted sign announcing, 'The Highland Alien Festival' at the side of the road.

'How long does this festival run, by the way,' asked Avalon.

'That's a point,' replied Ross as he pulled off the road and along a dirt track, 'it's usually for a month, so I bet it will be breaking up soon.' They drove towards the campsite where every tent seemed to glow with unfeasibly bright colours. Ross parked his car a little away from all the other assorted vehicles on the site and they got out into the warm sunshine. Avalon loosened his tie a little and said.

'We better make hay then before we lose potential witnesses,' and then Avalon's phone rang.

'Avalon,' he said abruptly.

'*Ah, Detective Avalon, it's Hamish Ramsey from the coroner's office,*' came a clear Scottish voice.

'Hello Mr Ramsey, I'm guessing you have something for me.'

'*Well, yes. Most of the fine detail is in the report but we did find an anomaly.*'

'Go on,' replied Avalon.

'*Well, death was due to blunt force trauma as suspected, with a large weapon but we also found a blow made by a different weapon and some hours before the first.*'

'So he had been attacked before he was killed?'

'*That looks likely,*' agreed Ramsey, '*there was also a dangerous cocktail of drugs in his system too, similar to the types found in the previous abductees, but considerably stronger we suspect.*'

'Were there signs that the victim was a regular drug user?' asked Avalon.

'*There were no regular needle marks, but that doesn't mean anything of course,*' replied Ramsey. He then added, '*There were a few marks on his wrists that may point to him being restrained at some stage but we are unsure how previous to death these were inflicted.*' Avalon thanked him for the information and then told Ross what he had said.

'That does explain why blood was found where he was kidnapped then. He was probably struck when he was abducted,' said Ross. Avalon nodded as they neared the camp. It was a rag-tag site, more like a refugee camp with temporary shelters and tarpaulins stretched over frameworks. Here and there stood a proper tent and even a few camper vans but the place was pretty untidy. Near the centre and under the trees was an area with straw bales and a large campfire where some people were cooking and close to that was a large military-style tent which had a telescope outside with binoculars hung from it. Avalon considered it looked a little more professional than the other shelters so he headed for it. As he approached the entrance, he noticed a man sitting inside on a deck chair reading a newspaper. He was in his early sixties and dressed plainly but quite tidily and seemed a world apart from most of the others at the camp.

'Ah,' said the man as he noticed them approach, 'strangers, enter do.' He had an English accent and spoke like a ham actor. 'Welcome to my little abode,' he pointed to a bench where Avalon and Ross sat. 'You two must be officers of the law, I did expect a visitation, eventually.'

'Why is that Mr...' asked Ross.

'Reid, Vincent Reid at your service,' smiled the man, 'well, it's quite obvious, three of our little flock go missing in the night, two return, and one remains hidden.' He placed the newspaper by his side. 'Can I offer you anything gentlemen?' Both detectives declined.

'I am Detective Sergeant Avalon and this is Detective Constable Ross, we are here to bring you some sad news I'm afraid.' Reid suddenly dropped the affable smile and looked a little more serious.

'Oh, what is it?' he asked.

'I'm afraid a body was found not far from here, it has been identified as Joel Price, the man who was reported missing from the camp.' Reid looked down at the floor and then up to Avalon.

'That is so sad, how did he die?'

'We're not sure yet but it looks like foul play,' replied Avalon. Reid shook his head.

'I don't know what's going on, we have run this festival for several years now and never has anything like this happened.'

'Did you know the deceased?' asked Ross.

'No not well,' said Reid shaking his head, 'but I know one person that did.' He stood and called to someone to bring a woman called Janey over. Janey was a tall, gangly woman in her thirties but with a pleasing, honest sort of face. Her mousy hair was braided, and she was carrying a bottle of something that was probably alcohol. She confirmed she knew Joel Price well as they usually met up at festivals of a similar type. She described him as a friendly chap but quiet. When she was informed he was dead, she became visibly upset and tears began to form in her eyes.

'I knew et,' she sobbed a little, 'a' bloody knew et.' She wiped her face with her sleeve.

'What do you mean?' asked Avalon.

'Well, he'd never leave es dog would he? They are never parted.'

'He has a dog?' asked Ross.

'Aye, he's been go'en loopy since Joel went missen'.'

'So why wasn't the dog with him when he went missing?' asked Avalon.

'The dog was with me, a few of us had a walk down to the burn late on so a' took him with me. Joel was oot of et as he'd been over do'en the vodka earlier.' She wiped her face again and regained her composure. 'The wee dog bolted after em when we heard em call out but all we found wis some blood.'

'Did he take any drugs with the vodka too?' asked Ross.

'What?' called out Janey, 'Joel? Drugs es et? Let me tell yea. Joel liked his vodka but he never took any drugs, he was well set against em.'

'This is important Janey,' said Avalon in a serious tone, 'are you sure he didn't take any drugs?' Janey stared right at Avalon and said,

'He wouldna' even take aspirin to get rid o' es hangover.' Avalon looked over to Ross.

'Well, thank you for your help Janey, Detective Ross will take your contact details in case we need anything else.'

'What about the wee dog?' she asked with concern. Avalon shrugged.

'Well, maybe you want to take it in, its future could be in doubt if it goes to a shelter.' Janey thought for a moment and then nodded. Ross took her details, and she left.

Reid looked at Avalon with a sad half smile.

'Have you seen any strangers at the camp Mr Reid?' asked Avalon.

'Well yes, of course, most of the people here are unknown to me,' smiled Reid and then added. *'Happiness grows at our own firesides and is not to be picked in strangers' gardens.'* Avalon thought for a moment then asked.

'Is that Jerrold?' Reid smiled again, this time with warmth.

'You didn't strike me as the literary sort detective.' Avalon just gave a slight smile.

'So what sort of people come to this festival Mr Reid?' he asked.

'Well, primarily we are here to witness visitations from people from other planets. Yes, yes,' continued

Reid nodding slightly, 'I know some people think we are moonstruck but some of us see things in the night sky we cannot easily explain.' He paused. 'This area is actually one of the most popular sites for UFO spotters. The sky is clear and there is no light pollution, it is a special place.'

'There seem to be a broad mix of types though,' added Avalon.

'Indeed, there are,' agreed Reid, 'but I have learned never to judge a book by its cover. Some come for the friendship, others for the peace and quiet. There are also those that see this as an alternative religion. Who are we to judge detective?'

'But don't you have to cover yourself with health and safety, about the numbers who attend and all that?' asked Ross.

'We do to a certain extent, the kind-heartedness of the landowner has to be protected but we don't have the resources to log everyone who turns up, or indeed leaves every day,' shrugged Reid. Avalon sighed, it was going to be a nightmare of a job tracking everyone down, but they would have to make a start. He looked towards the entrance of the tent and walked outside, he then turned and said.

'I think we will have to send someone up here Mr Reid, to get some details before anyone else leaves.' Reid nodded and then he seemed to have a thought and his eyes flashed from side to side.

'You know, there is someone you ought to talk to.' Reid stepped outside and looked around until he saw a blue tarpaulin in the trees. 'There is a man that had been sleeping over there on occasions. I am sure he has no interest in what we are about here and he seems to be

188

alone. I'm not saying he has anything to hide of course but he does stand out, simply because no one, not a soul has any idea who he is.' Reid shielded his eyes with his hand as if he was trying to spot the man. 'I can't see him but he's wearing one of those lumberjack style of shirts.'

'Thank you Mr Reid, we'll have a look for him,' said Avalon and he walked towards the blue shelter. Ross caught him up and asked,

'Shall I see if we can get some uniforms up here?' he paused, 'they'll probably be too busy but we could try.'

'We certainly need someone to log details, probably some DNA samples too if the forensics find anything,' agreed Avalon. Ross pulled out his phone as Avalon reached the blue cover. There was a man lying in the lee of the shelter and he was wearing a lumberjack shirt as Reid described but as Avalon bent down and spoke, the man bolted out of the rear of the shelter. He made it about five paces before Ross dived at him and bounced the slightly built man into a tree. He fell and looked up, Ross towering over him and there was a look of both recognition and panic in his face.

'Scobie you little weasel, when did you take an interest in little green men?' spat Ross as he dragged the man to his feet by the scruff of the neck. Weasel was a good description of the man, his gaunt, unshaven face had a 'pinched' look, and his tiny brown eyes darted everywhere in his panic.

'Mr Ross, what are ye doin' here?' he asked apologetically.

'I ask the questions Scobie. I ought to have known you would be where there is trouble,' Ross growled, still holding the man tightly.

'Who's this?' asked Avalon harshly.

'This is a petty little crook called Antony Scobie, the lowest of the low, even other crooks hate him,' explained Ross, never taking his gaze from the man.

'What are you doing here Mr Scobie?' asked Avalon with a serious tone, 'you don't look like the sort to be into extra-terrestrial anthropology,' he added.

'What did he just say?' asked Scobie to Ross. Ross reacted by banging the man against the tree.

'Answer the damn question Scobie,' he spat.

'Okay, Mr Ross, okay,' cried Scobie holding up a hand. Scobie sighed, then looking away from Ross said, 'I'm hidin'.'

'From who?' demanded Ross, Scobie hesitated just a slight amount, then answered.

'I... I owe some money and I don't have et.'

'So you came up here to see what you could rob then did you?' hissed Ross tightening his grip.

'No Mr Ross, I swear I'm just hidin' that's all.' The weasely man looked crestfallen, Avalon considered he might be telling the truth.

'Who do you owe money to Scobie?' demanded Ross pressing him tighter to the tree.

'If a tell ye, can a stay here?' asked the worried Scobie.

'Let him go,' said Avalon, getting closer to Scobie. Ross let his shirt go and Scobie slumped to the base of the tree.

'I haven't got time for this Scobie,' said Avalon calmly, 'you need to tell us why you are here or we'll take you in and make it plain where and when we are going to release you,' he added. Scobie looked up to Avalon and wiped his hand over his greasy face and

190

through his hair.

'Okay,' he began, 'I owe Rabbie Bee,' he sighed. Avalon looked over to Ross who nodded and said.

'Robby Bee is a small-time crook who likes to think he's Inverness's Al Capone.' Ross looked down at Scobie. 'His real name is Robert Bain, he uses scum like Scobie here to run errands for him.'

'Why do you owe him money Scobie?' asked Avalon as he crouched by the side of the man.

'I sold 'em some gear last week,' Scobie looked away and Avalon got the impression that 'gear' meant stolen goods, 'an' some o' et dinnae work.'

'I see,' mused Avalon as he stood, 'is there no honour amongst thieves anymore?' he raised his brows to Ross then looked back to the little man. 'You do know about several abductions from the camp, don't you Scobie?' he added as he walked slightly away and turned his back on the man.

'Aye, I heard but they're all crazy up here. If they see an hoolet they think et's a flyen' alien.' Avalon looked over to Ross with a questioning look.

'An owl.' explained Ross. Avalon nodded still with his back to Scobie. 'So what have you seen Scobie?' asked Ross. Scobie looked up to Ross, who was still standing close by glaring down at the man.

'A'v seen nothin' Mr Ross. A'v just been tryin' to keep out the way.' Avalon spun around at this and growled out.

'Detective Ross doesn't seem to like you for some reason Scobie, so unless you tell us something, I may have to take a walk and let him escort you into the woods.'

'Honest Mr...' Scobie attempted to prompt the

detective for his name but it didn't work, 'er, ef I knew anythin' I wid tell yers.'

'I think I believe you, I really do,' Avalon put on a false concern, 'but, you know detective Ross from old, that much is clear.' He looked to Ross and then crouched down at Scobie's side once more. 'And he doesn't believe you.'

'Too right,' laughed Ross, 'Scobie you backstabbing little toad, you know you saw something, that's why you were going to run isn't it?' Scobie shook his head. Ross reached down, lifted the man to his feet, and once more pinned him to the tree. Avalon stood too and noticed people were coming towards them to see what was happening.

'Right, Detective Ross. Cuff him, we'll take him to the station.' Ross let him go and reached into his pocket.

'Wait,' announced Scobie, 'I did see somethin',' he added with a sheepish look, 'am not sure it was anythin' but...' He paused and then said in a lower voice. 'A did see two guys hangin' around at night. On a couple of occasions, I saw just one.'

'So why was this significant?' asked Avalon.

'Well,' whispered Scobie, 'they were wearin' blue boiler suits.' Scobie looked for a reaction from the policemen, there was little. 'Well, ain't that odd up here? These people wear some odd kit, but boiler suits? When has that been the best clayths f'r watchin' spaceships?'

'Maybe,' nodded Avalon.

'What else were they wearing?' asked Ross. Scobie thought for a moment.

'One had a lightweight jacket, like a fleece an' he had an open face balaclava,' he paused as he considered

192

a little, then added, 'the other one had wellies an' a beard, but nae coat. He looked like he was straight out o' ZZ Top.' Ross looked at Avalon who turned to Scobie.

'You better be telling the truth, this is now a murder investigation and we wouldn't want anything to happen to you would we,' he said quietly. Scobie looked slightly shocked.

'Murder?' he asked. Avalon turned to Ross.

'You better make that call,' he said and for a moment, Ross looked questioningly, but then he understood and went off to ask for uniformed police. Avalon looked at Scobie. 'You can stay hidden here but if I hear so much as an 'I love aliens' pin badge goes missing I will fall on you, do you understand?' Scobie nodded. 'And I want you to keep your eyes open. Get it?'

'Yes, Mr, er...' nodded Scobie. Avalon glared at Scobie for a moment and then turned to leave.

'Avalon,' he said as he walked, 'Detective Sergeant Avalon. Remember the name.'

~~~~~~

Ross pulled into the car park and turned to Avalon in the passenger seat of the BMW.

'Why here?' he asked. Avalon shrugged.

'Why not? I said 'let's call at Drumnadrochit' and you asked 'anywhere in particular?'

'Yeah, but why a pub and why this one?'

'Can you think of anywhere better for local knowledge?' smiled Avalon as he got out of the car. Ross followed suit and used his remote to lock the car as they walked away. The double 'bleep' sounded off as they walked to the door of the medium-sized pub. 'I considered this one looked more like a 'locals' sort of pub,' he added. Ross smiled and opened the door for Avalon to enter. The public bar wasn't busy there was the barman and two customers, one was standing at the bar reading a newspaper, the other was seated with his back to a corner wall and looked around as they entered. Avalon walked closer and looked at the various bottles of single malt whisky on offer, just for future reference.

'Drink?' asked Avalon. Ross raised his eyebrows and looked towards the bar, Avalon couldn't quite make out what Ross was thinking. 'A half of this and...' he pointed to one of the hand pumps and then turned to Ross.

'Er, lager, half of lager please.' Ross stuttered. The barkeeper made no murmur or acknowledgement that Avalon had even spoken but he poured out the drinks and placed them on the bar. Avalon put a twenty-pound note beside them and said.

'And whatever these two chaps would like.' It was obvious that he meant the two customers. The man with the newspaper thanked him, as did the man on the chair, but the latter looked Avalon up and down.

'I'm thinking tax man or coppers,' he smiled. His accent was sort of local but with a broader edge, Avalon was beginning to tell the slight differences. It was unmistakably Scottish but broader than Inverness. He smiled back.

'What gave it away, the flat feet or the whistle sticking out of my top pocket?' The man in the chair smiled at this.

'I'm guessing the sound of the drums or the body found over at Abriachan,' replied the seated man

194

finishing his drink.

'You know about that?' asked Avalon.

'Aye, o' course we do. You can't keep something like that from the locals.'

'I suppose not,' agreed Avalon.

'I thought you weren't supposed tae drink on duty an' all that,' asked the man reading the paper without raising his gaze. Avalon looked at his watch and said.

'It's six-thirty, we have been off duty for half an hour,' he concluded. The seated man ordered his drink that Avalon had purchased from the zombie-like bartender and held the glass up.

'Sludge,' he announced. Avalon was lost for words. The beer looked fine.

'I'll ask him to change it if it's not right,' said Avalon pointing to the drink.

'It's a slightly sarcastic way of saying 'slange',' interrupted Ross with a smile, 'it's not spelled as it sounds though as it's Gaelic, but it means 'good health' or something like that.'

'It's Gaelic true, but did you know that is was used as a Jacobite toast to Bonny Prince Charlie?' explained the seated man. The man reading the paper turned for the first time and said.

'Don't get Walt started, he's been known to bore the tits off a stone pig.' He went back to the newspaper.

'Do you see what I have to put up with here,' began Walt. 'ill-educated locals, I could understand it if we didn't have schools.' He stopped to drink.

'So Walt,' began Avalon picking up instantly on his name, 'what do you make of the drums then?'

'I thought you were off duty?' he smiled.

'I am, this is just local interest from an Englishman to a Scotsman.'

'I see, well,' hesitated Walt, 'I'm not sure about it myself.' Avalon could see this man was more complicated than he at first seemed.

'Bloody hell!' burst out the man reading the paper, 'they've found the monster.' He turned with a broad grin on his face. 'Here, look.' He held up the newspaper and sure enough, the subheading read, 'Nessie found in Loch Ness.' There was also a small image that looked like a sonar scan. Ross went closer to read it.

'Aye, they found it all right,' he turned, and he too had a broad grin, 'it's a sunken prop from that old Christopher Lee film.' The man with the newspaper continued as he read the article.

'A Norwegian team who are plottin' the terrain of the loch announced that it was quite a surprise at first but it's in the exact place where it sank during filming for the 1970 movie, 'The Private Life of Sherlock Holmes'.'

'I remember that film well,' smiled Avalon, sipping his drink. He suddenly felt a nudge in his ribs, it was Ross and he nodded towards the door. Entering, was a stocky man in a white shirt that seemed to be covered in blood. It looked like he had either been attacked or been in a serious accident. There was blood all up his arms, all down his shirt and trousers and spattered on his face and in his hair. Avalon considered that the blood couldn't be his as he was walking fine and anyone losing so much would be unconscious or dead.

'Are you all right sir?' asked Avalon. The man glared at him for a moment and then looked back to the door.

'Me?' he asked putting one of his bloody hands to his chest.

'You seem to be covered in blood?' Avalon made it into a question rather than a statement of fact.

'Blood?' laughed the man, 'fence paint,' and he walked past Avalon to the bar. Avalon shrugged and went back to his place.

'Coppers then?' asked the man as he ordered his drink.

'They're investigating the murder at Abriachan,' cut in Walt.

'I didn't say we were investigating anything, and as far as I know, the case is a dead body not a murder.'

'Well you're not likely to catch the murderer if you can't tell the difference from blood and fence stain,' sniffed the paint-covered man. Avalon paid for a drink for him and the man raised his glass and announced. 'Sludge.' Avalon was ready and repeated it back to him. The man took a deep drink and then announced.

'I'm Jamie, thanks for the drink,' and he held out his paint-covered hand. Avalon shook it and luckily the paint was dry.

'Avalon and this is Detective Ross.' Jamie nodded. 'We are off duty anyway, so we are not allowed to make correct deductions about blood or paint,' explained Avalon with a serious face. Jamie smiled.

'What makes you think it's a murder then?' asked Ross.

'Well, his head was stoved in an' he was hidden in a copse of trees in a blanket. It would seem a pretty unusual suicide,' replied Jamie raising his eyebrows.

'Well, we can't confirm anything until the coroner's report comes out,' interrupted Avalon. He finished off his drink and Ross copied. Walt noticed this, and he offered to buy them another, Avalon refused but thanked him.

'We have got a few things to do before we call it a day,' he smiled. Walt looked at Jamie and said.

'They want to know what we think of the drums,' Jamie shrugged and said.

'You mean, is it really a ghostly drummer?' asked Jamie.

'I just wondered how the locals view it that's all,' added Avalon.

'Well, it's smoke and mirrors as far as I can make out,' replied Jamie.

'Meaning what?' asked Ross.

'Well, there's a boat on the loch with equipment to survey everything in it. If they find no evidence of a monster, there are going to be some tears around here.'

'So what are you saying? The drums are a warning?' asked Avalon.

'Not as such,' replied Jamie. 'More like insurance,' he smiled. Ross interrupted

'You mean, start a new legend before the old one dies?' he asked. Jamie shrugged.

'The Nessie legend won't die,' announced Walt, 'people come from all over the globe, most of them know they will see nothing but water, it's the feel of it, the place where it all happened...' he hesitated, 'or not.'

'Hmm, the same reason why people visit sites like Culloden? They won't see the battle still under way but they can be where it took place,' proffered Avalon, Walt nodded.

'Exactly,' he began to explain, 'MacBean's phantom drummer will never take over from the Kelpie, it just isn't well enough known, but it could add to the experience.'

'It's *all* crap to me,' said Jamie.

'Another Philistine,' grinned Walt pointing to Jamie. Then the smile subsided, and he said, 'Go and see a chap called Burnside.'

'He's off his head Walt,' interrupted Jamie.

'Aye he's weird, but he knows things about local legends,' and with this Walt winked.

'Do we have a full name or even an address?' asked Ross. Walt asked for a pen and so Ross gave him the notepad and his pen to write it down.

'I think you'll be wasting your time with that old crackpot,' said Jamie shaking his head, 'he lives up the hill near Walt, they're all mad up there.'

'You know nothing, you're just cynical about everything you can't explain,' replied Walt.

'Many thanks,' said Avalon as he read the name and address, 'we'll get off. See you around.' As Ross and Avalon left, the two men were still arguing about how people on the hill are different and Avalon considered this was probably something that happened every day. The two men did, however, wave as they left, the zombie, however, was still staring into space.

Ross was leaning on the top of the car by his door.

'Do you want to check this out?' he asked holding up his notebook.

'Not really,' replied Avalon shaking his head, 'let's call it a day, we can do a check on him some other time.' They drove back quietly and entered the station ready to go home but the duty sergeant told them that DI

Davies was still in the building. Avalon and Ross made their way to the main offices on the upper floors and towards the incident room. Davies was certainly still there. He and PC Kirk were checking on some CCTV videos of the robbery.

'How's it going over there?' asked Davies when he saw Avalon.

'Slow, very slow but it's early days,' Avalon slumped in a chair, 'we'll have to wait until the checks and the DNA samples collected by the uniform branch have been processed.'

'Yes, I'm sorry we couldn't send up more help but you know what it's like,' apologised Davies.

'I'm sure they won't complain about the overtime,' smiled Avalon. His face became a little more serious as he asked.

'How are you doing with the robbery?'

'The same really,' frowned Davies, 'very slow. We are having a meeting in the morning to bring all teams up to speed on this one. It looks like it had some real professional backing.' Avalon just nodded. He was ready for something to eat and a shower. He could still taste the beer on his tongue from earlier and considered a glass of single malt would be the first job when he got back to the B&B.

'How are you going with the search for a house?' asked Davies sitting by his side.

'Not good actually. Every time I find a flat they want a three or six-month contract,' frowned Avalon. Davies nodded.

'To be expected really, but something may crop up. Take Sunday off and have a look around.'

'But we are pulled out, I mean what with-' began

Avalon but Davies stopped him.

'Don't worry, it's just a day.' He turned to Kirk. 'You better get off too, we'll get back to this in the morning.' Davies stood as Kirk nodded and he walked to the door. He looked tired and stiff. 'Right, I'm off, I was supposed to be at home by five. Looks like I'm in trouble again,' and he made his way to the door. Before leaving he turned and said, 'oh, you will be in your new office Monday,' and he left with a half-hearted wave and no further explanation. Kirk switched off the computer and stood to put on her jacket.

'I wonder if it has a window?' asked Avalon to no one in particular. PC Kirk looked down at Avalon.

'I was thinkin' Sarge,' she said with a little doubt in her eyes.

'What is it O-K, I'm not in the mood for jokes I'm afraid,' smiled Avalon.

'Well, a' have this friend,' there was a pause, 'she rents a house near here and she has a spare room.' Another pause. 'She was thinkin' of renting it out, I could give her your number or I could ring her.'

'Thanks and all that,' smiled Avalon, 'but it may be inappropriate, although I'm not sure why.'

'Well, she nearly always works nights,' added Kirk.

'She sounds dodgy already,' laughed Ross, sitting and putting his feet on the desk.

'No, you filthy minded perve, she works en security, at the airport,' explained Kirk.

'Oh,' said Avalon not sure why that would make a difference, 'maybe it would work and it would help both of us out, I need a room, she gets some extra cash from the rent.'

'I'll give her a call.' Kirk dialled a number into her phone and there was silence for a minute. 'Angie? Hello, can you speak? Well, are y' still wanting to rent out that room?' There was a pause. 'No, he's one of the CID chaps down here, he's on secondment and needs a place t' stay for a few weeks.' Avalon wanted to tell her not to bother, but he was too late. 'How about Sunday?' she said, there was another pause, 'I'll bring him round then about half one.' A longer pause this time and Kirk laughed. 'Okay, I'll see y' Sunday, bye.' Kirk put the phone away and said, 'Yeah, she says go over and have a look and as the DI gave you the day off...' Avalon thought for a moment. Why not? There was no harm in meeting her. 'I'll give you her address and I'll meet you over there,' and Kirk jotted down something and handed it to Avalon. He read it and raised his eyebrows.

'Angioletta Carbonna? She certainly doesn't sound Scottish.'

'That's because she's Italian, she's a lovely person too and I'm sure y' two will get on,' explained Kirk.

'Is it just her at the house then?' he asked.

'Yeah, her parents aren't from here so she rented the house last year just after she got the job at the airport.' Kirk lowered her voice for effect. 'To be honest, I think she struggles to pay for et.' Avalon nodded.

'Well, I'll certainly have a look,' he smiled.

'Great, I'll see you there then. See you two,' and she left.

'Come on,' croaked Avalon raising himself from the chair with difficulty, 'we'd better get off too.'

Chapter Six

Detective Inspector Lasiter had a severe headache. For twenty-eight consecutive days he had gone to bed late and risen early and it was having its effect. He had taken some pills and was climbing out of his car to enter the station for yet another long day. Very few of the main cases were going well and though most of the staff at the station were under the same kind of pressure, here he was again, walking into the building and trying to raise himself enough to try to inspire the people around him to keep at it. Detective Chief Inspector Anderson was also pressurising him and Davies to get results but with more cases cropping up and no sign of any more help, Lasiter was feeling in a very poor state. The headache was just part of the problem, at home there were heated arguments with his family for the short time each day he was actually there.

As he entered the building and walked to his office, he gave no eye contact to anyone, hoping that if he didn't speak to them, they wouldn't tell him about another case that may have come in overnight. Once he was on the upper floor, he turned quickly into his office and closed the door behind him. Then he saw it, on his desk, a note from the Chief to see him as soon as he came in. He took a deep breath and walked the twenty or so paces to Anderson's office. He knocked lightly and heard the word 'Come,' and in he went to take on the wrath of the Chief or to become saddled with yet another case, or both.

'Sit down Robert,' said the Chief as he looked up. There was a polite smile but that was usual.

'Y're in early sir,' said Lasiter. He was, it was very rare for the Chief to be there before Lasiter, it must be serious.

'I woke early and so I thought I would come down and sort a few things out,' he looked down at his paperwork and then pushed it aside. 'I've been thinking,' he began, 'with the workload, we really need someone to take more responsibility, who is next in line for DI?' Lasiter was taken aback. This didn't seem as bad as he had expected, and a promotion would be good for morale.

'Er, well, et's a close thing really.' He thought carefully about how to put it. 'I think it ought tae be Andrew tae make the call, as B section have several excellent candidates. I mean C section has too, but we have just two with the correct paperwork if y' see my meaning?' It was difficult, most of the team were good enough, but to pick just one was something he didn't want to undertake.

'What about the new chap Avalon?' asked Anderson.

'Well, he seems excellent but o' course we can't promote him as he's on secondment.'

'Hmm, no, of course,' frowned the Chief, 'well if you think it best, I'll have a word with Andrew when he arrives.'

'I'll send him o'er if I see him sir,' smiled Lasiter. That was at least one bit of pressure he could forget about. Anderson asked him about the cases and then Lasiter left and returned to his own office. Lasiter had to now prepare for the morning meeting, there was a great deal to do and much to organise and the little chat with the Chief had already made him several minutes late. There was a knock at his door, as it opened, PC Kirk walked in carrying mail.

'Morning,' she announced as she entered. Lasiter didn't reply, he hardly ever did, as Kirk usually chatted incessantly but even she was quieter lately. Was the workload getting to the indomitable PC Kirk too? 'Anything special this mornin?' she asked as she dropped the single item of mail on his desk. Lasiter shook his head.

'Let's just get the meetin' out the way and then we'll think about the rest o' the day,' groaned Lasiter. Kirk continued on her way and left Lasiter with his thoughts. PC Kirk then moved on to DI Davies's office but as usual, he hadn't arrived yet. Davies was the sort of man you could set your watch by, he would be arriving in exactly two minutes, he always did, and Kirk knew that.

She didn't purposely try to avoid Davies because she disliked him, granted, she didn't particularly get on with him but he was good to work for, as he never changed his systems. She just thought he was *too* nice to be a true detective, a detective usually came in a package like Lasiter. She then moved on to the office of Detective Inspector Wick, of A section. This section usually worked in the south of the area, the sector south of the river but these days, the demarcation wasn't so clearly defined, as the amount of crime over the last few months had meant that there was a 'mix and match' policy. D section was smaller and usually dealt with internal investigations but Kirk rarely delivered them any mail. There was an E section, but it had been hastily put together for local matters and its staff changed on a daily basis, depending on who was available. She then walked along another corridor and down some stairs to check on the restroom to make sure that it was reasonably clear for the morning meeting. It wasn't her job, but she did it anyway. She had already sorted out the mail for the front desk and Chief Inspector Anderson, so the only mail left was for Avalon's office, she made her way to the bottom floor and the interview room at the rear of the building. As she turned into the passage where Avalon's office was, she saw one of her uniformed colleagues coming from Avalon's room.

'Have y' seen DS Avalon?' he asked. Kirk looked at her watch.

'No, he's usually here on the dot but they were late off last night. Problems?' she asked. The PC shrugged.

'I dunno, a phone call for him from forensics,' and the officer turned to leave. Kirk thought for a second and then said.

'Oh well, tell them we'll get him to call back, I'll give him the message when he comes in.' Kirk didn't consider that she had also been late leaving the previous night. It wasn't in her nature to factor in how busy *she* was she just got on with it. She looked down at the large sealed folder she had and decided to keep it with her so she wouldn't forget. With everything else done, she could now get on with her own work and she returned up the stairs.

'O-K!' came the usual greeting from the flat English accent of Davies. She turned to see DI Davies making his way to his office.

'Morning sir,' she called, as Davies disappeared around the corner.

Davies felt tired no more or no less than usual, but tired nonetheless. It was going to be a busy day, made worse by the fact that this morning's meeting would bring no solutions, no new clues, no extra lines of investigations to solve the security van robbery he and his whole team were working on. He now envied Lasiter, sure enough, Lasiter had a massive workload, but the security robbery could turn out to be the straw that broke the camel's back. He sat at his desk and opened his mail, thinking about the steaming argument he had with his wife the night before, read his emails and looked at the list of things to do he had made the previous afternoon. For a moment he thought he had been so tired he had copied down two day's work but after reading through them, he realised that it was indeed, just one day's items. He sighed and looked to see if there was anything he could cross off the list. There were two things that stood out. The first was the application for secondment of a young DC from Aberdeen. That could wait until Monday. The other was to get someone to clean out the interview room that Avalon was using as his office. Davies had gone in the previous evening to see if he and Ross where there but had found that they were at the UFO camp, but it struck him that the odd odour in the room was becoming stronger. What were Ross and Avalon doing in there that could create such a smell? He crossed it off. That could wait, indeed he could just ask Kirk to get the cleaners in there, yes that would do it. He sighed again, he could find nothing else to cross off the list, everything else was pertinent to current cases, or follow-ups on leads. As he sat there, he heard the Chief's voice outside the door.

'Ah, good morning Detective Avalon, how are you finding C section?' Davies heard the calm reply of Avalon. Then the door opened and in walked Anderson. What hell was going to visit him today he wondered?

~~~~~~

The day began pleasantly enough for Avalon, he ordered the Scottish breakfast whilst Jeanie asked for a short history lesson about his surname.

'Well yes, but you see the Arthurian legend has been altered through the years,' explained Avalon, 'the truth is, I don't know where it comes from.' Jeanie looked slightly disappointed at this but Avalon explained further. 'It's believed that the name is of Welsh origin but certainly, my branch of the family have lived between Kent and Norfolk for hundreds of years.'

'The opposite coast?' she asked.

'Yes, and the only historical basis for the Welsh connection, is from a dubious account by Gerald of Wales.'

'So do you have your own theory?' asked Jeanie.

'It's probably much more simple, the name could have come from the town of Avallon in Burgundy,' he smiled. Jeanie shrugged and collected the used plates.

'Well, you being a detective, should be able to uncover the truth.'

'It doesn't interest me that much, I once researched my own family back to the 16th century but all the history of my ancestors took place in Kent or Norfolk.'

'So no King Arthur connection?'

'No I doubt it,' smiled Avalon again, 'even Tennyson called it Avilion.' He took a deep breath and continued with, '*To the island valley of Avilion where falls not hail, or rain, or any snow*.' This seemed to content Jeanie and she took her leave to continue her work and Avalon sat in an easy chair relaxing before the onslaught of the day once more took hold of him. His first week in Scotland almost over, he felt so different to how he had felt in Wolverhampton and in some ways, he was looking forward to the next few weeks too. He didn't quite know why, as the workload was considerable but he was enjoying the experience. He was also realising that his unhappiness down south wasn't the fault of the Wolverhampton office that was clear now. It had been Avalon's approach to the environment, which had been flawed. Essentially, it had all been his own fault. He had blamed the job for his marriage problems, and the worse the problems became, the more he hated the job. A particular incident just after he moved there had also taken its toll on him, it gave him nightmares and brought on depressions, this caused him to have mood swings, eventually, it affected the way people saw him. He shook himself from his thoughts and realised he was running a little late, traffic build up due to a diesel spillage on the way in, made him more so. There wasn't a problem though as Ross almost always arrived after Avalon and it had been a late finish on the previous day. He parked the car, entered the building, and made his way to his office, or at least, the windowless box that was being used as his office. None of the rooms had windows of a normal style on the ground floor however, the building had obviously been designed to be secure, so the small windows were all high in the walls but the lack of natural light in the interview room was both depressing and claustrophobic. Avalon made his way upstairs to find out if there were any special orders on the notice board. It was something he did every morning until he felt confident with the systems. As Avalon entered the corridor, he saw Chief Inspector Anderson about to enter Lasiter's office.

'Ah, good morning Detective Avalon, how are you finding C section?' he asked with a slight smile.

'They're a good team Chief Inspector, I'm glad to be working with them.' Anderson nodded and entered Lasiter's office, Avalon continued to the notice board, wondering why the Chief was in so early. On the board, only thing of note or interest to Avalon was the morning meeting, so he then returned to his own office, that dingy box with its overpowering depression. It didn't help having a bottle of 'Dark Ice' aftershave in the filing cabinet and even though it had been hermetically sealed in two evidence bags, the odour still managed to float around the room. As usual, Ross was late, just a couple of minutes and he looked half asleep when he did arrive.

'Good god, you look like death,' announced Avalon.

'Late night,' replied Ross, and he slumped into his chair. Avalon poured them both coffee and sat back down to work out the day's procedure. He reminded Ross that there was a meeting in the restroom and then began to detail what he had planned but PC Kirk walked

210

in with the mail, a large folder by the look of it.

'Looks like either the coroner's report or the forensics,' said Avalon as he smiled to Kirk.

'On that note,' said Kirk, 'Sarah Underwood wants y' tae ring her as soon as y' can.' Ross looked up.

'I've been here four years, and she has never asked me to call her, how come you get her to ring twice?' he frowned. Avalon raised his eyebrows but Kirk answered for him.

'Because you don't have a sexy English accent.'

'Sexy? English? That's an oxymoron,' frowned Ross, even more deeply than before as Avalon slit open the packet and pulled out the forensics report on the dead man from the UFO camp. He thanked Kirk, and she left, then he opened up the report and read through the main points.

'Anything?' asked Ross.

'Not really, hardly any DNA material, just dog hair, two strands of human hair that have been tested and confirmed as being from two unknown sources and some blue fibres.'

'That seems odd,' replied Ross, 'you would think if someone was beaten up twice, that there would be some evidence on the body.'

'Hmm,' sighed Avalon reading more, 'well even if we get a match on the human hair, there is nothing to connect them to the murder. It looks like we are stuck.' He tossed the report onto the desk and leaned back for a minute. 'We should get someone to go over to Mr Nisbet's house to get a sample of his dog's hair to compare with that found at the scene.' He looked at his watch and said, 'Right, we better get off, the meeting starts in five.'

Most of the staff of B and C sections were there, Davies was running the meeting and some uniform officers were present too. Davies looked around and started the meeting.

'Firstly, I just want to say that I know you are all pulled out but I would like you all up to speed on this, just in case we need to re-arrange things at a later point.' He was standing in front of a large computer screen, which was being controlled by Lasiter. 'We have analysed all the CCTV footage from the security van robbery and I want to show you all we have, just in case it jogs any memories.' He turned and nodded to Lasiter. The screen showed two simultaneous images taken from two cameras and as it began to roll, a security van could be seen reversing towards the viewer.

'Here you can see the vehicle reversing into its usual spot to pick up the day's takings from the supermarket, just off Telford Street.' The van was seen to stop, and a guard climbed out of the passenger side. 'Here you can see the security guard leave the van from the passenger side to fetch the strongbox from the supermarket. Then he goes out of view for a moment. On the second camera, you see him approach the rear of the building and press the security bell. The door then opens and he enters.' Davies stopped and looked to those watching and then looked back to the screen. He then pointed to the bottom left of the screen and said,

'On this image you can just see the rear of a white van. It has been identified as a Mercedes Sprinter panel van with a stolen number plate.' He then pointed back to the right-hand side of the screen. 'You can now see the guard exit the rear door of the supermarket and cross the sight of the camera until he disappears from

212

view. He seems to take some considerable time before he reappears on the camera and makes his way back to the van.' He was quiet while this was shown on the screen. The view then went to one of the camera displays, the one with the security van. 'So now you see the guard walk up to the van, he bangs on the rear of the vehicle and the security door opens to allow the strongbox to be inserted. If you observe, the guard also drops in a canister.' It wasn't easy to see, but it was obvious something wasn't quite right. 'Then, the guard goes to the passenger door, opens it, and enters.' Here, the video was frozen. Davies looked at the audience and continued.

'This is the point that the Sprinter van comes into play.' He turned back to the screen as it began to play once more. 'From the left, you see another guard, who we will call guard two, run around the back of the grey security van to the driver's door and then the door opens. The driver can be seen being dragged out and dumped on the floor before the white van drives away and guard two jumps in to drive the security van. The van leaves in a hurry, leaving the injured driver on the floor.' The video ended. Davies leaned on a table. 'We now know that, off camera, the first guard, the *real* guard, was attacked with pepper spray and then beaten by the duplicate guard who we see return to the van. He probably isn't identical but as can be seen in the video, he is a close look-alike, enough to fool the guards waiting in the security van. It is likely that a gas canister was placed with the strongbox in an attempt to incapacitate the guard in the rear.' Davies took a break for a moment. 'As you saw in the footage, there was also another guard, guard two, hiding in the rear of the white

213

van to replace the driver, so all the doppelgänger had to do, was enter the passenger door, taser the driver and then push him out, where his accomplice knocked him unconscious.' Lasiter stood and continued.

'As y' have probably heard on the news, the driver and the first guard are hurt but recovering in hospital. We have no knowledge of the whereabouts of the van or the security guard who was in the rear of et.'

'So,' cut in Davies, 'with no good images of the doppelgänger, we have circulated images of the real guard to other police forces, in the hope that someone recognises anyone they may know that could double for him.' Lasiter then continued.

'The white van has not been found as yet but the number plates were stolen three weeks ago from Perth,' he explained. Davies then sat on one of the tables and folded his arms, before adding,

'We are keeping the doppelgänger part of the story from the media, just in case. We are considering that seeing as the security van was on its last pickup of the day and, going on what was usual for this run, there could be in excess of six-hundred grand in takings. With the third guard still missing, we have to look at his return as being a priority.' Davies then looked at some of the faces looking up at him and added, 'we've had no tips or inside information, this seems completely off the radar.' He then looked over to Lasiter, then back to his audience and said, 'the Chief is understandably anxious about this, particularly with the guard still missing. So...' he took a breath, 'are there any questions?' It was Wilson who asked the first.

'Aye, just one from me.'

'Go on,' nodded Davies.

'Well, the amount en the van doesnae seem all that much, ef they had pulled this at the weekend, et would have made more sense I'm thinking.' Davies nodded.

'True, and we have asked that question but the security company has explained that one to us. It seems that at the weekend or on busy days, three security vans pick up from around the city, on less busy days only a single van picks up from them all, including some smaller businesses. In theory, midweek is better to target a single van.'

'It still doesn't seem that much,' added Murrey, 'I mean how many are in for a share here? Four? Five?' Davies saw a few people nodding around the room.

'We considered this too. With this much planning, we think there could be a team of six or seven, so yes, we agree, it doesn't seem worth it for the risk and the work.' Lasiter stepped forward.

'We have considered that there could have been more cash en the van. This team seems to have inside information and et's possible that once the security company look at their paperwork, the amount could be higher.'

'Es there anybody we know of with this M-O?' asked Frazer.

'As I say, they seem to be off the radar,' added Davies, 'nothing like it before really. The Chief wondered if they had used our current situation as a good time to hit but myself and DI Lasiter have discounted it.'

'Why's that Boss?' asked McGill.

'Well, there is obviously a lot more planning than meets the eye to pull off something as audacious as this in broad daylight. This isn't something you can plan in a few weeks or even months. Even finding someone to play the part of the doppelgänger would take some time, plus studying the shift patterns of the employees of the security firm, etcetera.' There was more nodding, it was clear this had been in the planning for some time and the idea that it could be thrown together, just because the police were busy, didn't seem feasible. Davies took another look around the room.

'So that is how it stands,' he explained, 'I'm putting a regular team together for this as it is a priority, so it means yet more work for everyone else. We need to find the Sprinter van they used, the security van and the missing guard as soon as we can.' He stood and thrust his hands into his pockets. 'So if there is nothing else... right, thanks for your time,' and the meeting broke up.

There were no questions about the other cases and updates to other business. Everyone shuffled away very quietly, Avalon and Ross made their way back to the office where Avalon poured another coffee for them both. They sat quietly until Ross broke the silence with,

'What now?' Avalon shrugged then sighed, he eventually took a deep breath and answered.

'Well, we should have all the results collected from the blitz of the camp by the uniform branch, all except for DNA from the hair samples. Here is the forensic report and we should get the coroner's report soon, although I think we know what it will say.' Ross nodded and pulled over the forensics file. Avalon then remembered. 'Oh, and I better contact Miss Underwood.' He gave a wry smile to Ross who rolled his eyes and continued reading. Avalon rang her number.

'Hello, Sarah Underwood,' came her soft voice.

216

'Er, hello, it's DI Avalon, you wanted me to call.'

'*Oh, yes. Did you get the report?*'

'Yes, it's here in front of me. I have given it a quick read through but there is little to go on until we can match the DNA profile from the hair samples to someone. Oh, and the man that found the body had a dog, we'll get someone to collect some of its hair and get it to you.'

'*Oh right, yes, that would help.*' There was a very slight pause. '*I was actually ringing you about something else.*' Just for a second, Avalon's heart beat slightly faster. Even as he felt it, he knew it was stupid.

'Oh,' he said.

'*Yes, I was thinking about the evidence from the car wreck fires,*' Avalon's heart returned to normal.

'Go on,' he said in a flat tone.

'*Well, something was nagging at me and I couldn't quite make out what it was. You see, with the initial car fire, we found traces of sodium hydroxide on the plastic but because it was considered that the containers may have once contained the chemical, nothing was made of it.*' Avalon was silent he just listened. '*We also found traces of sodium hydroxide or something very like it, on parts of the melted plastic in the more recent fires.*'

'So you think that we could be looking for someone who uses it or deals in this stuff?' suggested Avalon.

'*Well, possibly,*' she replied. Avalon detected doubt.

'So you're not sure,' he asked.

'*Well, it's not that easy to come up with any other hypothesis. The issue is that the containers are used for*' *liquids. Sodium Hydroxide would be stored in very different containers,*' she eventually said.

'Which means you have an idea,' said Avalon smiling to himself, 'do you mind if I let my colleague listen in?' he asked her.

'*Well, I suppose so but this is totally off the record, you do understand?*'

'Of course,' agreed Avalon as he put the speaker-phone on so that Ross could hear.

'*You see,*' she paused again, '*I wondered if the sodium hydroxide had been put in the containers deliberately, rather than the containers being used to store it.*'

'For what purpose?' asked Avalon, looking over to Ross.

'*It has an unusual property, yes it's used for papermaking and to unblock drains but its common name is caustic soda.*' Avalon raised his eyebrows to Ross who shook his head.

'I'm not sure either of us follows you,' he replied. He could hear her doubt even through the speaker but eventually, she took a breath and said.

'*If the chemical was found in those containers, it must have been added to the liquid already in them. That means it was put in there deliberately. Sodium hydroxide breaks down DNA.*'

~~~~~~

Davies looked up as he heard a knock at the door.

'Enter,' he called, it was Avalon. 'James, what can I do for you? I am quite busy so please be brief,' he asked as he continued to write something onto a large

218

pad.

'Sorry, I realise...' he considered there was no point in beating about the bush, 'can I have a quick word about the 'drums',' he said as he sat in the chair opposite. Davies stopped writing and placed the pen on his desk.

'Ah, I wondered how long it would take for you to put two and two together about that,' said Davies apologetically.

'Well, I've known about it a few days,' Avalon admitted.

'We brought you in to work on that side of the case it's true but what with everything going quite crazy, we had to rethink the situation,' explained Davies.

'Yes,' nodded Avalon, 'I realise that, but what is puzzling me is, why DI Lasiter has put it out of bounds?' Davies leaned back in his chair and sighed.

'It was a decision we both took to be honest. The main reason was that it could cause people to lose the logical track and follow something that may have nothing to do with the case.' Avalon nodded and then said,

'With respect, Detective Inspector,' Davies realised Avalon was slightly agitated, 'you are not dealing with school children, these are professionals, they know what they are doing, and your answer is disingenuous. In my opinion, removing anything at this point is counter-productive and could compromise the surrounding investigations.' Davies leaned forward.

'With respect Detective Sergeant,' replied Davies in an abrupt manner, 'you are new here and don't fully understand how things work.' He stopped and sighed again. 'I'm sorry,' he said in a softer tone, 'I understand

219

your feelings James, but we are under such pressure from the Chief that we had to circle the main issues and remove those which seemed surplus to requirements. Even after we told the team to forget about the 'drums', some officers were still referring to them as if they may be tied to some of the cases.'

'They could be,' insisted Avalon, 'denying they exist doesn't stop people vectoring them into their calculations.' Davies Nodded.

'I realise that, myself and DI Lasiter argued about it but we eventually agreed to discount it.' He paused for just a second. 'Have you looked at the details of the drum incidents?' he asked wondering if Avalon had already gone against recommendations.

'No,' replied Avalon shaking his head slightly, 'I asked Ross to dig them out but I haven't had time to look at them.' Davies nodded at this then leaned back once more, this time picking up his pen and lightly tapping it on the edge of the desk.

'Okay, I'll make you a deal.' Avalon raised his eyebrows, he didn't think his new persona was someone to make deals of any sort but he listened. Davies continued, 'You will be moving to a new office on Monday, it's upstairs and much more salubrious than the rooms on the ground floor. We're putting a small team together, essentially splitting the section in two.' He paused to think it through. Avalon was wondering how this would work for him. Davies then continued. 'Take a look at the details concerning the drums. *If* and only *if,* you can find any reason that they may have anything to do with any of the cases that are pending, then dig a little deeper.' Davies stopped and stared at Avalon. He made no reaction. 'This must not take time out of your other work and it must not use resources that would better serve the main cases. Is that understood?' Avalon nodded. 'If you do find anything, I want to know, keep me posted at all times because if anyone finds out I have sanctioned something that isn't in our remit, we will both be in some deep trouble, clear?' Avalon nodded again. 'Anything else?' Avalon stood and left without a word but he wondered why he was being assigned to a new team. When he returned to the office, Ross looked up but Avalon ignored him and walked straight to the map of Inverness.

'What have you found?' asked Ross.

'Nothing really, it seems the section is being split and reformed into two smaller subsections.' Avalon was careful not to use the word 'we' as he had no idea if Ross was to be kept on the same team.

'Yeah, makes sense I suppose,' nodded Ross.

'How so?' asked Avalon.

'Well, they have done it before on larger cases, it's hard work though as the two teams will be expected to take on more duties,' explained Ross, 'to be honest, I don't mind if it gets me out of this place.' He thought for a moment then added, 'I really want to get back upstairs where there are some windows,' he smiled. Avalon sat and began to sift through the reports filed by the uniform branch on the people at the UFO camp, he also arranged for dog hair samples to be collected from the Nisbett's home.

It was a boring and seemingly endless task but it had to be done, to try and eliminate as many people as they could from the investigation. During a break later in the day, Avalon looked over the notes from the forensics case once more and read it in more detail, and then he made a connection. Why he had missed it the first time he couldn't understand but he immediately passed the report over to Ross and told him to read the last paragraph on the third page. Ross duly read it again.

'Only two human hairs were found not belonging to the victim,' paraphrased Ross, 'both hairs from two separate people, probably deposited around the same time. Fibre evidence consisted of one sample of blue threads, all matching and likely to come from the same source. This source has been identified as polyester fleece as is popular with outdoor clothing.' Ross shrugged, then Avalon watched him read it again but this time to himself and as he made his way through the passage, Avalon saw that he also noticed the relevant text.

'You see it then?' said Avalon with a slight grin.

'The fleece? That toady Scobie said...' Ross looked for his notebook and skimmed through the pages. He found the space pertaining to the interview with Scobie. He read it out. 'One had a lightweight jacket, like a fleece and he also wore an open face balaclava.' Avalon nodded.

'So it looks like Scobie may have seen our kidnappers,' he said. Ross looked directly at Avalon.

'We need to bring him in if that fleece he saw was blue, then yes, it's possible this could be our man,' agreed Ross.

'See if there is a uniform car that can bring him in if not, fetch him yourself,' said Avalon. Ross nodded and left the room. As Ross left, Avalon's phone got a text. It was his ex-wife, Carol.

'*Ring me when you get the chance,*' was all it said. He decided to leave that for later, in the meantime,

222

he did a background check on the person the chap in the pub had mentioned, and so he entered the name into the police database. It seemed that Harry Burnside had a police record, nothing serious but it may be wise to keep an eye on him. He then did a little reading up on Caustic Soda and after finding out all he could he rang Sarah Underwood.

'*Hello, Sarah Underwood,*' he heard her say.

'Oh, it's Detective Avalon again.'

'*Hello detective, what can I do for you this time?*'

'I have just been reading about caustic soda and I was wondering about your theory on the matter.'

'*Oh?*' she said as a question more than a comment.

'Well, as you rightly pointed out, this stuff can be used to break down DNA and if it was put into the car wrecks for that purpose, wouldn't the water in it slow down the process?'

'*Well, yes it would but knowing the properties of this chemical, can you see any other reason for it to be in there?*'

'But wouldn't the fire destroy any evidence, more so than the chemical?'

'*Not necessarily,*' replied Underwood, '*we have extracted DNA and other evidence from serious fires in the past, I would think that this was an attempt to make doubly sure. After all, the chemical doesn't burn but if it was added to the water in the containers just before the fires were started, the water would start to boil.*'

'I'm not with you,' replied Avalon.

'*When Sodium Hydroxide is added to water, it creates heat and under the correct conditions there is a great deal of heat.*'

'So how does that affect any possible evidence?' asked Avalon.

'*Well, in theory, the boiling, the fire, the washing away of particles from the hot liquid bursting out from the containers, and the caustic soda effects would help to destroy evidence I would think, but honestly? I think this is a very naïve way to go about it,*' she replied. She paused for a moment as if considering the idea. '*If I were to give an opinion on the matter, I would probably say the effort isn't worth the result.*'

'Well, thank you for explaining that and thanks for helping me out.'

'*Anytime detective, if there is anything I can help with, as I said before, please contact me.*' She said her goodbyes and Avalon heard the click as the phone went down. It still didn't seem like a good way to destroy evidence to him either, surely the fire would do the damage, the diluted caustic soda, even if it was hot, would tend to douse the fire to his way of thinking. Ross returned.

'There is a car a few miles away checking the area, they are going over to pick up Scobie when they have done. I told them to ask for the chap that runs the camp,' he said as he entered. Avalon nodded. As Ross took his seat Avalon said,

'I have just spoken to Sarah Underwood again.' Ross raised his eyebrows and gave a slight smile, Avalon ignored it. 'We are both of the same mind on the car wrecks. There was a very odd method employed to be rid of any evidence in those cars, and in my opinion they were more concerned about that than they were about the crimes these cars were used for.'

'What do you mean?' asked Ross.

'Well,' began Avalon, 'I think they put more planning into the disposal of the cars used than the actual crimes they were used to commit.' Ross nodded he saw what he was getting at.

'So we have to wonder why?' he asked. Avalon shrugged. Ross thought about it and continued. 'What do you want to do about it?'

'Nothing at the moment. At this stage, I think it's quite pointless to pursue it, but there is more here than a simple ram-raid I think.'

'Anything else?' asked Ross.

'Not much,' frowned Avalon, 'Burnside, the chap who we were told to see by the man in the pub, has a record, nothing heavy. Breach of the peace, that sort of thing,'

'Doesn't sound like there is anything there then,' said Ross.

'No, but the whole 'drums' thing isn't important at the moment, so we'll drop it unless something crops up.'

The two of them went back to checking details from the UFO camp murder and trying to eliminate possible suspects from the investigation. Just after lunch, the DNA results came in for the first batch of tests and Avalon was surprised how quickly they had received them. Ross wasn't.

'We have the most advanced forensics service in Europe, the English and Americans don't have it all their own way you know,' said Ross with a straight face.

'I already knew that,' smiled Avalon, 'but I wasn't aware that they could turn round samples that quickly.'

'They reckon they can do it in two hours at a

225

push but the backlog of work means it takes longer most of the time,' explained Ross.

'It's a pity some of your Scottish laws aren't *so* enlightened,' added Avalon dropping the smile.

'Like what?' asked Ross.

'Like the stop and search laws for instance,' Ross knew what was coming as Avalon continued. 'Why does Scotland have more severe Stop and Search laws than New York? It's pretty harsh for a population of five million people over the whole country.' Ross nodded.

'Yes, it's Draconian we know, and most police are against it as it has a negative effect on public relations.' Ross paused. 'What you have to remember is that Scotland has one of the highest murder rates in Europe, in fact, it's the second highest.' He paused again and leaned back. 'Drugs and alcohol abuse get the blame for it but I think the main problem is the justice system.' Avalon looked over to him and nodded. 'The courts are too lenient and unless it's revised, it's always going to be a problem.'

'I think that's true everywhere,' agreed Avalon, 'but yeah, there's no point in us working our nuts off catching them if the courts just make them wear a dunce's cap and stand on the naughty step.'

'Take a case recently,' shrugged Ross with a deep frown, 'a sixteen-year-old youth stabs another teenager to death and gets eight years. We may as well have made him write lines.' Ross stopped and then continued in a monotone voice. 'I must not kill my fellow pupils, I must not kill my fellow pupils...' he tailed off the repetitive phrase.

'It stinks but it must be what people want,' said Avalon.

'What they want?' asked Ross incredulously.

'Well yes, I don't hear the phone ringing for us to go out because a judge had been hung in the streets, I can't remember us being told to rush to Edinburgh because the public are storming Holyrood. They voted in the political system, so as far as I can see, this is what they want. They even had the chance to break away from Britain but they decided not to and if that isn't a statement of '*this is what we want*' I can't imagine what is.' Avalon seemed quite animated about the subject and for the first time, Ross was beginning to see into the 'inner' James Avalon. For his part, Avalon was surprised at the comment. He had a political standpoint, almost everyone did, but as a police officer, he wasn't supposed to show it or air it in public. He decided to defuse the comment slightly by making light of it. 'I'm thinking if the Scottish Assembly banned deep-fried Mars Bars or fish suppers there would be chaos,' he smiled to affirm the humour of it. Ross kept his face still, he showed no emotion one way or the other, he just said.

'Fair enough,' and went back to his computer.

The rest of the afternoon was spent going over the same files until the two hair samples from the forensics found on the body were confirmed as belonging to the woman called Janey, and a man known to be a regular drinking partner of the deceased man at the camp. There was nothing to link the dead man with anyone at the festival, except possibly the man seen in a boiler suit wearing a fleece. When the police car at the camp radioed back in, it was PC Kirk that brought the news. As soon as she entered she asked,

'What the hell es that smell en here?' she sniffed in the direction of each of the two detectives and then

227

added, 'one o' you's needs t' tak a bath.'

'Have you just come here to insult our designer aftershave or have you something for us Constable Kirk?' asked Avalon with raised brows.

'Oh aye, sorry,' she said and then followed with, 'the patrol car up at the camp says that Scobie has bolted, it seems he went just after you left the other day.'

'Shit!' exclaimed Ross, 'that little scumbag.'

'Thanks O-K, we need to put out a BOLO for Scobie, Ross will give you all the details.' Ross nodded and left to go with Kirk to file the 'Be On the Look Out' order. In the few minutes he had to himself, Avalon decided to call his ex-wife Carol who had sent him a text. He took out the phone and called.

'*Hello.*' He heard her voice on the other end.

'Carol, it's James, anything wrong?' There was a long pause. 'Oh sorry, you are at work, shall I call later?'

'*No I'm alone at the moment,*' she said and there was another pause.

'Something is wrong isn't it?' asked Avalon with concern.

'*Well, the truth is, I have no idea. I went round to your house last night to check up on everything.*' Avalon's heart began to sink. '*I checked on the bike, that was fine so I went to the house and for a moment I thought everything was as it should be but when I went into the main room,*' she paused again, '*well, there was something really odd.*' She stopped but Avalon didn't know what to say, she hadn't really said anything yet. The silence grew and so in an effort to break it, Avalon asked.

'Are you going to tell me, or should I fetch my Tarot cards?'

228

'*Sorry,*' she announced, '*I'm still trying to work it out.*' She paused again, this time just a few seconds then told him. '*Someone has broken in, painted the screen of your television white, then used a thick marker pen to draw a sort of target on it and written 'bullet entry point' in the centre.*' Avalon gulped, this was going to be difficult. '*Not only that, they have placed an unopened tin of spaghetti hoops in tomato sauce on the top of it, it's just sitting there.*' Yes, it was going to be very difficult to explain. She continued. '*It spooked the hell out of me and at first I thought there may be someone still in there but there wasn't and there is no sign of a break in.*' This time it was Avalon's turn to be silent. '*Did you hear me?*' she asked, '*I mean I haven't touched anything just in case.*' By now Avalon had formulated a plan.

'Just forget about it.' As he said it, he realised it wasn't much of a plan.

'*Forget about it? I think someone with a sick mind did this,*' she said anxiously.

'I did it,' he announced, 'I was drunk the night before and I got the idea that the TV was so poor that it ought to be shot at dawn.' There, he told the truth, well almost, he was perfectly sober when he painted the damn thing.

'*But what about the spaghetti hoops, you don't like spaghetti?*' she asked.

'I can't explain the spaghetti hoops, they just appeared,' said Avalon realising Ross had returned. 'Anyway, it's all fine, I have to go now. I'll ring you on Sunday, I'll be able to talk more then,' and he said his goodbyes. He put the phone back into his pocket and looked at his computer screen. 'What did you just hear?'

asked Avalon without looking up, knowing that some of the conversation would have been audible to Ross.

'Just the bit where you said, *'I can't explain the spaghetti hoops, they just appeared'*,' replied Ross without looking at Avalon. There was a good thirty seconds of silence until Ross finally looked around his screen and asked. 'Is there something you wish to talk about?' There was a slight smile on his lips.

'No thank you,' replied Avalon without taking his gaze from the screen.

~~~~~~

The door to Lasiter's temporary office was slightly ajar but Avalon still knocked and gently pushed it open.

'Och, James, tak' a seat,' he pointed to the chair by the desk.

'You wanted to see me?' said Avalon. Lasiter typed something on his computer then pushed the keyboard aside and looked at Avalon.

'Y' seem to be settling in quickly.' Avalon nodded and gave a weak smile, he knew enough about Lasiter to know that he hadn't asked him in to tell him that. 'The main reason I have asked t' see you es because of you movin' t' your new office.' His thick Scottish accent could be difficult for Avalon to understand sometimes but he deciphered enough to make out what he was saying. 'DI Davies and I have talked about one of the lads in B section gettin' a promotion, we're not sure exactly who yet but tae balance the thing up we are going to gae y' yer own team.' Avalon was surprised. 'We cannae promote y' o' course but with your experience y' should help out quite a bit.'

'When you say team...' it wasn't exactly a question but Lasiter understood what he was getting at.

'We thought two DC's and a PC in the office to coordinate it for y'.' Avalon nodded. It was more than generous but he knew there would be a catch.

'Of course, y' will hae t' expect a bit more tae do,' explained the DI and there was the catch. A much larger workload but that was to be expected, it didn't detract from the thought that, for the first time in his career, he would be running his own team. Inside he smiled.

'Who will it be?' he asked.

'Well, I would hae normally said Ross but I didnae know if you two got on all that well.'

'Yes, we had our slight disagreements but he's a good officer and he knows the case.'

'Aye, a' can see that would be best,' nodded Lasiter. 'Okay, Ross and DC Frazer then. Frazer can be a bit insular but she's got a quick mind and I value her as a detective,' explained Lasiter.

'I'll go with your suggestion,' smiled Avalon. 'Would PC Kirk be available for the PC job?' Lasiter smiled and then shook his head.

'If I gave y' her, the whole station would stop.' He looked down at a notepad. 'PC Dowd et's t' be. He's new t' the station but capable from all accounts.' Avalon nodded, Kirk would have been good, but he could soon knock this other PC into shape.

'The office should be finished sometime today so we think that everythin' should be up an' runnin' for y' on Monday mornin'.' Avalon nodded again but it didn't let the pleasure of the moment show. To him, this was proof that he had shaken off the past and he was a new person.

'We'll still be on the murder case I assume?' he asked.

'Aye,' nodded Lasiter, 'but there will be two other cases sent over. One is a violent attack on a woman, DC Ross knows about that one,' he looked down at his notepad once more, 'the other case es a missing person.' Lasiter noticed Avalon squint his eyes a little. 'I know it sounds tame, but there were signs o' a struggle at the scene. It came in yesterday and forensics are o'er there today.' Avalon nodded. 'They can wait until the mornin' though, so make some arrangements to get your kit moved en for Monday.'

'There isn't that much to move,' smiled Avalon.

'Is there anythin' y' need?' asked Lasiter. Avalon couldn't think of anything in particular but a slight detail sprung into his mind.

'Well, nothing specific but...' he hesitated as he was unsure whether to ask or not.

'Go on laddie, spit it out,' replied Lasiter, 'I can always say no.' The slight smile from the DI gave Avalon the push he needed but he would have to word it carefully.

'It's the little issue of the sounds that people are calling, 'the drums'.' He noticed Lasiter sigh. 'I realise that you put a stop to any investigation on this...' Lasiter interrupted.

'Et wasnae a stop as such. I didnae want our people wasting time with somethin' that had no influence on any o' the cases.' He took a pause and then gave Avalon a cold stare. 'Unless you have somethin' that no one else has found, I'm not likely t' change my

232

mind.' Avalon didn't, he was really just fishing around to try to see why Lasiter had made the decision to prevent anyone perusing it. Maybe Avalon was also curious why some people still considered the drums were linked to the spate of serious crimes of late, he was certainly considering that there *was* a link. Avalon decided at that moment that if he could find any more, he would look into it, otherwise, he too would forget about the drums of Drumnadrochit. He gave a slight nod. 'Okay,' added Lasiter. 'if you think o' anything' y' need just let me know,' and he went back to his work as Avalon left.

Returning to his office, he set about looking at what he would need to move. Certainly the maps were needed but they could probably be replaced, the filing cabinet wouldn't be required as there would probably be something for their use in the new office. Then he thought about the 'Dark Ice'. As much as he wanted to be rid of the smell he did consider keeping it. Maybe not. It would make the air in the new office as toxic as it was in the interview room.

'What are you doing?' asked Ross watching him look around the room.

'Oh, just looking what I need to move for Monday morning,' replied Avalon.

'Have they made a decision about who is working with you?' asked Ross. Avalon looked down at the detective constable to try to judge his mood, he couldn't, as Ross had a look of complete ambivalence on his face.

'Sort of,' began Avalon, 'a new PC called Dowd will run the office side and we get DC Frazer.' Avalon paused then asked. 'What's she like, as a detective?'

Ross raised his eyebrows.

'She's quiet, tough as hell, doesn't offer any information unless asked, but seems pretty good at what she does. I'm not sure she's much of a team player though,' replied Ross.

'That's not a bad thing, I like to have people who can work alone.'

'Is that it?' asked Ross staring at Avalon.

'Yes, did you expect more? I think it's more than adequate,' replied Avalon, taking another sweep of the room. 'It will leave us free if we need to follow anything up.'

'We?' asked Ross with a slight glare. Avalon looked back at Ross.

'Well, you didn't think I would punish DI Lasiter by making him take you back did you?' Avalon didn't smile, 'unless you want out?' he eventually added.

'No, no, I'll stay. You need someone to show you how to solve crimes,' and he went back to his computer. Inside, Avalon smiled but outwardly he kept a straight face and began to plan ahead.

Chapter Seven

Sundays were never a favourite day for Avalon. Historically, it was the day that family arguments were undertaken. He and his ex-wife had found Sundays to be the obvious day for disagreements and confrontation mainly due to Avalon having such high work commitments. A social life was pointless as he could never fully commit. He was always glad when Sunday had gone and the ubiquitous Monday came around once more, that special day when no pretence was, or could be attached to it, it was a 'work day' clear and simple. So when he found himself the proud owner of a shiny new Sunday, and a Sunday that he didn't have to work, he was like a child with a new toy. Saturday had been tedious at the police station, full of paperwork and reading reports, so as he sat at breakfast having absolutely nothing to do on this particular Sunday, it was both odd and exciting. He considered how he would plan the day out but of course he had one appointment he would have to keep. He was to be at Angioletta Carbonna's house to meet her and PC Kirk so that he could look over the room for rent, but that was hours away. Then a thought occurred. He was becoming quite happy with his new persona, Detective Sergeant Avalon had, at last, become the sort of detective he had always meant to be, but what of that ordinary Mr James Avalon? He had no idea, and no real plans for that side of the man. Several times he found himself saying 'Just be yourself' but he kept hearing a reply of 'who the hell is that?'

Most of his private life had been spent married to Carol and since then, there hadn't been much of a private life. He retired from the breakfast table and returned to his room, struggling with the idea of who he was and could *that* be changed? As he sat on the edge of the bed, gazing through the window, he began to take stock of his life. He knew he was a little too old to still be a detective sergeant, but he blamed that on his time at Wolverhampton. Being considered an outsider hadn't been great for his career and there were many more detectives in the department than was healthy for promotion, then he suddenly made a realisation that this might not be the reason he had been passed over. Was he just not good enough to stand out in the crowd? It could be, he may have been passed over because his superiors didn't have confidence in him. That was worrying because if it was true then the best course of action *was* to leave the force. He would now have to tread lightly, in his own mind he knew he could be on the verge of losing confidence in himself. He stood and walked into the shower room and turned on the cold water. He threw his clothes onto the chair and stepped into the shower, the chill made him wince but he continued. As he stood there, allowing the freezing water to take his breath, he decided to wake up every part of his being, he would walk out of that shower a complete man. Not just the detective he knew he could be but the man he wished he was. He turned the water off and stood there shivering, then he reached for the towel and dried himself. For some seconds he looked into the mirror and began to plan his future, staring unblinkingly into his eyes, eyes he didn't recognise anymore. He walked back into the room and glanced at the clock by the bed. Hours left yet. He looked in the wardrobe and began to consider what he should wear, it wasn't a long consideration however because it was clear that, except for his three work suits, the only other clothing he had, was a single pair of light coloured denim jeans and three tee shirts, one with a large Triumph logo across the chest. He knew this had to change. He had plenty of time to go into town and buy himself some new clothes, so he dressed the best he could and set off to purchase himself a new life.

By the time Avalon arrived at the house of Angioletta Carbonna, he was reasonably happy with the results of the shopping trip. Casual slacks, a new polo shirt and a smart jacket all of which he considered looked neither trendy nor old-fashioned but the main problem was, it was now raining, pouring actually. When he had first set off, the weather looked like it would be kind but gradually the sky had darkened and now the water was coming down by the bucketful.

The house was a pleasant looking, semi-detached bungalow on a small estate not far from the police station. From the outside, it looked ideal, a small patch of grass at the front, a drive at the side where two cars were parked and what looked like a small, but tidy rear garden. He was a little apprehensive but another part of him was looking forward to the meeting. He got out of his old Ford and couldn't help noticing that the two cars on the drive, presumably belonging to PC Kirk and Angioletta, were much newer than his. He walked up to the door and knocked, it was soon opened by the smiling face of O-K, otherwise known as PC Kirk.

'Allo. Come in, Angie is on the phone,' Avalon followed her inside. The rooms were furnished plainly but comfortably. They walked into the reasonably equipped kitchen and sat at the table, 'cuppa?' asked Kirk and Avalon nodded with a smile, 'I think et's her brother so she's takin' et in the other room,' explained Kirk as she poured his tea. Avalon was surprised how different Kirk was out of uniform. She wore the usual sort of clothes for her age but he wasn't used to seeing her with makeup and her hair down. It was like looking at a stranger. Her character was also different, gone was the tidy, hard-working PC Kirk, replaced by a woman who had a feminine side to her. And she smiled. She actually smiled a great deal, which was rather confusing to Avalon. 'Et's a nice wee hoosie don't y' think?' she asked as she sat.

'Yes,' nodded Avalon, 'to be honest it seems perfect.' He looked around the kitchen and realised it didn't look as if Angie was much of a cook. There were no obvious signs of a busy kitchen and on the worktop stood in pride of place, a top-of-the-range microwave oven. That gave it away for Avalon. He wasn't a fan of in-flight food unless he was actually in an airplane and so microwave cookers were not part of his kitchen repertoire. He was no 'bon vivant' and he would never manage a career as a chef but to him, if you had to eat out of tins then you should at least cook the food in a saucepan over a hob.

'Et's pretty close to work too,' replied Kirk, 'though I'm no' sure that's a plus.' She smiled yet again as Avalon just nodded. The door behind her opened and Avalon stood as he noticed the dark-haired woman, who must be Angie, enter. 'Oh, this es Angie, Angie this es Detective...' and she paused for a moment. It gave Avalon time to take in his prospective housemate. She was probably in her early to mid-thirties, with a typically Italian look. Dark brown, almost black eyes shone out from beneath raven black hair some of which was casually tied up at the back of her head leaving a multitude of dark waves cascading over her shoulders. Her skin looked immaculate with a slight Mediterranean hue and as she smiled, the corners of her eyes turned down slightly to give her a look of shyness. 'I cannae call y' Detective Sergeant can I?' insisted Kirk. It shook Avalon from his quick appraisal of Angie.

'No, course not,' he smiled, and he held his hand out towards Angie. 'It's Jim, Jim Avalon.' She took the hand and replied,

'Nice tae meet y' Jem.' Avalon was shocked, where was the sexy Italian lilt, the cascade of vocal intonation and the nasal resonance? He began to think for a moment that his ears had been corrupted by so many Scottish voices that he could no longer hear anything else, that even though she was speaking Italian, it was sounding like she was Scottish. In truth, her accent was even more pronounced than Kirk's and he realised he was standing there, silent, still shaking her hand with his jaw slack and hanging loose. He tried to hide it by saying.

'You're not local then.' She smiled, but it was Kirk who answered.

'She's a Weegie.' Avalon looked down at Kirk.

'Pardon?' he asked.

'A Weegie,' repeated Kirk. Angie smiled and sat at the table.

'I'm from Glasgow, a Glaswegian,' she smiled.

'We bathe are,' added Kirk laughing. Avalon was still no expert on the Scottish brogue but he could tell that Kirk had suddenly changed her accent.

'So you would normally speak like that?' he asked, as he joined them at the table.

'Aye, bet naebody up 'ere wed tell whit I wis sayen,' she laughed again.

'So,' grinned Avalon, 'you have to alter your accent here in Inverness so that they can make out what you say?'

'Not quite, but Inverness sounds posh tae us,' explained Angie with a slight giggle, 'so where are y' from?' she asked.

'Originally from Norfolk but I now live and work in Wolverhampton.'

'Ollie says yer up here for a wee spell an' then y'r off back,' added Angie.

'Yes, I'm here for about ten weeks, so if that doesn't suit, I understand.'

'No,' she shook her head as she smiled, 'that's fine, it'll help me oot,' she paused and then said, 'Ef y' want et o' course.'

Avalon was shown the room, he agreed everything was perfect and a price was settled upon. Angie then explained that she usually worked twelve-hour shifts from six o'clock at night, so they wouldn't see a great deal of each other. To celebrate they enjoyed a small glass of wine until the phone rang and Angie went off once more to answer it.

'She seems nice,' smiled Avalon.

'She es,' agreed Kirk.

'No boyfriends?' he asked but regretted it immediately.

'You're not her type,' smiled Kirk and Avalon wondered what she meant.

'I didn't mean it like that, I meant-' Kirk interrupted.

'I'm jokin',' she glared, 'no,' she then added, 'she used to hae a serious relationship back hame, but she came here for the job, an' she loves et but et doesnea mak' it easy f' her tae have any stable relationships.'

'I don't think she would have any problems in that department,' smiled Avalon.

'I don't think she's bothered tae be honest,' shrugged Kirk, 'she's close tae her family and that seems all she's bothered aboot.' Avalon nodded.

'I think that's all anyone needs,' he agreed.

'Aye you got family?' she asked. Avalon shook his head.

'Not as such. My father died twenty years ago and my mother remarried a man I can't get on with, so apart from the odd phone call, we don't actually connect much.'

'Nea brothers or sisters?' she asked. Avalon shrugged.

'One brother but he is in the navy, he works on ship maintenance so we hardly ever see each other.' He thought for a moment. 'When we meet up we just sit and get steaming drunk talking about old times, so even that is pretty superficial.' Avalon looked at Kirk who seemed to have drifted off. 'What about you?' She shook from her thoughts and said.

'A bit like you really, I mean I have a family but they think I work en an office.' Avalon frowned a little. She smiled and explained, 'Where I'm from et isnea a good idea to admit tae bein' a copper. They still don't know I work for the polis'.' Avalon didn't know how to react to this information, he just sighed and then inhaled deeply. Kirk looked him in the eye and then said. 'Er, listen,' she then looked down to her hands, 'I'm really sorry about that stupid thing I did when you arrived.' Avalon thought for a moment and then he remembered.

'Oh, the episode in the interview room with the two-way mirror you mean?'

'Aye,' she replied looking very embarrassed, 'et wis a stupid thing tae do. I just got a wee bit carried away when somebody suggested et.'

'It happens, as the new boy, I expected the uniform branch would be the first to put me on my toes,' smiled Avalon.

'How did y' know, that they were the other side of the glass I mean?' she asked looking at him again.

'I didn't, you're probably not the actress you think you are and to be fair, I did notice some PCs walk past. That corridor only leads to the interview rooms and the toilets. It was unlikely that three or four male officers would go to the loo together and they didn't have a reason to be in the other interview rooms I assumed they were the other side of the glass.'

'I can see why y' became a detective,' she smiled.

'Anyway, it's forgotten now,' he added.

'You impressed the lads that were the other side o' the glass I can tell you.' Avalon noticed her eyes soften.

'Well, I better get off, I'll have to make arrangements with my landlady and give her the news,' and he finished off the drop of wine left in his glass.

'Et's going tae be a big week, new office and a new home,' she smiled.

'Yep,' replied Avalon as he stood, 'but I think this place suits really well, thanks for setting it up for me.'

'My pleasure,' she smiled. Angie came back into the kitchen.

'Sorry about that. Work,' she shrugged.

'Well thanks, Angie, I think the place is excellent and will suit me perfectly. I want to pay you in advance if that's okay?' he said and pulled out his wallet.

'It doesnae matter about that now, ef I cannae trust a detective-' but she didn't finish the sentence.

'I insist,' smiled Avalon, and he gave her two week's rent. He then offered his hand, which she took and smiled. 'So I'll move over tomorrow evening,' added Avalon fastening his jacket ready for the deluge outside.

'Oh, I nearly forgot,' Angie cried out as she turned and opened a drawer, 'y' need this,' and she handed him a key. He nodded and thanked her once again and then made a dash to the car through the rain.

As he drove back to the B&B, he found himself wondering if he was becoming too confident with his new alter ego, he had found Angie attractive but he also wondered if Kirk had been trying to attract his attention too. He gave himself a ticking off for being too arrogant. He consciously made a decision to keep both business and pleasure very separate, he didn't want to make mistakes this time and he began to look at his future.

Once back at the B&B he went up to his room and sat in the window seat as the clouds lightened and the rain stopped. It was still overcast but a little more pleasant. He thought about the house he had just left, he knew he could make himself comfortable there and with Angie out when he was in, it was as good as having the place to himself. He was pleased with how things were working out and he saw that given time, he wouldn't want to go back to his previous life. In the past, being himself had been very counterproductive, but here in Scotland, it seemed different somehow. He made a decision that if the police force didn't like his new style, then it was tough, he was on secondment, which gave him a little more flexibility but even if it didn't work, Avalon no longer gave a damn. He was, however, beginning to like Ross, and he hoped forging some kind of rapport with him would help. He looked at the clock.

'Maybe it's time for a 'dram' in town,' he said to the empty room.

~~~~~~

Monday morning was a mix of two emotions, the first was excitement on starting with a new team, in a new office, and the second was trepidation. He had to begin as he meant to go on, so he tried to relax as he made his way upstairs to the new office. He was a little early as he wanted to sort out the room to his liking and as he entered he was pleased with what he saw. There were two large windows, admittedly they were the type you couldn't open, and they were tinted, but windows nonetheless. The view was towards the roundabout on the main road, which gave the perspective that there was

244

something going on in the world at large. The desks were almost in the position he wanted and it was simple to adjust them to where he thought it was best. It wasn't a large room by any accounts but there was enough space to get the job done. He then made his way to his personal locker downstairs where the items from the interview room had been kept and brought them up to the new room. Unfortunately, it included the 'Dark Ice' and not for the first time, he considered throwing it away but it could prove to be evidence later. After fifteen minutes DC Megan Frazer arrived, her humourless face seemed to nod without her head actually moving. She walked past him and looked around the room.

'Where do y' want me tae sit Sarge?' she asked looking at the desks.

'Wherever you want, first up, best dressed,' smiled Avalon but Frazer seemed confused by this, 'how about there,' suggested Avalon, pointing to the position by the cabinets. She nodded and sat, arranging the box of items she had brought with her on the table. PC Neil Dowd entered soon after and looked straight at Avalon with a much brighter countenance than Frazer, and asked.

'Es there anything you need for the office Sergeant?'

'Not at the moment but I'm guessing we'll need the coffee machine setting up.' Avalon pointed to the machine he had put by the door. Dowd looked at it and nodded then began to place the machine near a plug socket. 'You better take the desk by the door,' he added pointing to a small desk close to the entrance. Avalon then sat down realising Ross would probably be late but it gave him time to take in the room with people actually in it. Yes, it was small, that was clear, but it was better than the interview room downstairs.

'What d' y' want me tae start on Sarge?' asked Frazer apparently ready for the go. Avalon had noticed that she seemed to be sniffing something now and then. Was the Dark Ice leaving its lair already?

'Can you see if there is any news on the Bolo issued on Antony Scobie. We need to find him pronto.' Frazer nodded and picked up the phone and Avalon noticed Dowd looking expectantly. 'Oh Dowd... er,' he looked up to the coffee machine and noticed, although it was set up, it did not have water or coffee in it, 'can you get me the files and the log for the Abriachan murder?'

'The hard copies?' Dowd asked.

'Yeah,' nodded Avalon, 'the coroner's report should be in now as well.' Dowd nodded and went off to see the archive officer. Avalon was used to thinking for himself but he now had to make sure everyone else had something to work with. He smoothed down the maps he had placed on the wall and placed the pins back into the areas they had previously been. The door opened again and in walked Ross. He looked terrible as usual but he was so used to Avalon by now, he instinctively looked at the coffee machine.

'Power cut?' he asked nodding to the empty machine.

'I asked our PC to sort it but he omitted to add the coffee and water,' explained Avalon.

'He hasn't got the makings of a detective then?' frowned Ross derisively.

'I've sent him to get the files out for the murder case. I want to go through everything again,' explained Avalon. Ross shrugged and then asked.

'Is this me?' he pointed to the desk opposite Avalon's, 'I'm guessing this is me, seeing as it isn't covered in crap like all the other desks,' and he sat, placing his mobile phone and his car keys by the side of the computer keyboard.

'You don't sound your usual ebullient self this morning. Anything wrong?' asked Avalon.

'Nothing that a different lifestyle wouldn't improve,' he explained. Frazer had finished talking on the phone and replaced the handset, saying.

'Frothy Ross, they call him en the other sections.' She fixed her gaze on her computer screen.

'And we all know what your name is, don't we?' scowled Ross. Avalon could see there may be some tension between these two members of his team.

'Bloody hell, is this a Scottish trait? Do you have to let fly at each other before breakfast or what?' Avalon raised his voice a little and then looked from Ross to Frazer. 'What have you learned about Scobie?' he said in a quieter tone.

'Nothing Sarge. There have been no reports of anyone answering tae his description,' she explained.

'That little toe rag has probably gone to ground by now,' added Ross. Avalon had to admit, it looked doubtful they could find him.

'Do y' want me tae try an' rouse him out?' asked Frazer with a slight amount of confidence in her voice.

'What do you mean by that?' asked Avalon.

'I may be able t' find where he's gone, given a wee bit o' time,' she answered. Avalon nodded and said.

'Yeah, go for it, if you think you can,' she nodded and picked up the phone. She dialled a number and listened.

247

'Foley,' she began, 'I need some info,' there was a pause and then she added, 'y' know too well who et is, so don't arse me about.' There was another pause. 'We'll meet in the usual place, one hour,' she paused again and Avalon saw her eyes look up momentarily and in a hissing tone she concluded with, 'ye better be, or I'll be after you,' and she put the phone down. She looked up again to Avalon. 'A contact, I'll have tae go out a for a wee bit.' Avalon nodded, and she stood and left.

'What's Frazer like, as a detective I mean?' asked Avalon, slightly surprised by her telephone technique. Ross was looking out of the window and answered without turning.

'I think you asked me that before but, she's odd as you've seen. She makes Helena Bonham Carter look like a normal, balanced human being,' and then he added, 'she's probably good at her job too but I never turn my back on her.'

'I'm guessing you're exaggerating,' said Avalon. Ross turned from the window looked at Avalon and gave what seemed to be a list of attributes.

'Her family is from this area but she moved away, ended up working in fraud down in Aberdeen before coming here. Big on surveillance and I think long hours sat alone make her insular. She gets results but doesn't always let people into the loop. And no, I'm not exaggerating.'

'I see,' nodded Avalon, as he sat at his new desk,

'So how does she keep her position if she isn't a team player?' he asked.

'Well,' shrugged Ross, 'I suppose because what she does, she does well and she has lots of contacts. Hard as nails too. She has Lasiter on her side, he seems to think she's good if a little unorthodox.' Avalon made no comment he was considering if it was why he had been given Frazer, because no one could work with her. Ross continued. 'Frazer the Razor they call her and I wouldn't like to get the wrong side of her,' he smiled.

'We need to change that,' insisted Avalon, 'we need to get her to integrate, to become part of this team.' Ross nodded slowly as if he wasn't sure. There was a casual knock at the door and it opened. Lasiter walked in, wearing the usual tired frown that seemed to be a fixture and said.

'How's the new gaff?' Avalon nodded and said.

'Excellent, we're settling in fine.'

'It's slightly bigger than a pencil case but we are limiting the number of pencils,' added Ross.

'You're never happy Ross. D' y' want tae go back tae the interview room?'

'I didn't say I didn't like it, I'm just pointing out that we are looking for a small rodent to swing as we don't have room for a cat,' replied Ross with a fake smile. Lasiter looked over to Avalon.

'What a've come t' tell y' es that the security company in the robbery have come clean about the amount en the van,' he said as he leaned on the desk in front of him, 'they are now sayin' that they were supposed to have two vans on that run but they cut back due tae staff shortages.' Lasiter sighed. 'Et seems there could have been one point two million in the van.'

'Shite, it must have been carrying the Chief Constable's wages,' exclaimed Ross. Lasiter turned as if to berate Ross but Avalon broke in and added.

'Well, that certainly made it worth doing and crashes the theory that it wouldn't be worth taking a large team on.'

'Yeah,' nodded Lasiter, 'and it raises more questions.'

'Like, was it an inside job, maybe?' asked Ross. Lasiter nodded again.

'That's what we're thinkin', the gang must have known et was worth having, and they must have known months en advance,' he admitted.

'Well, it shouldn't take much to find out who is the insider,' added Avalon.

'Well,' sighed Lasiter, 'the security company isn't the most honest organisation to deal with and et seems they have over seventy staff including part-timers. There are also some casual staff so et's going t' be a long job.'

'So are we going to have to help out?' asked Avalon.

'Not at the moment, you stay on the murder and the other things you hae t' do. DI Davies and his team are putting extra time onto et f' now.' Avalon nodded and Lasiter asked. 'How's et going?' Avalon explained that they were pinning hopes onto the tiny bit of forensic evidence they had and were waiting to see if they could find Scobie. Lasiter looked less than pleased that there was no headway and left soon after.

'It looks like we better find something soon, or we may be demoted to cleaning Chief Anderson's car,' said Avalon, with a deep frown, just as Dowd returned.

'Here are the files, sir.'

'Thanks Dowd, put them on my desk.' Avalon set about the files, the coroner's report was put aside, and he passed some of the files to Ross. He told him to have another look through and see if there was anything they may have missed but both of them knew there wasn't.

Ross shrugged and scanned through the fine detail.

'You know,' he began, 'there seems to be no motive for this murder and yet he was abducted, beaten and then killed some time after.'

'I realise that, what's your point?' frowned Avalon as he began reading the coroner's report.

'I don't have one, except that we know two other people were abducted, but they weren't beaten.'

'It isn't confirmed that they were taken by the same people though,' explained Avalon.

'No,' began Ross, 'but it's likely seeing as they were both drugged, it's a UFO spotting festival, not a kidnapping festival.'

'Never assume. The first rule of detective work,' smiled Avalon. Ross sank his gaze into the files he did his best to read through the case notes and the detailed accounts from the camp. Avalon found nothing really new in the coroner's report until he came to the section dealing with compounds in the blood of the deceased man. Without looking up from the report, he said.

'Have a look at the case files on the previous abductions from the UFO camp and see if there is anything on the drugs found in the blood.' Ross typed on his computer and eventually reported.

'Er, it says, some compounds were found, one notable substance was Hyoscine hydrobromide. Other traces compatible with,' Ross paused for a moment as if gathering breath for the word and then continued slowly, 'Methylenedioxymethamphetamine,' and he paused as if he had conquered some impossible challenge.

'That's the drug 'Ecstasy', we came across it a lot in Brum,' frowned Avalon.

'Easy to see why they shortened the name,'

replied Ross.

'What's the other one?' asked Avalon.

'I'll check. Why the interest, is there a link?' asked Ross.

'Well, the coroner's report on the dead man says amounts of Hyoscine hydrobromide and a substance called Flunitrazepam were found in high amounts in the blood.' Ross went to work on his computer.

'Can you spell those out?' he asked and Avalon did so. Ross leaned back and read the screen.

'Flunitrazepam is sometimes called Rohypnol and has been reported on occasions as a 'date-rape' drug,' explained Ross.

'I think we can rule that out here,' insisted Avalon, 'anything else?' Ross read through quickly.

'Loss of sleep... addictive... and sometimes used for suicide.'

'Again, we certainly can rule that out,' said Avalon raising his eyebrows a little, 'what about the other drug?' Ross looked back at the computer and typed in some more keystrokes.

'Hyoscine hydrobromide, sometimes known as Scopolamine.'

'Seasickness,' said Dowd quickly.

'What?' asked Ross.

'Scopolamine, et's a treatment for seasickness, I go sailing sometimes and I'm told that et's supposed to work. Not that I suffer with et,' he explained, still typing on his computer.

'Well, I can't see that he'd be taking a seasickness cure even if he was planning a trip on the loch,' frowned Avalon.

'Apparently it's a widely used drug with many

252

applications, so he could have been taking it for any number of reasons,' explained Ross as he read further.

'I need more information on this,' said Avalon as he sat to his desk. 'I'll send an email to Sarah Underwood and see if she can come up with something.' He typed a message out and pressed 'send'.

'I think I've got it,' smiled Ross reading from his screen, 'The drug has been used in the past as a hypnotic.' Avalon looked up and said,

'So it may have been administered to have the same effect as the Ecstasy was in the previous victims?' Ross nodded at this and added.

'It would seem so. If you wanted to make someone think they had been abducted by aliens, this would be a good choice it seems.' Avalon stood and paced the room. Ross watched for a moment then said,

'Are you asking the same questions as me?' Avalon stopped pacing and said,

'Probably. Why would you want to make someone, seemingly at random, think they had been abducted by aliens?' confirmed Avalon staring into space.

'Is it me?' began Ross with a slight frown, 'or does this sound totally crazy?' Avalon cast Ross a slight smile as he said,

'I have to say, it's the biggest mystery since Justin Bieber made it big.' Ross looked at Avalon, who seemed very different this morning and then glanced down to his computer screen.

'Well,' piped up another voice, 'we have to assume it's a cover for some other actions.' It was Dowd, his comment had come from nowhere, and he was still staring at his computer screen. The silence that ensued made him stop what he was doing and look to both Ross and Avalon. 'Er sorry,' he stuttered, 'thinking aloud,' and he went back to typing.

'You may be right PC Dowd but it's what that other purpose might be? That is the crux of the matter here,' explained Avalon and he began to pace again. His phone rang. 'Avalon,' he answered and there was a pause, 'Yes, put her through.' Avalon's face visibly brightened as he said 'Hello,' to whoever was on the phone but the brightness lost some shine as he repeated 'oh' and 'I see,' several times. There then came a long pause, and he asked. 'Would this be more pronounced in someone who was not used to drugs or medication?' There was another long pause, and he concluded the call with. 'Okay, thanks for that. I'll keep you informed.' The phone was replaced on the receiver. 'That was Sarah Underwood. She says she is no expert on the subject and we should get other advice but she agrees with us about the Scopolamine. She says it probably depends on the amounts found but he could have been taking it as a prescription.' He then seemed to hesitate. 'She also says that the other drug...' it was obvious Avalon couldn't remember its name, 'can have some very serious side effects in some people.' Ross thought he knew what was coming. 'She says that there are paradoxical effects such as anxiety, depression, and aggressiveness, leading to violence. She thinks it's also likely that for someone not used to these sorts of drugs the results would be more critical and probably catastrophic.'

'Well, it fits. The woman at the camp said the victim never took drugs, even headache pills,' added Ross.

'Exactly, if the abductors were trying to induce

254

an alternative reality on him and the drugs had a bad reaction, then he could have become agitated and violent,' explained Avalon sitting down.

'And it looks like he was killed for it,' frowned Ross. 'So we probably have a lead on *why* he was killed,' he continued, 'but we still come back to why someone would want to turn a stranger's world into an episode of Doctor Who?' Ross stared questioningly but Avalon just shook his head.

'I don't know, maybe we need to talk to the chap who runs the camp again,' he said, 'but it seems we were right after all, they *are* all connected,' and he allowed a slight smile.

'Do you want me to put some pressure on Larry Olivier up at the camp then?' asked Ross.

'Who?'

'The man up at the UFO camp who talks like Shakespeare,' explained Ross.

'Maybe, don't go as far as shoving him in the boot of your car and chucking him in the loch though,' smiled Avalon. Ross seemed to brighten suddenly.

'Talking of the loch, have you seen the images of the scans that have been published?' he asked. Avalon shook his head. 'You should take a look, it's quite an eye-opener. There's a deep trench running along most of the floor of the loch.' Ross was searching the internet as he spoke.

'I gave up on that when they found the paper mache monster that sunk during the making of that film,' sighed Avalon. Ross looked over and told him to look at the image. Avalon admitted it was impressive but as he walked back to his seat, he said, 'It's an old geological fault line isn't it? Though you would have thought they

255

might have found some more interesting items.'

'Some years ago they found a whole bomber in there, this time just a few sunken boats and some abandoned cars,' shrugged Ross.

'What? No shopping trolleys? That's the indigenous marine species of canals and rivers around Wolverhampton,' replied Avalon going back to the coroner's file.

'Well, more significant was the fact they didn't find the monster,' concluded Ross looking over to Avalon. To his surprise, Avalon was staring into space with his mouth slightly open as if he had got six numbers up for the lottery but lost his ticket. 'What is it?' asked Ross. Avalon stared for a few more seconds then turned to Ross and asked.

'Did they find cars, or did you make that bit up?' Ross thought for a moment then stuttered.

'Er, I think, well I'm fairly sure they said a car or cars in the paper why?' Avalon didn't answer. He looked over to Dowd who was typing up some report or other and said abruptly.

'Dowd,' he thought for a second, 'What's your first name by the way? No matter, find the name of the company who did the scans and ask them if they found a car. If they did, get coordinates of where it is.'

'Oh no, not back to the car wrecks,' Ross was shaking his head.

'If there is a car, and it was used in a crime, then it may have forensic material in it. It's a long shot but worth checking,' insisted Avalon. He looked back over to Dowd who was already on the phone. 'Ask if they can send images over too.' Dowd nodded as he began to speak to someone on the phone.

'Listen,' insisted Ross looking across to Avalon, 'if there are any cars down there, they will be ancient. There are barriers up around most of the loch and the places that there aren't, it's too shallow to hide a vehicle.'

'Probably,' nodded Avalon, 'as I said earlier. Never assume.' He then looked up at the coffee machine and added, 'Time to wake up the coffee-pot I think.'
Dowd looked at Avalon and said.

'They're sending over the pictures by email, the guy there seems helpful enough.'

'Great,' said Avalon sorting out the coffee machine, 'at least we will be able to make a better decision once we see some images.' Dowd looked slightly apprehensive as he sat waiting for the images and Avalon noticed as he glanced over.

'Have you got a question PC Dowd?' he asked.

'Er no,' exclaimed Dowd with surprise, 'not really.'

'In my experience,' began Avalon as he switched on the machine and returned to his seat, 'not really usually means yes.'

'Well,' there was a long pause as Dowd fidgeted and wriggled in his seat, 'no, et's not important,' and he looked to his computer screen once more.

'Spit it out man, ask away. It's obvious there is something on your mind.' Dowd once again looked rather uncomfortable and glanced firstly to Ross and then back to Avalon.

'Well, don't take this personally, but...' there was another pause as Dowd seemed to be plucking up the courage to fire off a bombshell of a question, 'there is a really odd smell in here.' Ross gave out a slight noise, a mix of a laugh and a cough. He smiled at Avalon and said.

'We should make PC Dowd up to detective DS Avalon, he clearly has what it takes,' and then looked over to Dowd, 'that terrible smell is the new aftershave of Detective Sergeant Avalon. It's called 'Winds of England' and he bought it especially to impress Sarah Underwood from forensics, but he is so ashamed that someone will find out, he's hidden it in the bottom drawer of the filing cabinet and he calls it evidence.' Dowd looked over to Avalon.

'I... I'm sorry sir, I didnae mean any-' began Dowd but Avalon interrupted.

'It's alright Dowd, Ross is having another one of his little jokes you know, the ones that are devoid of humour.'

'So what es et?' asked Dowd glancing over to the cabinet.

'It was something I thought could be useful but as it turns out, I was mistaken. I think it's time to be rid of it,' admitted Avalon.

'Good,' smiled Ross, 'maybe I will start to get my appetite back.' Avalon was just about to tell Dowd to dispose of it when the PC looked at his screen and said.

'The email from the loch scans company es coming through.' The files were quite large, so it took a few minutes to download. 'The email says one particular image may be worth looking at,' explained Dowd, pointing to his computer screen, 'et says that image four shows what looks like an abandoned vehicle.' Avalon stared at the screen as image four began to open out, it was a colourful image, but he wasn't convinced. Ross stood and went closer to have a look.

'Almost five minutes to download and we get a red and yellow splodge. How does that look like a vehicle?' asked Ross glancing over Dowd's shoulder. Dowd turned his head to explain.

'The email says they think the vehicle is nose down in the mud, that's what all the ripples are in the image.' Avalon stood straight and stretched his back.

'Well it could be, is it worth getting a diver involved though?' he sighed.

'I don't think so, if you look where that is, it's by the main road. There's a traffic barrier all the way down and there has been as far back as I can remember, which means it's an old wreck, it must have got there prior to the barriers being put in place,' explained Ross. Dowd turned again.

'With respect, I don't think that's the case, why would there be mud ripples around et after all these years?' There was silence, Ross shrugged and went back to his desk. Avalon just stared down at the image. After almost a full minute he said.

'Right, let's see if we can get a boat and take a look.' He looked down at Dowd. 'Jot me down the coordinates so we can find it.' He then looked over to Ross. 'Know anyone with a boat?'

'Will the RNLI do?' asked Ross raising his eyebrows slightly.

'RNLI on the loch?' asked Avalon doubtfully. Ross just smiled and nodded then said,

'Oh aye,' and he picked up the phone.

~~~~~~

Avalon found the trip on the RNLI boat quite an

experience. The loch was big, he knew that, but when you were down there on the water, it became very apparent just how big. The waves were larger than he expected and the vastness was slightly overwhelming. The RNLI crew soon found the spot they wanted and carefully headed closer to the shore. When they were sure they were in the correct position, the skipper threw in a weighted buoy and the thing eventually bobbed in a fairly static spot. The wall of the valley here was steep and though Avalon would have liked a closer view, the edge was a sheer rock face. There was no shore to step on, just a few submerged rocks and the skipper of the boat considered it was too dangerous for the boat and crew to get in close. The skipper also explained that where the buoy was, the water was around 200 feet deep.

'How will we be able to find this place from the road?' Avalon asked. One of the crew of the boat explained how to take a simple bearing from three points and they worked out a rough place on the road. Ross said he thought there was a lay-by just above them, so they returned to the jetty and drove down to the place Ross had suggested. They got out of the car and lined up the reference points and considered they were close enough being parked in the lay-by.

'As I said, nothing has gone off the road here, barriers all the way, even in the pull in,' explained Ross. Avalon thrust his hands into his pockets and walked over to the edge of the sheer drop and leaned over the barrier. Beyond that, there was a wire fence to prevent anyone from falling down the sides of the loch. Avalon could easily see the orange buoy bobbing on the inky water below. He moved along the barrier as he looked down but could see no evidence of how a vehicle could get down to the water, but, just as he was about to climb back over the barrier, he saw something that piqued his interest. Some of the rocks on the edge of the drop had scrape marks on them, closer inspection showed the wire fence had a rough repair. He decided to examine the traffic barrier and Ross noticed him bend down to check the metal plates, when he stood he had a smile on his face.

'What?' asked Ross leaning on his BMW.

'This barrier has been tampered with and there are marks, scrapes on the rocks as if a vehicle had come through here.'

'But what about the Armco barrier it's fixed to the ground....' but Ross stopped as he noticed the supporting leg was showing repair to its base. Concrete had recently been poured around the leg as if to fix it in place. Ross examined it and then looked at the bolts and fixings of the barrier. 'It could have been an accident I suppose,' offered Ross.

'Well, that's easy to find out,' replied Avalon. Ross stood and then sighed. 'I know what you are thinking,' continued Avalon, 'but honestly, can you think why someone would go to all this trouble just to dump a car? There's more to this than meets the eye,' he insisted and Ross nodded.

'Yeah, okay. First, we can check with the council to make sure this isn't something they have done, but it looks pretty conclusive. I suppose we need police divers?' he said and then added, 'I don't envy you having to go to DI Lasiter to ask him.' Avalon was aware that Lasiter would be loath to give him any leeway on the burned-out car case but the tampered traffic barrier may hold some sway.

Back at the station, Avalon stood in Lasiter's office with DS Wilson seated in there, already having a grilling from Lasiter on some other case.

'Aye, but why the hell would I waste polis resources on this when essentially et's just a dumped car?' asked the frowning Detective Inspector.

'I'm sure that they wouldn't go to all the trouble of removing a part of the traffic barrier just to dump a car unless there was something in that vehicle that they didn't want us to find,' explained Avalon.

'He has a point,' agreed Wilson, 'removing the barrier and then replacing et es pretty conclusive.'

'You stay out o' this,' demanded Lasiter glaring over at Wilson. He then looked up at Avalon, still wearing a flushed expression and said, 'What ef the council had replaced a section recently?'

'We've already checked it, they haven't,' replied Avalon, 'they had a report that a support leg was damaged, so they removed it and replaced the leg without touching the barrier girders.'

'Aye, course y've checked it,' nodded Lasiter.

'And that wouldn't explain what seem to be clear marks of something scraping the rocks on its way into the loch,' added Avalon. DI Lasiter seemed to be thinking it through.

'Okay, give the Strathclyde Polis a call for advice. They have a training unit and know all about zero visibility diving,' Avalon nodded and turned to leave but Lasiter hadn't finished, 'and you better find somethin' solid after all this.'

Avalon returned to the office to find Frazer was back and sitting on the edge of her desk, chatting away to Ross. She stood as Avalon entered.

'Anything?' he asked.

'Yes, I think I've found him but I didnae want to go en there until I reported back.'

'So where is he?' asked Avalon as he sat down.

'A contact told me he thought he had been seen at his mother's house, so I got the address and sat outside. After about an hour I saw the upstairs curtains move and I'm sure et was him.'

'Did he see you?'

'No,' replied Frazer, 'I'm sure of et but I don't think he'll stay there long. Et's too obvious a place.' Avalon nodded and said.

'He's a crafty one though, the uniform branch checked his mother's house, I saw it on the report,' he tapped his chin with his finger, 'okay, you and Ross bring him in, there's no point in waiting.' With this, Ross and Frazer left. Avalon stood and walked over to the coffee machine then looked down at Dowd. He was reading something on the local news site.

'What's that?' he asked. Dowd looked up as if he hadn't realised he was being watched.

'Oh, er it's about the drums at Drumnadrochit,' he looked back at the screen, 'et seems they were heard again last night.' Avalon poured his coffee and walked back to his seat.

'What do you make of it?' he asked as he sat.

'The drums you mean?' asked Dowd. Avalon nodded as he sipped his coffee. 'Well, et's pretty new to me but everyone talks about et. There are quite a few think there es something spooky about et for sure,' Dowd glanced out of the window for a second and then continued, 'I'm no' sure I'm ready to believe et yet but

263

my dad used to say to me that dragons once lived. He said they lived because people didnae know what else tae call them, so they called them dragons which gave a name tae what they could'nae understand.'

'I don't follow,' said Avalon with a slight frown.

'Well, there was this place near where I was born called Dragon's Beach. The name comes from the medieval period. The legend told of a knight who slew a dragon on the beach. So you have tae ask yersel' where does that come from?' Dowd looked up at Avalon for a moment and then continued, 'imagine a whale was washed up on the sands, but y' didnae know what a whale was, would y' think et was a dragon?' Avalon raised his eyebrows and nodded.

'I see what you're getting at, you think people are seeing a whale and calling it a dragon?'

'Sort of,' nodded Dowd, 'I dunna' think et's a phantom drummer, but I cannae explain et away easily either,' he shrugged. Avalon considered Dowd had a more complex view on the world than would be expected.

'I can see I'm going to have to watch you Dowd, a thinking copper is a rare animal indeed,' smiled the DS.

Avalon walked down to the interview room that, until recently, had been his office. From his position behind the two-way mirror, he could see it was now clear of everything but the table and three chairs. At one side of the table sat Ross and at the other was Anthony Scobie, the look on his face told Avalon Ross was giving him a hard time. He turned to Frazer and asked.

'Has he said anything yet?'

'No Sarge, he has confirmed that the fleece the man at the camp was wearing was blue though and the colour probably matches the evidence found on the body.' Avalon left and entered the main interview room. Scobie looked up but before he could react he just said.

'Mr Scobie.'

'Mr Avalon,' answered the man, then he continued, 'ave jest bin sayin' t' Detective Ross I did'nae-' Avalon interrupted.

'Why did you run Scobie?' he asked.

'I had things to do, I just cannae stay-' Once again Avalon interrupted.

'I asked you if you would keep an eye out, you said you would and you have reneged that contract.'

'What contract Mr Avalon? I just said I would-' Avalon stopped him and continued.

'I don't take kindly to that kind of behaviour Scobie,' Scobie fidgeted on his seat, 'Detective Ross, do you by any chance have the contact number for a certain person who may be looking for Mr Scobie?' Ross answered without taking his gaze from Scobie.

'Aye, I think we have it somewhere.'

'Then let that person know he can come and collect Mr Scobie as we have done with him,' frowned Avalon and he began to leave.

'Wait, wait Mr Avalon,' Scobie sounded perturbed, 'Jesus,' he exclaimed running his hand across his forehead, 'what happened to the good cop bad cop routine?' he asked in a panic. Avalon looked at Scobie.

'Well?' he asked.

'Look, look Mr Avalon,' spluttered Scobie, 'I was tellen' the truth about not knowen who they were but I have heard somethin'.' Scobie wrung his hands, it was clear he was worried.

'Go on,' insisted Ross.

'There's word on the street that twa villains are en the area from Glasgie, I don't have any names but one of 'em es supposed to hae a tattoo o' an eagle on his right hand, an' I saw that tattoo on one o' their hands.'

'Not enough Scobie,' demanded Ross.

'A swear Mr Ross et's all a' know, I swear et, a' do,' pleaded Scobie.

'You double-crossed us once Scobie, I shall not take kindly to it a second time,' spat Avalon.

'A' know that Mr Avalon,' answered Scobie with a worried look. There was a knock at the door. It was Frazer.

'Sarge, have y' got a minute?' she said just leaning in the room. Back in the space behind the mirror, Frazer spoke.

'The man with the eagle tattoo es known t' me.'

'Go on,' said Avalon looking at Scobie through the glass.

'He's a violent offender from Glasgow, a bad man en many respects but other villains bring him en tae get things done,' Avalon looked back to Frazer as she continued, 'his name is Michael Sneaton and he's usually in partnership with his brother Franky. They're both wanted for questioning on several cases but they seem t' evade capture.'

'We need someone to search through their files then,' said Avalon.

'With respect sir, the Bodlien Library don't have enough space t' store their case files.' Avalon nodded.

'Okay, tell Ross to let Scobie go, this thing is suddenly taking another step up. Both of you meet me in the office.'

'So,' began Avalon sitting on the edge of his desk, 'we have a facilitator called Michael Sneaton somehow involved in this case. I want every scrap of every file on him and his brother sifted through. I want to know where they are now and what they're doing,' he turned to PC Dowd, 'Dowd, get me someone to talk to at Strathclyde Water Police, preferably a diver.' Then he turned to Ross. 'You and Frazer dig through any files on Sneaton and his brother.' Ross nodded and asked.

'What about Will Shakespeare?'

'Who?' frowned Avalon.

'The man who runs the UFO camp.'

'Oh, he'll have to wait, this comes first,' insisted Avalon and Ross nodded again and began typing on the computer. Avalon looked out of the window and added, 'It's likely that Sneaton isn't the main man here and if that is true, then this case is more than an abduction that went wrong.' Avalon thought for a moment as he heard Dowd talking on the phone. Eventually, Dowd looked to him and said,

'Sarge, I have a number for you to call,' and the PC handed him a card with the name Sergeant Colin Waters on it. Avalon looked up to Dowd who had obviously seen the irony in the name.

'Thanks,' said Avalon, and he rang the number. Sergeant Waters was the nearest deep-water diver on call for the area and was very helpful to Avalon but he was also very aware of the problems.

'You see Detective Avalon, if the wreck really is at that depth then we will need very specific equipment and being in Loch Ness brings its own set of issues.'

'You mean the visibility issue?' asked Avalon.

'*Well, that's just it. There is no visibility in the loch,*' explained Waters, '*I have dived it many times and even at ten feet you can just about see your hand.*'

'I see the problem,' sighed Avalon.

'*At fifty feet the most powerful lamp would not even let me see my hand, so at that depth, we may as well have our eyes closed,*' added Waters.

'So how do we go about it?' asked Avalon trying to sum up the details.

'*We need a full team,*' said Waters finally, '*I can get a special team together but I will need two in the water and four on the boat,*' Avalon was quiet, it was a lot of people to tie up, '*plus,*' continued Waters, '*we will need a radio link to a special recovery vehicle and the RNLI on site when we are down there.*' Avalon sighed again. '*I'll have to come over and recce the site too, when is best for you?*' Avalon thought that was a good idea and arranged a time the following day. As he placed the phone on the desk he was wondering how this would turn out. If he went ahead with such a large mission and all they found was a rusty 1957 Ford Popular, he was in for a hard time. He stood and walked to the window.

'Problems?' asked Ross. Avalon stared out towards the traffic roundabout, watching shopkeepers, builders, and school teachers, all going about their day and wondered if they had decisions to make. Probably not but he didn't think he would swap.

'Not really,' replied Avalon, 'I'm just hoping that my instinct is right on this one.' Ross thought about this. He had heard that some coppers ran with instinct but *he* never had that. He just worked with facts and made decisions based on sight, sound and smell. Was Avalon one of these instinctual detectives he wondered? Smell! That brought something back.

'So, is it time to be rid of the Dark Ice?' smiled Ross. Avalon looked down at him and then returned to his seat. He then looked over to Dowd who was typing something. He always seemed to be typing.

'Dowd,' said Avalon waiting for the PC to look up from the screen.

'Sir?'

'Go and find some welding gloves and then reach into the bottom drawer of the filing cabinet. There you will find, sealed in two evidence bags, a black bottle,' Avalon waited for this to sink in, 'carefully lift out the bag and take it to the Hazardous Materials section and ask them to dispose of the contents.' Dowd frowned. He realised Avalon and Ross had some sort of humour that he didn't quite understand but this was a little odd. He decided to test the water.

'So what's in the bottle?' he asked. It was Ross who answered.

'Hydrogen peroxide, but it smells like shite.' Dowd sort of got the hint and so he walked over to the cabinet and opened the drawer. As the odour escaped, he knew it was the background smell he kept getting a whiff of and he held up the bag.

'So what es et really?' he asked.

'Dark Ice they call it. The bottle describes it as 'Cologne' but I think they could be prosecuted for giving a false product description. Needless to say, it doesn't sell all that well. You can have it if you like,' smiled Avalon.

'No thanks,' grinned Dowd, 'the missis would throw me out if I stank o' this.'

'It's better than bleach,' announced Ross, 'bleach only kills ninety-nine percent of all known germs. This stuff goes all the way.' Dowd carried the bottle in the bags to the door.

'I'll put et in the bin I think,' and he left.

'You two are insufferable,' said Frazer.

'I can't imagine what you mean,' grinned Ross.

'Poor Dowd, he didnae know ef yer were kidding or no',' she added.

'Dowd has more up his sleeve than you would expect,' smiled Avalon and he suddenly thought of something, 'and while we are on the subject of Dowd, there is something he said earlier that I need to check on.' Avalon looked at Ross. 'Have you still got the number for Arnold Burnside?' For a moment Ross looked vague.

'The name rings a bell,' and he looked through his notebook, 'yeah, it's here.' Avalon copied down the number. 'I thought you had forgotten about all that.' Avalon just smiled then picked up his phone and dialled.

'Mr Burnside?' there was a pause, 'it's Detective Sergeant Avalon from Inverness police, I wonder if I could come over and have a quick chat with you?' Avalon was listening for a moment and then looked at his watch. 'About forty-five minutes?' he then said and, soon after, rang off.

'I'll be back as soon as I can, keep me posted,' he left and made his way to his car.

~~~~~~

The old Ford struggled with the short hill up to Burnside's house just on the edge of Drumnadrochit. The

270

single trackway didn't actually go all the way to the house, so Avalon had to walk about five hundred yards up a dirt path. The house was an old crofter's cottage that was getting ready for some attention and outside there were all manner of rusting relics and bits of metal. He knocked and a small, balding man, probably not that much older than Avalon, answered.

'Are you the polis then?' he asked.

'Yes, Detective Avalon,' and he showed his identification.

'Ah well, ye better come in,' and they entered the house. 'I wondered how long it would take y' to come,' he said as he offered a seat to Avalon.

'Why did you think that Mr Burnside?'

'Well, I'm guessing it's about the drums, I can't imagine you're here about anything else,' replied the man.

'Actually, yes, I was told to come and see you about the drums, it seems that some people think you are a source of local information.' The man stared at Avalon for a long moment without a reply, then he shrugged, and said.

'It's true but I'm surprised anyone around here has anything good to say about me. So how can I help?'

'I'm not sure you can Mr Burnside,' began Avalon, 'and I'm really here just to learn more about the legend.'

'Anyone could have told you that Detective, there was no need to come all this way for what is well known in the area.' Avalon could see there was no easy way to lie to this man, so he changed his approach.

'True, Mr Burnside. I want your opinion on the drums, I was told that you have more information, the sort of information I can't get from anyone else.' Burnside stared into Avalon's eyes and then, as if slightly embarrassed, he stood and walked over to a cabinet.

'Who told you that?' he asked turning to face Avalon.

'You know I can't tell you that,' smiled Avalon. Burnside thought for a moment, then opened the cabinet and showed a bottle to Avalon, which was clearly whisky, and he asked.

'Are you allowed?' Avalon shook his head. He wasn't one to refuse a single malt even if he didn't know exactly what it was but this time, he had to.

'Do you mind?' asked Burnside apologetically.

'No, of course not, you continue,' replied Avalon, and the man poured a measure then sat.

'Slange,' announced the man and Avalon resisted the urge to say 'sludge' and just replied,

'Good health,' and attempted to imagine how it tasted.

'Legends abound in these parts Detective, it's part of who we are. Those of us that know our heritage know why those legends remain with us,' Avalon leaned back a little. The man continued, 'our history isn't in the Jacobite rebellion and the Clearances, it isn't at Culloden or Bannockburn either. It's not even in the memory of the like of Wallace or Bruce.' He broke off for another sip, 'It's all about the land. It's about the hill, the glen, and the lochs. The land of the mountain and the flood as Hamish Maccunn so brilliantly put it.' Avalon had no idea what he meant, but he nodded and listened. 'Those legends abound because we have lost our way as a nation, as a people.' He stopped for a moment to take in

Avalon's reaction but Avalon was a master at hiding his feelings as his ex-wife could testify. Burnside continued, 'Nessie, the Loch Ness monster, is what we are left with, that and 'usquebaugh', the dram,' he held up his glass to make plain what he meant, 'ask a foreigner what comes to mind when you say 'Scotland'. These two things are why the Japanese, the Americans, and every other nation come here. Only when they arrive, do they fall in love with the other side of Scotland, the important side, the land... the country,' he paused in thought, 'and maybe sometimes its people, though I can't comment on that.' He quickly finished off his drink and pointed to the bottle on the cabinet.

'You sure you won't join me?' Avalon shook his head again, though he knew he would have enjoyed the drink more than the lecture. Burnside poured himself another and continued, 'My own name means Brown Wolf Hill and is likely a legend in itself, so, as you can see, legend is even in our names. And look at your name Detective, inextricably connected to English legend.' Avalon was beginning to think the man had nothing to say and was possibly one of those eccentrics that end up being arrested because they went shopping without any clothes on. He was just about to leave when Burnside changed tack. 'So Detective, when someone is tasked with preserving a legend, it is a very great office indeed.' Burnside sat once more.

'I don't follow Mr Burnside, I understand from my background checks that you are a partner in a Loch Ness business but I don't see how that makes you a curator of a legend. Selling 'I love Nessie' hats seems to cheapen it to my mind.' Avalon wanted the man to know that he had checked up on him, so probably knew of his past misdemeanours. The man nodded slowly.

'I do have a tourist interest in the area, I agree but what I know and what I do, are very different things.'

'As to what you know Mr Burnside, what do you know about the drum that seems to be heard on a regular basis?' The man seemed to recoil slightly, and he glanced away for a second. Avalon was tired of the charade, he wanted to leave, but he knew the man was hiding something. Burnside looked back to Avalon, finished the second drink in one gulp, and then said.

'I *know* it's not the drum making those noises,' he stood and moved to an internal door, from where he beckoned Avalon. As Avalon approached, the man barred his way and said.

'What I am about to show you must not be told to another person.' Avalon wanted to laugh but he nodded instead. 'Only a handful of very trusted people have been in this room Detective Avalon, I am only allowing you in because I think there is great danger in this.' Inside, the room was a large collection of artefacts of many sorts, many local interests but all very Scottish. Kilts, swords, armour, signs, paintings, some of which looked very old and in the corner, stood a large glass case which held something that took Avalon aback. He gulped slightly and asked.

'Is that the real thing?'

'It is Detective, and that is where it has sat for fifteen years.' Inside the case was an old drum. The hoops and the rope, which tensioned them, were worn and rotted but the main body of the drum was in reasonably good condition and it showed a faint but colourful coat of arms. He moved closer and read the motto but it made little sense to him.

'The skins were removed seventy years ago to prevent it from ever being played and it has remained hidden since. So y' see Detective, it simply *can't* be played,' he made great emphasis on the word 'can't'.

'So who would want to make people think it *was* being played?' asked Avalon.

'That, I cannot say,' replied Burnside shaking his head, 'but I don't think their motives have any merit.'

'Some say, that if the loch is scanned and there is proof that the monster doesn't exist, the drum will take over as the reason the tourists will come,' suggested Avalon. Burnside allowed a slight smile.

'Well Detective, for a year or so some people have maintained that Nessie has died as there have been no sightings. Some say she was never there. It hasn't stopped people coming. I don't think the drum could replace what the monster has brought to the area even if we wanted it to.'

'You're probably correct,' nodded Avalon, 'for someone who collects legends, you seem fairly non-committal towards the monster.' Burnside shrugged slightly.

'I find that you can't change what people believe in very easily Detective, so I don't try. I would, however, say that certainly, here in Scotland, some people may find that the 'Brollachan' isn't as dead as they think it is.' Avalon was about to ask what that was when his phone rang.

'Avalon,' he said.

'*You need to come back,*' It was Ross, '*we have been looking through the files on Sneaton and found something.*'

'Go on,' replied Avalon.

'*Sneaton was considered to be part of a gang that terrorised Glasgow three years ago. They were never caught though. Over a ten-month period, they robbed six security vans.*'

'Have you told Lasiter?' he asked.

'*Not yet,*' replied Ross, '*that's your call.*'

'Okay, keep it quiet until I get there, I'm on my way,' replied Avalon, and he put the phone away. 'Well, thanks for the information Mr Burnside, I have to go.' As Avalon quickly walked down the dirt track, he was sure he heard Burnside call out.

'Beware the Brollachan, Detective.'

Chapter Eight

The move from fishing to farming is quite a
change of direction and there are few people who would
consider it, but Daniel Cross knew he needed to get out
of an industry that he considered was entering a final
phase of a constant decline. He had owned his own
vessel and though he didn't like the idea of laying off his
crew, he knew that the time had come and no other
decision was realistic. He had considered selling up and
moving back to Aberdeen where he had been raised but
instead, with the money from selling the boat and a small
mortgage, he bought a smallholding and leased some
land close to the banks of Loch Ness. Unfortunately for
Daniel, farming wasn't quite what he expected and he
and his wife found themselves regretting the change and
looking for a way out. An opportunity arose when he
saw another boat for sale, not a fishing vessel but an
unusual river cruise boat that was in reasonable
condition. With the help of a friend who was already
running sea fishing trips from a small vessel, he
renovated the boat and had it moved to the Caledonian
Canal near Loch Ness. His friend eventually became his
partner in the venture, which they called 'Moray

Historical Cruises'. He rented out most of the land he had leased except for a small plot that had a large barn that provided a perfect repair shop for his boat, having mains power laid on. They even sold the smallholding to pay for the venture and moved to a smaller house just outside Inverness. The business didn't make the sort of money he was used to but he was back on a boat and with a well-rehearsed 'patter' with a touch of humour, he and his business partner had a pleasant time taking tourists on Loch Ness cruises. They provided an interesting and relaxed cruise, pointing out all the historical places and a few 'Nessie' legends.

The repair barn was just off the main road and on occasions, Daniel would stop off to check around the place. On one of these occasions he parked his Land Rover in the entrance and went to climb under the bar gate to walk the five-hundred or so yards to the barn. As he ducked under the gate, he noticed the chain that fastened the bar to the post was not in its usual place. He wondered if his business partner had been, but on closer examination, he saw that the chain had been cut with bolt cutters or similar. He rang his partner just in case he had been there but forgotten his keys. He told Daniel he hadn't and he should report it to the police but Daniel decided to check the barn first. He walked up the slope but as he neared the large door, he could see the lock was still in place. This too, however, had been cut through. He picked up a short piece of pipe, just in case there was still someone there and carefully entered the barn. To his surprise, it seemed almost as it had last time he was there some weeks previous. Nothing was missing and nothing had been left but it was clear someone had been in the place for some time. There was a smell that wasn't usual and there were bits and pieces of metal here and there. He decided to look in the cupboard at the rear but as he neared it he noticed even the small welding set was still where it should be. Inside the cupboard the few tools he kept there remained, though the angle grinder was missing its grinding disc. He looked back into the barn and wondered what had happed there. On the ground, there were signs of a vehicle being there recently as a few drops of engine oil testified to it, but nothing else seemed out of place.

He phoned the police who asked the usual questions about what had been stolen but as to be expected they thanked him for ringing and said that though they would record it as a break-in it was doubtful anyone would attend, as they were very busy. He was given an incident number and was told to ring them back if he did find anything had been taken.

He walked back to his vehicle thinking that he would have to go into town to buy a new lock for the barn and find some chain for the gate. He considered cutting a bit of old anchor chain to use, as the boat had a small anchor even though there was hardly anywhere on the loch it could be used, but old habits die-hard. The new lock was fitted the following day and a small length of chain was replaced on the gate and that was it. Daniel put it down to someone stealing a car and using his barn to break into the boot before they took it on the moors and set it ablaze. It was with some considerable surprise therefore when a car pulled into the tiny car park at the jetty at the marina and two men in suits came looking for him. As they approached, Daniel knew they were the police, and he said so to his partner.

'Good mornin',' offered the larger of the two,

'we're looking for Mr Daniel Cross.' Daniel suddenly knew his day was going to be odd.

'That's me,' he said.

'Mr Cross, I'm Detective Sergeant Douglas and this es Detective Norris, you reported that your barn had been broken into yesterday, is that correct?'

'Yes,' nodded Daniel, 'but as I mentioned on the phone, there was nothing taken.'

'That's as may be Mr Cross but we need to see that barn ef y' don't mind.'

'What, now Detective? I'm just about to start work.'

'If you don't mind Mr Cross, this es very important,' insisted the police officer. Daniel looked to his business partner, who nodded and told him he could manage and then Daniel went with the two detectives to the barn. He opened the bar gate, and they drove up toward the barn stopping the car a hundred or so yards from the building. As they got out of the car, they looked on the ground.

'Have you driven up here Mr Cross?'

'No, I usually leave the truck at the gate and walk up.' The detective nodded and walked into the field.

'I'd appreciate et ef you would follow me and take care not to walk on the track.' Daniel followed still wondering what was going on and when they reached the barn door he was asked to remove the new lock.

'Where es the old lock?' asked the police officer.

'It's on the bench in the barn along with the old chain from the gate why?' The detective didn't answer, he just carefully opened the door and took a peep inside.

'Are there lights?' the detective asked.

'Yes, just inside on the left.' The detective

280

carefully stepped in and turned on the lights though there was quite a lot of sunlight streaming in. He asked Daniel to stay by the door and carefully moved a little inside the barn and looked around. He pulled out a biro from his pocket and moved one of the shards of metal on the floor a little then from his crouching position asked.

'Have you touched or moved anything other than the locks and chain Mr Cross?' Daniel shook his head and replied.

'No, I just changed the lock and decided to clean up at some later date. What's this about Detective?' The detective stood and returned to the doorway switching off the lights. He nodded to the other officer and said.

'Thes es it, call et in.' The other officer took out a phone and rang a number.

'Hello, DC Norris B section. Can you send a SOCO team straight away?' He then tried his best to explain exactly where they were, as DS Douglas began to explain more details to Daniel.

'I'm sorry Mr Cross but this area es going to be off limits for a few days and...' he broke off as his phone rang, 'Allo, DS Douglas.' There was a pause and then he said, 'yes sir et looks like et, torn up bits of metal, most showing grey paint too.' He then looked as if he was listening and then ended with, 'aye, will do.' The detective replaced his phone in his pocket and then turned to Daniel again. 'Sorry about that Mr Cross, as I was saying, we are sealing off y'r barn for a few days as et es possible that this es a crime scene.'

'A crime scene? What crime would that be?' asked Daniel in utter surprise.

'I'm not at liberty to say and I would appreciate et ef both you and your business partner keep this quiet until our investigations are complete.'

'Of course,' replied Daniel with a startled look. The detective took a statement from him and as soon as a marked police car arrived he was taken back to where they picked him up. Daniel sat on the little bench at the jetty waiting for his boat to return from its first trip of the day and he considered what possible crime could have been committed in the barn.

Avalon didn't bother parking his car at the rear of the building, as it wasn't worth the hassle of going through the security gates, so he left it at the front of the police station instead. He was going to have to meet the police diver later and no doubt there would be other things he would have to sort out too. Once again he was a little early, so he was the first in the office but with the smell of fresh coffee invading the room he began to feel a little better. Gradually the office came alive with its inhabitants and as usual, Ross was the last to arrive.

'Jeez, you look worse than me today, what have you been up to?' asked Ross staring at Avalon.

'Oh, I didn't sleep too well, I'm on a camp bed until Friday as I can't get a proper bed delivered until then.'

'So you moved in then?' nodded Ross.

'Yeah, it feels great apart from the bed. The B&B was excellent, but it isn't quite the same as your own place.' Avalon thought back to the conversation he had with Jeanie. She had told him if he ever needed a place to stay again or somewhere for a visiting friend to just give her a call. If he was honest with himself he missed her fussing in the mornings. Breakfast just hadn't been the same, no full English or Scottish on the menu, just cornflakes.

'No, I can see that but I like to be pampered, I think I would have stayed at the B&B,' shrugged Ross. 'Not being able to sleep gave me time to think though,' said Avalon.

'Oh aye, there's always room for something new,' quipped Ross, 'is this about Sneaton?' he added. The previous evening, Avalon had returned from Drumnadrochit to find his team scouring through old records of the security van thefts that it was alleged Sneaton was involved with. They had decided that the Modus operandi was very similar to the robbery in Inverness and they had decided to let Lasiter know about it this morning so he could hand over the information to DI Davies and his team.

'No, it's not, it's about the Abriachan murder,' replied Avalon.

'So how did your insomnia help then?' asked Ross in what Avalon considered a slightly sarcastic tone.

'It's odd how when you are laid awake at night your thoughts seem clear and yet in the cold light of day they seem fanciful,' he eventually said.

'So, do we get tae hear or no?' asked Frazer slightly impatiently.

'I was trying to find a link to all the cases we have here and I couldn't find any, but then just as I was about to get up to make a drink, I had a thought that did seem to link most of the crimes.' He watched Dowd get up to pour everyone a coffee then continued. 'There is one aspect of most of these crimes that does link them and that is evidence or rather lack of evidence.'

'Not all that surprising, crooks these days understand about forensics and try to mitigate it,' shrugged Ross.

'Yes, but to the extent of the car wrecks?' asked Avalon, 'whoever left those cars burning did everything to cover their tracks and particularly to leave no DNA.'

'I refer the honourable Detective Avalon to my previous statement,' quipped Ross in an English accent.

'Then there is the theft of paintings at the magician's house, looking through the notes there isn't a scrap of evidence at the scene, no footprints no forensics.' Once again Ross shrugged and said.

'Crooks are getting clever.'

'But then there's the incident at the UFO camp, two men witnessed by Anthony Scobie and a few others dressed in boiler suits, why?' asked Avalon.

'Because,' began Frazer, 'like forensic suits they prevent a great deal of evidence being left behind?' Avalon pointed to her and said.

'Exactly, and if they were trying to prevent forensic evidence what else would they be wearing?' Ross sat upright with a start.

'Gloves,' replied Ross, 'and if they were wearing gloves that lying toe rag Scobie wouldn't have seen a tattoo on the hand of one of them.' There was silence for a few seconds.

'Jeez, then we have tae find him again? It looks like he knew who they were without seein' their hands,' sighed Frazer.

'It could be but either way, it seems like Mr Scobie is either leading us a dance or he knows more than he is admitting to,' agreed Avalon. Frazer turned to Dowd.

'PC Dowd, issue a BOLO on Anthony Scobie again, let's see if the uniform can find him,' she looked at Avalon, 'so why wis he hidin' up at the camp anyhows?' Avalon looked over to Ross.

'Well, he told us he had sold some dodgy gear to Robby Bee the week previous, and it didn't work so Bain was gunning for his money,' explained Ross.

'That's not possible,' announced Frazer, 'Robert Bain has been charged for aggravated assault an' he would be on remand at that time.' Ross looked over to Avalon who dropped his head into his hands. He sighed and then looked up.

'Okay, I cocked up, so let's find this little shit and bring him in. This time DC Frazer can interview him.' Just then the door swung open and in walked Lasiter.

'We are not having the meeting this mornin', DI Davies and his team are too busy but I want all C Section for a meeting.' They all nodded. 'What have y' got for me?' he asked with a tone that said there better be something. Avalon sighed again and then said.

'We have a lead in the murder case, it involves Anthony Scobie but we don't quite know what his involvement is yet.'

'I thought y' had brought him en?' said Lasiter.

'We had but didn't have anything to charge him with but new evidence has come up,' replied Avalon though he knew it wasn't exactly the truth.

'I need some progress on this, I dinna want any more ball chewing from the Chief,' he glared. Avalon tried to change the subject slightly.

'The missing person is resolved as the person has been found alive and well, the attack on the woman that Ross was working on has made quite a bit of headway thanks to help from DC Frazer and we expect an arrest soon.'

'Aye, et turns out et was her boyfriend, crime o' passion they call et. I can't see much passion en et though,' added Frazer.

'As to the abandoned car in the loch,' continued Avalon, 'I'm meeting a police diver later to find out what he will need for the recovery.'

'Let's hope et's a rope and a hook. I dunna want a large bill for this one,' frowned Lasiter. Avalon nodded knowing that wouldn't be the case. 'Well, fair enough, we seem to be making headway. DI Davies's team have had some luck too,' Lasiter moved towards the door and turned, 'a diligent PC noticed that a reported break-in looked suspicious. Et was at a large barn where nothing was taken so he informed B section about et. Turns out the security van was taken there t' be cut into and robbed. They found shards of steel with the same colour paint as the van and we're having et analysed with the paint from one of their other vans.'

'We think, we may have a link with that,' cut in Avalon.

'Oh aye, what's that?'

'We have been looking at possible suspects for the murder and a known fixer has been reported in the area,' Avalon stopped, remembering that the evidence came from Scobie, was this relevant now?

'Go on,' insisted Lasiter. Avalon considered how to word his next sentence.

'Well, we don't have any confirmation but the suspect we are looking for is Michael Sneaton. He usually works with his brother and they are suspected of being involved with similar offenses.' Lasiter looked upbeat about the information.

'I've heard the name, I'll look into et but DI

Davies has his sights set on someone else,' nodded Lasiter.

'Anyone we know?' asked Ross.

'Aye, well enough. Billy the Fish,' answered Lasiter. Ross frowned.

'A bit ambitious for Billy I would have thought,' added Ross.

'Et es but the way et's lookin', he could be involved,' replied Lasiter.

'Who the hell is Billy the Fish?' asked Avalon wondering if he had heard correctly.

'Ross will fill y' in on Billy, in the meantime get me confirmation that this Sneaton es involved,' and he turned and left. There was a communal sigh in the room.

'He seems in a good mood today,' quipped Ross.

'He's under the cosh, so is DI Davies,' replied Avalon, 'Davies particularly and when I saw him this morning he looked worse than Ross after an all-night session.' Ross just frowned. 'Well team, let's get back to it,' added Avalon changing the subject. He had heard plenty of rumours about Davies mainly suggesting that his marriage was on the rocks. Avalon was sympathetic there and he thought it was better to change the subject, rather than airing Davies' dirty washing. 'So who is Billy the Fish?' he asked. Ross began to explain.

'William Johnston, builder, property developer and crook, in no order of preference,' Ross leaned back and put his feet on his desk, 'he made a small fortune buying up land and building houses on it, crap houses that fell apart, I might add, but he made money. Then he was accused of building without permission and then managed to bribe his way out of it, but it drew attention to his dealings. Eventually, he was sent down for fraud and tax evasion and when he came out he was broke.'

'Aye he was, but he soon found his feet again didn't he?' added Frazer, 'he must have had cash stashed away 'cos he went straight back into business.'

'He had high connections though,' admitted Ross.

'What do you mean?' asked Avalon.

'Well, when he made his money, he would mix with the great and the good. He had loads of celebrity friends. He played golf with celebrities and dined out with them. If someone had their picture in the papers, you could almost guarantee he would be in the shot with them,' explained Ross.

'Most of 'em turned away from him when he was sent down,' added Frazer, 'but there were a few that didnae, some stayed loyal, en private anyways.'

'So why Billy the Fish?' asked Avalon curious about the name.

'Et comes from an adult comic, it's a character in one of the regular stories,' explained Frazer, 'he got the name because he opened a Koi carp centre and put most of his energy into that.'

'Aye, that and crime,' added Ross.

'So he's still at it then,' asked Avalon with a frown.

'Probably, but no one has managed to pin anything down,' admitted Ross, 'he's gone back into building too, Creative Construction he calls it.'

'I thenk et's more like Creative Accounting ef y' ask me,' frowned Frazer. Ross nodded with a smile.

The three of them went to the meeting, which was held in the old C section office. It was a little larger than Avalon's room but still too small to hold the expanded section. The meeting was for Lasiter to bring everyone up to speed about all the cases that the sections were working on and as always there were a few questions after. All in all it was a quick meeting and had some positive results for a change. Lasiter was still digging at Avalon though for more on the Abriachan murder and so as they returned to their office Avalon set up the rest of the day's work.

'Megan, I want you and PC Dowd to work on tracking down Scobie. We really need that snipe nosed...' he broke off, he didn't want them to see the fact that he had believed Scobie was telling the truth and was angry about letting him go, 'well, I don't need to tell you how important it is.' He turned to glance at Ross. 'Ross and me will meet the police diver at the loch.'

'Hang on,' interrupted Ross, 'how come she is Megan and I am Ross?'

'Sorry,' said Avalon in fake shock, 'did I not use your first name?' For a second he glanced to Frazer and then turned to leave. 'Come on then Diana,' and he walked out.

'Why do there have to be so many famous people with my name?' he sighed as he followed.

As they exited the building Avalon noticed there were two PCs by his car and one was writing something on a notepad. The officer writing noticed Avalon and Ross approach, he also noticed the keys in Avalon's hand.

'Problem?' asked Avalon. There was hesitation from the officer, a moment in time when he made two and two into eight and he quickly put the notepad into his pocket.

'Er, no Sergeant, we just er... we thought...' he made a half-hearted attempt to point at the car.

'You thought it had been abandoned didn't you Hendricks?' smiled Ross. Avalon visibly quickened his pace and got in the car. PC Hendricks stuttered and stammered an apology but Ross intervened as he too got into the car. 'No need to apologise officer, you were only doing your duty. Pity you didn't have time to have it removed.' They drove off leaving Hendricks wondering how he would explain this incident to the desk sergeant.

'I can't believe they thought it had been abandoned,' hissed Avalon.

'Well, it's not their fault, it could just be your parking and not the state of the car,' grinned Ross.

'We can't all afford a new BMW,' demanded Avalon.

'Oh, I can't afford it,' replied Ross, 'but neither can I afford the erosion of my self-esteem.'

'It's just a car,' he glanced quickly over to Ross, 'I don't think self-esteem comes into it.'

'You could afford it anyway, I bet that old bike of yours would fetch a bob or two,' said Ross.

'I had thought about selling it, I don't use it anywhere near enough but I don't think it's worth as much as you think,' Avalon replied.

'We could have a look on the internet when we get back, you ought to sell it and enjoy the money while you can,' suggested Ross, and he turned towards Avalon, 'you could be dead tomorrow.'

'Charming,' frowned Avalon, 'you certainly know how to lighten a conversation. Have you always been this miserable?' Ross turned back to the road in front of them.

'I'm always smiling inside,' he replied.

'Talking of smiling,' said Avalon in an effort to get away from the subject of his car, 'Frazer seemed in a better mood today, she was smiling as we left.'

'True,' nodded Ross, 'the last time I saw her smile she had her boot on someone's throat.'

'Well, they probably deserved it knowing Frazer,' replied Avalon turning onto the main road.

'Maybe, but the postman had only popped in to ask if we knew where Cavendish Street was,' said Ross without so much as a grin. Soon, they turned onto the A82 and headed off towards Drumnadrochit and the RNLI station. As they drove along the road, Ross looked down to a CD case on the glove shelf.

'Good film that,' said Ross picking it up.

'What is?' asked Avalon.

'Rush, it's about James Hunt and Nikki Lauder isn't it?'

'No,' smiled Avalon, 'it's a music CD, a Canadian rock band.' Ross stared at the case then said.

'Never heard of them,' and he began to take the CD out of the case.

'What are you doing?' asked Avalon.

'I'm going to listen to it.'

'The back speakers don't work,' replied Avalon prodding his thumb towards the rear of the car.

'The front ones do fine.'

'The left one makes a rattling noise when it's turned up,' added Avalon.

'I'm glad to see you take your music seriously,' frowned Ross placing the CD into the slot. He waited a moment and suddenly the disc came back out.

'Ah, it does that, you have to hold it in until it stops trying to eject,' explained Avalon. Ross just shook his head and pressed the disc back in. After several attempts to eject the offending CD the machine settled down to the idea it was required to fulfil its role as a CD player and sound could be heard through the speakers. Ross wound up the volume button and sat in stunned silence. It was probably no more than half a mile when Ross looked over to Avalon and pointing to the CD player asked.

'Is this playing backwards?'

'This, my friend,' smiled back Avalon tapping the steering wheel to the rhythm of the song, 'is music the likes of we shall not hear again.'

'Too right,' said Ross pressing the eject button. To his horror, the machine now held on to the disc and continued playing. 'How do I switch it off? Do I have to open the door or the window or something?' Avalon reached down and pressed the power button. The sound continued for a moment and then with a strange hollow echo, faded out.

By the time they reached the jetty of the RNLI station, Sergeant Waters and his assistant had arrived and as soon as the skipper was ready they set off to the spot where the orange buoy bobbed on the surface of Loch Ness. It wasn't that far from the jetty but there was quite a breeze and so one of the crew held on to the buoy to keep the boat on station. Waters and his assistant looked at the area and took photographs of the shore, a particular problem area for Waters.

'We're gonna need some sort of platform erecting on the water's edge because we won't be able to stand there without it.' Avalon nodded, 'More expense,' he thought then said,

'We have to do this at night but that isn't going to be an issue as you have zero visibility anyway.' Waters considered this.

'Yeah fine, but you'll need lights at the water's edge and at the top of the rock face.' He then turned to the skipper of the RNLI boat and asked about the depth and he informed the diver that after looking at the charts they had a depth of forty-five metres. Waters nodded, he seemed reasonably happy about this. Then he turned back to Avalon and asked.

'When do you want to do this?'

'As soon as we can, I have to okay everything with the Chief and we need to set up a road closure for the recovery vehicle so as soon as we can get everything in place.' Waters nodded.

'Okay, I'll keep a team on standby so let me know if it's off so I can stand them down.' When they had returned to the jetty and were back on dry land, Waters asked,

'So what's the story? What are you expecting to find?' Avalon shrugged.

'We're not altogether sure, but the vehicle may contain forensic material that may be linked to a case we're working on.'

'Hmm, seems a lot of work for an abandoned car,' shrugged Waters.

'They removed a section of traffic barrier to get it there,' replied Avalon raising his eyebrows.

'Ah,' exclaimed Waters, 'that explains why you are pulling out the stops, I did wonder.' As they parted company, Avalon promised to keep him and the RNLI informed and then he and Ross returned to the car and to off back to the station. As they sat in the car, Avalon put the keys in the ignition and turned to Ross with an expectant stare.

'What?' asked Ross, frowning at Avalon's apparent glare.

'You might want to cover your ears,' and he turned on the ignition. Before Ross could register the meaning of Avalon's warning a loud, high-pitched screeching sound came from the car speakers before the CD was catapulted out with the force of a child ejecting its first olive. As they walked up the stairs towards their office, Ross was still feeling the shock from the terrifying experience of Avalon's CD player, but he tried to put it from his mind and asked,

'When are you going to let DI Lasiter know about all the kit we need down at the loch?'

'I don't honestly know, I'm having second thoughts about it,' replied Avalon, 'I mean, what if it is just an empty, abandoned car?'

'You said it yourself, why would someone go to all that trouble to dump a car unless there was something in it they didn't want finding?' insisted Ross. Avalon nodded and entered the office.

'Where's DC Frazer?' asked Avalon as he entered. Dowd looked up from his computer.

'Oh, she's gone t' see someone about tracking down Scobie, she left me looking through some CCTV footage.'

'What are you looking for?' asked Ross.

'Scobie. This es the footage from the shop opposite his mother's house, she wants me tae see ef he went back after leaving here,' replied Dowd.

'She doesn't mess about does she?' sighed Ross.

'She's thinking on her feet, she's a woman of action,' smiled Avalon as he sat and checked his emails.

'Aye, that's the trouble, she probably beat up the shopkeeper to get those tapes,' replied Ross pointing to Dowd's screen.

'You are too harsh on her, she isn't that bad,' insisted Avalon.

'You wait until it's her turn to buy the milk for the coffee, you'll see a different side to her.' Avalon shook his head and leaned back in his chair.

'I tend to agree with DS Ross sir,' said Dowd, 'as she left, she seemed very angry and said et was to be hoped that the local PCs got t' him before her, or she might cut 'es balls off.' Avalon tried to ignore it and asked.

'So have you spotted Scobie then?'

'No, not yet sir,' replied Dowd. Avalon stretched his legs under the table and got ready for a long afternoon of paperwork.

When his reports were filed he decided to turn to the issue of the drums, after seeing the so-called 'Culloden Drum' his interest in the sounds were revived.

'Where is the file you told me about some days ago,' he asked Ross, 'the one that dates the sounds of the drum and the dates of crimes?' Ross looked up for a second and then said.

'It's not in the main database. Look under local, unsolved, and then look for a file called 'Cozy Powell,' he looked up again and added, 'one word, no capitals.'

'You have to be joking,' said Avalon.

'No,' replied Ross, 'that's what it's called. DS Wilson started it and it was he who named it,' Ross looked back to his computer before adding, 'he said as it was about a drummer then it should have a drummer's name.' Avalon shook his head in amazement and searched for the file. As it opened, he noticed it was a spreadsheet with dates in the column and coloured boxes for the dates the drums were heard with crimes tagged in the next column. It was a long table but Avalon looked at the detail noting what types of crimes were committed, how serious and how often the drums were wrong. Avalon heard Ross stand and walk around the small room.

'Found anything?' asked Ross. Avalon wrinkled his nose and slowly shook his head.

'Not really, there are so many non-conforming patterns that you can only come to the conclusion that it is totally random.'

'Didn't you find anything out from your trip to see Burnside?' asked Ross resting on the edge of Frazer's desk.

'Nothing,' confirmed Avalon, 'the man is a little eccentric but I'm sure of two things, the first is that he isn't involved, the second is that the sounds heard are not made by the drum.'

'Well, I always assumed that it wasn't the actual drum. It must have been lost years ago,' shrugged Ross. Avalon didn't comment, he thought of telling Ross but Dowd was in the room and he thought it best to keep quiet for the moment.

'So we have to consider why someone would want to sound off a drum at all,' he said.

'You still think there is a connection?' asked Ross.

'There's no doubt. The drum began about the

296

same time that this crime-wave started. What is clear is that the drum and the crime-wave are connected. We just don't see the connection yet,' insisted Avalon. Ross folded his arms and turned his head to look out of the window. It had begun to rain.

'Personally,' began Ross, 'for what it's worth I think you are right,' and he turned back to face Avalon. 'There isn't an option to it, but how to work this to a conclusion is a different matter.' Avalon nodded in agreement.

'So let's go back through this,' Avalon suggested, 'a crime wave begins, a drum is heard, sometimes when a crime is about to be committed, sometimes after. The person or persons unknown who sound off the drum must be in contact with the perpetrators, that is clear.'

'What if?' suggested Ross unfolding his arms, 'they are one and the same?' he hesitated a moment, 'and that is why there is inconsistency to the times of the drum?'

'Possibly,' agreed Avalon, he noticed Dowd had stopped working at his computer and was listening in, 'in that case, those same persons would not be able to predict crimes that were committed by other, independent offenders.' Ross also nodded at this. He walked to the rear of Avalon's seat. 'What if we take out all solved crimes from the list? Does that show anything,' he asked. Avalon didn't have the information needed for such a filter but he considered it was a good explanation.

'It could be the case but that would be difficult, as some of these crimes are quite petty and likely we won't know the outcome.' Ross thrust his hands into his pockets and returned to his desk. He sat on the edge of it for a moment and then once more, folded his arms. Avalon looked back to the dates and noticed something.

'Has no one been updating this file?' he asked.

'O-K was doing it. She agreed to take it over as, in her position, she tends to know what new crimes have been logged, she also has a friend who lives in the Drumnadrochit area,' explained Ross.

'Well, she hasn't updated it for a few days that's for sure,' frowned Avalon, 'the last entry is Wednesday.'

'It's not like it's official, or even her job,' admitted Ross, 'but it's not usual for her to miss something. She's probably too busy to update the file.' Avalon picked up the phone.

'Hello, it's DS Avalon, is PC Kirk about?' He paused as he listened, 'if you would please,' and he put down the phone. 'She's on the other phone,' he explained looking at Ross who stood and went to the map on the wall.

'You know, if we are even close and there is some connection with all this,' said Ross in an unusually serious way, 'it's going to mean that we have been made fools of.'

'What do you mean?' asked Avalon knowing the answer but wanting confirmation from Ross.

'Whoever is pulling the strings here, have had us running in circles, splitting sections, bringing in detectives, and all to cope with the extra workload that they are creating.'

'I sort of suspected it from the start,' frowned Avalon.

'So why didn't you say something?' asked Ross glaring over at Avalon.

'I'm the new boy remember,' glared Avalon,

'anyway, I did. I wanted to pursue the car wrecks cases, the protection rackets and the drums. Remember the 'Black Ice'?' Ross lowered his head a little.

'True, you did keep on about that, and all I did was complain,' Ross stood and paced in the little space that was available, 'so what now?' he eventually asked. There was a slight knock at the door.

'Come in,' called Avalon, it was Kirk, 'ah, PC Kirk, you could have just rung.'

'Och, it doesn't matter, I need the exercise. What do y' want Sergeant?' Kirk had resumed her 'local friendly' accent.

'I noticed you have stopped updating the,' he hesitated as he recalled the name of the spreadsheet, 'Cozy Powell file, any reason?' he asked. Kirk simply shrugged and said.

'Nothing to update.'

'You mean you haven't been informed of any further sounds?'

'Not exactly Sergeant, there have been no further crimes to add and, as far as I know, there have been no other drums reported. It's been quiet for some days.'

'How many days?' asked Ross.

'Well,' replied Kirk trying to think of the last record, 'I would say since the security van was robbed.'

'Oh,' sighed Avalon, and he looked over to Ross. 'Are you thinking what I am thinking?' asked Ross with a surprised look.

'Probably,' replied Avalon and before Ross could say anymore, he turned to Kirk and added, 'thank you PC Kirk,' and she turned and left. Avalon then looked at Dowd and said.

'Give me a call as soon as DC Frazer returns, we

299

have something to sort out.' Then he looked at Ross and nodded to the door. Outside the police station, Avalon walked up to his car and climbed inside. Ross then joined him in the passenger seat.

'Where are we going?' he asked.

'Nowhere. We need to talk,' said Avalon winding down his window, 'I'm guessing you have come to the same conclusion, that all this was set up by someone who was planning the security van job.'

'Aye, I was, but it seems a lot of trouble to go to for a security van robbery,' said Ross, 'in Glasgow, they just pull a shooter out and rob it,' he added.

'This isn't Glasgow and we are not looking at the run-of-the-mill villain I suspect,' frowned Avalon.

'Meaning?'

'The amount of planning here is off the scale. The way that most of the crimes look petty but are designed not to leave evidence, tells me that whoever planned it, couldn't afford to lose any of his team to something like a ram-raid,' insisted Avalon.

'Makes sense, it would also raise suspicion before the main event,' agreed Ross. Avalon sighed, then said.

'Something that Sarah Underwood said has now come back to haunt me,' Avalon tapped the steering wheel nervously, 'she said the methods to remove evidence in the car wrecks was amateur, or maybe she said naïve. Either way, it makes me wonder if whoever is in charge is new to this size of crime.' Ross just shook his head.

'No, that doesn't make sense, they have had us running around at their every whim,' he insisted, 'the planning, the timing, and the methods have been fairly faultless.'

'Not so,' insisted Avalon, 'take the murder at Abriachan, that was a miscalculation. I don't think that was ever supposed to be anything other than another abduction. They picked the wrong man, he wasn't taking drugs, so he resisted and was coshed for his trouble.'

'And they pumped him with drugs to make him think he was abducted but it had the wrong effect,' nodded Ross seeing what Avalon was getting at.

'Exactly, and then there was the protection racket where they chose the wrong target and someone threw them out. That may become important later as the only identifiable suspect was seen at that time,' Avalon looked over to Ross, 'what do you think?' he asked. Ross raised his eyebrows and looked out of the window with a sigh.

'It all seems plausible but I'm not sure all the pieces fit, for instance, the drums. Why have the drums banging away, it doesn't seem to make sense?' Avalon thought for a moment.

'I'm not sure, maybe it was to add to our confusion or maybe it was to play on the legend and get more of the public to pressurise the police. It could even have been a smokescreen who knows?' suggested Avalon.

'I suppose it could have even been a 'call to arms', a sort of way to let other offenders know anything they do that night will be blamed on the drums,' considered Ross. There was a silence and then Ross asked, 'so why Drumnadrochit?' Avalon made a slight chuckle and then said.

'I've been wondering about that and the only thing I can come up with is that the area is slightly more remote than trying to do it in Inverness. There are

301

enough people to hear it there and the land makes a natural crucible to echo the sound around the area,' his face suddenly darkened, 'and there is another reason I have just thought of.' Ross looked around.

'Is it a secret?' he asked. Avalon broke away from his thoughts.

'Oh, yes, sorry. Burnside has the original drum and I think whoever is involved with this, knows it's in Drumnadrochit.'

'MacBean's original drum? You have to be kidding?' Ross actually broke into a smile at this. He leaned back, 'wow, that must be worth a bob or two. It would certainly buy you a new car.'

'It possibly would but now I'm beginning to wonder if Burnside is in any danger,' frowned Avalon, 'maybe I'm just getting paranoid,' he leaned back and thought for a moment, 'I'll give him a call later. Any questions?'

'Yes,' said Ross, 'why are we having this conversation in your tatty old car?' Avalon looked around the car park at all the other cars. It was the oldest and the shabbiest but at the moment, it was private.

'I wanted to talk before we react. If we now go to Lasiter, we could lose most of this to B section.'

'But what's the option?' asked Ross, 'we can't not tell him, that's unthinkable.'

'I'm not suggesting that, I'm just saying that once we lay this on the line, we could be moved out of a prominent position, so the only way we can keep hold of it is by dropping a bombshell.'

'I don't follow,' frowned Ross. Avalon turned to him.

'I'm just about to go to Lasiter to ask if we can

302

have the go-ahead on a major operation to remove a dumped car from the loch. What we need to tell him is that we have a theory.' Ross stared into Avalon's eyes. There was something burning deep within them, a cold fire that seemed to be pure energy. He also detected the edges creasing as if they were about to smile.

'The security truck!' Ross cried out, Avalon allowed the smile to break free onto his face, 'you think that's where the security truck is,' repeated Ross.

It's possible,' nodded Avalon, 'it would make sense.'

'How long have you thought that?' asked Ross with a grin.

'Just a few minutes ago, but if Lasiter asks, we've been chasing it for days,' he smiled.

'But what if it isn't?' asked Ross with a little doubt. Avalon smiled again.

'Then I have egg on my face and Lasiter can put all the blame on me.'

'You're that sure?' frowned Ross.

'Not at all, it's just instinct.' There it was, that instinct again and Ross felt slightly troubled, after all, there were no real facts to say there was anything of interest in the loch. 'I think once I explain our theory,' continued Avalon, 'he'll be more than happy to sanction us pulling this vehicle from the loch, and if we are right...' he left Ross to consider the acclaim that would come from the find.

'He might still move this to B section though,' added Ross as an afterthought.

'Doubtful,' said Avalon, 'we have tracked this down as part of our murder case, this vehicle was our find and it's our job to bring it up.'

'Okay,' nodded Ross, 'we had better and talk to Lasiter in the morning. Can we go back to the office now, I don't want anyone to see me in this car?'

The following day, Avalon and Ross sat in Lasiter's office, waiting for him to react to their notes on their theory. Avalon had asked Ross to be there because he wanted him involved and maybe the support would be useful to convince the Detective Inspector. Frazer was back in the office following up on some leads she had found from the previous day but she was still no closer to finding Scobie. Avalon had told her that Scobie was now critical to the case due to the fact that he probably knew much more about what was going on than they had first suspected. He had also informed her of his and Ross's theory, if not all the details.

'Well,' announced Lasiter as he placed the notes on the desk, 'I can sort o' see where y'r comin' from but t' be honest you don't have a shred o' proof.'

'Admittedly, there is nothing concrete, but it is compelling and our feelings about this are that there is no other explanation,' explained Avalon.

'If I was sat at your side o' the table I would agree but I'm not. A spreadsheet and some circumstantial evidence isn't gonna make me think that this es the answer, but, I agree the idea has some merit.'

'Come on sir,' cut in Ross, 'can you really see any other reason that it's suddenly gone quiet?'

'No DC Ross, but ef I take this to the Chief as an alternative to standard procedure, he's gonna think I've lost what few marbles I had,' frowned Lasiter. Avalon then suddenly remembered he had promised Davies he would keep him informed of his progress, that was now out of the question if he wanted to continue with the vehicle recovery.

'So you don't think the Chief will see the logic of it?' asked Avalon.

'On a whim of a couple o' my section? Because that's all we have here,' his frown grew. Avalon sighed, he thought that Lasiter would have at least been more open to what they were trying to suggest. He looked over to the window, through the rain that was still falling from the previous day and considered if he still had doubts himself. He was still recovering from another poor night's sleep on the temporary bed and through his exhaustion he began to wonder if the effort was worth it. Nevertheless, he had given a great deal of thought to the case and he could find no other explanation of the events of the last week or so. Lasiter had picked up the notes again and was looking through them.

'You need tae find Scobie and we need to know ef the Sneaton brothers are in this area. DI Davies says he's closing in on Billy the Fish so it would seem there is a race on here.'

'What if they are all involved?' suggested Ross.

'Could be,' shrugged Lasiter, 'but my experience of Billy the Fish es that he would crap himsel' if he even knew who, and what, Sneaton was,' he placed the notes back down and continued, 'I dinnae think y' would get them in the same town never mind the same job.' He leaned back then concluded with, 'Scobie is too stupid tae be anythen more than a pawn in this, so en my opinion I cannae see these being linked.'

'Unless we still haven't found the top man,' suggested Avalon.

'Aye, that's a possibility but until a' have a

name...' he raised his eyebrows and pushed the notes back to Avalon.

'So that's it?' frowned Ross.

'I need somethen to take to the Chief or he isn't gonna sanction thousands of pounds of taxpayers' money to salvage some scrap,' insisted Lasiter. Avalon sighed deeply,

'So give him what we know,' he began as he stared at Lasiter, 'there *is* a vehicle in the loch that is sitting perpendicular to the road, just at a point where a section of barrier has been removed and then replaced recently. We know the vehicle cannot have been there much more than a few days, due to the settling of the mud and silt shown on the sonar readings,' Avalon paused to see Lasiter's reaction, 'that means the vehicle has been placed there to hide it and therefore, it must be potential evidence. Not only that Detective Inspector, you once came to the theory that many of the recent crimes were linked, and frankly, I agree with you.' Lasiter nodded.

'Aye, an' I still think they are but et doesnea tak' a genius to see that. What matters es that the Chief sees et enough tae sanction the operation.'

'Then take what we have to him,' began Ross, 'evidence could be being eroded at the bottom of the loch every hour we wait.' Lasiter nodded again.

'Okay, but ef he laughs at me, you'll no' get a second bite o' this one.'

'We'll take that chance,' glared Avalon. Lasiter sighed deeply and then looked back to Avalon.

'I want y' tae carry on organising the recovery of the vehicle, I will do my best to clear everythen y' need for et but don't hold yer breath,' Avalon nodded and looked over to Ross. 'So what are y'r theories about the links of the crimes?' continued Lasiter. Avalon looked back at the DI and then raised his eyebrows a little.

'I'm not sure, I have everything in place but I'm guessing that a plan was formed to make us extra busy and we would be spread so thin that it would take time to put resources together to solve the security van robbery. They must have put a team together to commit as many crimes as they could, without getting caught. They probably practiced the car burnings a year earlier to be sure no evidence would be left anywhere.' Lasiter nodded.

'Sound theory.'

'Not everything went as they planned though,' continued Avalon, 'and the protection racket scam backfired, so they dropped it. It's likely that they also did the abductions and obviously, that went wrong,' Avalon looked to Ross and then back to Lasiter, 'beyond that, it is all theory and until we get to see what this vehicle is, I can't offer much else.'

'Okay, you're more or less thenking the same conclusion as me. Like I say, I'll do what I can,' replied Lasiter and then he added, 'so why are y' still sat here then, aye y' got nothen tae do?' The two detectives got the hint, made their way back to their office and sat down quietly. Both Dowd and Frazer looked at them and wondered why they were so quiet.

'What's wrong with you two?' asked Frazer. Avalon rested his head in his hands and his elbows on the table.

'We've just been told the Christmas Party has been cancelled,' frowned Ross. Frazer shook her head and said.

'It's a shame you've got nothin' better tae look forward too,' replied Frazer.

'Well, that's easy for you to say but we're not as antisocial as you,' sighed Ross. Frazer looked at him wide-eyed and demanded,

'I'm not antisocial, just because I don't want tae spend any time with you doesn't make me antisocial.'

'You live out in the middle of nowhere in a little farmhouse with no other people near you, that seems antisocial to me,' offered Ross.

'That's because I don't want tae listen to yapping dogs and lawnmowers all day, that doesn't make me antisocial,' Avalon decided to intervene and said.

'Quiet you two, I'm trying to be miserable and all you're doing is cheering me up.' Frazer scowled at Ross and then continued with her work. Just forty minutes later Avalon's phone rang.

'Avalon,' he said, and he sat motionless for a moment staring into space and then replaced the receiver back on its cradle. With a slightly shocked look he glanced over to Ross, 'We're on, the Chief wants it doing straight away.' Ross just sat glaring back until Avalon broke the silence.

'Megan, it's going to be a long day, don't consider that you'll be in bed much before dawn, if then. If you've anything to do I suggest you go and get it sorted.' She furrowed her brow and thought for a moment then announced.

'No, I donna think so. What's on?'

'We will probably be recovering the vehicle from the loch but it will be early hours of the morning,' explained Avalon, Frazer just nodded, 'DI Lasiter cleared it with the Chief and it's all hands to the pumps.'

'Talking of pumps,' began Ross, 'if this rain doesn't stop it's going to be a miserable night.' Avalon glanced at the window and could hardly see the roundabout a few hundred yards away.

'True, it's like a set from a Ridley Scott film,' frowned Avalon.

'So what do we need to do first?' asked Frazer.

'Dowd,' began Avalon, 'contact the Council and explain we are going to be running a recovery operation and will require a road closure planning. We will send them further details when we know the times but they must keep it quiet and put up signs saying emergency road repairs or something,' Dowd nodded and picked up the phone. 'Megan you contact any recovery companies that we use, ask them if they have got anything that can pull a truck out of mud on a loch bed and raise it up a twenty-foot cliff edge,' he thought for a moment, 'before you do, you better ring the security company and ask how heavy their vans are so that you can let the recovery company know. Give them a clue it may be in the middle of the night too,' he turned to Ross, 'we need someone to build a scaffolding platform on the loch edge with access from the road and we need lights,' Ross nodded, 'you will probably have to work with them to make sure they put them in the right place, with a ladder to get down from the road,' Ross frowned but picked up his phone, 'I'll contact the RNLI and Sergeant Waters to tell them it looks like a goer.'

It was late in the afternoon when Lasiter came to see Avalon.

'You got a minute?' asked Lasiter, and he left the room. There was only Avalon and Dowd in the office but it seemed Lasiter wanted a private chat. As they walked down the corridor Lasiter began to speak.

'How's et going?'

'Pretty well given the short notice,' replied Avalon, 'Ross is down at the site sorting out the staging and some lighting, the recovery company have four men ready with a truck and a crane that has a large jib so I would say, failing stormy weather, we should be ready.'

'Good,' nodded Lasiter, 'the Chief is backing this completely, but I have let DI Davies know what we think we have,' Avalon swung quickly round, 'don't worry, we're not taking you off et. Et's only right he's aware o' what we are doing.' Avalon nodded.

'I promised to tell him how we were getting on but I totally forgot,' frowned Avalon.

'Oh?' questioned Lasiter.

'It's a long story, anyway, I suppose he needs to be there, what we find could alter his investigation,' agreed Avalon.

'I told him there was'nae any need to be there. He looks really tired, ill really,' frowned Lasiter as they continued walking.

'I know he's under a lot of pressure to get results,' offered Avalon.

'We all are but Andrew has more pressure from many areas,' Lasiter didn't elaborate but he turned off into the rest room. He sat and Avalon joined him, 'so what's the plan?' Avalon took a deep breath and began to explain.

'It looks like one o'clock in the morning is an optimal time for the road closure, there is less traffic then and signs have been placed at either end to warn people the road will be closed for emergency maintenance. The recovery company think the job could take several hours, even after they are connected to the wreck. I have asked the divers to start earlier, at midnight.'

'Why so long?' asked Lasiter.

'When I spoke to the driver of the recovery truck and told him it was likely to be a large van, he said that it would have to be drawn out slowly and once it reached the surface, they would have to allow the water to drain out,' Lasiter nodded at this information, 'we then have to secure it so that chains can be fitted for the crane to lift it out. The plan is to rest it on the road and then get a better lift to place it on the recovery truck. The other thing is, I have asked Frazer to arrange for forensics to be on site.'

'Aye I was just going tae suggest that,' agreed Lasiter. Avalon sensed he wanted to say something.

'Doubts?' he asked.

'Not doubts as such,' replied the DI. 'et's just that ef what comes out o' the mud o' the loch is a security van, then et gives more validity to your theory and if it ends up that you are right, we have all been played for silly buggers,' Avalon nodded.

'We know, we have talked about it.'

'But thes all comes back on me. I was the one who forced Andrew tae put a stopper on the drums,' sighed Lasiter.

'If it makes any odds, I would have done the same thing.'

'Aye laddie, probably so, but other people may not see et that way,' he stood, 'anyway, that's another story. I'll see y' down there o' course,' and Lasiter walked away. Avalon returned to his office and waited for the others to return. Eventually Ross and Frazer walked in, almost at the same time and Ross said everything was just about ready but he complained about being wet and cold. Frazer explained that Sarah Underwood was at an inquest that afternoon but she had promised someone would be on site for the recovery of the vehicle. Dowd went home at shift time and Avalon suggested that Ross and Frazer went home to get a few hours rest before the 'fireworks'. Frazer said she was going to eat and said she would meet them at the site on the A82 later.

'Do you fancy a pint?' asked Ross. Avalon nodded.

'Why not? I won't be able to sleep anyway,' he smiled.

Chapter Nine

Driving out of Inverness both Avalon and Ross were very quiet, they had set off earlier for a drink at the pub but decided that coffee would be of more benefit. They then considered food but neither had an appetite. For Avalon, his doubts on what they would, or wouldn't find at the bottom of the loch, had ensured that food wasn't a priority, but he suggested they call at a service station to buy several sandwiches for later in the morning. As they turned onto the A82, into what seemed the darkest night of the year, they soon came to the road barrier that announced the road closure and briefly spoke to the uniformed officer on duty there before continuing. At least the rain had stopped some hours previously and there was little or no breeze to interfere with what they had to do. From the passenger seat of Ross's car, Avalon looked to their left at the vast, black mass of Loch Ness, here, at its eastern end, it stretched out and widened considerably as it traced its way across the country down the Great Glen. Still, they sat in silence, with no other audible company than the droning engine noise of the BMW, heading towards Drumnadrochit. It was eventually Avalon that broke that silence.

'You're married aren't you?' he asked. Ross was a little surprised, and it was a few seconds before he replied.

'Yeah, five years this July.'

'Any children?'

'No,' replied Ross shaking his head, 'we did consider it but Lucy is a teacher and we just kept putting it off until she was settled in a job she wanted to keep,' Ross shrugged and glanced over to Avalon, 'that never seemed to happen,' there was a little more silence before Ross asked, 'have you got any?'

'Children?' laughed Avalon as if the question was ridiculous, 'I couldn't even keep a marriage together,' he sighed a little and then added, 'I once regretted not having a family, I considered it might have held us together but I don't think it ever does. The problems remain and now I'm thankful we didn't.'

'It's not the best sort of job for happy marriages, even DI Davies seems to be having some troubles at home.' Avalon didn't comment, they just returned to the silence once more. As they neared the lay-by where the recovery was to take place, the lights at the site could be seen in the distance, creating a bubble of glowing mist that Avalon found welcoming on such a starless night. As they drove through the site to the bottom end of the lay-by on the Drumnadrochit side, they found a few other cars parked. The crane and the recovery truck were already in place and the crew were readying it for the operation. Close by, several people were looking over the side of the scaffolding, down to the loch. Avalon and Ross made their way to that point. It was Waters the police diver and another of his team. His boat was already in the water and tethered to the scaffolding at the platform below. The system had been well designed. From the roadside the scaffolding was fashioned into a tower with a ladder that dropped to the platform, just a foot or so above the level of the water where wooden planks made a solid base. The area looked about six by ten feet and was illuminated by a powerful light suspended from the tower. Other lights on the tower illuminated the area at the top and several other lights on stands brought the whole lay-by to almost daytime light levels. A mobile generator was sited at the upper end of the lay-by, along with various heavy chains, ropes and strops. Avalon shook the hand of Sergeant Waters.

'Any problems you can foresee?'

'Not really,' replied the diver, 'my chaps seem happy with the setup and the RNLI people are all set to go,' he handed Avalon a walkie-talkie and said, 'keep it on channel eleven and you will hear everything we are doing.' Avalon nodded and checked the radio channel before placing it in the pocket of his heavy coat. Waters returned to continue his preparations and Avalon walked over to the police van that had been parked close by as an operational headquarters. It was occupied by the uniformed officer who was coordinating the roadblocks from the radio in the van.

'Everything ready?' he asked, as he sat.

'Yes sir,' replied the police officer, 'both ends are secured.' Avalon nodded and looked at his watch, realising there was still over forty minutes before they were set to begin.

'Still got doubts?' asked Ross as he entered the van and sat in the seat opposite. Avalon shrugged.

'I've no doubts that we'll find something, but I have doubts about what is down there.'

'It could come back to haunt Lasiter if we do find something,' Ross suggested. Avalon shrugged slightly and said,

'I don't think so, dropping the investigation into the 'drums' wouldn't have any consequences here.' Ross was about to add something but they both looked back as another car arrived.

'Looks like Lasiter is here now,' announced Ross craning his head to watch the car stop. Indeed, it was the Detective Inspector, with his usual frown and as he left his car, he came straight over to the van.

'Everythen' okay?' he asked.

'DI Lasiter, we were just talking about you,' said Ross, returning his gaze back to Avalon.

'Y' mean you were havin' a joke at my expense,' replied Lasiter.

'Not at all, quite the opposite,' replied Ross.

'Yeah, yeah, a' spent too many years as a Detective Constable to know how you lot spend your time laddie,' sighed Lasiter. Ross looked over to the DI with a slight tilt to his head and said,

'A detective constable? I thought you came out of the womb as a DI.'

'Less o' the lip an' tell me how you're goin' with this case?' he perched on the edge of one of the seats and continued, 'if you spent less time checkin' the colour o' y'ur belly button fluff and more on police work, Avalon here might not have tae do everythin' himsel',' Avalon gave a quick glance toward Lasiter and said,

'He makes a decent cup of coffee though.' Lasiter gave a slight grin and Avalon continued, 'we're waiting for the divers to ready themselves and then we should be good to go.' Lasiter nodded and left the van to have a

316

look at the scaffolding tower.

'He seems fairly upbeat,' said Ross with a slight smile.

'He does, but I suppose like us, he wants to know what is down there.'

Several minutes later, another car arrived, it was Frazer who immediately checked in with Avalon and then went to talk to Lasiter, so Ross and Avalon walked over to see if Waters was ready.

'Yes, everything's set, we're just waiting for the RNLI to confirm they are in position and ready.' As if on command, the lifeboat appeared from the gloom of the loch, with its lights casting dancing reflections on the rippling black waters. Avalon turned up the volume on his radio and watched Waters descend the ladder onto the platform below. He gave the command to begin and the four crewmen in the divers 'rigid-hulled inflatable boat', better known as a Rib, moved slowly out to the buoy that had been previously placed and checked by their sonar. The divers entered the water and from there on, Avalon knew it was just a waiting game, as no part of the operation could be rushed. He turned the radio volume down, as various crackled commands were sent to and fro from the divers to Waters who was coordinating the dive from the platform. Avalon turned to look at Lasiter, who was close by and said.

'Well, all we can do now is wait,' and he sat on part of the Armco barrier looking back at the road. He soon began to feel cold however and decided to walk around to warm up, but the frustration of the wait made him return to the command vehicle, where Ross and Frazer soon joined him. Lasiter had returned to his car

317

where he could be seen making phone calls. After twenty minutes, Avalon heard Waters on the radio calling for him, so he and Ross quickly made their way to the scaffolding tower, with Frazer following along.

'What is it?' called down Avalon. Waters looked up and tried to shield his eyes from the lights above.

'We are at the vehicle and my men are beginning to attach strops to the axle. We are going to raise it slowly with cables from the recovery truck winch until we can get the chains from the crane jib on the strops.' Avalon wasn't quite sure what he meant, but he gave the 'thumbs up' sign as two of the recovery crew began fixing a steel roller to the scaffolding. Avalon had a thought, and he called down to Waters.

'Have they been able to ascertain what type of vehicle it is?' Waters looked up again.

'It's pretty dark down there but they have confirmed it's a large van.' Avalon nodded, then pulled back from the edge to allow the recovery crew to continue and he saw Lasiter walking towards him and Ross.

'Anythin'?' he asked.

'We now know it's a van,' smiled Avalon.

'Thank Christ for that,' sighed the DI.

'They are attaching it to the crane as we speak but it's going to be a slow job.' Lasiter nodded and then looked directly at Avalon.

'Have y' got a minute?' Avalon understood as Lasiter took him aside and spoke quietly, 'how are you gettin' on with Frazer?'

'Fine,' nodded Avalon, not sure why he was being asked, 'she's a good worker and has a few tricks up her sleeve.'

318

'Good,' nodded Lasiter, 'some people don't quite get what she's about but I think she's got a lot to offer. Keen as mustard too.'

'I agree sir, I certainly have no complaints.'

'Aye, okay,' he nodded again and seemed to be relieved, 'I'll be in my car if you need me,' he said and he walked off. Avalon joined the others, still wondering about Lasiter's questions.

'Well,' said Ross, 'I'm gonna see if I can get a cuppa from the recovery crew. They're running a kettle from the generator, coming?'

'Maybe in a mo, you two go, I'm going to talk to the crane driver.' As Ross and Frazer walked to the recovery crew truck, Avalon moved over to the crane and asked the driver to explain the procedure Waters was about to undertake. Once he understood it, he made his way to the recovery truck and was given a hot cup of tea but Frazer and Ross had gone, they had returned to the scaffolding and were looking down at the operation. Avalon still had some doubts and stayed out of their way, deciding to sit on some wooden boxes by the crane, just as another vehicle arrived. It was a small, unmarked white van, which Avalon guessed was the forensics personnel. To his surprise, he saw it was Sarah Underwood who climbed out of the vehicle and approached Lasiter's car, then returned to where Ross and Frazer were. Avalon found himself appraising her, the way she walked, the way she dressed, and the way she took in her surroundings. He felt guilty about it at first but then, he *did* find her attractive, so he put it down to a natural inquisitiveness. From where he was, he didn't think he could be seen, but he noticed Ross's eyes scanning the site and pointing to the van, and then in the

319

direction of the recovery truck. They had spotted him, Sarah began to walk towards him, walking casually with her hands in her pockets and said.

'Good morning.'

'Hello, I was under the impression you were busy,' smiled Avalon.

'I was, but after a truck shed its load on the A9 as I was coming home, it made me so late, I phoned my colleague and said I would come straight here. It made sense as I was going to be late anyway,' She sat at the side of Avalon, on one of the other boxes.

'I don't suppose they would have argued with you.'

'No, they didn't,' she smiled, 'I'm regretting it now though, I haven't eaten since breakfast.' Avalon suddenly remembered the food purchased earlier.

'There are some sandwiches in Ross's car, I'll get them for you,' and he stood.

'Oh…' she paused, 'no thanks, I'll wait until I get home now.'

'They're not doorstops or anything, we bought them from the service station on our way up,' she shook her head.

'No, no thanks, it's quite alright. I can manage.'

'They are fresh and still sealed, cheese and tomato and cheese and pickle I think.'

'Really, I'm grateful but I can't eat them,' she insisted.

'Oh,' said Avalon a little crestfallen, 'Is it some sort of food allergy?' he asked and then held his hands up in a submissive manner. 'Sorry, it's none of my business,' and he returned to a seating position on the boxes. There seemed to be a slight smile playing on her lips as she said,

'It's quite alright, no, not a food allergy. I have a vegan diet.' For several seconds, Avalon scoured the corners of his memory for information that would bring him a definitive explanation of what 'vegan diet' meant. He knew it was similar to vegetarianism, but that was all he could find.

'Oh,' he said to give himself time to think and then gradually it came to him, 'so you don't eat anything made from animal tissue?' he eventually asked.

'Well, it's more complicated than that but you have the idea,' she smiled.

'So I bet that is pretty difficult to keep to?' he added.

'Not at all,' she replied, but the smile had gone. He wondered about changing the subject but before he could, something dawned on him, like a bright light in his mind, something about Miss Sarah Underwood that could be explained by this particular piece of information.

'So that's why...' Avalon realised his mistake as soon as he had begun, a probable reason why she didn't accept dates became clear to his detective mind. She turned to face him.

'That's why what Detective Avalon?' she asked with a very questioning look. Avalon was tired but not that far gone that his brain couldn't think quickly.

'Why you can't eat the cheese and tomato sandwich,' he said as if that was what he was going to say all along. As he turned away from her, he saw Ross coming towards him. Ross leaned on the truck and announced.

'The vehicle is near the surface and they're going

321

to swap the lift over to the crane.' Avalon nodded,

'So we should see it soon then?'

'Yeah, but they think it could take another thirty minutes to drain it for a full lift,' added Ross.

'Okay,' replied Avalon, 'we better let the DI know.

'I'll tell him,' nodded Ross and he left to find Lasiter. Avalon noticed from the corner of his eye, Sarah watching Ross walk away, not just looking, but as if she was 'examining' him. It seemed, although she had refused a date, she certainly found something interesting, or even attractive about him. Avalon looked away as she turned and said.

'So, I had better go and have a look, oh and the recovery team have a kettle. It's not the same as a hot meal but it may warm you up.'

Avalon looked down at Sergeant Waters on the platform as the divers returned to their boat and gave him the sign they were ready for the crane to begin the lift. Waters called on the radio for the crane driver to begin. There wasn't much light on the chains coming out of the water but the diving team had two powerful flashlights hung by lanyards on the scaffolding and Waters was shining one at the chains. It was a slow job but within a few minutes, a shadowy shape could be seen swirling in the water. To everyone's shock, through the mud and silt of the loch, the van could be clearly seen to be white and not the grey colour of the security van. Avalon's heart sank a little but as the number plate became visible, he climbed down the ladder and took hold of the other flashlight and trained it on the plate.

'Ross,' he called back up to the top of the

scaffold, 'check this number with the stolen van used in the robbery.' Ross began to jot it down but Frazer seemed to say something to Ross and he called back.

'It is, Frazer remembers it.' Avalon switched off the lamp and nodded to Waters as he climbed back up the ladder.

'Well, it isn't what we expected, but it's a start,' he smiled. Lasiter seemed pleased too but was impatient to get the van on the road to have a look inside. Sarah Underwood was already suiting up in her white coveralls ready to examine the interior.

By the time the dripping van was hanging, nose down over the road, Waters was standing by Avalon.

'It isn't the one you were looking for but you never know, it may have some forensic evidence.' Avalon thanked him and Waters went back to stand his team down, so they could change and get warm, but there seemed to be a problem.

'What's wrong?' asked Avalon as he neared the diver.

'I'm not sure, the lads in the boat are going on about a 'contact' in the water. I'll go and see what the matter is.' Waters climbed over the barrier and down the ladder, Avalon followed. On the platform, the diver's boat came closer and one of the team jumped onto the structure.

'What the hell is going on Buckly?'

'Well, our sonar is showing somethen' else down there,' he replied in a thick accent, 'we're askin' the RNLI to check et with their equipment.' On the water, the lights of the lifeboat could be seen moving into the position of the buoy until a voice cut in from them.

'*Confirmed, contact at the same coordinates.*'

323

With this, Waters turned to Avalon with a slight smile.

'It seems DS Avalon, you have another vehicle down there.'

As Sarah Underwood examined the inside of the white van, the divers and the RNLI stood down for a rest and a hot drink but there seemed very little of consequence to be found in the vehicle. The van was to be placed on the recovery truck to be taken to the police compound and another truck was on its way for the second vehicle.

'There isn't much in there,' began Miss Underwood, 'we can do a better job when we get it back but I see little point in getting your hopes up Detective.'

'The next one could hae more en et though,' replied Lasiter.

'Or it may be nothing to do with this case, it could be a coincidence,' added Avalon.

'That's et Avalon, keep raising my spirits.'

'Sorry sir but it is a possibility.'

'We'll know soon enough,' said Sarah, removing her white coveralls, 'I think I could do with that cup of tea now.'

Waters briefed Avalon from the command vehicle whilst sipping on a hot drink from a very large thermos flask he carried.

'There is a possibility that this second vehicle could have been pushed into the mud from the weight of the first van, so it could take a little longer to get out. When does your road closure end?'

'Officially at 0500 hours but we can squeeze a little more out of it if needed,' admitted Avalon.

'If there are no issues, we should be done by then but you never know,' he took another sip of his drink, 'the only problem is, that we don't know if the second recovery truck has a winch, so we are going to try to do the full lift with the crane. The driver says we can't do it in one go as it will only lift about half the height we need, so we are going to use the extra chains to lock the vehicle to the barrier while we lengthen the jib cables.' Avalon tried to make sense of what Waters was saying but he wasn't sure, he just voiced concern about the strength of the barrier. Waters shrugged and said that the driver was confident as the vehicle wouldn't weigh much submerged in the loch. Avalon nodded as Waters continued. 'Buckly will coordinate this time, I'm going down there with the other reserve so I'll try to keep you up to date on the radio,' he was about to get up and leave but he hesitated, 'I was going to let the RNLI people go as the weather is perfect and I don't think there'll be any traffic on the loch at this time.' Waters then left and so Avalon went to find Ross and Frazer to explain what was happening, he found them drinking more tea by the crane.

'The other truck is on ets way Sarge and should be here en fifteen minutes or so,' explained Frazer. Avalon nodded then explained what was going to happen, and they all walked over to the scaffolding.

'Another long wait then,' sighed Ross as Waters and his team pushed off and headed for the buoy in their boat. Avalon went to find one of those sandwiches from Ross's car, as he passed Lasiter's vehicle, he noticed the DI was asleep in the driver's seat. He decided not to wake him, there wasn't much to tell anyway. He took the food and headed back to his team passing Sarah who was sitting in her car.

'You can have one of these if you change your mind.'

'No thank you and I won't,' she smiled, 'have they started out for the other vehicle yet?'

'Yeah, just. I'll take these to the team,' he replied nodding to the food. As Avalon walked back to Ross and Frazer, he considered that he had information about Sarah that no one else had and he didn't know if he should tell Ross or keep it to himself. He decided on the latter as he may get a little fun out of it later. He handed out the sandwiches.

It didn't take much longer than the first time for Waters to confirm that they were connected to the vehicle and that it felt like another van. The team were fairly upbeat about this and by the time Lasiter returned, looking like he was still half asleep the vehicle was reported as being close to the surface. The second recovery truck was in place and the crane was running out its cable as the unseen vehicle was tethered to the Armco barrier by several cables and strops.

The lift of the vehicle from the water would soon begin and everyone gathered around the scaffolding tower to watch. As the crane was connected and the securing cables were released, the chain began to lift slowly from the water but from the roadside, there was little to see. Avalon and Ross decided to climb down to the platform with Buckly, Ross directed the second flashlight onto the area of water where the vehicle was expected to surface. It was tense and Avalon couldn't help the doubts still lingering in his brain. True, all the signs were favourable but there was still the possibility that this wasn't the security van. Soon, the water around the chain began to swirl as the vehicle came close to the surface but Buckly halted the lift to allow the divers to leave the water and return to the boat. The message came from the boat that they were all aboard safely and were returning to the RNLI jetty and so, Buckly gave the order to continue the lift. As the vehicle broke the surface, it was clear to all that it was indeed the security van and Ross flashed Avalon a broad grin. Avalon looked up to the road edge and saw Lasiter speaking with Frazer and nodding, his face showed relief for the first time. Avalon looked back to where Ross was directing the flashlight beam and could see clear indications of where the rear door had been ground and cut away, but they would have to wait until it was on the road to examine it closely. When the vehicle was a few feet out of the water, the lift was halted again to allow water to drain from the inside and the crane driver brought it closer to the loch edge until it grounded on the slope. There it sat until the water emptied and Avalon leaned on the scaffolding with a deep sigh. Ross turned off the torch and smiled to Avalon.

'Well done, a good call boss,' Avalon didn't know if Ross calling him boss was more gratifying than being right or not.

'It was a team effort, we came to this conclusion based on work we all put in,' nodded Avalon, 'it's nice to know we were on target though.' He then allowed himself a smile too.

'I gather this es what you were after,' said Buckly, turning to Avalon.

'Yes, and we couldn't have done it without your team, thank Sergeant Waters and the rest of the men please, inform them we have struck gold.'

'I will,' smiled Buckly as he reached for his radio but there was a terrific splash out in the loch, for a moment Avalon thought the chains had broken and the van had plunged back into the water.

'What the hell was that?' called Avalon as he noticed the vehicle was still held on the chains. Ross and Buckly shone the flashlights out across the water and by chance, caught the sight of a wave heading towards them. Avalon and Ross managed to heave their feet out of the way as the water washed over the platform and the vehicle moved around on its chains.

'What's going on down there?' came Frazer's voice from above.

'We don't know,' called back Ross, still scanning the black waters for the sign of something out there.

'Sergeant Waters, come en,' called Buckly on his radio.

'*Waters, over.*'

'Sarge, are you still on the loch?'

'*No, we are at the jetty, we saw a wave, is everything alright there? Over.*'

'Yes, but there might be a craft or something on the loch. Over,' replied Buckly.

'*Okay, I'll send two out to have a look around. Out.*' Ross eventually switched off the light and looked slightly worried.

'Maybe we should go up the ladder,' he suggested. The three of them returned to the road where there were questions from Lasiter and Frazer but no one had any answers. Soon after a car arrived, it was Waters and another member of his team from up at the jetty.

'I have two of my team out there but after speaking to them on the phone, they are sure there are no other vessels on the loch,' he explained.

'Then what just happened?' asked Ross.

'My best guess is that disturbing the mud caused a release of methane or something to escape. The resulting bubble broke the surface and caused a wave,' offered Waters. Some nodded, others still looked out into the pitch black of the loch and if anyone had any other ideas or were looking for another explanation, none were offered.

It took just over thirty minutes to bring the vehicle from the water and carefully rest it on its wheels, the correct way up. There were several obvious areas of damage and the rear crew door was torn to shreds around the area of the locking mechanism. Avalon took out his handkerchief and carefully opened the door, which resisted a little. He shone a small flashlight inside and saw a considerable amount of chaos in there. Smashed cash boxes and money containers, a few various tools and other unidentifiable items all mixed in with some mud and silt were heaped up near the front bulkhead in an untidy pile. To his side, stood Sarah once more suited up to examine the interior and when Avalon considered it was safe, he allowed her to climb in. She carefully made her way to the front, examining items as she moved, until she came to the main pile. It took a little time for her to bend down, remove two cash boxes and turn back to face Avalon. From under her mask, he clearly heard her say,

'There is a body, it looks like the security guard.'

~~~~~~

Detective Inspector Lasiter explained that anyone who had been at the vehicle recovery did not need to be in the office until lunchtime but Avalon was back by ten thirty. The reason was as much to do with his temporary bed as the wish to sift through the findings from the recovery. He expected PC Dowd to be in the office but not DC Frazer.

'Hell Frazer, why are you here at this time?'

'Probably the same as you Sarge, anyway Dowd phoned me earlier,' she frowned looking over to the PC.

'I'm sorry DS Avalon but no one told me you wouldn't be in, I just thought-' Frazer cut him short.

'It's okay Dowd. At least et was good news,' then she looked over to Avalon, 'he rang to tell me that Scobie had been found.'

'Where is he?' glared Avalon.

'Down en the cells,' she replied. Avalon sat in his chair and turned on the screen of his computer.

'We need to interview him as soon as we can.'

'Well… I have taken the liberty with that one sir,' She looked a little doubtful and then continued, 'I had a few words with him this mornin'.'

'Is he still conscious?' frowned Avalon.

'Aye but I was tempted,' she replied.

'So did he tell you anything we didn't know?' asked Avalon giving her his full attention.

'Some,' she nodded slowly, 'but with him it's hard to tell how much es lies and how much es bigger lies.' She thought for a moment and then explained, 'I told him that we were going tae pin two murders on him as we had no other suspects. He seemed surprised that there was another body, but I refused to let on where et was found.' Avalon nodded and asked.

330

'Did it make him talk?'

'Not at first, but I made some crap up about the Sneaton brothers looking for him and that put him en a rare panic,' she sighed before continuing, 'he then said he needed to phone legal, so I informed him he hadn't been charged and he was free tae go. He then panicked even more and said he wanted tae talk tae you.'

'To me? I wonder why that is?' Avalon smiled and then continued, 'I better go and see him then.'

Scobie was sitting in the first cell at the back of the building looking very unsure of himself when Avalon walked in with Frazer.

'Mr Scobie, how nice to see you again.' Scobie looked up and with a flushed face, he said,

'Mr Avalon, we need tae talk. I have somethin' tae tell you but you have tae make me some assurances.'

'I am here to formally charge you Mr Scobie, you seem to tell more lies than a career politician, so anything you have to tell me will be at your trial,' frowned Avalon.

'Charged, with what Mr Avalon? Detective Frazer said I was free tae go, anyway, I had nothin' tae do with any murders honest.'

'Tell that to the twelve good men and true,' he replied.

'I dunna know what you just said but I have tae talk tae you,' insisted the man. Avalon sat and glared for some time at Scobie.

'Last time we met, you told us you had dealings with Robert Bain and yet Robert Bain was on remand when your 'business' was supposed to have happened.'

'Aye, that was a wee porky Mr Avalon but when you know what a' have tae tell you-' Avalon cut him short.

'Then tell me and I'll see if the information is worth my time.' Scobie looked at the floor and began to wring his thin hands as if he was about to confess all his sins. He coughed and wrung his hands once more before he eventually said.

'I'll tell you what I know but you have tae believe me Mr Avalon, I don't know what es goin' on with the murders.' Avalon continued his fixed glare at Scobie, which did little to comfort him, the man was visibly distressed.

'A few weeks ago I was out an' about an' I saw a Forestry Commission van, y' know one o' those wee green jobbies wi' the trees on the side,' he paused to wring his hands a little more, 'et seemed tae me that the two guys en the van didnae look like forestry types, they looked more like villains, ef you catch ma' drift. When they got out an' went into a building, I noticed the driver had a tattoo on his hand but I didnae know who he was, so I went tae have a closer look,' he paused for a moment, 'I had a peek inside and I was surprised tae find et open.'

'You mean you broke en?' interrupted Frazer.

'No! Well, not really...' he sighed, 'yeah, alright, I broke en, I suppose when dead bodies start appearin' my breaking and enterin' ain't that important,' he looked at Avalon. 'I'm no killer Mr Avalon, Detective Frazer here will tell y' that, so if this gets me off the hook, so tae speak, I'll tell you like et happened.'

'Just get on with et Scobie,' growled Frazer. Avalon looked unmoved, so Scobie continued.

'Et's really odd but en the back they had some big speakers, y'know like en a disco or somethen.'

'Loudspeakers in the back of a Forestry Commission van?' asked Frazer shaking her head, 'are you making this shite up Scobie?'

'No, I swear detective, et wes what I saw.'

'So someone steals a Forestry van and makes off with some equipment from a music shop, so what?' hissed Avalon hiding his interest. Scobie nodded and swallowed hard.

'I know et sounds weird an' I thought that too, so I picked up a few bits...' Scobie looked sheepishly at Avalon, 'just for my trouble you see an' then went tae have a look en the front,' at this point he looked down at the floor and then back to Frazer and Avalon, 'that van belongs tae...' he hesitated for a split second, 'Rabbie Bee.'

'How would you know that Scobie?' asked Frazer with some venom.

'I know the van, I've been en et several times an' I recognised some o' the stuff en there, I also remembered that Rabbie kept a weapon, a big spanner under the driver's seat, et was still there. I mean et had fake plates but et was the same van. It was even still painted white inside.'

'Go on,' insisted Avalon. Scobie gulped once more and then continued.

'When I got back I asked around, y' know tae see ef anyone knew any villains en the area with a tattoo o' an eagle on his right hand, that's when I was told et sounded like Sneaton. I was scared an' so I did a runner and went off tae hide at that camp, ef Rabbie Bee an' Sneaton were after me I needed to disappear. I didnae think anyone would look for me there,' he began to wring his hands once more as he continued, 'I buried my personal stuff under the shelter I made an' waited for the whole thing tae blow over but then I saw them, the two guys from the forestry van, lurking about en the shadows at the camp.'

'And were they dressed as you described?' asked Avalon.

'Aye, the very same. One o' them was obviously Michael Sneaton, as he fit the description, I didnae know the other face with the beard but he looked like someone Sneaton would employ,' Scobie began shaking his head. 'I just panicked, I ran down into the wood and followed the burn until I was clear.'

'Were they wearing gloves?' asked Ross.

'Aye, a' think so.'

'So how come you were still there when we came then?' asked Avalon with a deep frown.

'I went back for my stash, et was all the cash I had, et was just my bad luck that you were there, I recognised Mr Ross an' so I hid en the shelter.' Avalon was silent, he eventually stood and made to leave, but Scobie continued.

'I'm as good as dead ef they find out Mr Avalon, I need you tae gimme some protection.' Frazer was still seated and her glare told Scobie she was likely to harm him if he didn't tell everything. Scobie looked up towards Avalon who was obviously impatient. 'Honest, I don't know anymore and I don't know what tae do.' Scobie was terrified, that was clear. Avalon turned to Frazer.

'Is Bain back on the streets?'

'Probably,' she replied, 'I would say he got bail, I can check.' Avalon nodded, he was beginning to see some light at the end of the tunnel.

Avalon was still standing by the window, staring out towards the traffic roundabout when Ross arrived in the office. He noticed Avalon's hands were clasped behind his back, which he had previously noticed was a habit that Avalon had when he was deep in thought.

'Am I late?' grinned Ross seeing the clock said one thirty.

'Eh? oh it's you,' said Avalon as he turned.

'It's quiet in here, where is everybody?' asked Ross as he sat. Avalon paced back to his desk and also took a seat.

'Dowd is on lunch and Frazer has gone to arrange surveillance.'

'On who?'

'Robert Bain,' answered Avalon, 'he's out on bail,' Ross raised his eyebrows but said nothing, 'Scobie has been found and has imparted some interesting details.' added Avalon.

'Don't believe anything that lying turd has to say.'

'I don't think he's lying this time,' replied Avalon in a very calm tone.

'Go on,' shrugged Ross.

'If I was to tell you that one of Bain's vans had been painted in Forestry Commission graphics and had some 'over-the-top' stereo in the back and was driven by a hardened criminal from Glasgow, what would your conclusion be?' Ross kept his face perfectly neutral as he answered.

'Well, one of two things, either Scobie has taken to dreaming up plots for daytime television serials, or we have a lead on who has been naughty over the past few months.'

'I'm thinking the latter,' said Avalon. Ross nodded, leaned back in his chair, and considered the situation.

'I just don't see Bain being the driving force of this though, it must be the Sneaton brothers.'

'From what Frazer tells me, the Sneaton's wouldn't likely employ someone like Bain though, he's too small time for them,' said Avalon.

'Maybe,' agreed Ross, 'but who else do we have?'

'Our major problem at the moment is much closer to home.'

'How so?' frowned Ross.

'This isn't our case, we've no doubt now that all this is connected and the security van robbery is Section B and DI Davies's case. Unfortunately, we have to hand this information over. We can't hold onto it anymore,' explained Avalon, Ross seemed to take a few seconds to take it in and then his body language showed the disappointment he was feeling.

'Isn't there a way we can be kept on this? I mean, we've put in so much to see someone else benefit from it...' Ross became lost for words.

'It isn't a competition, we are all here to get the job done, no matter how that ends up,' explained Avalon.

'Yeah, I realise that, but getting a result is why we do it, but there's no satisfaction, no result if we hand it over now.'

'Well, maybe you have to look at it from a different angle, take satisfaction from what help we can give to the other sections,' replied Avalon, 'I'm disappointed too but we have to move on. I'll see if Lasiter is in, it's his decision.' Avalon left to find Lasiter.

'Aye, you're right laddie and I wes thenking about it on the way here, we have to hand what we know over tae DI Davies and his team,' agreed Lasiter, but he paused to think for a moment, 'I do however, consider that the Abriachan murder es separate and still the domain of C Section, so I want you tae stay with et. I'll talk tae Davies about et and get some thoughts of his and then we'll talk later.'

When Avalon returned to his office, Dowd and Frazer were back and by the sound of it, Frazer was considerably upset.

'What's the commotion about?' asked Avalon. Frazer turned to him and she looked furious.

'I spent an hour going through proper channels tae set up surveillance on Robert Bain's properties, to be told by DS Douglas of B Section, that we can't do it as they have plans of their own.' Avalon nodded.

'It's their case, but I have spoken to Lasiter and he says we are still working the Abriachan murder.'

'But Bain could be a suspect,' demanded Frazer.

'Then get me proof that he is, because at this moment, all we have is a story that we obtained from a notorious liar and thief,' announced Avalon, raising his voice slightly. Frazer went quiet and slumped in her chair. Avalon saw the realisation of the truth appear on her face. 'So let's look at what we have,' he continued, 'fibres at the crime scene that could be a match to a similar jacket *allegedly* seen to be worn by one of the two men at the camp. The two men were also *allegedly* seen driving a van *allegedly* owned by Robert Bain.'

'So by the amount of 'allegedly' in your statement, I assume we need to verify Scobie's story first?' said Ross. Avalon raised his eyebrows and then said,

'As it stands we are just surmising a theory that may explain a link. We need evidence as you well know so let's try to find some.'

'What about a trip to see Bain?' suggested Frazer.

'We could try it,' agreed Avalon.

'That still seems like treading on B Section's toes,' insisted Ross.

'It is but we are pursuing our own case which DI Lasiter wants us to continue with and as Bain is out on bail, he may want to cooperate a little more,' smiled Avalon. Ross shrugged, it was clear he was still aggrieved about having to take a back seat.

'So how do you want tae do this?' asked Frazer.

'Tell me about Bain,' said Avalon.

'Small-time crook,' shrugged Frazer, 'never anythen' big, started off as a door-to-door scammer but was sent down for burglary. Learned his trade inside and then came back on the streets bigger and stronger.'

'Is that it?' asked Avalon.

'I think he was running a buying and selling business but he's also turned to violence in recent times, as you know, he was on remand for aggravated assault. He's probably just been lucky enough to evade the courts until now,' added Ross.

'Aye,' explained Frazer, 'I heard he had a couple of petty crooks 'done over' for trying tae fleece him.'

'So the security van and murder still seems out of character for him?' asked Avalon.

'Probably, unless he has shifted his sights,' nodded Frazer folding her arms.

'So where would he most likely keep a van hidden?' Avalon was making it clear this was the route he wanted to take.

'He has a small yard down by the docks,' offered Frazer.

'Okay,' announced Avalon, looking directly at Frazer, 'we start there but I want you to go down and see Scobie, I want the address of the building where he saw Sneaton and accomplice enter when he saw them in the van and I want the nearest guess he can make of the correct number plate for that van,' Frazer nodded and left for the cells and Avalon turned to Ross, 'we need to try to find Sneaton, send out a BOLO with a full description, making sure that he is regarded as highly dangerous.' Ross got straight to work. 'I'm going to give Miss Underwood a quick call,' he reached for the phone and dialled the number.

'*Hello, Sarah Underwood.*'

'Hello it's Avalon here, sorry to bother you I know you must be busy.'

'*That's alright detective, I suspect you are after some information.*'

'Yes,' replied Avalon with a slight hesitation, 'you see, technically this is not my investigation, it's just that we are struggling to link the Abriachan murder to specific suspects.'

'*Oh, I see. Well, we are still working on the vehicles but I can give you a little information,*' she paused and Avalon could hear the distinctive click of typing on a keyboard, '*as I intimated on site, the white van has produced little forensic evidence but the security van is another matter. The perpetrators must have thought you'd never recover that van as they have left a selection of forensic evidence.*'

'Such as?' asked Avalon fishing for other

339

information.

'*Well, the extreme cold of the loch has preserved everything in good condition, including the body of the security guard. There are several fingerprints and even blood but very little in the way of fibres.*'

'Have you any clues to how the guard died?' he asked.

'*Nothing solid but I suspect asphyxiation, as we found a CS gas canister in the rear,*' she explained, '*the coroner will confirm the cause of death, but it's my best guess.*'

'What about the blood?'

'*It's too early to say if it came from the guard but we are testing that at the moment,*' she admitted.

'Well thanks for the information, let's hope there is more to come,' replied Avalon, and he said goodbye.

'Anything from Sarah?' asked Ross. For some reason Avalon's mind suddenly flashed back to Sarah watching Ross with interest early that morning. Was it Ross's look or was it the way he *was*? Avalon simply didn't know but he would guess it wasn't his charm.

'Er, not much. She is guessing the guard suffocated from CS gas.'

'Shit, CS gas? That's serious stuff to throw in a vehicle,' frowned Ross, 'these are pretty heartless bastards if they used CS.' The door to the office swung open, it was Lasiter.

'Avalon, you got a minute?' Avalon followed Lasiter down the corridor and into his office, 'sit down.' he said and Lasiter sat in his own seat, 'I have had a meeting with DI Davies and told hem what we know but I have also informed them you are still on the Abriachan murder.'

340

'How did he take it?' asked Avalon with trepidation.

'Fine, he sees et like we do, as a separate case,' Lasiter seemed to be thinking about something.

'Is there…' Avalon paused slightly, 'anything else sir?' Lasiter seemed to come back into the room from somewhere.

'Oh, I wes just thenking about the sound of the drums over at Drumnadrochit. That still seems tae be a loose end.'

'Well,' again Avalon paused, 'we think we may have an idea about that,' he said with a slight smile.

'Go on,' frowned Lasiter.

'If Scobie was telling the truth, and that is still to be confirmed, there is something he said that I held back because there is no evidence. If our next few lines of inquiry come to fruition, then I may be able to solve that little mystery.' Lasiter thought about what Avalon was getting at and at first he began to doubt, but the detective sergeant had been correct about the security van. Rather than berate him for keeping information back, he smiled and said.

'So you don't believe it was the drummer's ghost then?' Avalon returned the smile and replied.

'No sir, the only spirits I believe in are single malts.'

~~~~~~

An old Ford Mondeo came slowly to a halt outside a small yard in the Inverness dock area. A well-built man in his thirties got out of the passenger door and looked around, before bending back into the car for a

341

moment. He then walked to the gates of the yard, followed by a slightly built woman in a suit and the two of them tried the gates, they opened. From the small building on the site, a burly man approached them and there was a short discussion. The burly man returned to the building and the two people returned to the car. The driver of the car got out and joined the other two. He was slim, about six feet tall and had an air of authority about him, he lead the other two back towards the building. They entered.

'Detective Sergeant Avalon, I'm always happy tae help officers o' the law, take a seat please,' smiled the chubby man with a red face. 'What can I do f ' you?' Avalon remained standing, as did Frazer. Ross had remained outside.

'I'll be blunt Mr Bain, this isn't a social call. I am here because I have a few questions to ask you,' Bain tilted his head to one side and said,

'I'm sure y' are aware that I can't discuss my case until I appear in court.'

'This isn't to do with your recent brush with the law Mr Bain, this is a separate issue.'

'I'm sure you'll understand that as I'm on bail et wouldn't be en my interest to speak to you.'

'Do you own a green Volkswagen Transporter van registration number Sierra, Hotel, five, five-' but Avalon was cut short.

'I did own a vehicle like that, but et was white not green and doesn't have the same registration as you have there,' he looked up from the registration number Avalon had on a notepad, 'were there not three o' you Detective?' Bain looked to the burly man who was close by, 'I'm going to have tae ask you tae leave Detective,' he insisted looking back to Avalon.

'My other detective constable had to make a phone call back to HQ, as to the van, I gather you mean you have sold it?' Avalon watched the burly man make his way to the door.

'Please leave detective unless you have any *official* business.' Avalon turned and walked outside, just behind the burly man and he met Ross coming back.

'Did you make that call DC Ross?' asked Avalon. Ross looked puzzled for a second and then said.

'Oh, aye, you were right too.' Avalon nodded. Bain stopped by the door as the burly man moved behind him. Avalon raised his eyebrows to Ross, who nodded towards a small workshop the doors were closed, so Avalon couldn't see what was inside.

'If you have sold the van, it wouldn't be in that workshop would it?' asked Avalon with a matter-of-fact voice. Bain glanced at Ross for a moment and then back to Avalon.

'It's in there waiting for the new owner to collect it but unless you came with a search warrant...' Bain was making it clear he was losing his patience.

'I'll be back in a moment Mr Bain,' smiled Avalon and the three detectives walked back to the car.

'Did you get the registration?' he asked Ross.

'Yes, Scobie was pretty close,' he replied as he took out his phone and dialled. 'Detective Ross here, can you check a registration number for me?' Avalon waited a few seconds looking back to the building where the burly man still stood as Ross dictated the registration number. Bain it seemed had returned inside the building.

'Yes,' said Ross replacing his phone in his

pocket, 'it's still registered to Robert Bain.' Avalon nodded and made his way towards the burly man.

'Where is Mr Bain?' he asked, but the man stood silent and glared. Avalon made to pass him but the man attempted to prevent it, in a second Ross and Frazer had him on the ground and handcuffed. Ross escorted him to the car as Avalon knocked on the door and entered.

'You're persistent detective but I'm sure you realise you can't just go arresting my employees without cause.'

'Your *employee*, was preventing police officers from carrying out their duties, and don't presume to lecture me on law,' insisted Avalon.

'As a' see et, he was preventing you from coming into premises you have no authority tae search,' replied Bain. Avalon was beginning to realise Bain had a few tricks up his sleeve and putting pressure on him may not work very easily. Avalon's new 'self' was getting too cocky and was in danger of becoming a liability. He hesitated and that could be seen as a weakness, he had to think quick. He nodded at Bain and sighed a little for effect.

'Then if that's how you feel Mr Bain, we'll go through proper channels and serve a search warrant on the premises,' and without waiting for a reaction, he turned and walked out of the building to where Ross was waiting, 'he isn't playing ball.'

'It *is* the van boss,' insisted Ross, as they quickly returned to the car, 'you can even see traces of green paint.' As they joined Frazer, and the handcuffed man in the car, Avalon said to Frazer.

'We have to get a search warrant. Let him go.' Frazer shrugged and took the cuffs off the man who

344

exited the car with a smile. He slowly walked back to the building in the yard as Ross spoke.

'You realise of course, that by the time we get a warrant, that van will have gone.'

'That's why you and Frazer are going to drop me off at the end of the road and then keep your eyes on that van,' Avalon gave Ross the car keys, 'I'll ring Dowd and get a car to pick me up, I need to check the address that Scobie gave us as the place Sneaton and his friend visited.' Ross looked a little surprised and then handed the keys to Frazer.

'I am not driving this car, it's enough being seen in the passenger seat, without being seen driving it.' Avalon was about to rant and berate Ross for his bad timing but he resisted and just said.

'Whatever, whoever. Just don't lose that van and try not to let them see you.'

It was PC Kirk who came to pick up Avalon, and she seemed quite glad about the excursion.

'Well et's been a pretty boring day today, so when the desk put your request through, I volunteered,' smiled Kirk, 'where to?' Avalon showed her the address on a notepad, 'Merkinch? Are you sure?'

'That's the address I was given why?' asked Avalon, hearing a little alarm in her voice.

'Detective Avalon, not all of Inverness es as easy goin' as where you and I live. There are some places where certain people just shouldnae go.'

'I don't follow,' frowned Avalon.

'Well tae put et bluntly, in some areas not far from here, if you're not wearing a Fred Perry shirt and track suit or if you drive around en a marked police car, you might not get a proper Inverness welcome,' she looked straight at him, 'and you have the added target bonus of being English.' Avalon just smiled and said.

'Maybe I should have kept Frazer with me.'

'Do you still want tae go?' she asked but Avalon just smiled and pointed ahead saying.

'*Carry on, carry on. Brace for another attack. It's looking like hell but you never can tell. Carry on old man, carry on.*' Kirk just stared at him open-mouthed. 'It's a poem,' he grinned, and she started the car, not knowing if Avalon had lost his wits or not.

The address was an old dock building close to the trading estate and Avalon told Kirk to stay in the car and near the radio. The building was boarded up, but he found a way in at the back. There was nothing much to see, though it was obvious it had been used recently and so he carefully ventured to the upper floor. His phone vibrated in his pocket, he took it out and read a short text message. It was from Ross, and said, simply, 'Van is on the move.' He put the phone away and continued. In the first room, he found a wooden chair and an old mattress and considered someone had been living rough there, but in the corner, he found something that changed his mind, a crumpled piece of 'duct tape'.

Kirk almost jumped out of her skin when the knock came on the window. It was Avalon, so she popped the door locks to open.

'Radio in, we need a team to seal off this building and a forensics team here as soon as possible.'

~~~~~~

346

It was strange for Avalon to see his car from another perspective. He was in a borrowed pool car as he slowed to a halt behind the old Ford Mondeo, it looked strangely out of place on the deserted road in the gloom of the evening. He saw Ross get out of the driver's seat and come to him.

'You ended up driving it then?' he said. Ross just stared at him.

'Frazer drives like a lunatic,' he then pointed over to some waste ground but by now it was almost dark and difficult to see, 'the van is over there, I think they are going to torch it.'

'They?' asked Avalon as he got out of the car.

'The big bloke we cuffed earlier is the driver, he just drove around for about an hour and then ended up here.'

'So he knows you followed him?' asked Avalon with a frown.

'No, that's just it, we lost him in traffic, it was just luck we saw him turn down here sometime later.'

'So who else is here?' asked Avalon.

'We think it's Bain, he turned up ten minutes ago in another vehicle, probably to drive him back.' Avalon nodded.

'Okay, let's move before they damage the van.' Frazer stayed with the cars, Avalon and Ross crossed the waste ground until they could see the white van in the gloom. A hundred yards or so away was another car with two people inside. Avalon and Ross moved carefully behind it and then one went either side. Avalon tapped on the window which slowly opened.

'Ah, Detective, you again,' it was Bain but this time, he looked less than confident.

'Don't tell me Mr Bain, you are waiting for the new owner to turn up to collect his van.'

'Why yes, you have et exactly,' replied Bain, with a fake smile. Avalon smiled back this time.

'We are not on your property this time and by the powers of 'Stop and Search' I want you two to get out of the car and come over to the van.' They all walked over to where the van was parked and Ross produced a flashlight so they could examine the vehicle. There was nothing in the rear of the van to Avalon's surprise and so he walked to the front.

'What made you want to sell the van Mr Bain?' he asked, as he opened the driver's door.

'I didn't use et much,' shrugged Bain.

'Strange, because it looks like it's had a recent re-spray,' commented Avalon as he got inside and pulled a pair of forensic gloves from his pocket.

'Not that recent, six months ago I think. As a' say, et didn't get used much,' replied Bain still calm and collected, seemingly disinterested in the detective's actions. Avalon looked around the interior and slowly let his hand drop beneath the seat and there, he found a large spanner.

'Well well, Mr Bain, I rather think this spanner is a little on the large side for working on this vehicle,' and he carefully placed it on the passenger seat. 'Robert Bain, I'm arresting you on suspicion of being an accessory to murder. You don't have to say anything…' Avalon read him his rights as Ross slipped handcuffs on him and Frazer detained the burly man. They called for a car to take them to the police station. The whole time, Bain just smiled and said nothing.

Back at the office Lasiter came to see what they had found.

'You are gonna struggle to make this stick Jim,' he frowned.

'I know but I needed to impound that vehicle and put pressure on Bain,' replied Avalon, as he typed at his computer.

'You realise that ef forensics find nothen' in the van the Chief will kick yer arse for compromising the other investigation?' pointed out Lasiter.

'Yes, I know,' replied Avalon, and he stopped typing, 'but what do you want me to do, wait until he makes a deathbed confession? He may be a petty crook but he's pretty cool under pressure and he was going to set the van ablaze, he had petrol in the back of his car for the job.'

'You don't have enough tae take this tae court though, Bain knows the system and with all the good work you have done on thes case, you are now gonna throw et all up in the air.' Lasiter was angry and Avalon decided to try to calm the situation.

'We do have a plan and it's risky I'll grant you, the problem I have, is that with B Section working on the main case, my hands are tied somewhat.' Lasiter shook his head and paced what little space there was.

'I hope you know what you're doing Avalon but ef you cannae give me some news soon, I'm gonna let Bain walk.' Avalon glared at Lasiter for a moment but Lasiter turned and left. To Avalon's surprise, the DI's visit hadn't annoyed him as much as he expected. He was actually feeling good, he felt really alive, and though he couldn't understand it his thoughts moved to Sarah Underwood. Was it because he was thinking about forensic evidence? He doubted that, but maybe he wasn't her type anyway, he had seen her watching Ross after all. He casually turned to Ross and asked.

'Do you work out?' Ross was flabbergasted.

'What?' he asked.

'Do you work out, you know, down the gym or something?'

'Er, no…' Ross was stuck for words, 'I er… I jog a bit when I have time and I play badminton… what has this got to do with anything?'

'You seem to keep yourself pretty much in shape. I was thinking of getting more exercise, that's all. I think I need to get fit.' He patted his stomach to make a point and then continued typing but it seemed an empty gesture as Avalon wasn't overweight. Frazer looked over to Ross and raised her eyebrows and Dowd made no eye contact with anyone, he didn't want to be involved. Ross thought for a moment, was this Avalon's sense of humour gone sour? He tried to test the water, to see if Avalon had a punch line.

'I think you need to improve your diet rather than work out.' Avalon curled his bottom lip and stopped typing again then he stood and said to Ross.

'I'm assuming the plastic barrels you found at Bain's yard were empty.' Once again this took Ross by surprise. Why was Avalon swinging from one subject to another? Was the pressure becoming too much?

'Er, yes, we have sent three of them over to forensics to be checked but it seems Bain has been dealing legitimately in moulded plastics for just over a year.' Avalon nodded.

'Let's hope there is something of interest from the forensic tests then.'

'What happened down at the address Scobie gave us?' asked Ross still unsure about Avalon's state of mind.

'It may turn up something but my instinct tells me that's where the UFO camp abductees were held. If so, it could be a murder scene.'

'When will we know?' asked Ross. Avalon shrugged,

'Sometime tomorrow I hope.'

Chapter Ten

Once again, Avalon hadn't slept well, he had been awake so early, he heard Angie arrive back at the house from work. The temporary bed had as much responsibility for the insomnia as his mind, constantly buzzing with the case. A message on his phone from the company who were supposed to be supplying his new bed saying there would be a further delay was the catalyst that pushed him into a thoroughly bad mood. He tried to calm down as he drank his first coffee and looked out of the kitchen window at the grey clouds scudding by. Angie had showered and gone to bed by the time he had risen, he wondered if he would ever get to see her and have a casual chat. It was the same in the evenings, he came home to a quiet, empty house, and though it was relaxing in a certain way, he did think that an evening with a bottle of wine and a pleasant chat would be something to gladden his heart. As it was, the thought of what was missing from his life did nothing to lighten his mood and by the time he arrived at the station, he was just about as glum as DI Lasiter seemed to be on a regular basis. He walked up the stairs and into the office. Dowd had just arrived and was just finishing booting up the coffee machine.

'Morning sir,' said Dowd, Avalon just nodded. Was he turning himself into Lasiter he wondered? He decided he didn't need to apologise for his mood and so he sat without saying a word. He looked through his notes and began to devise a strategy for the day's work as Frazer arrived.

'Mornin',' she said to the room in general but only Dowd answered as she slumped in her chair and switched on her computer. Avalon looked up to Frazer and reconsidered what Lasiter had asked him about her, was she a good detective or was it that she was just useful if handled correctly? He wasn't sure, he certainly didn't think she had the deductive ability that Ross was beginning to exhibit. She caught him watching her, she certainly seemed aware of what was going on around her.

'What is et Sarge?' Avalon's mood meant he wasn't about to apologise for staring at her, nor was he about to make up some excuse.

'Do you think we are going about this in the right way?' he asked. She glared back at him for a moment and looked to her keyboard as if she was deep in thought. Then she looked over to Avalon and said.

'Can I speak freely?' Avalon nodded, 'I thenk tae crack this one, we need a bigger hammer. Your idea of putting pressure on Bain tae make him implicate others won't work. He has too much tae lose.'

'So,' asked Avalon, 'what would you do?' she glanced over to Dowd for a second, and then, back to Avalon.

'Find out what Davies has on Billy the Fish and go after him as well.' Avalon shook his head and stood.

'I'll not do that, it's Davies who has to follow that lead, his team worked for it, and they have to conclude it. How would you feel if DS Douglas and company took on our cases?'

'I'd kidnap their families and hold them to ransom,' replied Frazer with a straight face, Avalon looked astonished, 'it's a joke,' said Frazer, 'I thought you and Ross liked humour?'

'Well, I'm probably not in the mood for it today,' frowned Avalon trying to brush over it just as his phone began to ring, he quickly lifted it and said.

'Avalon,' there was a short pause, and he concluded with, 'Yes, I'll come now,' he put the phone down and then added, 'DI Davies wants to see me.'

'Here's your chance then,' said Frazer.

Davies's office seemed cluttered to an impossible degree and the man himself looked tired and drawn.

'Hello James, take a seat,' he said in a friendly tone but there was no eye contact and no smile.

'You want to talk,' said Avalon, as he moved some files and lowered himself into the chair that he had been resting on.

'Yes, it's about your decision to charge Robert Bain,' Davies looked at Avalon for the first time, 'I wish you'd told me about your plans, I could have informed you that this would upset the apple cart.'

'With respect, Detective Inspector, I'm running a separate case to you and I wasn't aware that I had to liaise before I acted,' replied Avalon calmly.

'No, but you were aware that B Section has a very large stake in this whole scenario.' Davies looked agitated with his reply, it was clear to Avalon he wasn't good with any type of confrontation, not ideal for a

354

detective and, today of all days, Avalon wasn't in the mood for this kind of conversation.

'I was under the impression that your main suspect was William Johnston, not Robert Bain,' said Avalon.

'He is but we think that Bain and Johnston have some connection and now that you have brought Bain in, you may have jeopardised our investigation,' Davies was sharp in his manner but remained calm. Avalon sighed and looked down to the floor. He nodded slightly and then said.

'I think that these two cases are so interlinked we just can't make headway with two teams, we probably need the Chief to make a decision,' Davies looked surprised at this.

'I really don't think that's necessary,' Davies looked around his room as if he was stuck for words but finally he said, 'In any case, I don't want to take the credit from what you and your team have achieved, finding the security van could be the breakpoint of this whole case.'

'That's as may be but for me and my team to reach further into this nest of vipers, we will need to look into Johnston's files and that is going to bring us into further conflict,' insisted Avalon. It was now Davies' turn to sigh, and it seemed like his composure was taking a great deal of controlling.

'Okay,' he eventually said, 'I admit we don't have much on Johnston as it stands but we are seriously considering our options. We're going to bring Johnston in as soon as we can but we're waiting for the report from forensics on the van, just in case it helps our cause. The preliminary report should be here later today so I

can tell you more then. If you can just wait for us to-'
Avalon interrupted him.

'No DI Davies, I can't give you any guarantees. Speak to DI Lasiter if you wish but I have to continue unless I am told otherwise,' and he stood to leave.

'Avalon! James...' called back Davies but Avalon had left the office.

Ross had arrived late as usual and was quickly informed by Avalon, as were the rest of the team, about the meeting with Davies. Avalon had made it clear that he would continue with the case unless told to stop. Ross was surprised by Avalon's reaction but said nothing and by noon, most of the building was aware that there had been a blazing argument between Lasiter and Davies. Only Avalon knew what it had been about.

The preliminary forensics report from the two vehicles found in the loch made interesting reading, even if it was to confirm what they had already guessed. There were four separate fingerprints found inside the security van or on items in there and another in the white van, two of the prints matched and belonged to a person not on the police computer and remained as 'identity unknown'. Fortunately, the other three prints were confirmed as belonging to known criminals, one being Michael Sneaton and another being a Richard Crane, a convicted burglar. It was clear, from his criminal record identity photograph that he was the doppelganger for the security guard, as there was a close resemblance. The final prints belonged to a man with a violent past whose notes announced that he sometimes took to wearing a beard.

'It looks like he could have been the guy that was

with Sneaton in Bain's van,' announced Ross, pointing to the image of Crane. Avalon nodded but remained quiet as he read through the report. It stated that the DNA extracted from the blood found in the security van didn't match the guard, neither had it been recognised by the Police database. It had most likely come from one of the perpetrators through injury, as it matched tissue samples found on the twisted metal previously found at the barn. Avalon looked up from the report and leaned back in his chair. Ross sensed there was something on Avalon's mind but didn't think the time was right for questions. Instead, he offered his thoughts on the crime.

'So it looks like the security van robbery has moved forward with this.'

'Yeah,' nodded Frazer, 'but catching Sneaton es not going tae be easy. We haven't found hem or his fleece jacket yet and that es about the only theng that can link him to the Abriachan murder.' Avalon went back to reading through the report but there was still no smoking gun. He couldn't find anything that could help them with their own investigation. Finding the security truck was a blessing for B Section, but it had done nothing to advance their own case. He stood and poured a coffee, just as Lasiter entered. The DI looked agitated and it was a few moments before he actually spoke.

'I can't see anythen' en the report that helps your case,' Avalon looked at him but made little reaction and returned to his seat. Lasiter looked at both Ross and Frazer before moving his eyes back to Avalon. 'I had a bet of a shouting match with Davies earlier. I think we have tae take a back seat for a few days,' he paused for a moment and then continued, 'I'm sorry tae do this but the security van robbery es a priority.' Frazer threw a pencil at the wall narrowly missing Dowd and she slumped back in her chair.

'So what has Davies got on Johnston,' hissed Frazer, 'that makes this so important because as far as I can see, we have more on Bain than he has on Billy the Fish?' Lasiter glared at Frazer.

'You call him *DI* Davies, DC Frazer,' but Frazer just shook her head at the reprimand. Lasiter calmed a little and then explained the evidence B Section had was fairly circumstantial.

'They've found a partial fingerprint, DNA on a shard o' the twisted metal and several fibres at the barn where they suspected the van had been breached. The blood and tissues have brought up nothing on the database, DI Davies thinks the print belongs tae a known associate of Johnston called Hamish Todd but et es impossible to verify. They have kept surveillance on him but from what I can gather he es keeping his nose clean.' Ross made a chuckle at this information and said.

'So that is it? That's *all* they have?' Lasiter glared at Ross.

'For your information DC Ross, they have only been running the investigation for just over a week and they have another five cases at the moment,' he growled.

'Aye true,' replied Ross, 'about the same time we have been on our cases.' Lasiter strode up to Ross's desk and leaned on it facing him.

'And as soon as y' can tell me you've solved et I'll give you a gold star an' apply for a 'detective of the year' award for you.' Lasiter was clearly furious and Ross knew it but the younger man was also displeased that they were about to be sidelined. He retaliated.

'True, we haven't solved it but we have suspects

for the murder and we found the security van, what has B Section got?' Lasiter banged his hands on the desk and Ross recoiled slightly.

'Damn it, Ross! Do you really think Scobie will take the stand against the likes of Bain and Sneaton?' Lasiter let the words sink in, 'you have the same as DI Davies, nothing.' He then stood and turned from Ross, making his way back to the door, 'yeah, you found the van an' that was great work but that's half the problem. Most of B Section are less than happy about your...' he seemed to struggle to find the correct words, 'ability tae find evidence.' Ross then looked as if he was going to explode and so Avalon decided the time was right.

'Just a moment Ross,' he interrupted, 'I'm somewhat concerned that we are being passed over because B Section aren't happy DI Lasiter,' Lasiter looked at Avalon with a slightly aggressive scowl, 'and if that is true there will be repercussions from this.' Lasiter was trying to calm himself down and the team could see that, but it wasn't working very well.

'For Christ's sake Avalon, I would have thought you of all people would see that es not the case,' but Avalon hadn't finished.

'With all due respect sir, I think that you're wrong, we have a suspect who is clearly involved with at least one murder,' he held up his hands, as if to accept there were issues, 'and granted, Scobie isn't an ideal witness but think what halting this case could do.' He paused to test Lasiter's reaction. There was none, so he continued. 'We have a van over at the forensics lab being tested and we have a meeting with the Crown Office and Procurator Fiscal Service later today. This case is going reasonably well, holding it back will destroy it.' Lasiter nodded after a few seconds but his features remained glum.

'I'm aware of how much progress you've made but my hands are tied,' and for a moment Lasiter's face became calm, 'remember, you're here temporarily Avalon. The rest of us won't be shuffling off tae the West Midlands en a few weeks,' he turned and left the office. There was silence except for a crash as Ross's pager struck the door and smashed into a hundred pieces. Avalon considered that Ross was slightly overreacting, but he had to find them something to do.

'Well, what else needs attention?' he asked. Both Frazer and Ross looked at each other and then over to Avalon, eventually, Ross said,

'I can't take this so easily,' then he stood and left the office.

'Are you running out too?' asked Avalon, as he looked over to Frazer. She was slumped in her chair in an almost reclined position.

'What's the option?' she asked with disinterest. Avalon thought about the 'options', Ross had clearly got a problem with inactivity but Avalon knew that going against Lasiter would be as good as handing in his notice. What was this 'new Avalon' going to do he wondered?

'I suppose we could get out that bigger hammer you spoke of earlier,' he eventually replied. Frazer sat up a little.

'Meaning?'

'Meaning, it may be time to take a few risks.' Frazer had a hard look, she was no beauty, but neither was her look unpleasant, she looked capable and business-like with an air of confidence. Avalon could see she wasn't the sort to walk out because things get difficult but what he was about to suggest was going to be tricky to justify. She stared without blinking and then, with a slight sniff, she said,

'Ef you are going tae suggest that I risk my whole career on the whim of an English detective I have only recently met, on a case I have been told tae leave alone...' she quickly looked over to Dowd who had somehow remained silent through the episode, 'we had better get started,' and she gave, what could be considered, a slight smile. Avalon stood.

'Right then, we need to pay a visit to one Hamish Todd, last known address, Leachkin Road.'

'How do y' know that?' she asked. Avalon nodded to his computer as he stood.

'I was checking it on the computer as we were talking.' As the two detectives left the office, Avalon looked back at the PC still at his desk. 'We're off out to do some shopping Dowd, carry on.'

~~~~~~

Ian Ross stood at the bar of the pub, he ordered a pint of lager and went to a quiet corner to think. Since his time in the police force he had really only enjoyed his job on two occasions. Once when he first became a detective and once when he worked on his first major case with Lasiter. Since then, the job had seemed hard work, filled with stress, little free time and not enough money, so he had slowly resigned himself to the drudgery of it. In recent months, the workload and pressure had increased along with the tedium and the tiredness. Some of that dark cloud had dissipated when

Avalon joined the team. Certainly, they hadn't hit it off straight away but gradually Ross had seen that Avalon had the same goals, the same ethics, and the same humour as himself. That was now destroyed with the news that the case was to be sidelined for a few days. It made a nonsense of the job, it made the whole process just another 'box ticking' exercise for those in charge and he was surprised that Avalon had taken it so calmly. Obviously Avalon wasn't the copper Ross though he was. He sipped his drink as his phone rang but he simply ignored it and looked around the pub. It didn't take his mind off the issue however and he could feel anger and bitterness welling up inside. Some of that anger wasn't just because of the events of the last hour, there were other issues blocking the clear thinking of his mind. Issues that were much closer to home. The car he had seen near his house on several occasions for instance, he had checked the license plate and the owner was someone he didn't know. Maybe it was time to get out of CID and go back to the ordinary police work, but then again he never enjoyed that either. He took another sip and considered getting drunk but that would be another nail in the coffin of his home life, which was quickly going down the same route as DI Davies. The phone rang again, so he took it from his pocket and looked at the display. It was Avalon trying to get in touch but Ross placed it on the table and ignored it. He leaned back in the seat and pretended to relax but it was just that, pretence. Inside he was wound up like a clock spring, considering all the problems, wondering if it had all been worth it. The phone buzzed again, this time it was Frazer with a text message that said 'Important, get in touch.' If he could ignore the DS he was damn sure he could

362

ignore a lowly DC. The phone then went quiet, for some reason this felt as bad as if it was going off all the time and just as he was about to pick it up and ring Frazer, it went off again. This time it was Avalon and Ross answered it as casually as he could.

'DC Ross,' he said.

'Where the hell are you?' asked Avalon.

'The pub,' replied Ross, he could hear Avalon sigh deeply.

'Are you fit to drive?' Ross looked down at the glass he had barely reached the half pint level.

'Yeah, why?'

'Get over to the office, find the records of Hamish Todd and print off his photo,' Avalon paused as if he was with someone, *'then, find the phone number of the business owner who identified one of the protection scam attackers and ask if they can take a look at the photograph,'* there was a pause, *'got it?'*

'Yeah, but what's this about?'

'I'm with Frazer, we came to talk to Todd, he isn't at home but you'll never guess what I found when I opened the letterbox flap of his flat.'

'Another dimension?' asked Ross. There was another pause where Ross could almost hear Avalon shaking his head in disbelief.

'Not quite but just as dangerous,' replied Avalon, *'the depressing odour of Black Ice.'*

'That doesn't mean anything,' insisted Ross.

'I know, that's why I need you to get this done as quick as you can, we're going to do some more fishing around.'

Avalon sat quietly in his car waiting for Frazer to

363

return. She had suggested walking around the area to see if she could spot B Section surveillance while there was still some light. Davies's team were probably still watching Hamish Todd but they had seen no evidence of anyone close by. It wasn't long before he noticed Frazer in the side mirror coming towards the car with a small plastic, carrier bag. She returned to the passenger seat and said,

'I've got a few things from the service station and some bottled water,' and she passed one of the bottles to Avalon, 'seen anythin'?' she asked. Avalon shook his head and checked his watch it was almost dark and it looked like they were going to be there some time. Frazer opened a packet of something and asked.

'Do y' want a sweet?' Avalon looked over to a packet she was holding. Avalon took one and as he ate it, he thought about some sort of conversation to try to get to know her more and to make the time pass quickly but couldn't think of a subject. Frazer solved that problem.

'You were married weren't you Sarge?'

'Yeah, until the dreaded 'detective virus' killed it. How about you?' he asked.

'Sort of, I have a partner,' she replied. Avalon wondered if the partner was male or female but wanted to avoid the straight question so he asked,

'Children?'

'Nae fear, I struggle enough tae find time tae be with him without adding problems.' Avalon nodded, she seemed to be confirming the partner was male.

'Can I ask a personal question, there's no need to answer if you don't want?'

'Aye, fire away,' she said as he took another sweet.

'Do you think that Ross is attractive,' he hesitated, 'from a woman's perspective, of course.'

'That's a pretty odd question, I'm no' sure how to answer et.' Avalon saw the incredulous look on her face and tried to explain without giving too much away.

'It's just that when I have been out with him, some women seem to look him over and I just hadn't seen him as a 'woman's man' for want of a better expression.' Frazer gave it some thought and eventually replied.

'I suppose he's not a bad-looking lad and I'm sure some women would see somethen' en em but he's definitely not my sort o' thing,' she said with a slight smile, 'he thinks he's Adonis mind you, but that's Ross.'

'But he's married isn't he?' asked Avalon.

'Yeah, but most men like tae think they still *'have it'*, if y' know what I mean and present company excepted?' Avalon shrugged with a little embarrassment as his phone rang, which was enough of a distraction to justifiably end a conversation he wished he had never started.

'Avalon,' he answered abruptly. It was Ross.

'You were right, it looks like Todd is one of the men involved with the protection scam but you are gonna need an ID line up to confirm this.'

'Yeah, I realise that but it gives us enough reason to bring him in,' replied Avalon. He thanked Ross and put away his phone. 'He's the one,' he said to Frazer, 'all we have to do now is bring him in.'

'But Sarge,' began Frazer, 'technically this isn't our case.' Avalon looked at her with a slight smile.

'Technically,' he began, 'it *is* our case seeing as we are still investigating the protection scams.' She nodded and thought for a moment.

'I just think that Davies will hit the ceiling if we bring someone en that they're watching, they may even try to stop us.'

'Options?' asked Avalon.

'Let's tell Lasiter, he can be an arse when he's poked, but he's also a good DI,' she insisted.

'Do you think it would be better coming from you?' asked Avalon considering the regard that Lasiter had for her abilities, 'not that I wouldn't like to drop this in his lap myself.'

'I'm not on great terms with him but aye, okay,' she agreed looking at her watch, 'can we sleep on et? I would rather see him en the office than ring him at home.' Avalon nodded but the prospect of that temporary bed for another night didn't enthral him.

~~~~~~

Avalon didn't know if he was getting used to the bed or becoming more tired but he had slept better than any other night he had spent at his new home. As he sat in the office, waiting for Frazer to return from seeing Lasiter, he wondered what had happened to Ross. He was always late but this morning he was considering giving the DC a ticking off. Maybe it was just his impatience waiting for Frazer to return that made him angry, she had been gone almost an hour and he was wishing he had gone to Lasiter himself. The phone rang.

'Avalon.'

'Can y' come to my office straight away?' It was Lasiter and his phone had rung off without waiting for a reply.

'Come in,' called Lasiter as Avalon knocked. Lasiter sat at his desk with Frazer seated opposite and they both looked up as he entered. Lasiter was about to tell him to sit but he realised there wasn't room.

'When this es over we have to talk,' Lasiter said and Avalon detected some anger in the tone. 'DC Frazer has explained what you found last night and under the circumstances, I have taken the liberty of talking with the Chief.' Avalon swallowed, he was suddenly feeling thirsty and wondered if he had drunk enough coffee to prepare him for what might come next.

'The Chief?' said Avalon not really meaning it to sound like a question.

'Course,' began Lasiter. 'y' won't have heard. DI Davies has collapsed, he's been taken to hospital for tests. DS Douglas is in temporary command of B Section as he knows the case.' Avalon was shocked, he knew Davies was struggling but this sounded more serious than he had considered. 'B Section had been trying tae find a link with Todd and Johnston,' continued Lasiter, 'but apart from Todd spending time at his warehouse, they had found very little.' Lasiter looked down to some notes on his desk. 'The Chief thinks, that with the information you gathered last night, there es reason to bring en both Todd and Johnston for questioning and tae get Todd in an I.D. lineup,' he continued as he looked back to Avalon, 'he es en a meeting with DS Douglas at this moment arranging for B Section to bring them in as soon as Todd arrives at Johnston's warehouse.'

'Can we be there?' cut in Avalon.

'I don't think, under the circumstances, that DS Douglas will agree to that,' frowned Lasiter. Avalon made no other comment on the matter. He listened to

Lasiter go on about sections needing to work together and not to tread on each other's toes, but inside he wanted to bang the desk and tell Lasiter what he thought. As he walked back to his office, he calmed down a little, but he was ready to give Ross a dressing down if he was there. He wasn't, there was just PC Dowd, and *he* said nothing. Frazer took up her place at her desk and asked.

'So what are we supposed to do now?'

'I'll give forensics a call and see if there is anything they can tell us about Bain's van. You give Ross a call and find out what the hell he's up to.'

Though Sarah Underwood was extremely busy, she explained that they had found no forensic evidence in the rear of the van but there were a number of fibres and residual DNA samples in the cab. She also explained that it could be some time before they were able to process all the material. She did, however, think that the most promising evidence would come from the large spanner that had been kept under the seat.

'Could it be the murder weapon?' he asked.

'*I can't say until all the DNA has been checked,*' she replied, '*but we have found very small blood and tissue samples on it.*' Avalon was slightly more upbeat about the case as he put the phone down but Ross had still not arrived.

'Ross?' he called to Frazer, she shrugged and said,

'Not answering his phone. Do y' want me tae go and fetch him?' Avalon thought for a moment, he didn't know what Ross's problem was but he couldn't afford to become side-tracked with it.

'No,' he eventually replied, 'we need to finish the reports from last night.'

When Ross eventually arrived, he looked in poor shape.

'Where the hell have you been?' called Avalon before Ross even had time to close the door.

'Sorry boss, I had a few problems,' he replied.

'Whatever they were, they're nothing to the problems you have now,' growled Avalon. Ross looked straight at Avalon and there was fury in his eyes.

'Look, I'm sorry I'm late so if you're gonna report me do it but don't give me any sanctimonious bullshit about letting the team down.'

'Go home,' said Avalon without any emotion.

'What?' frowned Ross.

'Go home, you're no good to me. I want people who value the work they are doing, not people who give up when things get rough,' he added. Ross glared at Avalon, then turned and left slamming the door behind him. The office went back to the silence there had been previously but in the back of his mind, Avalon couldn't help thinking he should have dealt with the situation differently. Yes, there was pressure, there was also a great deal going on in his mind but Ross *was* part of his team and he should have thought more about that. He was thinking about telephoning Ross when the phone on the desk jumped into life.

'Avalon,' he announced.

'*It's Lasiter,*' came the answer. '*B Section has arrested Johnston and Todd, they're bringing them en. We're arranging for the witness tae come over and identify Todd.*'

'Can we have a look at the premises?' asked Avalon.

'*SOCO are securing it, so I doubt it. You could*

369

try I suppose.' Avalon put down the phone and looked over to Frazer.

'Do you fancy taking a look at the warehouse where Johnston was arrested?'

'Aye, why not? I suppose there could be somethen tae see,' replied Frazer as she stood. As they walked towards his car, Avalon noticed Ross's BMW at the rear end of the car park and he thought he could see Ross in the driver's seat.

'Here, you drive,' called Avalon throwing the keys to her, 'I just have to do something.' He waited until she moved off and then he walked to the BMW. Ross was in the seat and he had his head slumped on his arms across the steering wheel. Avalon lightly tapped on the passenger window, Ross slowly looked across and unlocked the door. Avalon sat in the passenger seat as Ross returned to his position leaning on the steering wheel.

'You want to talk?' asked Avalon quietly.

'No.'

'Okay, what do you not want to talk about?' asked Avalon. Ross turned his head towards Avalon, he looked tired and under a great deal of pressure.

'It's personal,' he announced. 'I have some problems that I have to sort out.' Avalon nodded.

'Okay, I have to get off,' said Avalon as he got out of the car. He turned and bent to look back inside. 'You know how to reach me if you change your mind,' and he closed the door.

'Is that Ross's car you just got out of?' asked Frazer as he joined her in the passenger seat of his own car.

'Yes,' he said staring out of the window. Frazer

got the message and started the car.

The SOCO team weren't totally happy to allow Avalon into Johnston's warehouse but he put a strong case for allowing it. He and his DC were given forensic suits and asked to log anything they found, then they carefully threaded their way through the building like two animated snowmen, glowing white and feeling that the exercise could be a complete waste of time. They eventually found themselves at the office where two Scenes of Crime Technicians were still processing the room and looked aggrieved at having visitors. Avalon and Frazer tried to ignore their glances from behind their masks and moved to one side. They were now in Johnston's inner sanctum and it was clear the man had an ego. There were many photographs in the office, on his desk there was one of an overdressed but good looking woman, who was possibly a wife or a girlfriend, there was one of an expensive-looking sports car with Johnston by its side and one other photograph of a man Avalon didn't recognise but was emblazoned with a signature.

'Who's this I wonder,' asked Avalon pointing to it. Frazer craned her neck and said.

'It's Miles Tyler, the actor from one of the more popular soaps.'

'He likes to flaunt his celebrity friends,' said Avalon looking at some other photographs that adorned the walls of the office.

'Is that?' began Avalon pointing to another picture but he couldn't remember the name of the man.

'Aye, some famous golfer or other,' replied Frazer, equally unable to recall his name. The image showed Johnston with his arm around the shoulders of the man, both smiling for the camera.

'Well, there seems to be nothing here Sarge,' announced Frazer, looking through some paperwork strewn over the desk. Avalon had to admit, his hope of finding some connection with the Abriachan murder seemed doubtful, maybe there was simply no connection with the case and without B Section giving any clues to why they were after Johnston, it was difficult to implicate him in the security van robbery either. Avalon watched one of the SOCO team dusting another photograph for prints, as a business card fell from its back. Avalon stooped to pick it up, wondering if it held a clue. It was just one of Johnston's own cards for his business but on the back it had a contact written in biro. It seemed to be the name and number of a supplier and so Avalon gave it back to the man dusting for prints but took a quick look at the photograph.

'What is that?' he asked. The man shrugged and replaced the photograph back on the cupboard but Avalon couldn't help thinking he had seen the image before. It was a group shot of about twenty people with Johnston in the line-up, some minor celebrities Avalon recognised and some he didn't. He picked it up as Frazer stood by his shoulder and looked at the photograph.

'That, Detective Sergeant is Billy the Fish's charity organisation. His attempt to seem legitimate,' explained Frazer with a laughing tone in her voice, 'Johnston and his cronies got together tae raise money for charity and yes, the Fraud Division have examined et and yes, et es above board.' She pointed to one of the men in the photograph. 'He even mixes with politicians,' and she walked away. Avalon replaced the photograph and after a few more minutes of fruitless searching, they left. As they returned to the car and Frazer started the engine, Avalon seemed to be thinking.

'You're quiet,' she said.

'I just can't help feeling I have seen that photograph somewhere before.'

'Highly possible,' agreed Frazer, 'there's an enlarged copy of et en one of the pubs en the town. That's where et was taken. The landlord had et put up on the wall to commemorate the occasion.' Avalon nodded, he did think he could have recalled it when he and Ross were out. 'So what did y' expect tae find at the warehouse?' she asked.

'Oh, I don't know, maybe some connection with Drumnadrochit or the chemicals found in the car wrecks,' sighed Avalon, 'I think it was just an instinct thing, I thought if Davies and B Section had something on Johnston and he had connections with Bain, there may be some connection to Sneaton.'

'Aye, well, I thenk everyone would like tae find somethen' on Sneaton,' nodded Frazer.

Avalon was surprised to find Ross waiting in the office when they arrived back. Avalon nodded to him but said nothing. Ross seemed to have superficially pulled himself together and was eating some biscuits from a packet but the confidence had gone, there was no intensity in his eyes, nothing of the old Ross there.

'Did I miss anything?' asked Ross.

'Not much,' replied Avalon quite unsure how to proceed with him, 'where's Dowd?' he asked. Ross just shrugged and shook his head and carried on eating. Frazer seemed to read the situation and announced,

'I'll see ef I can find him. I want him tae sort my reports out,' and as she left, Avalon looked over to Ross.

'Want a biscuit? They're chocolate,' and he offered the packet to Avalon, who took one.

'How are you feeling?' he asked. Ross shrugged again and said.

'I've been better, but life goes on.' It was clear he wasn't ready to talk about it and Avalon thought it was better to change the subject. He couldn't bring anything to mind, but as he looked into Ross's eyes, he couldn't see Sarah Underwood seeing anything in him at the moment. He considered bringing up the subject to cheer him up.

'Do you know what a vegan is?' he asked short of other subject matter for small talk.

'Yeah, someone who doesn't eat meat or dairy,' replied Ross, with a suspicious look.

'I was thinking of trying it out,' he smiled, taking another biscuit.

'You? Do without bacon sandwiches, eggs, cheese and all the other things you like?' questioned Ross.

'It can't be that difficult, there are plenty of other things to eat.'

'Ice cream, butter, beer, wine-' continued Ross but Avalon interrupted.

'Beer and wine, what about whisky?' he asked in shock. Ross just stared at him and continued.

'Cake, chocolate, Hob-Nobs,' he continued pointing at the packet of biscuits on the desk. Avalon looked at the packet and simply sighed.

'Oh, not as easy as I thought then,' frowned Avalon. Ross shook his head and said.

'I don't wish to pry but why the sudden interest in 'working out' and becoming a vegan, is there a woman involved?' asked Ross but Avalon noticed a change in his speech at the end of the question. Ross seemed to take in a deep breath and Avalon could see a dark cloud cover his features. 'I have to go, it was a mistake to come back,' he stood and made to leave.

'Ross, for Christ's sake, talk to me,' demanded Avalon. Ross turned and Avalon could see tears welling up in the corners of Ross's eyes. Ross stopped, he tried to control himself and then, in a faint but clear voice said.

'I think my wife is seeing someone else,' and he fell to his knees, tears streaming down his face.

Avalon had bustled Ross out of the building without anyone but PC Kirk seeing them and into his car. They had left the station and Avalon was just driving, he drove over the Kessock Bridge as he couldn't think of anywhere to go. As soon as he found a lay-by to park, he pulled over and looked at Ross. He was more composed but he still looked miles away and Avalon could feel some of the pain he was feeling. Was it empathy, or a return of a fear that Avalon had once felt himself.

'So tell me,' asked Avalon, 'are you sure, are you absolutely sure?'

'Course I'm sure I'm a sodding detective,' spat Ross.

'Yeah and a good one but when it's personal, we don't always see things in perspective,' added Avalon. Ross took some deep breaths and tried to calm himself before speaking.

'Yes, I'm pretty sure, just a few things that I have noticed but they all add up to one conclusion.'

'Have you talked to her about it?' asked Avalon. Ross shook his head. 'I'm not sure anyone can advise you but I would certainly talk to her. Bottling it up will make it worse. I regret to my eternal shame I didn't talk more to my wife.'

'I'm too angry to talk to her,' insisted Ross.

'But you are angry about something that may not be,' insisted Avalon. Ross shook his head.

'I can't talk to her yet.'

'Probably not, I understand that but don't let this fester in your mind,' replied Avalon. He thought for a moment then said. 'I'll have a word with DI Lasiter and get you some time off.'

'No! Don't do that,' demanded Ross, grabbing Avalon's arm, 'I need to keep busy, I don't want to spend time at home.' Avalon looked at him and nodded. Ross continued, 'I feel better now you know, I'll sort myself out, I won't be a liability.' His gaze was intense and Avalon believed him. To give Ross something to concentrate on, as they drove back Avalon told him everything that had happened, everything but the news about Davies. He decided that was something Ross didn't need to know yet.

'So what do you think?' asked Avalon, when he had finished. Ross sighed and looked out of the side window for a moment and then back to Avalon.

'Well, I know my brain isn't working on all cylinders but I can't help thinking that there is still a missing piece of this puzzle,' answered Ross.

'To use your jigsaw analogy, I think we have the box it goes in but all the pieces are down the back of the sofa.' Ross gave the first sign of a smile and nodded then said.

'Oh, and you can't have seen that photograph at the pub, well not with me anyway. I don't go in that one. I don't like the company.'

'Oh,' replied Avalon, 'so where did I see it before then?'

'Dunno,' shrugged Ross, 'I can't think of anywhere else.' Avalon was pleased that Ross was clearing his thoughts, he sounded and looked more like his old self. There was still a distant look to his eyes but activity seemed to be the best option at the moment. He took the turning to make his way back to the station and asked Ross if he felt well enough to return to the office.

'Yeah, I'll be fine,' he nodded. Avalon thought of something as he pulled to a halt in the car park.

'I have a present for you,' and he reached into his jacket pocket and dropped a coin into Ross's hand with a slight smile across his face. It was a single pound coin.

'What's this for?' asked Ross with a puzzled look.

'You forgot I took it, when I showed you the trick with the disappearing coin.' Ross nodded.

'And some people say Scotsmen can be tight,' he said as he looked at Avalon with a slight smile but Avalon looked distant as if a light was pulling him towards it, 'what's wrong?' asked Ross with some concern.

'I remember where I saw that photograph,' and Avalon pulled out his phone, dialled, then looked at Ross, his face becoming animated, as several thoughts seemed to ripple through his features, 'something suddenly makes perfect sense,' and he turned to face

377

forward. 'Frazer, it's Avalon, where are you?' There was a pause. 'Good, meet us in the car park straight away, oh and see if you can find some bolt cutters.'

~~~~~~

The door opened much less and more slowly than Avalon had expected and an unsure face, half peered from behind it. The eyes showed fear and apprehension, a marked contrast from the previous encounter with them. They looked at Avalon, then to Ross and then to Frazer. They came to rest on Avalon's tatty Ford with a realisation that this was the visitation he had dreaded. The door was opened fully, and the man seemed to have an apologetic aura about him as he spoke.

'Detective Sergeant Avalon, you had better come inside.' The four of them made their way to the sitting room and the man asked them to be seated. 'I'm sorry I can't offer you refreshment, I'm alone at the moment.'

'That doesn't matter Mr Tennant, we have a few questions we would like to ask you,' said Avalon with an official tone. Frazer pulled out a notebook and a pencil.

'I was expecting you at some stage detective,' said Tennant in monotone.

'So you didn't consider running?'

'Oh yes, I considered it,' began Tennant, 'but where would I run to? I have known this moment would come for some time and I have considered all the options.'

'So you will be happy to answer our questions?' asked Avalon. The man nodded.

'Of course.'

'Are you involved with the security van robbery

that took place in Inverness?' Tennant gave a slight smile and then just as quickly, it faded to the look of a condemned man.

'Yes, I planned it. Are you going to charge me now?'

'Not at the moment,' replied Avalon, 'as I said, we just want to ask you some questions.' Tennant seemed confused by this but he nodded and said,

'I'll answer anything you wish to know.' Avalon knew his questions would have to be well thought out and he considered several options.

'What can you tell us about the body found at Abriachan?' Tennant began to shake his head at this.

'You must believe me Detective Avalon, if I knew people would get hurt, I would have never had done this.' He linked the fingers of his hands and looked at the floor. 'My ego got in the way, I thought I was working with artists, I wasn't. I employed sociopaths and idiots. What a fool I was,' he looked up, 'I was given a snippet of information about the security company over a year ago and I really wanted to commit the perfect crime, to make the money disappear without a trace. To do that, I had to create confusion and chaos. That was my mistake. I needed people to do that and you can never trust anyone else to choose the right people for the job.'

'So you didn't directly employ these people?' asked Avalon.

'No,' replied Tennant shaking his head, 'I left that to Johnston,' he made a stifled laugh, 'and what a mistake that was.'

'Who else was involved?' asked Avalon in a quiet voice.

'You must know that detective, or you wouldn't be here now,' and then he saw what Avalon had to do, and he nodded. 'I see, you need me to confirm some details. Bain of course was involved, I said from the start that was a mistake but as to the minor players...' he shrugged and looked back to the floor.

'So, can you outline your original plan?' Avalon was appealing to Tennant's ego and if the man realised it, he didn't show it, he visibly brightened at the chance to explain.

'It was a simple plan really, I needed to have as few of your people as possible on the case, I had to be sure you were overworked and so, after I heard of an old legend about the Culloden Drummer, I used that as a means for the confusion. Johnston asked that idiot Bain to sort that side out, to paint a van like a forestry vehicle and equip it with a public address system. That way we could drive it to a quiet spot on the hillside, play the sounds of the drum and then simply drive off without anyone suspecting, but stupidly Bain used one of his own vehicles. I also suggested the abductions and how to do it without leaving evidence but the fools bungled that too. As soon as I heard about the killing of that poor man from the festival, I told Johnston it was off.'

'So you called a halt to it?' asked Avalon seeing genuine sorrow in the man's face.

'I can be a tartar detective but I'm no murderer,' frowned Tennant, 'they still went ahead with it and so I went to see Johnston to stop it but he said it was too late, someone he had employed had taken over,' Tennant looked up and said, 'Sneaton, he called him, I don't recall his first name.

'So you're saying that you had nothing to do with

380

it apart from the planning?' asked Avalon.

'I wish I could say that but now two people are dead, if I hadn't been so conceited they would still be alive.'

'Do you know who actually killed the man from the festival camp?' Tennant nodded and said.

'I was told by Johnston that it was the man he employed to double as the guard, I don't know his name, however.'

'Have you any idea how the guard in the security van was killed?' Avalon asked.

'I suspect that must have been incompetence detective. I think they must have used too much sleeping gas, I did insist on my initial planning that the correct amount would have to be calculated,' insisted Tennant.

'They used CS gas,' added Avalon. Tennant looked shocked at this information. He shook his head and looked to the floor once more.

'That poor man, what a horrible death he must have suffered,' he whispered.

'Do you know where the abductees from the festival site were taken to?' asked Avalon.

'I don't know the fine detail, that was my error, I should have taken more control over it,' explained Tennant. Avalon asked about the security van and whose idea it was to hide it in the loch.

'It was my idea, it was something I thought of quite early, that was why we had to add to your confusion. I needed to create time to remove the barriers and push the vans through the gap and then refit them. The idea was to have the vans drive down in the middle of the night, when there was less traffic and refit the barriers shortly afterwards,' he looked up, 'I considered that was the genius of the plan, they would never be found. I just didn't count on the sonar scans of the loch and a particular English detective.' Avalon stood and moved away from him and nodded to Ross. Ross looked directly at Tennant and began a phrase he knew all too well.

'Mr Tennant, we are arresting you for your part in the security van robberies that took place...' and as Ross read the magician his rights, Avalon found the whole situation a complete anti-climax. He knew at that moment, the act of arresting Tennant would be the end of his time at Inverness, he knew he should have kept to proper procedure and given the information to B Section. It was too late now, and he looked down at Tennant as Ross wound up his 'caution'.

'I assume the robbery that you reported here didn't really happen?'

'Correct, I needed a way to know how much the police knew, it was unfortunate that the day you arrived here I had just heard about the death at Abriachan. That was the main reason I was in a terrible mood.' Avalon simply nodded.

'So why *didn't* you run Mr Tennant?' asked Avalon, as Ross stood Tennant up.

'Many reasons, I would have liked to have thought that I could have just stepped into one of my cabinets and with a flash and some smoke, disappeared forever but that, as we know, is just not real. In our modern world, it is very difficult to simply disappear forever without vast amounts of money to facilitate it and I have little of my own. Show business is fine when you are at the top, this was to be my final and greatest trick, instead it has been my downfall.'

'The robbery would have provided a considerable sum I would have thought?' added Avalon.

'Not after people lost their lives, I wouldn't take blood money and I couldn't have lived with it on my conscience,' he said and looked up to Avalon, 'I realise you must be thinking I am trying my best to wriggle out of this, particularly as you have experienced the worst side of me, but I am no monster, I am truly sorry that anyone was injured.'

'It isn't me you will have to convince Mr Tennant,' replied Avalon as he nodded to Frazer and she led the man into the hallway, but he stopped and turned to Avalon and asked.

'If you don't mind me asking Detective Avalon, what exactly pointed to my involvement?' Avalon shrugged slightly.

'Not one specific thing, but remembering where I had seen this photograph helped,' and he nodded towards a framed photograph on the wall.

'I see,' began Tennant as he looked at the image, 'an association I will regret for the rest of my life.'

At the door, the police car had arrived that they had called for and Tennant was taken to the station with Frazer in attendance. Avalon and Ross stood at the doorway, watching the blue flashing lights move down the drive.

'Now we wait for the flack,' announced Avalon thrusting his hands into his pockets. Ross nodded and handed Avalon something. 'What is it?' asked Avalon keeping his hands in his pockets.

'It's that pound coin, you're probably going to need it.'

~~~~~~

Frazer walked into the office and looked around, there was Dowd but no one else.

'Where's the boss?' she asked.

'Oh, the DS said he was going out for some air, I think he said the car park.' Frazer left the office and made her way to the rear of the building where she found Avalon, sitting on a low wall, looking up at the sky.

'Praying for divine intervention?' she asked. Avalon looked at her and smiled,

'Not really, just thinking.'

'About what?' she asked sitting by his side.

'Oh, this and that,' he replied.

'How's Ross?' she asked.

'He's got a few issues to sort out some things he has to get cleared up. I convinced him to take some time off and fortunately, he agreed.' He looked at her and asked, 'did you find anything out about Davies?'

'They're saying et was exhaustion.'

'It figures, that and divorce seem to be the main ailments of the detective,' he replied and looked up to the sky once more. Frazer looked up too, and said,

'Et's always an odd time in a case don't y' think? Et all comes together, and you feel cheated.'

'Cheated?' asked Avalon looking back to her.

'Yeah, et's like winning a first prize in a competition, just to realise you would rather have had the second prize,' she explained.

'There's still a lot to do, we have to find the Sneaton brothers and the rest of the gang, so don't get too complacent,' said Avalon standing up.

'Aye, but that es just a tidy up. Every division in

384

the UK will be lookin' for them now,' she said.

'These 'tidy ups' as you call them, can be a long job and then there's loads more paperwork,' insisted Avalon.

'Et won't take long, some of the guys are already sayin' you've got the luck o' the devil.'

'Really?' frowned Avalon, 'I would like to think it's down to skill rather than satanic luck,' and he looked down to her raising his eyebrows a little.

'What did Lasiter say tae you by the way?' and she too stood but then apologised. 'Sorry Boss, I didnae mean to pry.'

'That's alright, he didn't say much, he just said the Chief will be seeing me soon. I suppose he's leaving the talking and the arse kicking to the DCI,' explained Avalon. She nodded.

'He's bound tae see reason an' I'm sure Lasiter will put a good word en for you.'

'Hopefully, come on, we better get back to it,' smiled Avalon, and they made their way back to the building. Avalon's phone began to ring.

'You go on I'll take this out here,' and he turned back into the car park. 'Avalon,' he announced.

'*Hello, it's Carol.*' He was taken aback, but it lifted his heart, it seemed ages since they had spoken. '*Can you talk?*' she asked.

'Yeah, of course, how are you?'

'*Fine thanks, how are you getting on?*'

'Great, this is just what I needed, I feel a like a new man.'

'*You certainly sound well,*' she said.

'How's life in the West Midlands?' he asked, with a slight smile on his face.

'*Oh, you know, the same old. Nothing much changes.*'

'You seem like you have something on your mind,' he said feeling that she had a question. His instinct was correct again.

'*Well, I do have a question actually, I mean I know I shouldn't think I have to ask but I thought it was only right.*'

'Go on,' he said hesitantly.

'*Well...*' there was an uncomfortable silence, '*I have met someone, nothing big, but I thought I ought to ring and tell you, I didn't want it to crop up later in an uncomfortable way.*' Avalon could feel his temperature dropping, his stomach felt tight, but he managed to say.

'Well, we are divorced, I mean it's your life, erm, is it serious?'

'*I wouldn't say serious, but-*' he interrupted her.

'Look, you have to move on with your life, we both do, just be careful, that's all. Don't latch on to someone else who'll make your life a misery.'

'*You didn't make my life a misery we just-*' he interrupted her again.

'Look, can we talk about this later? I have to go, someone is calling me.'

'*Yes, okay, call later when you get time.*'

'Will do, take care,' and he ended the call. He wanted to vomit, he felt like he needed to scream. Instead, he put his phone in his pocket, bit lightly on his finger, and headed off back into the building.

The Avalon Series, by Peter Gray.

The Drums of Drumnadrochit
By Peter Gray.

Introducing Detective James Avalon, a man in turmoil. Both his private and professional life is at an all time low and to make things worse he is seen as a liability to his senior officers. He has to make a change in both aspects of his life, but how? Though he is still on good terms with his ex wife she is beginning to despair with his lack of compromise in his life until a chance meeting with another officer shows promise of opening new doors to his future.

Auld Clootie
By Peter Gray.

James Avalon faces a new menace in the second book in the Avalon series. Change and upheaval within the police forces sees him struggle with the problems of a reorganisation of the team. Trouble visits once again in the shape of a major crime that seems to have no clues or motives and Avalon has to work with limited resources to solve a crime linked to religion, ritual and legend.

The Brollachan
By Peter Gray.

After just twelve months based in Inverness, Detective Inspector James Avalon now feels more at home than any other time in his career. With his personal life still a shambles, Avalon takes solace in the landscape and his work, but when a woman disappears from her car in plain sight, he wonders about the accuracy of the report. When a body is found, the case becomes more serious. Is the woman's disappearance linked to the body or does Avalon need to reassess his methods?

The Black Clan

By Peter Gray.

When Avalon becomes embroiled in the world of secret societies and Masonic rituals he soon finds out how far up the food chain the rot has climbed. Once again the Inverness detective is on the streets and this time he's angry.

Caledonian Flame

By Peter Gray.

In the final book of this series, Detective Avalon finds the streets of Inverness quiet enough to risk some time off. His boredom however, forces him to dip his toe into a few old cases and that in turn opens a whole new can of worms.

Out 2019

See website for details.
www.avalon-series.co.uk

Also by Peter Gray

A Certain Summer

Sam's Kingdom

With Feeling

Please visit:

www.petergrayauthor.co.uk
www.acertainsummer.co.uk
www.avalon-series.co.uk

www.trickyimppublishing.co.uk